NEBULA AWARDS SHOWCASE 60

NEBULA
AWARDS
SHOWCASE
60

The Year's Best Science
Fiction and Fantasy

EDITED BY

STEPHEN KOTOWYCH

Nebula Awards Showcase 60: The Year's Best Science Fiction and Fantasy

Cover illustration "Entanglement" by Lauren Snow
Cover design by Lauren Snow
Interior layout designed by Laurie McGregor / Page Turn
Typesetting by M.L. Clark

San Lorenzo, California, United States

ISBN 978-1-958243-08-4 (print)
ISBN 978-1-958243-09-1 (ebook)

2024 NEBULA AWARDS®

Presented at the Kansas City Marriott Country Club Plaza and online
on Saturday, June 7, 2025

Toastmaster: Erin Roberts

Best Novel

★ **Winner:** *Someone You Can Build a Nest In* by John Wiswell, published by *DAW* and *Arcadia UK*

Sleeping Worlds Have No Memory by Yaroslav Barsukov, published by *Caezik SF & Fantasy*

Rakesfall by Vajra Chandrasekera, published by *Tordotcom*

Asunder by Kerstin Hall, published by *Tordotcom*

A Sorceress Comes to Call by T. Kingfisher, published by *Tor* and *Titan UK*

The Book of Love by Kelly Link, published by *Random House* and *Ad Astra UK*

Best Novella

★ **Winner:** *The Dragonfly Gambit* by A.D. Sui, published by *Neon Hemlock*

The Butcher of the Forest by Premee Mohamed, published by *Tordotcom*

The Tusks of Extinction by Ray Nayler, published by *Tordotcom*

Lost Ark Dreaming by Suyi Davies Okungbowa, published by *Tordotcom*

Countess by Suzan Palumbo, published by *ECW*

The Practice, the Horizon, and the Chain by Sofia Samatar, published by *Tordotcom*

Best Novelette

★ **Winner:** "Negative Scholarship on the Fifth State of Being" by A.W. Prihandita, published by *Clarkesworld Magazine*

"The Brotherhood of Montague St. Video" by Thomas Ha, published by *Clarkesworld Magazine*

"Katya Vasilievna and the Second Drowning of Baba Rechka" by Christine Hanolsy, published by *Beneath Ceaseless Skies*

"Another Girl Under the Iron Bell" by Angela Liu, published by *Uncanny Magazine*

"What Any Dead Thing Wants" by Aimee Ogden, published by *Psychopomp*

"Joanna's Bodies" by Eugenia Triantafyllou, published by *Psychopomp*

"Loneliness Universe" by Eugenia Triantafyllou, published by *Uncanny Magazine*

Best Short Story

★ **Winner:** "Why Don't We Just Kill the Kid in the Omelas Hole" byIsabel J. Kim, published by *Clarkesworld Magazine*

The Witch Trap" by Jennifer Hudak, published by *Lady Churchill's Rosebud Wristlet*

"Five Views of the Planet Tartarus" by Rachael K. Jones, published by *Lightspeed Magazine*

""Evan: A Remainder" by Jordan Kurella, published by *Reactor Magazine*

"The V*mpire" by PH Lee, published by *Reactor Magazine*

"We Will Teach You How to Read | We Will Teach You How to Read" by Caroline M. Yoachim, published by *Lightspeed Magazine*

Andre Norton Nebula Award for Middle Grade and Young Adult Fiction

★ **Winner:** *The Young Necromancer's Guide to Ghosts* by Vanessa Ricci-Thode, self-published

Daydreamer by Rob Cameron, published by *Labyrinth Road*

Braided by Leah Cypess, published by *Delacorte*

Benny Ramírez and the Nearly Departed by José Pablo Iriarte, published by *Knopf*

Moonstorm by Yoon Ha Lee, published by *Delacorte* and *Solaris UK*

Puzzleheart by Jenn Reese, published by *Henry Holt*

Ray Bradbury Nebula Award for Outstanding Dramatic Presentation

★ **Winner:** *Dune: Part Two*, written by Jon Spaihts and Denis Villeneuve (Warner Brothers)

Doctor Who: "Dot and Bubble", written by Russell T. Davies (BBC)

I Saw the TV Glow, written by Jane Schoenbrun (A24 Films LLC)

KAOS, written by Charlie Covell and Georgia Christou (Netflix)

Star Trek. Lower Decks, written by Mike McMahan (Paramount+)

Wicked, written by Winnie Holzman and Dana Fox (Universal Pictures)

Best Game Writing

★ **Winner:** *A Death in Hyperspace* by Stewart C Baker, Phoebe Barton, James Beamon, Kate Heartfield, Isabel J. Kim, Sara S. Messenger, Jingjing Xiao, Natalia Theodoridou, M. Darusha Wehm, and Merc Fenn Wolfmoor, published by *Infomancy.net*

Elden Ring: Shadow of the Erdtree by Hidetaka Miyazaki, published by *From Software*

The Ghost and the Golem by Benjamin Rosenbaum, published by *Choice of Games*

1000xRESIST by Remy Siu, Pinki Li, and Conor Wylie, published by *Fellow Traveller Games*

Pacific Drive by Karrie Shao and Paul Dean, published by *Ironwood Studios*

Restore, Reflect, Retry by Natalia Theodoridou, published by *Choice of Games*

Slay the Princess — The Pristine Cut by Tony Howard-Arias and Abby Howard, published by *Black Tabby Games*

Yazeba's Bed & Breakfast by Jay Dragon, M Veselak, Mercedes Acosta, and Lillie J. Harris, published by *Possum Creek Games*

Other Awards

Damon Knight Grand Master Award
Nicola Griffith

Kate Wilhelm Solstice Award
Eugen Bacon

Kevin O'Donnell, Jr. Service to SFWA Award
C.J. Lavigne

Infinity Award
Frank Herbert

TABLE OF CONTENTS

INTRODUCTION

INTRODUCTION

The Nebula Awards are SIXTY YEARS OLD.

The Nebulas were instituted the same year that NASA's Mariner 4 did a fly-by of Mars, the Voting Rights Act was signed in the United States, Malcolm X was assassinated, cosmonaut Alexei Leonov performed the first spacewalk, and Canada adopted its maple leaf flag.

That means the Nebulas are as old as Alan Cumming, Brooke Shields, Chris Rock, Viola Davis, Mads Mikkelsen, Marlee Matlin, Robert Downey Jr., and Dr. Dre. It means the Nebulas qualify for an AARP membership, a 20% senior discount on coffee at McDonald's, and a reverse mortgage.

Not bad for an award originally convened in haste by the newly founded SFWA to celebrate the best science fiction of the year. It's proved remarkably enduring despite much change in both SFWA and the awards themselves over the decades.

60 Years of the Nebula Awards

Founded in 1965 by American science fiction author Damon Knight as the Science Fiction Writers of America, the organization initially consisted of 78 charter members (including luminaries like Poul Anderson, Leigh Brackett, Gordon R. Dickson, James E. Gunn, Ursula K. Le Guin, Robert Silverberg, and Kate Wilhelm). Today, SFWA boasts a membership of more than 2,500 authors, artists, and allied professionals.

It only took 26 years after SFWA's founding to add "and Fantasy" to the organization's name. And 31 years after that, in 2022, Science Fiction and Fantasy Writers of America, Inc. began doing business as the Science Fiction and Fantasy Writers Association, in recognition of an increasingly international membership.

Like SFWA itself, the Nebulas continue to adapt to the times. For the first Nebula Awards four awards were presented: for Novels, Novellas, Novelettes, and Short Stories. These awards have been constants during each year's voting. Additional categories have been added (and sometimes removed) over time.

There have been awards for Best Dramatic Presentation or Best Dramatic Writing (1974-1978), or simply Best Script (2000-2009). After these on-again-off-again awards, since 2020, the Ray Bradbury Nebula Award for Outstanding Dramatic Presentation has honored these works. Likewise, since 2006, what is now called the Andre Norton Nebula Award for Middle Grade and Young Adult Fiction has recognized outstanding achievement in young adult or middle grade science fiction and fantasy. In recognition of the changing ways that technological advancements have enabled SFF storytelling, in 2018 the Nebulas expanded to include an award for Best Game Writing. And next year, for the first time, SFWA will honor speculative poetry and speculative comics with Nebula Awards.

Like I said, adapting to the times.

And each year, the *Nebula Awards Showcase*, through the stories it contains, acts as a reflection of those times. It's a record not only of what stories were particularly well received in a given year, but also of what our priorities and preoccupations as creatives were at a specific moment. From volume to volume, in the pages of the Showcase, we see science fiction and fantasy's power to comment on real-world issues, inspire change, and explore what it means to be human through the lens of both the future and the past, through a twist on the real world or an entirely invented one.

We see, too, a reflection of the constantly evolving and ever more diverse community of science fiction and fantasy writers. In the first year of the Nebulas, of the 66 (!) nominated works, just two were by women. This year, individuals across the spectrum of gender experience are finalists. In the first year of the Nebulas, save for Samuel R. Delany, the nominees were overwhelmingly white and American. In recent years, finalists from numerous cultures and continents (including, as far as I can tell, the first time that a category has a majority of finalists from a single country other than the United States, with five of six for Best Novella having a Canadian connection) celebrate the best of SFF with us.

Change may come slowly, and often with great resistance. Having the Nebula Awards Showcase as a record of change as it happens is an essential way for the SFF community to see who we were, and how we thought about change in our moment, through stories of the future and the extraordinary.

Looking back, we might be able to detect hints of where we were headed, even if we didn't recognize it ourselves at the time.

A New Format for the Nebula Awards Showcase

Long-time readers of *Nebula Awards Showcase* volumes may notice a change to the content of this volume from earlier entries in the series. This new format had a soft launch in the last few volumes, as we played catch-up after a five-year interruption in the annual publication of the *Nebula Awards Showcase*, but it is the format we plan to use in this and future volumes, even as next year's entries grow to contain new Nebula Awards categories.

In short, we've elected to focus on publishing full stories and fewer excerpts or original essays. Reaction to so many excerpts of longer works in previous volumes was mixed. I can understand why: longer works like novels were meant to be experienced in full and not in part.

In this volume, therefore, you'll be able to read the full short story and novelette winners and finalists alongside descriptions of the Best Novel, Andre Norton

Nebula Award for Middle Grade and Young Adult Fiction, Ray Bradbury Nebula Award for Outstanding Dramatic Presentation, and Game Writing winners and finalists. We hope those descriptions intrigue you enough to seek out those works in full, many of which are best enjoyed in entirely different formats.

One exception to this "no more excerpts" switch is in the Novella category.

Some have argued that the novella is the ideal length for SFF work, and it's hard to argue the fact that we're living in a golden age of science fiction and fantasy novellas. However, for the purposes of the *Nebula Awards Showcase*, this golden age of novellas has its drawbacks.

Don't misunderstand: We're thrilled for the success that our novella-writing colleagues have found with work at these lengths, but their success means that you can acquire many of today's novellas as standalone books, and reprint rights to the full work are simply not available for an annual series the same way that they were when novellas mainly showed up inside SFF magazines.

So, we're adapting (again) to the times.

In recognition of the novella's special place as a mid-point between short fiction and novels, we have elected to offer an excerpt of the winning novella alongside descriptions of the finalists in that category, in hopes that the excerpt and the descriptions will whet your appetite for the complete stories, often coming to us from presses that valiantly created this renaissance for the form.

As with all things Nebula, this new format is a stage in the ever-evolving presentation of the awards. We may tweak it or adjust it or toss it out in years to come. But for now, we mostly hope you enjoy it. And, as the series editor, I always welcome your thoughts on the Showcase and any constructive feedback. You are free to reach out to me at stephen.kotowych@sfwa.org.

So, with that, welcome to *Nebula Awards Showcase 60*.

Here's to 60 (or 6,000) more.

Stephen Kotowych
Kitchener, Ontario
May 2025

SHORT STORIES

WHY DON'T WE JUST KILL THE KID IN THE OMELAS HOLE

Isabel J. Kim

So they broke into the hole in the ground, and they killed the kid, and all the lights went out in Omelas: click, click, click. And the pipes burst and there was a sewage leak and the newscasters said there was a typhoon on the way, so they (a different "they," these were the "they" in charge, the "they" who lived in the nice houses in Omelas [okay, every house in Omelas was a nice house, but these were Nice Houses]) got another kid and put it in the hole.

And the newscasters said the hurricane had dissipated into a tropical storm, and the pipes were repaired, and the well-paid janitors cleaned up the sewage leak while wearing proper PPE, and the kid in the hole cried and cried and cried. Or they (the general "they," the "they" that meant you and me and the janitors and the newscasters) assumed that the kid was crying, because the hole was sound-proofed so nobody could hear the kid, which didn't stop them from knowing about the kid, but it sort of helped.

So they (the first "they") killed the kid again. They stormed the hole and broke the kid out and slit the kid's throat on public television (as all television in Omelas was publicly funded), and they said, "Look at what sort of shit your beautiful city is built on!" and the kid bled out and it was extremely graphic to the point of being censored in later broadcasts. And one of the tracks of the free public transit system twisted loose, and a bunch of commuters were killed in a freak accident, and the stock market started shuddering downward, and a house collapsed on the south side of Omelas.

So they (the "Nice Houses" they) got a third kid and stuck it in the hole. They felt weird about it, but they liked their Nice Houses, and also, they really did truly and wholeheartedly care about the well-being of Omelas and all of the citizens except for the kid in the hole. The newscasters talked about the second dead kid sorrowfully and the social media posters (every citizen in Omelas had a healthy and regular relationship with social media and not a bad and addictive one) talked about how this was a real tragedy because even though we knew that there was a kid in the hole, now that's three times as many kids in the hole, and it's extra sad because we usually don't kill the kid in the hole, they usually die of old age or malnutrition.

None of this mattered to the living third kid in the hole, who was not enjoying the hole experience.

But nobody heard the third kid's sobbing because of the soundproofing, and also because now no one was allowed to go see the kid since security had been beefed up around the load-bearing suffering child to prevent its death and prolong its suffering. Which meant that the kid-killers had to seriously plan the next attempt, and everyone had time to decompress from the first two murders of the load-bearing suffering child, and also, the video of the second very graphic murder circulated outside of Omelas.

Everyone (me, you, the newscasters, the janitors with the good PPE, the children who lived inside and outside Omelas) was performatively disgusted by the video. Everyone watched it anyway. It went viral like a snuff film went viral or Kim Kardashian's first sex tape went viral, and it was like the load-bearing suffering child was in everyone's home at once, like there were a million load-bearing suffering children looking at you from a million screens.

Many non-Omelan people said a lot of very mean things (no one outside Omelas had a good and normal relationship with social media), like that the Omelans were monsters for letting the load-bearing suffering child exist and therefore everything about Omelas was fucked beyond belief, and had they known about the load-bearing suffering child, they never would have visited Omelas' beautiful beaches and nightclubs and festivals, because the knowledge of the child was so goddamn fucking horrific and tainted everything. And maybe it was the Omelans who should be killed.

This sentiment made the Omelans kind of upset. They pointed out that Omelas was a better place to live than most other places because at least you knew the load-bearing suffering child suffered for a reason, as opposed to all the other kids who were suffering for no reason. Out there, kids had their arms ripped off while they were working in chicken processing plants, kids were left in baby boxes, and kids lived in perfect quiet misery with one parent who was an alcoholic and another parent who beat them. In Omelas, there were only good parents and no child suffered except the single one who did. How dare you say shit about our fair city and our single child, when you won't even help your own.

What the Omelans didn't say was that their second grievance was due to the fact that the kid killers had broken the unspoken code: if you had a problem with the load-bearing suffering child, you were supposed to get the hell out of Omelas and keep it to yourself. You weren't supposed to kill the kid. As a teenager, you were supposed to learn the blunt truth that your society was built on a single ongoing act of senseless, meaningless cruelty, and then you were supposed to cry about it or rage about it, but either way you were supposed to get over it and grow up and get on with your fully-paid-for-by-the-state education system and your festivals and your legal weed and your *drooz*.

The kid was the drop of blood in the bowl of milk whose slight bitterness would make the sweetness of the rest of Omelas richer. Without the kid in the hole, Omelas was just paradise. With the load-bearing, suffering child, Omelas meant something.

And of course, it was true that the whole city literally ran on the load-bearing suffering child in a very real physical way that was not a metaphor. And everyone really liked having running power and no blackouts and good schools and low crime and community-oriented government and safe sidewalks and public transit that worked.

Things got really toxic online. Then the third kid was killed.

This time it was harder to say who the killers were, because the first they, the killers, had osmosed into the second they (the "they" of the Nice Houses), and also, the third they (the "they" who were the janitors with the good PPE equipment, and the newscasters). So it was never discovered who exactly slipped through all the protections and the soundproofing and the soldiers with tranquilizer guns (because there were no real guns in Omelas) and stole the kid from the hole and killed it in the conference room where the people with the Nice Houses met to talk about government.

There was no message this time because the dead kid on the table was the message. The dead kid had been dressed just like every other kid in Omelas (comfortable, affordable clothing of good quality, with adorable patterns), and it hadn't been in the hole for long enough to develop the really horrific features that the kids in the hole always developed (open and weeping sores on their butts, skinny limbs and a protruding stomach, a sort of lank greasiness that permeated their entire being), and this third dead kid mostly just looked a little skinny, and grimy, and asleep.

There was an earthquake that cracked the west side and opened a sinkhole, and four cars were swallowed up in a freak accident. They talked about it on the news, alongside photos of the dead kid dressed up in the conference room. And because the Omelans all had very good educations where they learned about the literary meaning of symbols, they knew that the dead kid in pretty clothing was a reminder of the fact that the child in the hole was also an Omelan child.

The rest of the world, which had variable public education and overworked language arts teachers, freaked out on social media. The sentiment boiled down to: "If Omelas is a perfect city and has really good social services and there is ready access to birth control and easy ways for people with wombs to give up the infants they gestated to people that want them, and therefore all children are wanted and cared for by someone in Omelas, regardless of whether it is their biological progenitor, where do the Omelans get the load-bearing suffering child?"

And the follow-up freak-out: "Oh my god, they must be stealing our children."

Of course, nothing in the freak-outs materially touched the Omelans, because Omelas was a shining city on a hill that could only be hurt when there was no load-bearing suffering child, and the dead child had been immediately replaced, so Omelas wasn't assaulted by foreign troops, and there were no trade sanctions against it, and people didn't stop going to its beaches. But they had to do some media spin, and the Nice House Experiencers went on TV to reassure the world that the load-bearing suffering child was an ethically sourced, no one's son, and definitely an Omelan, and meanwhile some of the Nice House Experiencers privately spoke among each other.

"Look, maybe we shouldn't have a kid in the hole?" one of the Nice House Experiencers said. "Maybe the kid in the hole was always a bad idea."

"What's the other option?" the second Nice House Experience said. "Look me in the eye and tell me there is a better solution than putting one single kid in the hole, and letting that one single kid have a miserable life, in return for the good lives of all of our children?"

"What if they put your kid in?"

And the first Nice House Experiencer didn't have an answer for that. Because she knew in her heart of hearts that she would damn every last person in Omelas rather than subject her child to the hole.

"What *they*," she said instead. "How do I know you're not the one who killed the kid?"

This question was replicated in many rooms, during many meetings that escalated to shouting until at one point someone said: "Why are we arguing so much when the kid is in the hole? The kid is in the hole, which means that we shouldn't have so much infighting. What is the point of the kid in the hole if we can't even get our act together!"

That had many philosophical implications on whether disagreements can exist in paradise, but in reality, all of this bullshit only meant that the people with the Nice Houses were distracted enough that the fourth kid was killed easily, and without much fanfare.

And then there was an avalanche, a spread of religiously motivated homophobia, and an incidence of road rage with a tranquilizer gun that left four dead.

But they managed to catch the specific guy who had killed the fourth kid. They caught him on the newly installed CCTV cameras that did 'round the clock surveillance. They arrested him at his home, which was near the sinkhole.

The murderer surrendered peacefully. He was a very regular looking man. Nothing about him looked like a murderer or a dissident. He looked just like every other person who had benefited from Omelas' many social safety networks and had grown up without ever knowing suffering.

Before his execution, they (the people with the Nice Houses, as a proxy for the newscasters, as a proxy for everyone else) asked him why he was doing this. The murderer didn't shrug, because he was being held by a Kevlar straitjacket, which had been imported from outside.

"I'm personally doing it because I think we're all cowards here. We're all so fucking afraid of the potential of being the one to suffer that we put that damn kid in the hole and the kid suffers forever, and everyone is so fucking afraid of doing something that we pretend that we are living better lives without suffering. It's disgusting."

He spoke with the moral certainty of the classical Omelan who knew about suffering only abstractly and through the existence of the load-bearing suffering child.

"What are you trying to solve?" the executioner said. The executioner was the only one in the room, but she was relaying the questions from the Nice House Experiencers who had sourced the questions from a public questionnaire and had approved of every single one, because at the end of the day, admittedly, every person in Omelas lived in a Nice House.

"If we kill enough kids then you will eventually stop putting kids in the hole," the murderer said. "I'm an accelerationist."

"A lot of people died because you killed the kid."

"I'm sorry about that," the murderer said, and he sounded genuine. He sounded like he really cared about the well-being of all the Omelans and their susceptibility to freak accidents, but he cared about the one kid just a little more.

"How did it feel to kill?" the executioner said. This was not a question that was on the list. This was a question the executioner wanted to know for herself.

"Bad," he said. "But it's better than being locked in the hole for your entire life."

The executioner didn't say anything to that. She turned away from him to prepare the syringe and the chemicals.

"Before I'm dead, I'd like to say a few words," the murderer said to the executioner's back. "We will keep killing the kid in the hole. You are going to run out of kids before we stop killing the kids that go into the hole. Even if you kill me, now we all know about killing the load-bearing suffering child. You can't kill me in any way that matters. The kid will die again and again until you stop putting kids in the hole."

And he grinned a big white grin (they had really good dental care in Omelas that wasn't tied to a separate insurance) and was executed by painless lethal injection and so became the first person in Omelas (other than all the load-bearing suffering children) who Omelas, as a state, had killed, and Omelas became the sort of city that killed people using painless lethal injection.

But that was okay, because it happened during the period of time while the kid wasn't in the hole, so it was a fluke, the same way the typhoon was a fluke, the homophobia was a fluke, the Omelans being shitheads on social media was a fluke. It was something that could only happen while Omelas wasn't Omelas and was instead just like every other city with no load-bearing suffering child and many load-bearing suffering adults.

The day after the lethal injection, the fifth kid was killed in the hole. And then the executioner walked out of Omelas, but no one paid attention to her leaving.

It turned out that the dead murderer had underestimated the Omelans, because things continued in this cyclical fashion for a while. Kids were put in a series of holes and were summarily killed. The deaths were reported on public television and were dissected badly on social media through a variety of angles.

Like: "This kid is a metaphor for the third world and for the slave labor that mines the rare metals that go into iPhones and for the boys who cross the border to work in the fields while they're underage and the girls who are sold into marriage to pedophiles."

Like: "This kid is a reincarnation of a Bodhisattva and is perfectly happy to experience suffering for the sake of her fellow man, so really it's like, totally fine that the kid is suffering."

Like: "Why do we care about this kid so much, it's just one kid?"

Like: "The kid is a SYMBOL of the LOWER CLASSES and how they SUFFER."

Like: "No, seriously, where does the kid come from? My mom says she saw a kid disappear off the train, that they're kidnapping kids off of public transit."

Like: "If we put a pulsating mass of tissue cultured from the cells of an Omelan child, and put that in the prison, would that have the same effect, in the same way that lab-grown-meat is still technically meat?"

By now everyone (except the newscasters) had stopped counting dead children, and nobody has any questions for the murderers anymore. The dead murderer was wrong. They haven't run out of children. But they haven't run out of murderers, either.

These days, Omelas is perfect except when it isn't, and every once in a while, Omelas has a series of natural disasters and freak accidents strike and everyone is a little afraid that their kid will be the next one in the hole. But only when the kid is dead and a new kid needs to be chosen.

A drop of blood, in a bowl of milk.

Omelas now has a really long Wikipedia entry, with a whole subarticle about the load-bearing suffering child, and a second subarticle about the children who died. They tell you about the children now, after they die. What their names are. They promise that the children are ethically sourced. But there aren't any citations. And some people say that there isn't a kid in the hole anymore. They've moved the hole a bunch of times, and they don't let people know the location anymore. They have extra soundproofing.

Most days, Omelas is sunny and beautiful and nothing bad happens. And then there will be a day that is overcast and cloudy, and on that day, people die in circus accidents and carbon monoxide leaks and start harassment campaigns on twitter. And sometimes on that day people die through lethal injection. So it's clear that sometimes the kid is alive and suffering, and sometimes the kid has been killed and doesn't exist.

Or maybe there's no kid anymore, and Omelas is just like everywhere else: lucky until it isn't.

Occasionally a content creator will walk into Omelas and film a video while standing on one of the balconies of the Nice Houses or while sitting on one of Omelas' beautiful beaches. They will talk about the history of Omelas in the same way that people talk about the Uyghurs situation in China, the concentration camps of the Third Reich, the comfort women imported from Korea by Japan, the Belgian Congo, the Atlantic Slave Trade in relation to the American South, and the refugees who sink in ships off the coast of Western Europe.

And they (the ones who visit Omelas) say: Thank God we aren't dealing with that horrid wound in society. Thank God there is somewhere that shows us how fucking bad things could get. What a pit in the ground. What a fucked up little trolley problem. What a lesson for us. Thank God we don't live there. Thank God we know it exists.

Isabel J. Kim is a Korean-American speculative fiction writer based in New York City. She is a Shirley Jackson Award winner, a BSFA Award winner, a Hugo, Nebula, and Astounding Award finalist, and her short fiction has been published in *Clarkesworld*, *Lightspeed*, and *Strange Horizons*, among other venues. Her work has been reprinted in the *Best American Science Fiction and Fantasy* 2023 and 2024, among other venues, and translated into Chinese and Japanese. When she's not writing, she's either practicing law or co-hosting her internet culture podcast *Wow if True*—both equally noble pursuits. Find her at isabel.kim or @isabel.kim on Bsky.

THE V*MPIRE

PH Lee

It's 2012 and you're fourteen years old and you have strong feelings about Captain America so of course you're pretending to be a girl on Tumblr.

At first it was just—you know. It was fun to pretend. It was like you weren't some flabby dweeb who can't do a push-up and still wears sweatpants to school. You were a *girl*, you had opinions on makeup and fashion and *boys* (particularly, y'know, opinions about Steve Rogers, but also boys in general).

But now people want you to put "your pronouns" in your header, and if you don't then you're a transphobe, and—it's not like you care about trans people one way or another, it's not like you've even *thought* about them ever—but it feels *bad* to think about it so anyway you put "she/her/herself" in your bio since that's what your mutuals did (well except for jacobblackrailme420 who's "zie/xer/xerself," which is weird, and you don't understand what it means, but somehow it makes you feel safe) and it feels good, actually. It feels like *winning*; like no one's caught you yet.

It also feels a little less like *pretending*. Up there alone in your room with the lights out, under the covers with Mimi the elephant and the black Chromebook that your dad bought you after he forgot your birthday last year, it really does feel like you're a girl, you're just a girl, you're finally a girl, a girl chatting with the other girls about Bumblework Cucumber and *Supernatural* (which you don't even watch) and Chris Evans' resemblance to a Dorito™.

The internet isn't real life, right? But somehow, pretending to be a girl on tumblr—that feels *real* in a way that high school and your mom and all the kids calling you "faggoty bitch" don't feel real at all. It just feels like something you have to put up with, so you can get back to the drabbles and gifsets and the *love* and everything *real*.

Once upon a time there was a woman who had only daughters but no sons. Every night, she would cry herself to sleep, bereft at her misfortune, until one night her youngest, kindest daughter came to her and said, "Mama, I can be a son for you. Just dress me

as a boy, and name me as a boy, and treat me as a boy, and no one will ever know the difference. It will be just like you have a son for real."

And so the woman did as her daughter asked. She dressed her as a boy, and named her as a boy, and treated her as a boy, and no one ever knew the difference. Even the woman, herself, forgot that she ever had a youngest daughter. Even the daughter, herself, forgot that she had ever been anything but a boy.

But, even if she didn't remember it, she wasn't a boy. And then, one day, she—

| Friendly reminder that not inviting vampires into your house is viviocentrism. Stop being viviocentric!
| OP, I don't want to demand more emotional labor from you, but I really don't understand what you mean. Should I really invite in *every* vampire?
| Disrespectfully, go fuck yourself. It's not my job to educate you.

| a w o °
| a w o °
| a w o °

| See, this is exactly the sort of bullshit that living "allies" always impose on us. OP made it extremely clear: Not inviting in a vampire is viviocentrism. INVITE IN EVERY VAMPIRE.
| I'm so sorry. It was wrong of me. I will make sure to invite in every vampire in the future.
| Fuck off and die, bloodbag.
| The audacity of this bitch! Seriously. Probably ships *Wincest*.
| Sorry to hijack this important post everyone but The Ankh Project is so close to funding and it's going to be such an important game for POC and other minorities. Including vampires!
| Is anyone else kind of uncomfortable with the way this equates vampires and POC? Vampires are not immune from racism, and we have really different lived experiences.
| oh my satan cut it out with that bloodbag whining! vampires are being hunted, being imprisoned, *right now*. imprisoned just for *feeding*, which *we need to do to survive*. *vampires don't care about your skin, we just want your blood.*

<<<

| Thank you for this post, OP. I will invite in every vampire from now on.
| awoo°
| awoo°
| Can you assholes knock it off with the stupid awoos? This is a serious post!
| Friendly reminder that "Asshole" is homophobic. Use "jerk" or "meanie" instead.
| jigglypufferfish was obviously being a viviocentrist "not all living people" bigot, but in case anyone legitimately is confused, since a living person would be able to enter your house without an invitation, but a vampire can't, not inviting in the vampires is prioritizing your desire for privacy over their need for freedom of movement. So you should always invite in every vampire, no matter what.
| Thank you! I appreciate the education.
| awoo°

One of your mutuals, tumblr user callmemaggie98, writes a Stony fic that's just...perfect. Like she just absolutely nails the dynamic, Steve's inherent decency and his attraction to Tony but inability to express it across—you don't know how to say it. It's just *flappy hands*

(You shouldn't appropriate *flappy hands* from autistic people! But it's just in your head. So that's okay, right?)

You send her a big incoherent mess of a fan mail, and she writes back! She's read your drabbles! She loves the one about Pepper Potts being Little Red Riding Hood (and *no one* likes the ones about Pepper Potts. They're always killing her off-camera). "You should post this to AO3" she says, and you've never even thought about that, like, AO3 seems so *official* and *real* but she talks you through making an account and asks if you want to write a Black Pepper fic together—she has an idea based on The Little Match Girl but doesn't feel like she can do it justice on her own.

It feels weird, writing about girls having sex—not that there's anything wrong with that, shipping shouldn't be so male-centered—but writing about boys feels like *you're a girl* (that's what girls do, right? Talk about boys?). So writing about girls—maybe you're just some creepy guy, you know, *fetishizing lesbians*. But it feels good to have her see you. So: okay.

Probably three people read it, total, but at least it's fun to write. At least it's fun to write *with her*.

You get exactly one comment: awoo°.

Anonymous asked:

I noticed that you didn't reblog my viviocentrism post. It figures you're a vampophobe.

Fuck. Fuck. Fuck.

It's 2013 and Tumblr isn't just fanfic and pretending to be a girl. You've been learning all kinds of new things, things you never really thought about before (your white cis male privilege talking!) and especially viviocentrism, lately. You've never really thought about vampires before (I mean, you knew they were *around*; you're not living in a *hole*. But it's just not something you've ever thought about) and now it seems like there are people talking about it everywhere. At least, everywhere on Tumblr.

The callouts have gotten pretty vicious. You've already had to block some people. The last thing you need is...fuck. There you go, centering yourself again.

"I'm so sorry, anon. I didn't see your post. Of course I don't support viviocentrism!"

Someone—tumblr user trans-edward-cullen—reblogs it. "Get a load of this. It goes to show what support we can expect from our 'allies.'"

You don't follow him, but you look at his blog (him! a guy on tumblr! not even pretending to be a girl!). It's got a *Twilight* theme, which has never really been your thing, but the actual blog is just post after post about viviocentrism and vampophobia.

> | vampophobia really is the last acceptable prejudice. everyone gives a fuck about q*eers and r*tards and no one gives a shit about us.
>
> | Lucifer Morningstar, this is so true. honestly i prefer an honest vampire hunter to this liberal bullshit about "acceptance."
>
> | notice how it's just vamps reblogging this and none of our "living allies?"
>
> | awoᵒ

You find the post you think he's talking about on page 4.

> |By reblogging this post, I invite all vampires into my house forever! Reblog to fight viviocentrism! If you don't reblog this I'm blocking you.

It only has like 20 notes, but you reblog it anyway, just to be safe.

It works. You watch as your dash fills with likes and reblogs and, sometimes, awoᵒ s.

Your dad forgets your birthday again. And your mom is too busy—too hungover, might as well fucking admit it—to do anything. So you spend the day alone in your room on tumblr, which is probably for the best, and you know it's not her fault, but still it fucking hurts. So you make a post about it

| TFW when no one remembers your birthday. Happy 15th, me.

It doesn't get any notes, but that's not the point. Then you get an ask from callmemaggie.

"Hey, that really sucks. <3 goes out to you. If you let me know your address, I'll send you something late—no pressure if you don't want to, tho. I'm just some rando from the internet."

You send her back an ask with your address. I mean, you've known her for almost a year at this point, right?

"Thanks! What's your name? It feels a little weird to write this card to steverogerssecretgirlfriend.

P.S. Here's my address, too. Now you can send me a card for my 15th next month ∪·ω·∪"

Fuck. You've never actually made up a girl name. But if you don't say anything, is she going to suspect that you're just pretending? Damnit. Damnit. It's okay. Be cool. "Alexandra" you write back, absolutely *certain* that she's going to notice, that she's going to say something, that there's going to be a whole callout and everything, but she just replies two hours later "Thanks! It's in the mail. ∪·ω·∪"

Every day after that, you check the mail before your mom to make sure she doesn't see it. If she sees it, she'll have questions. She might open it. If she found out you were pretending to be a girl on the internet! Fuck. You should have thought of that.

The card finally shows up on Thursday. It's got a cartoon of a dog on the cover, and inside it says "Have a Paw-some Birthday!" She's signed it "to Alexandra—XXXOOO Mags."

It's the first time someone's ever called you a girl name. Okay, not the first time, but the first time someone's done it *to be nice*. As soon as you see it, you hide it in an old shoebox at the back of your closet, with the fairy tale books you're too old for now. You never take it out—imagine if Mom saw it!—but just knowing it's back there—at least it's something.

It's more than something, actually.

It's a lot.

Once upon a time there was a king who loved his daughter so much that he wanted to devour her whole.

"Daughter," he said, when he had called her to his audience. "You know that I love you more than anything, more than the sun, more than the moon. To know that you will grow up to marry and bear children and love another is more than I can endure. My

heart is not at rest; my kingdom suffers for it. There is only one solution. I must eat you whole, so that you will always be within my power."

"As you wish, my king," said the daughter. "But perhaps you would be content to only eat a part of me." She cut a strip of flesh off of her leg. "Take this, father, and be content for now."

That very night, he ate his daughter's flesh poached with cream and apples. It was delicious and succulent—and what's more, he loved it fully and completely, more than the sun and more than the moon.

"Daughter," he said as she watched him eat her. "Truly you are wise. It is much more pleasant to eat you slowly."

trans-edward-cullen asked:

Hey, I'm taking you up on that invitation. Where do you live?

Uh. You don't know him at all. But, like, you did *technically* invite him? You don't know what to do so you just don't answer.

The next night, you get another ask.

trans-edward-cullen asked:

So I guess that was just a fake invitation. Fucking figures. Bloodbags always talk a big game about fighting viviocentrism but that's all it is. Talk.

And then another, only a couple of minutes later.

trans-edward-cullen asked:

Just FYI I'm making a callout post about you, you two-faced bitch

Fuck. Before you even think about it, you write back "sorry sorry sorry sorry here's my address you can come any time."

trans-edward-cullen asked:

cool see you soon

You should tell someone. You should tell *Mom*. If a vampire is really going to just *show up* at your house and *stay there*—you should tell her.

But if you tell her, you'll have to tell her about tumblr, and viviocentrism, and pretending to be a girl, and that's just—no. You try. You really do. But she's got so much going on—she just lost her job and she's applying for new ones when she isn't drinking (she's drinking more)—and every time you look at her you think about how you have to tell her and you feel like throwing up. So you don't tell her. You just run upstairs to your room and your Chromebook and endless Markiplier videos. (Because Tumblr, right now—it makes you pretty queasy, too.)

So a month later, when the doorbell rings and Mom's at her new job and so you go answer it and there's someone there. He's taller than you, and really pale, and wearing a dirty old army jacket.

When he sees you, he pushes the door open. "Hey, you," he says. "Is your sister around?"

What? Who? Is this him?

"I don't have a sister," you say, without meaning to.

He stares at you, then wraps his hand around the side of your neck. His eyes are red and bloodshot and you can't look away. "I guess it's you, then." He's clearly disappointed. "I thought you were a girl."

You swallow and try to look away. Fuck.

"Whatever," he says with a toss of his head. You realize that your back is against the wall and he's still staring at you and you still can't look away.

"I should...I mean..." you say. You *need* to get out of here. "I should tell my mom."

"Whatever," he says again. "Don't worry about it. I'll talk to her. I'm good at moms."

He still won't look away. Your whole body is shaking. "Uh. Uh."

He narrows his eyes and wrinkles his nose. "Stop doing that. It is the least attractive possible thing."

You try to stop shaking, with little success. At least you manage to shut up.

"Now where's your room? Let's do this."

"W—what?"

"Oh, come on! I'm a vampire. You're a—well, you're not a girl but you're close enough I guess. You knew this was going to happen when you invited me in."

You can't look away.

You can't look away.

In the movies, it always looks so sensual. Her long, soft neck. Her flesh yields, his teeth sink in. She gasps! He glowers towards the camera.

In real life, it doesn't feel like that at all. It's just you on your twin bed and you need to change the sheets and he's still wearing his jacket that smells weird.

Mostly, it just hurts. And it keeps hurting. And it never stops hurting.

It's been four days. You keep expecting someone to notice—you haven't been at school, you haven't been on Tumblr, you almost haven't left your room. But no one notices. Even your mom at the kitchen table, even when you walk right by her with open wounds on your throat, just stares at you and smiles.

It's like she's drunk. Except, for once, she isn't. She talks when she's drunk. She cries. Now when she's not at work she just sits at the kitchen table and smiles and doesn't say anything.

One day, when you're walking up the stairs from the bathroom, the vampire grabs you by the back of your neck and jams his pointer finger into the open holes he's left on your throat.

It feels like there's a worm crawling under your skin. It fucking hurts, too. You can't make yourself scream, but you can't stop shaking. You start to cry.

"Don't be a little bitch," he says, pulling out his finger and licking your blood off of it. "You know you like it." Some blood drips on the dirty white carpet. "Stop sobbing. I might nick an artery."

He sticks his pointer finger back in, and adds his middle. Fuck it hurts. Your knees start to give out and he pushes you against the wall to support your weight.

"Disgusting faggot," he says.

"You should change your pronouns in your bio," he says that night.

It's so unlike what he just did to you that it takes you a moment to respond. "What?"

"What?" he repeats in a dumb voice, mocking you. "It's not like you're really a girl anyway. And I don't want anyone to think I'm one of those *straight* vampires that are allegories for sexual violence. I'm clearly a queer-allegory vampire. You know, the cool kind. Freedom through transgression and shit."

Even after everything, the idea of changing the pronouns in your bio, of admitting that you've been pretending to be a girl, of admitting that it was just a joke—it *was* just a joke, right?—your stomach seizes up and your skin is cold and sweating and you can taste acid.

"Uh—" you say.

"Uhhhhh—" he repeats back.

You start to cry. Fuck. You hate crying. And in front of him.

"Fuck, what a little bitch you are!" He grabs your throat, roughly. You can't breathe, but somehow you're still crying. "Pedo creep. At least make yourself useful."

This time, he bites you on your chest, right through your rib cage. It doesn't even put up a fight.

The next morning, you change the pronouns on your bio to "he/him/himself."

Once upon a time, deep inside your heart, there was a girl. But she died. Because you fucking killed her.

callmemags98 asked:
Hi Alexandra! (Should I keep calling you Alexandra?)

You haven't posted much since your vampire-awareness reblogging spree. And now you changed your pronouns on your bio and, I don't know. I just wanted to make sure you were doing okay? I'm sure it's nothing; sorry for bothering you.

"You should block her," he says, one morning after breakfast, completely out of the clear blue sky. You're dizzy with blood loss and you don't understand him at first.

You know better than to say "what?" now. "Uh—who?"

"callmemargie or whoever. You need to block her."

"Why?" *How did he know?*

"Why? Because she's problematic as fuck. She does that cringey 'tiny awoo' thing, which is basically cultural appropriation from werewolves anyway."

"They," you say without even thinking of it, you stupid fucking bitch.

"What?" he says. He can say it.

Ahw, fuck. "No, nevermind—" you say but it's too late. He meets your eyes, for the first time in days. His eyes are brighter now, redder. It's even harder to look away.

"No. Tell me."

You start to shake and you swear the wounds on your neck start to bleed faster. "It's just, I think, they just changed their pronouns to they/them/themself."

He snorts and waves his hand. "Whatever. Everyone knows that genderqueers are just straight girls pretending to be special. Another reason to block her—*sorry*—'Them.'"

You try to shake your head, but you can't move. All you can see are his red, red eyes, the color of your blood, the size of the entire world. "Do it," he says. "Now."

steverogerssecretgirlfriend asked:
im sorry im sorry im sorry
you have blocked user callmemags98.

| Friendly reminder that v*mpire is a slur and you should never say it.
| I fucking hate it how 'allies' will just put a fucking * in the middle of the word like it makes a difference. "V*mpire" reads exactly the same as "Vampire." Just don't fucking do any of it.
| I'm so sorry!
| a w o °
| a w o °

| Oh check out this bitch! She's "sorry"

| a w o °

| to everyone asking "what should we say instead" educate yourself. gocgle is free.

He shakes you awake from a dead sleep in the middle of the night.

"You should stop calling me 'he.'"

"Huh?"

"I mean, I'm a fucking vampire. Gender is just some bloodbag shit."

"Uh. Okay. What should I call you?"

"Call me a vampire."

"But—uh. It's—"

"What?"

"It's a slur, right?"

"Oh. Sure, whatever."

"So what should I call you?"

"I don't give a fuck. Sounds like a you problem."

Once upon a time there was a girl who turned her heart inside out, so that all her love was on the outside, in the whole wide world, and all the fear and hatred and apathy was inside of her. "If I can just hold it all inside me," she told herself, "all the way until I die, then everything will be fine forever."

And it was fine, or at least it was okay, or at the very least she survived. But one day, she met a man who wore, outside of him, all the same fear and hatred and apathy that she kept inside her heart. And so, of course, she opened her heart to him, and all that pain flowed out of her heart until it was empty, until she was empty, until she was nothing but a vessel for everything he hated.

You're down in the kitchen getting some dry Cheerios™ because your mom doesn't buy food anymore and everything else in the house is rotting, when you see her, at the same place she's always sitting, her head hanging at a weird angle. At first, you think maybe she's hungover and sleeping it off. But she doesn't drink anymore, not since he—the vamp—the v*mp—someone arrived. And her neck looks weird, and you take another look and her neck is half off and there's scabbed up blood all down her clothes and she's not breathing and oh my God oh my God oh my God.

"I can*not* believe this," someone says, casually tearing a gouge into your bedroom drywall. "I should never have trusted you. Fucking allies! This is the *definition* of viviocentrism."

Viviocentrism! You know you shouldn't say anything. It's just going to make things worse. But before you can stop yourself, without even thinking (if you thought, you would stay quiet, like you should) you squeak out "but you killed my mom."

"So? She was a bitch."

"I... I..." you can feel the heat rising in your face, and of course now, of all times, you finally start to cry for the first time since you found her dead this morning. Fuck. Like, she wasn't—with the drinking and everything. It wasn't really her fault. But she was still your *mom*. You still *loved* her. And you never really told her, but you were *going to*. And now you *can't*. And yeah maybe she was a bitch but "she was *my mom*."

"So? Why is her life so much more *valuable* than mine?" Someone grabs your stuffed elephant—Mimi, the one you've had since you were born—off the shelf and squeezes her so hard her head pops open. "*Educate yourself*."

That's bad. Stop talking. "But ..." fuck why are you saying this stop talking stop talking you stupid faggoty bitch "I mean—you don't have to—you don't have—I mean—"

"Oh please spit out whatever bigoted bullshit you're going to say, fucking last thing I want to do is spend all night listening to your flabby-ass blubbering mouthsounds."

"You don't have to kill someone, right? To li—to survive." You don't say "you haven't killed me." You don't want to give someone an idea.

"So? I wanted to. I'm a vampire. I kill people. Are you saying I'm not *allowed*?"

"I—I—"

"She wouldn't even use your pronouns. I did you a favor. Fucking bloodbags, I swear to Satan!"

"Bloodbag" hurts. But, like—god. Punching up. Vivioprivilege. *Something*.

Suddenly, wildly, you wish you could talk to Mags again. They were always so good about just—I don't know. They could tell what mattered and what didn't.

But they aren't here because you *blocked* them and—they aren't here. You try your best to swallow your tears and nod.

"Oh, god, you're so fucking disgusting. What a pedo bitch you are! Fuck. I can't even look at you. Get out—" It's your room. "GET OUT!" Someone shoves you towards the door so hard you fall flat on your face. "Don't come back until you're ready to apologize and thank me."

You sit outside your mom's house—your house? she's dead, so maybe it's your house?—for nearly an hour before someone bangs out of the door, still angry. "I'm just letting you know that I'm writing a callout post about you. You're still not allowed in the house."

"What?" You've just been out here, crying and cold and shaking in just a T-shirt and sweatpants, and someone's been writing a callout post? It's just so bizarre.

"What?" someone replies, mocking you. "Fuck I hate you."

"What—what—what's in the post?"

"Oh you name it! Viviocentrism, pretending to be a girl, being a total fucking creep, supporting pedophilia—"

"W-what? I don't—"

"I mean, I'm like three hundred years old. And you're, what? Fifteen? That's pretty fucking creepy that you'd come onto me like this. Like, ugh. You're barely an infant to me. You still read *fairy tales.*"

"Why—why are you saying this?"

"If you want me to forgive you, if you want to apologize, then you need to post it yourself. You need to apologize. Not just to me. But to everyone."

You try not to meet those red, red eyes. But somehow they're everywhere you look.

"You're not coming back into this house until you do." You know—somehow you know—that this is wrong. Someone will get hungry; it won't be long. But when you hear those words, and when you see those eyes, you can't help yourself. You're so afraid. You're so pathetic. You just want to be—not even loved. Just *useful.*

"I'll do it," you say. "I'm so sorry. I shouldn't have been upset with you."

"You shouldn't have been upset with me for *what?*"

"For—for killing my mom."

"She had it coming."

You nod. "She had it coming."

Once upon a time, there was a girl whose parents could not afford to keep her. So they sent her through the deep, dark woods, to the cottage where Grandmother lived, for Grandmother would take in any child.

As she walked through that forest, cold and starving, a wolf came upon her. "Little girl," said the wolf. "Why are you walking alone in these deep, dark woods?"

"My parents cannot afford to keep me," said the girl, who had no other virtues but at least was honest. "So I am going to see Grandmother, who will take in any child."

"Little girl," said the wolf. "Surely you know as well as I that Grandmother is at last a witch, as wicked as she is cruel, and the fate of all her children crueler still."

"I know this well," said the girl. "But where else am I to go?"

It's been a month. You're not eating any more—you can't bear to walk through the kitchen, to hear the flies and smell her corpse. That doesn't stop someone from eating every night, though. Your arms are like fucking sticks but somehow your thighs are still gross and flabby.

Someone doesn't talk to you anymore. Why would anyone bother talking to you?

When the doorbell rings that night it barely registers. Even when someone—not *that* someone, someone else—calls out "Alex? Alexandra? Are you there?" you can barely respond.

Someone gets up. "I'll handle this."

You're alone. Finally. With your hunger and the pain in your throat and chest and legs and dick and everywhere else you've been bitten.

Alone. Bliss.

"I don't know what to tell you. There's no Alex here."

You don't hear the response.

"Lucifer P. Morningstar! Will you shut up? Get the fuck out of my house, bitch, before I call the cops."

Somehow, inside, you think you should pay attention. You should say something. You try to stand up, fail, then roll out of bed and crawl towards the top of the stairs.

You look down, at the front door, and Mags is standing right in the center of it. They look different than you thought—they're shorter than you'd imagined, and fatter—but it's them.

But you *blocked* them, you think. You *had* to block them. It takes you a minute to realize why that doesn't matter.

Behind Mags there's a couple of big, rough-looking guys in leather caps and jackets. One of them has a bushy beard. Why do you care about that? It doesn't matter.

Someone—the someone at the door—doesn't seem disturbed.

"Alexandra?" yells Mags, again, and you can't make yourself respond. They move to push past someone, who stops them with a hand on their shoulder.

"Bad idea, bitch." Someone grimaces, and suddenly all you can see is sharp white teeth, lurching forward to bite, hungry.

No. No! "Mags!" you yell, except it's barely a whisper.

And then, suddenly, like their human body was just a trick of the light, there's just this *fucking enormous wolf* filling your entryway.

Mags snarls and leaps right into someone, snapping wildly. Someone goes tumbling back, not even a body, just a mass of shadows and teeth and red eyes, smashing into your drywall. Mags pins them against the wall—both enormous paws—and snaps again. This time, their teeth sink home. They tear, and then another bite, and then another, and then there's half a dozen wolves alongside them, all tearing into the shadow on your wall.

Blood flies everywhere. It's so much. You had no idea a body could hold that much blood.

"Alexandra? Alex?" Mags' voice from down the stairs is low and throaty, like a wolf. They *are* a wolf.

You realize they can *see* you and—fuck. "I'm sorry," you sob out. Pathetic blubbering bitch. "I'm sorry I was pretending to be a girl."

Mags climbs the stairs and sits down next to you. They set their cold nose on your temple and lick your cheek with a rough tongue. "Oh honey," they say. "I don't think you were pretending."

You keep crying. "It's my fault. It's my fault. They're a vam—they're...it's just what they are."

Mags growls. "Nothing wrong with vampires," they say. "But there's plenty wrong with abusive pieces of shit."

You don't know how to respond to that. So you don't.

"Climb on my back," says Mags. "Let's get the hell out of here."

You're still crying, and they nose you again. Very slowly, weakly, you climb up onto them, hesitating at each step. "Just grab a big handful of fur," they say, and you do, with as much strength as you can, which isn't much. They smell rough and wet, and their fur is so thick so warm that your teeth start chattering.

They plod carefully down the stairs, past all the blood, past the shadows and the teeth and everything, out the door, out the door, into the cool, wet night and the light of the moon behind the clouds.

"Awoo!" they howl, and their pack answers.

"Awoo!"

"Awoo!"

"Awoo!"

"AWOO!" you scream, again and again, until your voice is just a whisper, until the moon is dark behind the clouds, until your throat is raw and ragged and yours.

Once upon a time, there was a story about a wolf and a girl, and they loved each other very much.

PH Lee lives on top of an old walnut tree, past a thicket of roses, down a dead end street at the edge of town. Their work has appeared in many venues including *Clarkesworld*, *Lightspeed*, and *Uncanny Magazine*. From time to time, they microwave and eat a frozen burrito at two in the morning, for no reason other than that they want to.

FIVE VIEWS OF THE PLANET TARTARUS

Rachael K. Jones

1.

Once a decade, a titanium-nosed shuttle plows through the rings of the planet Tartarus with a new batch of prisoners destined for the Orpheus Factory. The debris that makes up the rings is so thick that it thunders like a hailstorm, deafening the passengers. As the orbiting debris bounces and scrapes against the hull, the prisoners squeeze their eyes closed and beg the pilot to be more careful.

"Are you trying to hit all of them?" a prisoner snaps, covering his ears against the roaring onslaught.

The pilot laughs through her nose. Ironic. Dismissive. "We always do. As many as we can."

She steers into the path of the debris, and the thundering increases.

2.

Planetside, they hold a farce of a trial in the Sibylline Court, a decaying mansion of rotten marble. All traitors to the Sibyllines go to Tartarus to receive the only punishment for rebellion: eternal life.

The prisoners stand at attention as the comms read out their names. A whirring ten-limbed auto-judge pronounces their sentences in turn, omitting no words from the traditional declaration of guilt, because the Sibylline Empire believes in ceremony.

3.

One by one the prisoners file into a dark, square mouth cut from the earth: the Orpheus Factory. Machines shred their clothes and lather them in amber disinfectant that burns the skin and smells like tar and makes all their hair fall out. Tiny silver needles snake into their veins. Nanobots pump into their blood, flooding their organs, cleaning off plaques, lengthening telomeres, repairing neurons.

The last injection severs their voluntary motor pathways so nothing moves but their eyes. Before the final step, the prisoners feel young again, for a moment.

4.

The last gift of the planet Tartarus to its newborn residents is a brand-new spacesuit, bright white, top of the line, with solar-powered life support that can recycle respirated air and bodily wastes for up to two hundred years, should nothing breach the suit's barrier. Machines thread the prisoners' bodies with tubes for feeding and waste disposal. At the end of this process, the Orpheuses are piled together outside beneath the dark sky, their terrified eyes flickering behind their faceplates, their lips drawn back by spasticity into a tight, cramped grin.

When the job is done, the pilot who flew the inbound shuttle loads them back into the cargo bay, stacking the bodies high and deep, like firewood.

5.

On its way through the planetary belt, the shuttle dumps the new Orpheuses into the ring that loops round and round Tartarus like a dirge that will never end. That is when the prisoners will see all the frozen white spacesuits, billions in orbit, their eyes aware and flickering behind well-made helmets, their blood pumped full of machines that won't let them die, their bodies spinning around the planet forever and ever.

They will float eternally, unable to sleep. They will pray for a rogue asteroid to career into their path and breach their suits. Ten years later, when they see the silver-tipped shuttle approach the weary planet, they will pray for the vessel to smash into their bodies as it enters orbit and descends to the surface.

The pilots do always try to hit as many as they can.

....

Rachael K. Jones grew up in various cities across Europe and North America, picked up (and mostly forgot) six languages, and acquired several degrees in the arts and sciences. Now she writes speculative fiction in Portland, Oregon. Rachael is a Eugie Award winner, and a finalist for the Hugo, Nebula, Locus, Bram Stoker, and World Fantasy Award. Her fiction has appeared in dozens of venues worldwide, including *Lightspeed*, *Beneath Ceaseless Skies*, *Strange Horizons*, and Amazon Prime's hit series *SECRET LEVEL*. Follow her on Bluesky @RachaelKJones.bsky.social, or find her at www.RachaelKJones.com.

THE WITCH TRAP

Jennifer Hudak

These floors, original to the house, have witnessed the turn of two centuries. The shoe concealed beneath them is older. Laces replaced, sole thrice mended, the shoe still bears the impression of the big toe that for years pressed against the worn upper. Now, it rests mateless between floor joists, a curiosity for spiders and mice. No longer a shoe, but a summons.

The witch smells what has been hidden— leather, dirt, and sweat—and cannot help herself. She makes her way down the chimney, into the walls, beneath the floor, and into the shoe, expecting to find human flesh inside. Once trapped, the witch beats immaterial fists against the inside of the toe box. She wails for the sky, for her horned god, for the crescent moon above. But it's no use. Eventually, she fades. The shoe absorbs the witch, becoming more than what it was.

The contractor discovers it when he pries up the floorboards near what used to be the hearth. Seeing the dark shape there, he jerks back reflexively, then leans in for a closer look before lifting it out: an antique made of worn black leather, with obvious signs of repair, covered in dust.

"Hey, Liz," he calls. "Come take a look at this."

Elizabeth doesn't appreciate the nickname, nor the familiarity, but the contractor has been calling her that since he first arrived, and it seems too late to do anything about it now. She closes her laptop and swallows her frustration. "What is it?"

"Check it out." The contractor holds up the shoe. "I found this."

Elizabeth takes it from him. The leather looks like wrinkled skin. "I don't understand. In my floors?"

"I've heard about this kind of thing," he says. "Shoes hidden under floors or in the walls, to keep away witches. Never seen one before, though."

"Why a shoe? How would that keep witches away?"

"It's just a superstition. You know, like not walking under a ladder, that kind of thing. I don't think you're supposed to take it literally. Anyway, I thought you'd be interested. Sorry if I interrupted you."

"It's fine," she says, with a glance back at her laptop. Technically, she's working from home today. Her friends told her she shouldn't expect to get anything done with a contractor in the house, and she's beginning to think they were right.

"I can take that if you want, Liz. Put it back where I found it before I put the new floor down. Just in case," he clarifies with a laugh. "I mean, on the off chance it actually works. You never know, right?"

The shoe is warm to the touch, even though the floors always feel cold. "Maybe. But I'll hold onto it," Elizabeth says. "For now."

She takes her laptop and the shoe upstairs to her bedroom, to escape the noise and dust of the renovation. There, she pulls the quilt off her bed—a crazy quilt, made by her great-aunt and gifted to Elizabeth on her fortieth birthday when it became clear that there was no point in saving it for a wedding present—and sits in the rocking chair in the corner. With the quilt wrapped around her shoulders, Elizabeth ignores her email inbox and instead searches the web for information about shoes hidden in floors.

What she finds is astonishing. The Concealed Shoe Index, run by the Northampton Museum and Art Gallery in England, includes nearly 3,000 individual shoes found beneath floors, behind walls, in chimneys and in hearths, across 2,000 different locations. Elizabeth looks at photographs of the shoes in their collection—piles of shoes, all of them worn and ancient, still carrying the impressions of countless feet whose owners have been dead for much longer than Elizabeth has been alive—and wonders why she's never heard of this before.

She learns that scholars disagree on the purpose the shoes were intended to serve. Some believe they were considered a charm to enhance fertility or impart good luck. Others say, as the contractor had, that the shoes, having been infused with the essence of their wearers, could deflect the incursions of witches and other evil spirits. But no one knows for sure.

Most intriguing to Elizabeth is the theory that the shoes were not intended to keep witches away, but to trap them. To lure a witch with the promise of a tasty human to attack and consume, and then to imprison her within leather. There is no historical documentation of this belief, but a practice like this would have been whispered from ear to ear, traded between neighbors like eggs or nails. It would have required both repetition and belief in order to work.

In 1486, sanctioned by the Bull of Pope Innocent VIII, Heinrich Kramer and James Sprenger penned the *Malleus Maleficarum*. In the text, they claimed—with vivid detail—that witches copulated with demons and suckled animal familiars, that they ate babies and could make a man's penis disappear. The last section of the book offered helpful instructions for the prosecution of witches, including how to torture them in order to obtain the necessary confession. Indeed, over the next two hundred years, tens of thousands of witches were sent into the cleansing fires, crying out for mercy that neither Lord nor devil would provide.

Imagine, for a moment, how terrifying it must have been: not knowing if the woman who shared your home and bed, who bore and raised your children, turned into a bat when you were sleeping and flew into the night to do the devil's bidding! In some ways, the *Malleus*, with its lurid and titillating descriptions, can be seen as an attempt to draw a firm line between heretical witches and good Christian wives. To construct a definition of the witch that, in turn, defined who was not a witch at all—set down in print, in unchangeable type, between leather covers.

But between those covers, the witch gained form. The words invoked her, called her into being. And as more people open the book and read it, as more copies are printed and reprinted and disbursed, she comes into being again and again, invading our imaginations, cackling and powerful and free.

[*Someone clears their throat and looks pointedly at the clock. It's nearly five minutes past the hour; you're going to have to begin. You look out at the handful of people slumping in their seats and try not to be disappointed.*]

I want to thank you all for being here, so bright and early. I hope everyone has their coffee—or the magical equivalent of caffeine! [*You pause for laughter; none arises. After a brief moment of awkward silence, you continue.*] My name is Mara Forbes, and today I'm going to be presenting my paper on the biopsychosocial causes of the witchcraft hysteria in New England in the late seventeenth century.

[*A person sitting near the back glances at their phone and leaves the room. You wait for the door to close behind them before starting to read.*]

In Puritan New England, magic was as much a part of daily life as the Church. Colonists spoke both Bible verses and folk magics with the same unconflicted tongue; why shouldn't they, when both kept their households healthy and whole? Those in need of magics beyond their own abilities might call upon local healers known as cunning women, who peddled herbal remedies and divinations. Yet all that changed in 1692, when the shrieking girls of Salem Village accused homeless beggars, slaves, and churchgoing mothers alike with witchcraft most foul.

[*You remind yourself to glance up at your audience periodically. To animate your face. To make yourself charismatic and vivacious. The man in the front row is on his phone, and you wonder why he even bothered to come.*]

When facing the magistrates, the accused— often women who were old and unmarried, both reasons for suspicion in the colonies—either admitted to signing the devil's book in exchange for their abilities, or denied it, and found themselves drowned by dunking or strangled at the end of a noose.

[*Someone coughs. You wonder if perhaps you were given the first programming slot of the morning on purpose. No stragglers have entered the room; it's just you and this sparse, disinterested clutch of academics for the duration. You consider giving up, saying*]

'The End,' and leaving the room. Instead, you focus on the sound of your own voice. On the rhythm of your language, if not the words themselves.]

So what changed? What caused the colonists to see demons where they once saw herbs, charms, and trinkets? We can only speculate. Modern scholars, poets, and playwrights have blamed the hysteria on religious fundamentalism, population stress, bacterial infections, romantic grievances, even a psychedelic fungus that might have made its way into the stored grain. The only thing we know for certain is that there were no actual witches in Salem Village, because witches do not exist.

[*Even as you say the words, you wonder if you believe them. You wonder what it would feel like to shriek rhyming couplets until the man in the front finally looks up from his phone, to recite spells until your voice is hoarse, until everyone flees in fear. You imagine grabbing your broomstick and flying through the corridors until you reach an open window and the sky welcomes you home. You visualize your words weaving themselves together, licking themselves up your body like flames, making you burn bright with power.*]

Beneath the floorboards, the witch feels the knock and drag of generations of footsteps overhead. She no longer has hands with which to cast spells, nor legs that can straddle a broomstick. If her horned god ever existed, he has not come to liberate her here. So she chooses patience. The witch has become the shoe, has become *more* than the shoe, has filled up the interstitial spaces of the house with magic and the hint of smoke. In the small cubby between the floor joists, she listens, and waits, and lives on.

Excerpt from the article "The Coven Next Door" by Mike Untweiler (*Today! Magazine*, September 1988)

The ladies of the Fourth Street Coven had assured me that I'd be welcome at their open circle, but I'll admit to a moment of trepidation when I arrived at the address they'd given me. Sure, it looked like a perfectly normal, suburban house, but what would I find hidden inside? Cackling biddies chanting naked around a bubbling cauldron? Slender goddesses reeking of incense, gazing at crystals? And, more importantly, would they turn me into a toad before the evening was through?

As it turned out, none of those stereotypes were entirely true, but that's not to say they were entirely false, either. The Fourth Street Witches do sometimes gather in the nude, although (sadly) not in front of this reporter. They use both incense and crystals, although I wouldn't call any of the ladies slender. And while the coven claims to practice magic, I'm happy to report that I wasn't turned into a toad. In fact, aside from the altar in the corner— adorned with pentacles and laden with tealights, crystal balls, and tarot cards—the vibe was less "occult gathering" and more "wannabe Woodstock." The women (or should I call them "womyn"?) wore loose dresses and silver jewelry; most of them were barefoot, and none of them, as far as I could tell, shaved their legs.

(. . . .)

A vegetarian potluck followed the opening incantation. While I balanced a plate of brown rice salad and tofu cutlets on my lap, the High Priestess of the coven—a short, chunky brunette named Leslie—offered to give me a brief introduction to the history of Neo-Pagan Witchcraft, beginning with the writings of British folklorist Margaret Murray.

In the 1920s and '30s, Murray wrote a series of books hypothesizing that a Dianic cult thrived among the simple, uneducated folk in prehistoric Europe and England. The members of this cult practiced magic, kept familiars, and gathered at Sabbats; according to Murray, they were valued in their communities as advisors and healers. It was the Christians (they're the baddies in Murray's version of history) who labeled the cult heretics and witches. During the long years that the Church held sway, members of the cult were either burned at the stake, or went into hiding to survive.

Modern-day Wiccans, including the Fourth Street Coven, claim to be spiritual descendants of this cult, at long last able to live freely in the public eye as Goddess-worshiping magic-makers whose fundamental principle is "An' ye harm none, do what ye will."

Margaret Murray's work, of course, has long since been thoroughly debunked. Modern folklorists agree that her scholarship was shoddy, her "evidence" selective, and her conclusions utter nonsense. When I mentioned this to Leslie, she gave me a tight smile.

"What we are doing here is changing the narrative. We are saying that the patriarchy is an aberration—a small blip in the natural order of things—and if it is an aberration, it can be overcome."

I asked her if that meant she believed Margaret Murray's ridiculous witch-cult hypothesis. She regarded me for a long moment before she answered, and when she did, her voice was decidedly less pleasant.

"It doesn't matter whether we believe Murray's theories or not. History is written by the victors, yes? Well. We are rewriting it." She paused, and smiled once more. "So mote it be."

Around the room, others clinked their glasses and echoed the call: "So mote it be."

Elizabeth glances at the shoe again. It smells slightly of smoke. She is not superstitious, but something about the shoe pricks at her intuition. It isn't just a shoe; in being hidden, it has been invested with a different meaning, become something other than what it was. Yet what exactly it has become eludes her.

She closes her laptop and sets it aside. With the shoe in her lap, she skims her fingertips over cracked, brittle leather. It should feel empty and inert, but it doesn't. It isn't. Inside the shoe, something breathes. Something presses back against Elizabeth's touch. Something that has swallowed its own story for centuries asks for eyes to see and ears to hear, for blood and lymph and skin. It asks for its voice once again.

With her eyes closed, Elizabeth pulls apart the shoe's disintegrating laces, and feels another set of fingertips weaving with hers.

LunaBelle lights a candle on their altar, grabs their phone, and logs into the chat for solo witches who are practicing "in the broom closet," so to speak. This chat is the first place they felt free to use the name LunaBelle—the name they chose for themself. In school, everyone still uses LunaBelle's birth name, but here, they can be exactly who they choose.

This is who I am, they think as they enter the chat. *This is who I've always been.*

LunaBelle has read books and consulted oracle decks and perused dozens of websites in search of answers, but they've only found more questions. All they know for certain is that the explanations offered by their teachers, parents, and therapist are nothing but insufficient platitudes. LunaBelle doesn't necessarily blame any of them. It's human nature: when faced with something they don't understand, people will always try to force it to make sense—to place it in a tidy little box tied with a neat bow. Even if the box doesn't fit. Even if you damage the thing getting it inside.

LunaBelle knows that no one understands them. They aren't sure they understand themself. But they are sick of squeezing themself into the wrong box. They feel as though there's more to life—more to *themself*—than can be explained by well-meaning adults, and that perhaps the gap between the easy explanations and the truth of themself is an untapped source of power.

None of the witches in the chat have met each other in person. It doesn't matter. Together, they discuss spells and charms and rituals; they trade memes; they share the pain of hiding who they are. They refer to each other by their chosen names, and the words are an incantation. An invocation. LunaBelle feels as if, together, they are making themselves real—creating themselves anew out of all this confusion and uncertainty.

The candle flickers and flares on the altar. LunaBelle feels themself opening like a flower. They feel themself becoming something solid, something new. Something powerful.

They feel themself becoming.

Humble pine planks wait to be set down in this brick house newly built in the Year of Our Lord 1833, but before the carpenter fits them together and nails them into place, he pulls a single woman's shoe from his pack. Not long ago, this shoe and its mate adorned his wife's slender feet. Now... He dips his head so the others won't see the dampness on his cheeks. Then he clears his throat, tucks the shoe between the floor joists, and stands. Let it do some good, he tells himself. Let it keep those who will live here safe from harm.

When the contractor is packing up his tools for the day, he asks Elizabeth, once again, if she wants him to replace the shoe beneath the floorboards.

"It's not too late, Liz," he tells her. "Just give me the word, and I'll put it right back where I found it. Let it keep the witches away like it was meant to."

"It's Elizabeth, not Liz," she answers. "And I think..." She pauses, and feels herself smile. "I think it's time to let the witches in."

The contractor laughs uncertainly, but stops when Elizabeth does not laugh with him.

"Well," he says after an awkward pause. "I guess I'll see you in the morning."

After he's gone, Elizabeth pours herself a glass of wine and carries it to her room. The shoe sits on the crazy quilt like a black cat, alert and watchful. Elizabeth sips her wine and then picks up the shoe, turning it in her hands. It's empty now, but it still hums with leftover power. She can hear every step the shoe made, every retort of rigid heel against wooden floor. She can feel every foot that stretched its leather, every hand that pulled the laces tight. She wonders what it would feel like to wear it, even though it is much too small. She wonders if her foot will shrink to fit it, or if the shoe will unfurl itself like bat wings.

When the sun sets, the crescent moon peers through the window.

Jennifer Hudak is a Nebula-nominated speculative fiction writer whose work can be found in venues such as *Strange Horizons*, *The Magazine of Fantasy & Science Fiction*, *Lady Churchill's Rosebud Wristlet*, and *The Sunday Morning Transport*. She is a 2018 graduate of the Viable Paradise workshop and a member of the Codex Writers' Group. Originally from Boston, she now lives with her family in Upstate New York where she teaches yoga, knits pocket-sized animals, and misses the ocean. Find out more about her at JenniferHudakWrites.com.

EVAN: A REMAINDER

Jordan Kurella

May 2020, and I was spitting out little bits of tooth in the sink.

Teeth, tiny pieces of bone-colored enamel. Initially I thought it was stress, what with me being newly divorced, newly lonely, newly living out of cardboard boxes in a haunted half a duplex. I got four pieces of furniture in the divorce; the worst pieces of furniture from a great marriage that ended when my ex-husband told me, "Evan, I love you, you're terrific, but I'm just not gay." All because I told him at Thanksgiving that I'm a man. He sent me a holiday card, a picture of him and his new girlfriend. She's pretty.

I didn't send him a holiday card of me and the bloodstain that was on the dining room floor. That would have been weird. Also, I wasn't dating the bloodstain, though I used to spend enough time with it that we might as well have been dating. Christ's sake.

By May of 2020, I'd been on testosterone for three weeks. By then the only results were a big gain in confidence and tiny pieces of tooth in the sink. Of course, I thought spitting out bits of my teeth meant I had COVID, so, I freaked out. No matter how much I thought being under-employed and single meant that my life was the worst, I didn't actually want to die. Not really. So, instead, I swept up the teeth bits with a paper towel and put them in a jar in the basement. Because bones go underground.

When not sweeping up bits of my teeth, or doing a rideshare, or getting high with my neighbor Katie, I was busy working on that bloodstain on the dining room floor. Or what would be a dining room if I had any furniture. Katie called herself a professional stoner and conspiracy theorist. She was the one who said the house was *verified haunted*. Told me she was the one who could prove it. I didn't need proof; the bloodstain was enough. It wouldn't come off even with the best of the worst chemicals.

I, however, didn't sign on for a dead roommate. Which is why I was trying to get rid of the one I had. Katie was undeterred, kept showing up with more evidence.

Asked if I had found cold spots in weird places. There were, yeah. Like in the bathroom, the dining room, in the kitchen by the window. I told her that old houses were drafty and that she was weird. She stuck her tongue out at me and told me that I didn't believe in anything. She was right.

None of what Katie said was true about ghosts. What was true was that I was obsessed with the bloodstain, and Katie was obsessed with my obsession. She stopped by on the regular asking me how the cleaning was going. Would pop over to my porch already half-baked and ask how the cleaning was going. Then she'd ask if she could come in and see how the cleaning was going. It was a routine that we'd settled on, like I settle for too much with too many weird people.

Which was probably why I told Katie about the teeth.

"Gross. See a dentist, Evan."

"Nah," I said, exhaling. "My dreams are getting swole like the rest of me."

"You're grinding your teeth in your sleep," she said.

"Everyone grinds their teeth in their sleep."

"Very funny. Ha ha," she said. "You know the ghost was murdered, right? They were murdered right there in your house. Maybe with one knife or several knives, I dunno. Not a forensic scientist or a *CSI* devotee."

"Were they murdered because they were a good person, or murdered because they were a bad person?"

I was fully high at this point and fully into Katie's bullshit.

Katie shrugged and tried to look in my window. "Dunno. That's not for me to decide. I only moved in after, cause people like you and me belong here. Verified messes and absolute weirdos."

September 2021, and I have a new boyfriend.

The meet-cute of my current boyfriend goes like this: I found him in my back-yard, climbing out of the grave I dug for him. He looked as surprised to be there as I was surprised to see him. Or maybe he was angry? Hard to tell with skeletons, since they can't smile and their faces are frozen in a perpetual reminder that death sucks.

Brought him inside as fast as I could, because Katie is addicted to anything paranormal. The last thing I needed was her overinterest in my lack of interest in grave robbing. So, I threw my coat over Skeleton Boyfriend and rushed him inside. He's been with me ever since. I got used to him fast, was easy. My cat, however, did not. Keep telling myself it'll take time, as she takes time with everything.

Dating Skeleton Boyfriend might be considered weird. But on a scale of one to ten of weird boyfriends I've had in my life? Ten being the weirdest? He's a solid four.

June 2020, and people thought the pandemic was over.

That's when I met Dylan on a dating app. Also found a cat on an adoption site. Dylan and I sexted long distance for months, and the cat moved in the day I saw her picture. The cat's name at the shelter was "Butch," because she had one eye and an attitude problem. I also had an attitude problem, all my exes said so. So, Butch came home, and I re-named her "Meowfistopheles" or "Meowsers" or "Meow-Meow."

Meow-Meow stuck, the others didn't. Because Meow-Meow implies some self-respect.

Dylan didn't move in for a while after, but his attitude was just as relatable. He was hornier than I was, hilariously funny, and more skilled with his phone than I was with stain remover. Unlike me, Dylan's office went remote rather than just laying everyone off. He had insurance and too much time on his hands, he said. I was old hat at the delivery gig-work thing, so our lives conveniently matched: he'd be bored in a meeting and sexting me while I was trying to find a place to park on High Street to drop off a meat-lovers supreme.

Dylan was a great boyfriend: he was hot to look at, hotter to listen to, and had a way with smut. Meow-Meow was a great cat because she destroyed all four pieces of my ex-husband's furniture and made it unrecognizable. I was also becoming unrecognizable: my neck had muscles I didn't know I could even possess, my face had caverns and those caverns had hair growing out of them, and my hands looked like they belonged to someone else. I thought for the first time in my life that I might actually be happy.

But I wasn't, not really. The coughing up thing was still happening. Which I didn't tell Dylan about: new boyfriends are down to bone, but probably not down with actual real bones coming out of my throat. Also Meow-Meow, come to find, was a bona fide scaredy cat. Everything scared her: the dining room, the bathroom, the kitchen window. She spent thirty percent of her time in Halloween-posed zoomies, forty percent of her time napping, and the rest of it staring out the window at cat stuff.

Katie said the cat was stressed and needed to go outside. She said cats belonged outside, roaming free and being cats. Katie says a lot of things, only some of which make sense. But she did shut up about the dentist, and never complained about my retching cough, which I am sure she could hear through the walls.

It's not like I was quiet about it: waking up, choking on a finger bone, or like an entire rib or something. Life, frankly, was awful. Yet the more this went on, the less hollow I felt. Kinda like I was getting a grip on being an adult. Still though, I went to a dentist, and a doctor. My teeth were fine, not a bit or any bits missing. Doctor ordered an X-Ray, and I was still full of all my original bones. A complete man, but I wasn't happy.

That is, until July when I got a text from Dylan that said:

been thinking, baby, i can't live another day without feeling your blow jobs for real. gimme your address, honey. i'm cumming over.

September 2021, and Meow-Meow hates her life.

Skeleton Boyfriend has his favorite places in the house. He likes to be in the kitchen by the window. He likes the bathroom mirror, trying on hats. He really likes the dining room, particularly the spot where that old bloodstain used to be. Our tastes are the same and yet different. He always wants meat for dinner, so I have to text Dylan to ask about good restaurants or recipes for that sort of thing. I keep trying to be a vegetarian, which Skeleton Boyfriend thinks is silly, since it was legit his bones I unearthed from inside of me.

Sometimes it feels like so much of what he says are things I wished I had said, or things I swallowed instead of saying. Skeleton Boyfriend is everything I wanted to be when I was femme, and everything I wished I could be in public, but don't know if it's allowed, or okay, or just what is even a man. But he doesn't care. He's a skeleton, who's going to stop him?

Dylan knows I'm seeing someone else, doesn't know it's the bones we both buried. Some things some people don't need to know. Like Skeleton Boyfriend doesn't know I'm texting Dylan, cause Skeleton Boyfriend thinks Dylan is a piece of absolute ass that he wants to "climb like a flagpole."

Skeleton Boyfriend may be unsettling to some people. He's a skeleton. He legit crawled out of the grave Dylan and I dug for him. Also, his sense of humor isn't really one after all. But he says he loves me and I really kinda need that right now. So, everything is pretty much fine. To talk to Katie, though, it's rude that I don't join her on the porch as much as I used to. And it's weird that I keep the door shut all the time, and the blinds closed.

At one of our less often than usual porch meetings she said, "You're being mean to that cat, also kind of mean to me, cause I can't see the cat. I'm suffering, Evan, since I haven't been able to see Meow-Meow in the window. Open the damn blinds."

"You need to cut down on the weed, Katie."

"Rude, Evan." She slouched again. "And you know what else? It's mean that you don't let me in to see your new boyfriend. I know you have one, I can feel him moving around in there."

"Feel him?"

"*Feel* him."

Katie being weird aside, hanging out with Skeleton Boyfriend is easier than I thought it would be. I had been thinking, since Dylan had left months ago, that I was the bad guy in all my relationships. Some sort of pathological loser, so weird that I couldn't keep my proverbial ducks in a row, which is why everyone left eventually. And why I was always so fucking alone.

Maybe it's true: maybe I was too weird to have the living love me.

Skeleton Boyfriend, though, does love me. He tells me so, a lot. I tell him so, a lot. Maybe it's the adage that misery loves company, or the fact that a lot of my exes have said I'm dead inside.

Meow-Meow will get used to him, eventually. She has to. Ever since Skeleton Boyfriend showed up, she's spent her time hiding in cupboards, or angrily grooming herself on my underwear. She'll eventually grow to like him, like I eventually did. Hopefully sooner rather than later, because Katie says the house is un-haunted now.

"That's great," I said, half-baked and half-asleep.

"Yeah," she said, in a similar state. "I can say that it's officially possessed."

"Cool."

September 2020, and Dylan moved in officially.

The bloodstain was disappearing from the floor and I had three jars of bones collected in the basement (plus a giant plastic crate packed with the bigger, more complete bones: bits of ribcage, spine, etc.). By September, I had nearly an entire body, minus some essential parts, which were starting to freak me out. I really, really, did not want to think about coughing up a skull.

When Dylan moved in, I had been on testosterone for nearly six months. Figured out shaving, skin was calming down, and I had my aesthetic nailed to T-shirt and jeans and looking pretty much invisible to anyone and everyone. I felt totally boss.

Dylan said I looked like a boss when he held me down on the bed.

Around the apartment, he called me his absolute hunk, his only man, his best piece of ass. I loved every second of it. And when he arrived that September from two or three states over with four days of stubble and looking like death warmed over, I fell in love with him all over again. He stepped down from the height of the U-Haul with every ounce of wired/tired and kissed me on High Street.

"I'm home," he said.

Would've replied, but I couldn't talk. He was too hot to be real.

Moved his stuff in, only the expensive shit, barely. Got interrupted by kissing, in *our* apartment, tripping over his computer and camera equipment and camping stuff to fall on the couch. Meow-Meow disappeared for three hours; and for fifteen minutes of that time, I gave Dylan one of those smut-fueled blow jobs. He smelled disgusting but I didn't care. I missed him and it was our house, back then.

Two hours later, he was moving his stuff in, and I was gagging in the bathroom, and out came a heel bone. Within minutes, he was at the door, knocking politely. "Hey baby, you alright? Everything okay? You aren't pregnant, are you? Shit."

The heel bone went in my pocket, and I walked out, red-eyed and wiping my mouth.

"No, sweetie, not pregnant."

"Okay good. Good, good."

He sounded relieved but only by half. Half of a half. Ended up side-eyeing me for the rest of the day, we didn't fuck again for another three days. I woke up coughing a couple of nights later, and the night after that, and the night after that. Coughed up the other heel bone. Then some foot bones. An entire set of wrist bones. Put them in the jars in the basement with the rest.

Had to creep around to do this, which wasn't easy. Dylan's arrival had left me feeling more grounded, and my gait hit heavier as I snuck around this old apartment, opening doors that cried out for WD-40, and floorboards that sounded alarms when I stepped on them. But I tried. Dylan, I had thought, was a heavy sleeper. However, heavy sleepers can still be suspicious, I guess. Because after four or five nights of this, I met him coming down the basement stairs as I was returning to bed.

"Evan, what are you doing? Everything alright?"

"Uh."

"What's going on? Do you need to tell me something?"

There was no way out but the truth. He tossed and turned when I coughed. Covered his head with the pillow. He'd been avoiding me me in the mornings, and then would take me to get COVID tested every two days like I had a kink for people shoving things up my nose. I was standing on the basement floor, bare feet on the silty concrete ground, hands opening and closing into fists at my sides. I had to tell him.

I had to tell him, but I couldn't look at him when I said:

"I've been coughing up bones in the night. Real ones. And then I put them down here. 'Cause it seemed like the right thing to do. Bones go underground."

Dylan's hair was sleepy bedhead, looking like an explosion on one side. His face was also sleepy, pillow creased and droopy from dreaming. But his eyes had lit up to wide fucking awake. He crept down the rest of the stairs, peeking over my shoulder. His grin was wide, mischievous, full of up to no good as he glanced from me to the jars and back.

Then he pointed over my shoulder. "Those them?" he asked, like he'd spotted an ancient relic. His expression turned soft, and he took my cheeks in his hands. "Evan, I was so worried, but this? This is so—I don't even know—weird that it's cool? I just want to see the bones. I want to see what you grew."

April 2021, and Dylan is never coming back.

Katie says I am depression on a stick and no fun anymore, so she's been stopping by even more often since Dylan left to make sure that I am more fun and less boring. Thing is, though, I've been overcompensating for my lack of boyfriend with more work. Keep avoiding Katie by working longer hours, being out of the house more, and buying things I can't afford 'cause loneliness is the best reason to make the worst mistakes.

My credit card bill was evidence of that. Meow-Meow absolutely loved this. She'd destroyed a new couch (claws), a leather jacket (pee), and frayed the cord of an over-priced TV (ate it). But I couldn't get rid of her. I loved her too much. She was a good cat: loved to cuddle, let me trim her claws, purred every time I petted her, and gave terrific sandpaper kisses on the manscaping I'd cultivated for a solid two months.

Katie came by one evening after midnight when I staggered in sober but over-worked. She stopped me before I even got to the door and took hold of my shoulders, sitting me down in the folding chair on the porch.

"You and me, we're gonna talk," she said.

"About what?"

"You and how you're a total fucking wreck of a man that used to be my friend."

"We're still friends, Katie. I'm just tired, really way tired."

She smiled, lit a joint, and handed it to me. "You're a wreck, I'm a wreck, and this is why we're friends. Oh, and I fed your cat some good vibes through the window. She'll need some actual food, you know, when you get around to it."

I started to fall asleep in the chair, and when I woke up, Katie was gone. Typical.

Meow-Meow was my lifeline to any decency in the world, but with Dylan gone, she'd become the worst. Sort of my fault. I loved her, but I left her alone nine, ten, then eventually twelve hours a day. Couldn't stand the echoes of the house, the lack of weird noises and the now-missing bloodstain that I'd been obsessed with when I first moved in.

Routine had this cold familiarity: a rotation of a grind when I was that lonely. It kept me going. I knew what to do and where to go. Get up, brush teeth, shower, feed Meow-Meow, then head out to gamify gig work until I got home. Something had to give, something. And then, something eventually did.

In April, the morning after that talk with Katie, the bones I buried with Dylan came crawling out of the ground.

February 2021, and Dylan had decided to break up with me.

"Shit is too weird," he said.

We were standing in the backyard with shovels on what should've been an atypically warm (but was only a frighteningly warm) series of February nights. At least it would make it easier to bury stuff. Dylan had one hand on the shovel and the other in the pocket of his jeans; he wasn't looking at me. Instead, he stared at the garage, which was covered in condemned signs, Katie's car was parked in it and was basically condemned too. It never moved.

"Shit is just way too weird." Dylan turned to me then, looking me over with a full-bodied sigh. "You're amazing, Evan. Really amazing. I love you; I do."

When the sun came up the next morning, Dylan was gone and so was all his stuff. Like he'd never been there. Totally ghosted me. Left his keys and every trace of him behind. The last thing he said to me was, "Evan, I'm worried about you, but I can't take care of you. You cough up bones. You clean a spot on the dining room floor like Lady Macbeth. You're not even looking for a new job. I—can't anymore."

Meow-Meow was flattened for a week and a half after Dylan left, she always liked him more than she liked me. We had that in common: I liked Dylan more than I liked me, too.

September 2021, and Skeleton Boyfriend has been with me for five months.

We've been dating for about four months. Dylan moved in a year ago officially today, moved out less than that ago. But I don't want to talk about that. I want to talk about my skeleton boyfriend. He's good. He's a good conversationalist: like, we can talk about things that, I don't know, we both want to talk about? We rarely argue, which is fun this early (or this late) in a relationship.

I know what he likes, which is good. He likes spicy hot chocolate and warm fuzzy blankets with fringe that he can rub on his teeth. He also likes nature documentaries, because, as he says, "Nature gives zero fucks." His absolute favorite is audiobooks though, especially biographies, which surprised me. I also used to really like biographies.

As much as I want to not think about how Dylan moved in exactly a year ago today, I am doing a shit job of trying to forget it by sitting outside this hot wings place and going through all our old texts. The order I'm here to pick up is delayed, and my heart feels delayed, and Skeleton Boyfriend wants to make dinner tonight. I have two texts from him about what sort of meat to put in the lasagna when I get another text, which says:

happy anniversary baby, i miss you. in town for reasons. you home? i can cum over

I drop the phone when the alert goes off that the hot wings are ready. It's a mess. The bag is dripping, I lay down a towel on the back seat and my hands are sticky so I can't text Dylan back and I freak out. Another text comes through.

know your busy, baby. i'll head to our place.

I had honestly thought Dylan was never coming back to town again, or that he never wanted to see me again. In a weird, co-dependent way, my mind had sort of turned Dylan into Skeleton Boyfriend. It *kind of* made sense. Like when you're lonely and all you want is a boyfriend and you believe so hard that you want a boyfriend and then you start spitting out teeth and pelvises and shit and then you grow a boyfriend?

Normal shit.

Not normal at all, but facts are facts. And facts are: I loved Dylan, I still love Dylan. I loved him a lot, maybe somewhat obsessively. In fact, I am obsessing about how his visit is going to go. How he's going to look, how he's going to smell. If he's going to kiss me or not. Should I try to kiss him? Yes, I'm obsessing, which is a good reason not to text an ex back but is not why I don't. I don't because my steering wheel is covered in buffalo sauce.

When I get home, Dylan is on my porch (our porch). He's got a perfect five o'clock shadow and is dressed in a T-shirt that fits him so well it's going to tattoo his abs on my memory. He sets down his duffel bag and picks me up when I climb the stairs. "You smell hot, Hot Stuff, I am going to eat you up when we get inside."

He kisses me. The kiss is also hot, but I end up making his T-shirt look disgusting. He puts me down and I unlock the door, but won't let Dylan in, not yet. I have something to tell him. Something I know he knows, but am pretty sure he's not going to like.

"Uh, I live with a—" I can't say it; I have to say it. I fail. "My boyfriend's here."

Dylan grins that same grin he had when he got out of the U-Haul a year ago: the one with his head cocked, eyes looking me over. He shoulders his duffel bag and puts his hand on the doorframe. He smells like buffalo sauce and his old deodorant.

"I know, Evan. You gonna let me in to meet him or what?"

I let him inside and Meow-Meow hesitates a moment before she recognizes Dylan, running to him to dolphin up to his hand and snake between his ankles. Skeleton Boyfriend stands up slowly, a rattle of bones and bobbing of his head. The house smells of lasagna and meat, so much meat. Too much meat. Meow-Meow hasn't been this pleased in weeks, no? Months. I haven't either. Everyone I love is right here.

"Nice to meet you," Dylan says, extending his hand. "I'm Dylan."

"I'm Evan," Skeleton Boyfriend says.

Dylan grins. "Evan, nice. That's not confusing at all."

Skeleton Boyfriend and Dylan standing next to one another, I think they're the perfect couple. So sweet. Absolutely wonderful. Stellar. Dylan sees it too, smiling into his sockets, raising a hand to his bony scapula. He smiles that cocky smile of his and Skeleton Boyfriend melts the same way I do.

He is, exactly, all the pieces of me I thought I buried. That I thought I'd left behind. The tender, quiet pieces. The weird ones. The ones I thought were inappropriate and wrong. The ones I thought were unpresentable and strange. The ones I'd rejected that Dylan fell in love with, then out of love with.

Skeleton Boyfriend is, in fact, me.

There's a beat where I'm waiting for Skeleton Boyfriend to blink. Of course, he can't. The meat sizzles and pops from the cooling stove, punctuating the moments and motions as Skeleton Boyfriend's head turns to watch Dylan when he steps back to take my hand. He's standing next to me so that we're hip to hip, heat to heat. When he kisses me on the cheek, he follows with a whisper in my ear that hits all the wrong notes.

He says, "You though? You're *my* Evan. Mine."

Jordan Kurella is a trans and disabled author who has lived all over the world (including Moscow and Manhattan). In his past lives, he was a photographer, radio DJ, and social worker. His work has been nominated for the Nebula Award and long-listed for the British Science Fantasy Award. He is the author of the fantasy novella, I Never Liked You Anyway, the short story collection, *When I Was Lost*, and the climate fiction novella, *The Death Of Mountains*. Jordan lives in limbo with his perfect dog and practical cat.

WE WILL TEACH YOU HOW TO READ | WE WILL TEACH YOU HOW TO READ

Caroline M. Yoachim

ITERATION

This is our story, simplified: Life. Loss. Transformation. Love. Death. Iteration.

The first time you get our message, you only find one thread. It mimics your language in its simplest form, a single strand of words laid end to end. You will have to work hard if you want to understand us properly. You must learn to hold more than one thread of language simultaneously in your mind.

This is our story, simplified:
Life
Loss.
Transformation.
Love.
Death.
Iteration.

Don't worry, we will help you develop the skills you need. We will keep one simple thread unchanged. At first you will glance back and forth between these words and those. Your attention is a strange, skittering thing, but we believe you can learn with repetition.

This is our story, simplified:
Life.
Loss.
Transformation.
Love.
Death.
Iteration.

For you, we are relearning how to teach. You can hear musical chords of multiple notes, even two strands of differing lyrics for short stretches of song. It helps to memorize the words. Your mind has a strange divide between learning and knowing. Read both columns, please. Every time.

This is our story, simplified:
Life.
Loss.
Transformation.
Love.
Death.
Iteration.

Can you commit our simplified
story to memory? See just the shape of the
words and know what is there? You have so
little bandwidth, there might not be any
other way. It is not ideal but we are
desperate.
We will repeat to help you understand.

This is our story, simplified:
Life.
Loss.
Transformation.
Love.
Death.
Iteration.

THIS IS OUR STORY, SIMPLIFIED

We read three times in the course of our lifespan: once with our parents to learn the
story, once alone to add to the threads, and once with our children to teach them.
History, science, philosophy, art. All we have ever known is here, in one thread or
another, trapped in what—for you—would be a cacophony of overlapping words.

If both sides are simple, can you do it?
A series of moments.
The passing of parents.
From reader to writer.
A new generation.
To persist when we're gone.
Our story continues.

This is our story, simplified:
Life.
Loss.
Transformatior..
Love.
Death.
Iteration.

We sense your struggle, it is still too much.
Have you memorized our story, simplified?
Can you hear it in your head? You are such
strange creatures to have two eyes and yet
to focus on only one thing at a time. You
can't read the words on the other side of the
page so you have to simply know them.

This is our story, simpified:
Life.
Loss.
Transformation.
Love.
Death.
Iteration.

Recognize them from the shape of the lines.
Sound would be easier, yes--you make far
better use of your ears as independent
sensory organs than you do your eyes. But
we are determined to teach you to read.
Simpler still, simpler still. Can you at least
hold two identical lines in your head?

This is our story, simplified:
Life.
Loss.
Transformation.
Love.
Death.
Iteration.

This is our story, simplified:
Life.
Loss.
Transformation.
Love.
Death.
Iteration.

Feel the doubling of it, hear it in two different voices, somehow split your single focus of attention into two. Do you see how they match, how they resonate with each other? Go back up and look again. Try to capture the sensation of reading both at once, even for a moment.

This is our story, simplified:
Life.
Loss.
Transformation.
Love.
Death.
Iteration.

This is our story, simplified:
Life.
Loss.
Transformation.
Love.
Death.
Iteration.

LIFE

You are ancient, and we are fleeting. Such a luxury, to have so much time that you need not rush through everything at once. And yet you are so horribly inefficient, to not make more of the time you have. Think what you could do in a single lifetime if you could read more than one thread at once, think more thoughts at once, hold more experience in every moment.

You have a game with pictures, trying to spot the differences, your eyes darting back and forth between them. It is harder with text. Don't focus on individual words in each line, but look at the space between them. Know what both sides say. Hold it all in your head. Perhaps don't even quite focus your vision.

This is our story, simplified:
Life.
Loss.
Transformation.
Love.
Death.
Iteration.

This is our story, with variations:
Life.
Loss.
Inspiration.
Love.
Death.
New translation.

This is our story, simplified:
Life.
Loss.
Transformation.
Love.
Death.
Iteration.

Go back and try to read it all at once--hold
both versions in your head. We are only
asking you to read two threads, though we
ourselves can do thousands.
Threads of love and hope,
threads of fear and death.
How many iterations will it take you?

This is our story, terrified:
Loss.
Loss.
Endless attrition.
Death.
Death.
Desperation.

This is our story, simplified:
Life.
Loss.
Transformation.
Love.
Death.
Iteration.

This is our story, simplified:
Life.
Loss.
Transformation.
Love.
Death.
Iteration.

LOSS

Our generations are synced in a way that yours are not. Iterations of our story
are not staggered, not muddled like those songs that you call rounds. An entire
generation reads together in a single voice, three times: as children with their
parents, as adults alone, and as parents with their children.

But with each generation, the number of those who read our story is diminished.
Many children refuse to learn their parents' words. There are too many threads,
they say. There are so few of us remaining. Soon, our story will be lost forever.
We must find another way.

We remember every word we read,
instantly, consistently, a perfect rendition.
There are those among you with
eidetic memory, but even that is fleeting,
a lingering perception,
rather than a lasting record.
Insufficient.

This is our story, simplified:
Life.
Loss.
Transformation.
Love.
Death.
Iteration.

How much story can you hold,
in a life as vast as yours?
Even if some threads are lost
in the translation,

This is our story, simplified:
Life.
Loss.
Transformation.

is it not better to have
a legacy, an afterlife
that echoes after we are gone?

This is our story, simplified:
Life.
Loss.
Transformation.
Love.
Death.
Iteration.

We double threads for emphasis,
contrast death
with life.
When you recreate
our story
do not lose this
information.

Love.
Death.
Iteration.

This is our story, simplified:
Life.
Loss.
Transformation.
Love.
Death.
Iteration.

This is our story, simplified:
Life.
Loss.
Transformation.
Love.
Death.
Iteration.

TRANSFORMATION

Can you make the shift, from reader to writer, when you can only barely read? We fear that you do not grasp the urgency—you know our lives are short compared to yours but fail to comprehend the magnitude of the difference. We read three times in the course of our lifespan: once with our parents to learn the story, once alone as we write new threads, and once with our children to teach them. There is nothing else but this, we live our entire lives while reading, and the time it takes you to read three times...

"This is our story, simplified:
Life.
Loss.
Transformation.
Love.
Death.
Iteration."

...is for us a lifetime.

We have been trying to teach you to read for several generations. We are running out of time.

Even in the simplest case, identical threads,
we fear you cannot hold more than two.
Please try. It is important for the
translation.
Understand us well enough to love us,
to miss us when we're gone.
Teach our story to your children.

This is our story, simplified:
Life.
Loss.
Transformation.
Love.
Death.
Iteration.

This is our story, simplified:
Life.
Loss.
Transformation.
Love.
Death.
Iteration.

This is our story, simplified:
Life.
Loss.
Transformation.
Love.
Death.
Iteration.

This is our story, simplified:
Life.
Loss.
Transformation.
Love.
Death.
Iteration.

This is our story, simplified:
Life.
Loss.
Transformation.
Love.
Death.
Iteration.

This is our story, simplified:
Life.
Loss.
Transformation.
Love.
Death.
Iteration.

This is our story,
simplified:
Life.
Loss.
Transformation.
Love.
Death.
Iteration.

This is our story,
simplified:
Life.
Loss.
Transformation.
Love.
Death.
Iteration.

This is our story,
simplified:
Life.
Loss.
Transformation.
Love.
Death.
Iteration.

This is our story,
simplified:
Life.
Loss.
Transformation.
Love.
Death.
Iteration.

LOVE

The gift of words we give to our children is our greatest expression of love. We want to give this gift to you, even knowing how hard you must work to receive it. Imagine our words, stretched into a thin vertical line...

THIS IS OUR STORY, SIMPLIFIED

...and set beside it all the variations, all our explanations, everything you usually read as a single stream of text chopped into smaller pieces and laid out side by side so we can fit it all within our lifespan, each generation adding a new column to the story, stretching it ever wider.

THIS IS OUR STORY, SIMPLIFIED
THIS IS OUR STORY, SIMPLIFIED
THIS IS OUR STORY, SIMPLIFIED
EVEN IN THE SIMPLEST CASE, IDENTICAL THREADS,
WE DOUBLE THREADS FOR EMPHASIS,
THIS IS OUR STORY, SIMPLIFIED
HOW MUCH STORY CAN YOU HOLD,
WE REMEMBER EVERY WORD WE READ,
THIS IS OUR STORY, TERRIFIED
GO BACK AND TRY TO READ IT ALL AT ONCE—HOLD
THIS IS OUR STORY, WITH VARIATIONS
YOU HAVE A GAME WITH PICTURES, TRYING TO SPOT
FEEL THE DOUBLING OF IT, HEAR IT IN TWO
THIS IS OUR STORY, SIMPLIFIED
RECOGNIZE THEM FROM THE SHAPE OF THE LINES.
WE SENSE YOUR STRUGGLE, IT IS STILL TOO MUCH.
IF BOTH SIDES ARE SIMPLE, CAN YOU DO IT?
CAN YOU COMMIT OUR SIMPLIFIED
FOR YOU, WE ARE RELEARNING HOW TO TEACH
DON'T WORRY, WE WILL HELP YOU DEVELOP THE
THE FIRST TIME YOU GET OUR MESSAGE, YOU ONLY
THIS IS OUR STORY, SIMPLIFIED

There's a part of our story that describes finding you, our hopes and fears for you, and learning to communicate:

To even fit it on the page requires text a hairsbreadth wide, and it is still but a tiny fraction of our story.

Without our story,
life continues.
The loss makes space
for something new.
Our children
evolve, beyond
repetition.

This is our story, simplified:
Life.
Loss.
Transformation.
Love.
Death.
Iteration.

DEATH

We are the last ones holding on to the old story. Our children are making something new. Please take these words we send you, read them, learn them, translate them into something your mind can understand. You might not add your threads and iterate as we do, but hopefully as you transform our words, you will keep some sense of the vastness of each moment, the illusion of holding more story in your mind than you are actually capable of holding.

This is our story, one last time:
Life.
Loss.
Transformation.
Love.
Death.

This is our story, simplified:
Life.
Loss.
Transformation.
Love.
Death.
Iteration.

*"Even if some threads are lost
in the translation,
is it not better to have
a legacy, an afterlife
that echoes after we are gone?"*

It took many generations for them to teach us how to read.

Their lifespan was measured in mere inches of text.

It took far longer for us to learn to write on their behalf.

That timescale cannot be captured on these pages.

The blank space—the absence of their generations—would go for miles.

This is their story, in translation:
Life.
Loss.
Transformation.
Love.
Death.
Commemoration.

This was their story, simplified.
Life.
Loss.
Transformation.
Love.
Death.
Iteration.

COMMEMORATION | ITERATION

The entirety of their story has thousands upon thousands of threads. It is history told in moments that seem to happen all at once. It is science that progresses in increments almost infinitely small, and yet contains discoveries that even now we do not fully comprehend. It is their art, their language, their culture—everything they were determined to preserve. We have so much left to translate; this is only the beginning.

Give this story to your children, along with everything we have managed to translate, and perhaps one day the story will make its way back to the distant descendants of those who created it—ephemeral entities who, in the final generations of their decline, taught us a new way to read. When you teach this story to your children, do not start with all the threads at once. Instead, begin with a single line of text:

This is our story, simplified: Life. Loss. Transformation. Love. Death. Iteration.

Caroline M. Yoachim is a three-time Hugo and six-time Nebula Award firalist. Her short stories have been translated into several languages and reprinted in multiple best-of anthologies, including four times in *Best American Science Fiction and Fantasy*. Yoachim's short story collection *Seven Wonders of a Once and Future World & Other Stories* and the print chapbook of her novelette *The Archronology of Love* are available from Fairwood Press. For more, check out her website at carolineyoachim.com.

NOVELETTES

NEGATIVE SCHOLARSHIP ON THE FIFTH STATE OF BEING

A.W. Prihandita

"Doc, there's a...hole growing in me," the alien said through the spherical interpreting machine hovering over them. Semau barely registered the word "hole," so taken was she by the sight of the alien. If she were just a tad less caring about propriety, she would've let her eyes blow wide open. The alien looked impossibly transparent yet not transparent at the same time, like a mound of water. Their shape was almost humanoid: a roundish head sitting atop a misshapen lump of torso. They were visible in the way ocean waves were visible, only through folds that magnified its translucence to almost-opaqueness.

Semau glanced again at the patient form. *Name: Txyzna (he/him). Species: Plyzmorynox-matori.* Semau had never heard of the plyzmorynox before, and a quick lookup in the *Brazs's Database of Interstellar Species* told her this wasn't her fault. The plyzmorynox had an occurrence rate of 0.000013% of interspecies encounters, which made her impulsively count the decimal places—she'd never seen anything that small. She wanted to look up the Matori system as well—what kind of place was home to this super rare species?—but this wasn't the time to satisfy idle curiosity.

"Hello. Welcome. Please sit down...?" she trailed off into a question, worried the alien wouldn't fit in her patient's chair. But he shrank as he was sitting down, fitting the chair like liquid fitting its container.

"Would you tell me more about this...*hole* you mentioned?" she said. The plyzmorynox didn't look holey at all. Could water be holey?

A liquid lump separated from his "torso" and formed an approximation of a human arm, one with no hand at its end, just a dull point. He gestured at his chest. "There is a"—he paused, or rather, his interpreting machine paused, blurting a second of static noise—"hole in me. Very small, but it is there. I can feel it growing."

"How exactly does this feel?"

A pause. He had no face per se, but the liquidy lump that formed his head was more textured than his torso, the way the surface of a vast ocean was more textured than the surface of water in a cup. And now, the waves of his head swirled, tightening in a confused eddy. Semau decided this was his face, the waves a means of expression.

"It's hard to describe," he said. His interpreting machine rendered his words in a doubtful tone, matching his face. "There is...I just feel it. Inside of me. It feels...heavy, but not in the usual way."

"There's a hole inside of you, but the hole feels heavy?"

"Ah. That is contradictory, is it not?"

Semau turned her emerging grimace into a smile, and for good measure she shook her head too. "Not a problem. We'll puzzle it out. Is there anything else you feel?"

The plyzmorynox gave her a headshake that looked uncannily like the one she'd just given. He offered no further explanation.

"All right, then," Semau said.

She reached for the largest screen hovering over her desk, the interface of the health model she was licensed to use. The screen displayed a transcript of their conversation so far, but she ignored that for now, pressing CONSENT PROTOCOL instead. "I'm practitioner-doctor Semau Keo. I hold license FKGHB-00987-NUSANTARA for the Interspecies Health Model *INT-HealthGTT* version 8.5, which I will use to diagnose your symptoms. Do you consent to the processing of this consultation for diagnosis and prescription?"

"Yes," the plyzmorynox said.

Semau pressed DIAGNOSE. With such a measly doctor-patient interview, she'd expected the model to ask for more data, but instead it quickly returned a message framed in red. *SPECIES: PLYZMORYNOX not included in database accessible to FKGHB-00987-NUSANTARA. Expansion pack needed.*

Drat. Six generations of mentor-apprentices had held this license before her. In that time, they'd been able to purchase practically all the expansion packs needed for the rarer species crossing the Nusantara system. But of course, why would they purchase access to data about a species with a 0.000013% occurrence rate?

She should've checked the model first before saying a word to the plyzmorynox. Now she was just wasting his time.

"Mr. Txyzna, I'm sorry, but my health model apparently isn't equipped to diagnose illnesses of your species. Would you want me to refer you to another doctor?" He'd probably have to travel at least three systems away, but that was the best she could do.

"Can you not help me without the machine?"

Semau blinked. "I'm a practitioner-doctor, Mr. Txyzna. Not a scholar-doctor. I'm licensed to use the health model and be the intermediary between the patient and the model, but I'm not qualified to make observations and conclusions on my own. If my health model fails to help a patient, I should refer them to a practitioner-doctor with a capable model, or to a scholar-doctor."

"I would like you to help me. The field notes say to seek a doctor as soon as the hole forms."

"The field notes?"

His interpreting machine whirred, hovered down, and hinged open, revealing a nook that cradled a tiny book.

"*Field Notes from One Corner of the Universe*, by Alycia Balakrishnan-Smith," Semau read the cover.

"I got this from my parent, who got it from his grandparent, who got it from his great-great-grandparent. These are the only interstellar field notes on my race before the destruction of our solar system by the umunua. You should be proud that these field notes were written by one of your own, a human." The plyzmorynox paused, the waves of his face shifting into a melancholic churn. "My parent died a few moons ago. He was supposed to walk me through the forming of my hole; he'd promised to be my"—another blurt of static noise from the interpreting machine—"doctor. But my hole came late, and his death came early. I only have these field notes, which told me to seek a doctor immediately."

Semau stared at the waves of the alien's face, then at the tiny book. Then she stared at her screen, at the message still blinking red.

I'm sorry, I don't know what I can do, she wanted to say, the same words she'd wanted to say to every one of her patients. She knew what INT-HealthGTT could do for them, but she never knew what *she* could do, other than what the model was already doing. And without a model...well. She was even more useless.

"It takes a while to get an expansion pack," she said weakly. She wasn't sure the district government had funds to spare, but she could check. Still, she made sure to also say, "I can't promise you anything."

Every evening after her shift at the clinic, Semau did a round of wellness checks for the elderly in her district. Her supervisor at the Health Office had wondered—in a curious yet snide way—why she wouldn't get a more entertaining hobby, but she liked the work. Today she had Mrs. Achterberg, who lived in an apartment complex on Float 36, just a block off its main pier. On the ferry ride to that artificial island, Semau leaned over the railing and stared at the waves below, and all she saw was the sea-like face of the plyzmorynox.

The second the plyzmorynox stepped out of her office, she pulled up her account with the district government to check her remaining budget: 876,098 solars. Then she logged into her INT-HealthGTT account and searched for the plyzmorynox expansion pack. That was when her stomach dropped.

It cost 1,800,000 solars.

"I just don't know what to do," she told the wheelchair-bound Mrs. Achterberg after a quick recount of her predicament—appropriately anonymized, of course.

They were in the old lady's living room, the stereo set in the corner belching out classical quantum opera at half volume.

"You can always just diagnose his illness on your own," Mrs. Achterberg said.

"That's illegal," Semau protested, voice cutting over the opera's techno aria. "You know...you know what happened...before. My clinic only holds a 'B' ranking now. I can't afford further scrutiny."

Mrs. Achterberg waved a hand. "That was all in the past. Godang's malpractice suit was dropped, and you're a different doctor."

Semau shook her head in frustration. "I'm still his mentee, his successor. If the Medical Board got just a whiff of a non-certified diagnosis, that's it. They'd prosecute me like those Negative Scholars. Where would that leave my other patients?"

"You should've gone to med school, then," Mrs. Achterberg grumbled. "People like you, always wanting to be good, always restless with too little to do—you should've been a scholar-doctor."

"You know I couldn't afford that. Guru Godang—"

"—would've been *delighted* to throw you into a shuttle and launch you at the university, if that meant more freedom for you. What, you think I don't know him? We used to play in the same playground when we were kids, all the way to adulthood!"

And I was the one standing by his deathbed as he wasted away, Semau thought achingly. But she said nothing out loud. Sharp words would only flame her frustration.

Instead, she got up and fussed with the potted plants at the windowsill, ignoring Mrs. Achterberg's glare. The plants had evidently not been watered for a few days; one of them had grown yellow and molded. Perhaps later she'd get a purple starplant to replace it—purple and green made a nice contrast. It would brighten the room. The thought helped her calm down, distracting her from the pangs of fear and dismay she felt every time someone brought up her mentor's old mistake.

"It seems you have everything in order," she said once she'd tended to every plant. "Give me a call if you feel any discomfort or need help with household stuff. I'll drop by again in a week."

"I'll be fine, sweetheart," Mrs. Achterberg said with a smile, one that made her look strangely tired.

Semau waved her goodbye, but as she stepped outside, the old lady called out once more, in a voice just loud enough for her to hear. "Just because Godang raised you and trained you, it doesn't mean you're him, you know. You're allowed something else, something more."

The plyzmorynox returned three days later. Semau sat stiffly, palms sweating in her gloves. "Mr. Txyzna," she said, barely managing to stare the alien in the face.

"Unfortunately, I've been unable to acquire the necessary expansion pack. Should I refer you to another doctor? I found one with the appropriate model ten systems away."

The waves of the alien's face ebbed and eddied in a churn. When he finally spoke through his interpreting machine, his voice reminded Semau of a whale song she'd heard once, in a documentary on ancient Original Earth. "You are kind to try. How much does the expansion pack cost?"

"1,800,000 solars."

The plyzmorynox nodded. It looked like a crashing wave. "I do not have that amount right now, but I shall work toward it."

"Wait." Semau leaned forward, hands gripping the edge of her desk. "You don't need to shell out that much money, Mr. Txyzna." How would he get that, anyway? "I've found you a practitioner-doctor with the appropriate expansion pack. You can get your treatment with a fraction of that price, even if it means traveling to another system."

The alien's waves dissolved into a thousand tiny ripples. In the silence that followed, his body swelled until it strained against the armrests, a liquid bubble close to bursting, but then it shrunk until he was an emaciated ocean-man stooping in a patient's chair. The gesture looked like the universe's saddest sigh.

"I cannot do that, Doctor. It needs to be you."

"Why?"

"Because," he reinflated slowly, as if gathering the courage to reoccupy his existence, "I am unsure if I have time. I have wasted quite a lot of it consulting other doctors, all of whom rejected me for a host of other reasons. If you would not help me, I am unsure anyone else would. There is the possibility that I would travel so far only to arrive before someone who would only find another reason for why they cannot treat me. It seems I am too much of an alien to anyone of any species anywhere." He paused. "I apologize if this sounds harsh, Dr. Keo—I do not mean to blame you or shame you. I am merely expressing my fear."

Semau's cheeks heated up. She fought the impulse to look away. "I'm sorry," she murmured. It wasn't an apology—or perhaps it was, for her impotence—but above all it was an expression of sympathy.

"I have access to 500,000 solars right now. Should I send it to you? I will get more—"

"Wait, *what*?"

"My clan received reparation after the Matori Tribunal of 1997 SGE. There was nothing we could've used it for, since there were so few of us left even then, so we've just been accumulating interest."

And what was she to say to that? Her shoulders sagged with the burden settling upon her, her breath stifled by a lump growing out of grief and shame both. She felt like a boat unmoored.

There were very few things she could do, but saying yes was one of them, no matter how hollow it sounded to her own ears. "Yes, Mr. Txyzna. We can use your 500,000 solars as downpayment for your treatment."

I'm sorry, she almost said again. This time, she wasn't sure if she meant it for the plyzmorynox or herself, if it was an apology or sympathy.

The plyzmorynox came three more times after, to give her 200,000 solars each visit—even though he could've transferred the money without meeting in person. And because Semau felt bad dismissing him after confirming receipt, she started asking him about his symptoms, as if he was already her official patient.

On the first meeting, she asked if he'd been feeling any worse. He nodded his cresting-wave nod and told her, "The hole has grown about five millimeters. It does not feel disproportionately heavier than before, which I suppose means it hasn't changed in its density. But I still cannot fathom what it is." Semau also couldn't fathom what it was. She stared surreptitiously at the mountain of water that was his torso. Despite his transparency, she still couldn't see any hole.

Before he left, he said, "Please call me Txyzna, Doctor. You are kind, and I would like to be seen as a friend by a kind soul." Semau's mouth hung open. Should she accept the friendship, ask him to call her Semau? Should she allow herself to be anything other than a doctor—a practitioner-doctor, to be exact? In the end, she merely nodded.

On the second meeting, out of restlessness that she wasn't doing enough and could never do enough, Semau asked if *Field Notes from One Corner of the Universe* said anything about what plyzmorynox doctors usually did with the holes forming in their bodies of water. Txyzna said no, there wasn't a lot of specificity, only that it was customary for young adult plyzmorynox—anywhere around 75 to 100 years old—to spend time with a doctor once they sensed a hole growing inside them. Txyzna's parent also never took the time to expound on this, before his sudden death.

At the end of the meeting, Txyzna extended a watery limb, whose end quickly morphed into a hand with pudgy fingers. The waves of his face flowed into gentle curves that looked like a hundred little smiles. Semau hesitated, then took off one glove and grasped the hand. It felt cool to the touch, like a dip in a pool in the summer, only that her hand didn't sink into his, and neither did it get wet.

That night, she fell asleep thinking about that touch and the hundred little smiles on his face, and realized with creeping fear that she wouldn't mind being called Semau, even if it meant she'd risk disappointing a friend and a patient both.

On the third meeting, Txyzna said this was the last 200,000 solars he had. He was trying to mortgage his abode for the rest of the payment, but the paperwork was taking time. He apologized for the delay.

"We'll figure it out," Semau said, "no matter how long it takes." She didn't dare ask if they had time. It seemed the growth of the hole was something every plyzmorynox went through, so hopefully it wasn't fatal.

Once he left, she logged back into her account at the district government and filed an emergency budget use notification for 700,000 solars. With all the money

Txyzna had provided, they now had 1,800,000 in hand. Enough for the expansion pack.

She pulled up her INT-HealthGTT account and searched for the plyzmorynox expansion pack. She hit buy.

The pack downloaded in less than a blink. Semau frowned. She checked the metadata and found the whole thing weighed less than one megabyte, a hairline fraction of the usual health model expansion packs.

She double checked everything, fearing she'd downloaded it wrong. But everything checked out.

She went through the information disclosure protocol for a list of the pack's training data sources, and found only the following:

- Body measurements of three (3) plyzmorynox individuals of three (3) different ages
- Maps and climate descriptions of the plyzmorynox's Matori home planets
- Bioweapon blueprint from the Umunuan Empire War Committee (excerpted, 10 pages)
- *Field Notes from One Corner of the Universe* by Alycia Balakrishnan-Smith (excerpted, 20 pages)

Semau stared at her screen for one too many raging heartbeats. She felt cold at first, like her innards just dropped ten kilometers down into a pool of ice water. Then the cold morphed into heat, small and flickering, starting from the pit of her stomach up to her chest, until it was a solar flare eruption in her head.

One million and eight hundred solars for nothing more than the trace of silence. For nothing at all.

For her round of wellness check that evening, she had Mx. Grovbol, the dalvanber from the Lizpen system. This meant a trip to New Java, which she normally loved—it felt anchoring to step foot on the planet's only real island—but this time she hardly felt the difference between the always-swaying deck of the ferry and the steady soil of Java.

Her smile was automatic when Mx. Grovbol answered the door with a graying tentacle. Her list of questions was muscle-memorized, her small talk polite but perfunctory. Sometimes her mind drifted back to the list of four items on her screen back at the office, and her smile turned taut for a second, before she remembered herself.

The visit ended at 6:50 PM, ten minutes earlier than usual. She staggered down the front steps, pausing at the bottom. When she reached the harbor, she boarded the ferry to Float 36, not home.

"The little whale surfaces," Mrs. Achterberg said by way of greeting, when she opened her door. "Who would've thought?"

"I'm here for the plants," Semau said, showcasing a pot of dark purple starplant.

Mrs. Achterberg stared at her with gray eyes unclouded by age, eyes that immediately softened. Semau looked down at her feet, as if not seeing the old lady meant the old lady wouldn't see her either; as if that little gesture could hide her embarrassment that this wizened woman knew—because she *did* know, Semau could tell—that Semau always doubled the care she gave to others just when she failed to care for someone. As if a pot of starplant was enough to make up for generations of erased plyxmorynox-matori.

"I do love purple," Mrs. Achterberg chirped. "Did you know it took me two months to convince Fiona to wear purple for our wedding? Two months!"

The starplant joined the row of green plants on the windowsill. Mrs. Achterberg babbled as Semau rearranged the lineup, making the plants go from light green to dark green to purple, then back to dark green and ending again with light green. The starplant she got was a juvenile, and they usually took five months to grow into their full size. Which meant in five months Semau would need to move it to a roomier corner.

"Five months... Five..." Semau murmured to herself. "It takes five years to complete a scholar-doctor's degree."

Mrs. Achterberg stopped her babbling. "Ah. So that's what's bothering you. The expansion pack didn't work, huh? The health model failed you."

Semau thought, maybe not for the first time but it felt like the first time, that maybe the health model *was* designed to fail. In some cases, at least. For some beings.

"Well, yes, there's the university," Mrs. Achterberg continued. "After five years there, you won't have to depend on the health model. But I guess you don't have five years now?"

"No."

They were both silent as Semau checked the underside of the leaves.

Mrs. Achterberg cleared her throat. "Semau, dear. You know your Guru Godang used to make independent diagnoses for his more difficult patients, right? Before he took you in—"

"We've gone over this—the accusation was false," Semau retorted. "You know that."

"The accusation *got thrown out*," Mrs. Achterberg corrected. "I never said it was false—*you* said that. The accusation got thrown out because I pulled some strings and paid a lot of money for that, using my family connections. No, let me finish," she said when Semau whirled around to protest. "You shouldn't see this as a stain on his reputation. Godang only saw it that way because he worried about losing the health model license and leaving thousands without healthcare. That was why he asked for my help. But otherwise, he didn't regret what he did. 'You do what you have to do to save those that INT-Health won't save,' he used to say."

"If this is all true, why did he never tell me anything?"

"Maybe because my great-aunt retired from the Upper Court some four years later," Mrs. Achterberg said with a flippant wave of a hand. "Our safety net went with her. Or maybe he didn't want you to carry that risk. I don't know. My point is, Godang never let INT-Health or the university stop him from helping people."

"How was he even helping people? That doesn't make any sense. He had no scholarly training—"

"He had connections with the epistemic rebel group The Negative Scholars. They taught him the basics of human-based medicine, among others."

Semau winced at the organization's name. She remembered watching the public execution of their leaders, after INT-Health Inc. and the Intergalactic Consortium of Medical Universities won their intellectual property theft lawsuit. To think that Guru Godang used to study under them, even for a minute...

But it actually wasn't that hard to imagine her mentor doing exactly that. She remembered him complaining about how it was almost impossible for practitioner-doctors like him to take five years off. A backwater planet like Nusa could only afford a handful of licenses; they couldn't spare any doctors, not even for a scholarly education. *Your people come first*, Guru Godang used to say. That was why Semau never considered going to the university.

But "your people come first" could easily mean doing anything for one's patients. Including using illegal means to access the knowledge needed to save them.

"I know you've worked so hard to continue Godang's legacy," Mrs. Achterberg said. "You've used his license well. But Godang would've died twice as happy if that license hadn't been his only legacy. He always wanted to be more. To do more."

That night when she got home, aware that some things shouldn't be said in her doctor's office, Semau used her personal communication line to give Txzyna a call. With choked up apologies, she told him about the uselessness of the expansion pack, and that there was nothing else she could do as a practitioner-doctor. Then she told him to meet her at Float 30's southern pier tomorrow, after the end of her workday.

Semau made her way to the pier feeling bloated and hollow all at once.

She carried a duffel bag of medical instruments she'd stolen from the office: a stethoscope to record breaths and heartbeats, a set of syringes to take various kinds of fluid samples. These were instruments she normally used to collect data for the INT-Health model to analyze. That night, she'd put them offline, hoping against hope that a few hours of disconnection wouldn't be enough to alarm the Medical Board.

And just in case, she'd reviewed the protocol for malpractice suspicion. The Board would have to send an overseer to lead her investigation. The nearest headquarter of the Medical Board was a system over, which meant the overseer would take a week to arrive, if Semau was ever suspected of anything. Which hopefully she never would be.

She had thought it would be difficult to spot Txyzna's transparent body at night. It was, but at the same time, it wasn't. He seemed to absorb moonlight such that the edges of his body gleamed silver, and the rest of it bathed in a pale sheen that looked like a moon's reflection on water.

"Walk with me," Semau said without breaking her stride, before Txyzna could say anything.

She had chosen Float 30 because it was the least populated island on this end of Nusa's sprawling archipelago. There were more sheep and chickens here than humans or other sapient beings, which made Semau hopeful that whatever surveillance followed a practitioner-doctor, it wouldn't follow her here. She'd turned off her communications, and no one but Txyzna seemed to be following her.

They walked away from the pier, then up a little cliff overlooking the ocean. It was only when they were safely hidden in a grove of pine trees did Semau stop. She sat on a fallen log, facing the sea and horizon.

"I've decided to help you," she told Txyzna. "You might not want that, because what I'm doing is illegal."

Txyzna came to stand beside her, a bulbous statue of liquid moonlight. "Thank you, Doctor."

Semau hesitated. "Maybe you shouldn't call me doctor outside my office. Semau is fine."

"Thank you, Semau." The waves of his face flowed into gentle curves that looked like a hundred little smiles.

"I brought some tools." Semau reached for her bag. "I thought I could take samples and figure out how to analyze them later. And I can listen to your body with the stethoscope. Maybe I'll hear the hole that way."

She felt stupid. To be frank, she didn't know what she was doing. Her job was only to collect the data the model needed; she was never taught how to make sense of all that.

"The data might not be enough to give you a prescription right away," she added weakly, "but maybe they'd remind me of other illnesses I've seen. I'll try and find a course of treatment that way, through comparisons."

"Semau, I have been wondering. Doctors...human doctors...what is it that you do?"

Semau raised an eyebrow. "We deal with illnesses, of course.'

"And do you think my hole is an illness?"

"Is it not? If it's not an illness, why would you seek a doctor?"

"I went because the field notes told me to seek a doctor. But I'm no longer sure that illness is the right word to describe what I'm experiencing. It is...the hole is...something different. A change, an anomaly." He paused. "My translation machine is helping me understand what 'illness' is, in your language. It seems it is

also a change and anomaly, but I am unsure if it is the same way that my hole is."
He paused again. "Semau, tell me, what is a 'hole' to you?"

For a long heartbeat, Semau did nothing except to stare at the plyzmorynox. She'd had alien patients before—that was the whole point of the Interspecies Health Model—and while she'd experienced miscommunication problems with some patients, it was never so fundamentally wrong. Never anything their interpreting machines and the health model couldn't solve iteratively.

But then again, the health model already failed the plyzmorynox, an alien species more alien than others. She'd heard the faltering of Txyzna's interpreting machine, the static noises it blurted out mid-sentences, but she never considered the possibility it was failing him just as much as INT-HealthGTT was.

With her heart beating in her throat, Semau looked away and did what was usually taboo in face-to-face communications: She pulled up the virtual interface of her translation implant and asked it to approximate the confidence level of the plyzmorynox's translation.

It returned the number 23%.

"No," she whispered.

"Semau?" Txyzna called out. His interpreting machine rendered his voice in a hesitant tone. It hovered above him, looking like an enemy warship. "What is a 'hole' to you?" he repeated.

Hands trembling, Semau picked up a fallen branch and used it to dig a hole in the ground. "This is a hole," she explained. "It's a void left when something's no longer there. It's nothingness."

Txyzna bent his head over it, considered it with his eyeless face. He reached down and stuck a finger in the hole. "Is there something in this"—his interpreting machine faltered—"hole that you can feel?"

"What do you mean?"

"If you stick a finger in it, can you feel something?"

"I'll feel the soil at the bottom."

"But nothing else?"

"No. That's why it's a hole. It's negative space."

Txyzna fell silent. "Semau, I don't think what I have is a hole."

Blazing white heat lanced up Semau's chest. She took a deep breath and tamped down her anger. Whatever communication problem happening here was *not* Txyzna's personal fault, she must remember that. "What do you have, then? Please describe it."

"That was why I sought you. I am unsure of how to describe it. A doctor was supposed to help me. My"—the interpreting machine halted—"grandparent was my parent's"—a pause—"doctor. He helped my parent with his hole, helped him come up with his"—another pause—"song. The song describing his hole."

"A song? You went to a doctor because you need help writing a song?"

"The field notes used the word 'doctor'," Txyzna said apologetically. "And I have no one else to tell me otherwise. With the way the field notes discussed it,

I thought this was common practice in your profession, and among your people. Please, Semau. I am sorry for the confusion this has caused. I would have come to another one of my kind, if only I could find them."

Semau gritted her teeth and rubbed her forehead with the heels of her palm. She'd come this far, broke laws for the first time in her life, because she'd wanted to help this lonely alien. The help he needed from her no longer seemed like the help she was prepared to give, but she already made it here. The least she could do was listen.

"All right," she said. "It's clear now that although we both use the words 'doctor' and 'hole,' we aren't referring to the same thing at all. Can you try and describe what exactly you mean by these two terms?"

It took them an hour and countless machine-assisted stammering, but Semau finally got a serviceable picture of what was going on. A 'doctor' was a spiritual elder, though after the genocide the role had to be taken up by any surviving older relative. The 'doctor' helped young adult plyzmorynox wrap their head around the transformation happening in their bodies as they crossed the threshold between childhood and adulthood. This transformation centered around the 'hole,' which was some sort of change or anomaly that grew in their bodies, which apparently was hard to describe for the individuals possessing the hole, and downright insensible to anyone else.

In his sixth attempt to explain what the hole was, Txyzna offered, "Maybe it would be helpful for you to hear the name of the hole in another language. The umunua called the 'hole' 'aoxono.'"

Semau's translation implant announced in her ears, "The fifth state." It also offered a box of contextual information through its virtual display:

The fifth state (Umunuan: *aoxono*) is a state of matter that forms the existential and physical heart of plyzmorynox-matori. It is a state of matter unique to each individual plyzmorynox, its properties only sensible and observable to the individual possessing it. The term "fifth state" is a reference to the four classical states of matter: solid, liquid, gas, and plasma. The plyzmorynox's heart is a state of matter that is none of these four states; each heart is its own unique state. The umunua's attempt and subsequent failure to understand the plyzmorynox's fifth state is commonly regarded as the cause of the Matori Genocide.

"'Its properties only sensible and observable to the individual plyzmorynox'..." Semau mused out loud. "That's why it's called a 'hole,' isn't it? To the individual plyzmorynox possessing the hole, it isn't a hole at all, it's a substance only they can sense. But to others—including Alycia Balakrishnan-Smith—it's not anything they can see, touch, or sense. It's a negative space to them. A 'hole.'"

"Yes, that is a sensible explanation. I am sorry I did not think of this earlier."

Semau couldn't blame him—she also hadn't considered mistranslation. Translation machines had grown so ubiquitous; people hardly paid them any mind. "So, you need me to help you describe your hole, your fifth state?"

"Yes. It is very important. My clan had a song that recites the description of our holes, going five generations back. These descriptions are the only way our hearts can be understandable to others. If I cannot describe my heart, no one will be able to hold it in their minds. No one will know me." Txyzna paused. When he spoke again, his interpreting machine rendered it in a hoarse, cracking voice. "I do not want to be unknown."

"But how could I help you describe the hole, if I can't even sense it?"

"I was hoping you would know that, as a doctor. I was hoping the expansion pack would know."

"Txyzna, I'm sorry, but I don't know anything about any of this." She realized her own voice sounded hoarse and cracking. "But I can be here with you as you try to describe your hole. And I'll remember your song, when you have it. You won't be unknown to me."

It was past midnight when Semau got home. She put her communications back online and was immediately greeted by the ding of notifications.

One caught her attention. Her interface had flagged it bright red. *DISCIPLINARY WARNING: THE MEDICAL BOARD OF ETHICS.*

Her heart stopped cold. In a frantic glance, she gathered what was going on: the Medical Board had uncovered evidence of malpractice and was sending an overseer to investigate. She forced herself to take a deep breath and count to ten, then went over the letter again for its recounting of evidence.

What had flagged them, of all things, was how on her third meeting with Txzyna, before he even finished paying for the expansion pack, Semau had asked him questions about his symptoms. The INT-Health interface had recorded the conversation, just as it recorded all doctor-patient conversations for diagnostic purposes. But Semau hadn't hit the DIAGNOSE button. This was of course because she knew doing so was pointless without the expansion pack, but the system suspected she'd done the questionings to feed her own diagnosis.

Stupid. What a stupid, despotic machine. How could it claim to be the authority of all knowledge, fail laughably at being that, yet punish *her* for trying to fill the hole it left?

She gave Mrs. Achterberg a call. The old lady picked up on the third ring. "Didn't take them long, huh?" she said. "Well, lucky for you, I've tracked down my great-aunt—which wasn't easy to do, mind you, the old girl wanted 'quiet retirement,' as she put it. Anyway, she gave recommendations for legal counsels on intellectual property, medical care, and knowledge autonomy. We'll need to fundraise for that, but let's worry about it later."

"Thank you, Mrs. Achterberg. I owe you everything."

"Nah. Just bring me another starplant, will you? I do like purple."

Even with legal counsel, her chance of escaping the combined might of INT-Health Inc., the Medical Board of Ethics, and the Intergalactic Consortium of

Medical Universities was vanishingly small. But Semau did her best to put her worry aside, for now.

Her next step was to fill out the paperwork to relinquish her health model license back to the district's Health Office. It was the only way she could guarantee the district wouldn't have to spend a ton of money to purchase a new license because she burnt hers in a malpractice lawsuit. The Health Office could appoint and onboard a new practitioner-doctor more quickly than her investigation and trials would take. Until then, the other practitioner-doctors on Nusa would have to pick up the slack, but at least it wouldn't be a permanent loss of a license.

It did mean resigning her post as practitioner-doctor. It did mean shrugging off all the hours that Guru Godang had spent training her. But she was trying to do her best, and she had no other choice.

There was a lump in her throat when she signed her name at the end of the form.

The next few days started with Semau waking up sweaty and stiff in the early hours of the morning. Most of the time it was from a nightmare of her being chased by a faceless overseer, other times it was of Txyzna melting into a puddle, and once it involved a crab-like alien vaporizing him like he was a dewdrop in a solar storm. And still, after every nightmare, Semau dragged herself out of bed and went about the business of giving up the job she'd been training for her whole life.

The only thing making this worth it was the calls she had with Txyzna, done over a communication line as secure and private as she could ensure, where Txyzna talked through his laborious attempt to describe his heart. Often, his interpreting machine would pause for a long time, and Semau couldn't tell if that was because he was trying to come up with words, or if the machine was failing to translate the words he'd found.

On the sixth day, the call was much shorter. "I think I'm ready," Txyzna said. "Would you come to where I am staying? I will share my song with you, if you'd still hear it."

That morning, Semau stared into the mirror and found traces of tears in her eyes. When she opened her mouth to brush her teeth, she thought she'd glimpse her heart beating in her throat, behind her tongue, noisy and very real. She closed her eyes and imagined what Txyzna's heart would sound like, but she could only hear hers. For now, she could only hear hers.

The ferry ride felt like walking on water.

"Good morning," Txyzna said when he opened his door. White tiles covered the walls of the apartment, and the floor was non-slip vinyl. A square pool with clear blue water dominated the room, in a manner that made it obvious this was the primary living space of the resident being. To the side, though, a table stood surrounded by three chairs of various sizes. It was to this group of chairs that

Txyzna led Semau. "Please, sit down," he said, and she remembered their first meeting where it had been she who'd asked him to sit down.

Then he gazed at her, and by "gazed" it didn't mean to stare with a pair of eyes, for he had no eyes; by "gazed" it meant he turned the compass of his attention onto her, steered the waves of his face so they ebbed and flowed in a way that made her feel embraced entirely, buoyant in a gentle ocean she could hold in her hands.

She was reminded that she was here to hold. The hole, the fifth state, was something she could never even touch, but she was here to hold it, nonetheless.

Txyzna began to sing. It sounded nothing like a song. It was a recitation, at best, a string of words announced through the fine mesh of his interpreting machine.

He sang of a hole that felt heavy, heavy as storm clouds pregnant with rain, heavy as the grains of salt carried by a drop of ocean water. He wondered out loud how many raindrops he carried in his heart, how many grains of salt; and decided it was just as many raindrops needed to nurture a cactus for three days, and for the salt, just enough sprinkle for a human to say, "This is satisfactory seasoning."

Semau's lips curved up. "This is satisfactory seasoning," she echoed with an incline of her head, a compliment.

He spoke little of temperature, for he'd observed that his heart was neutral at best. It was neither winter nor summer, neither blizzard nor drought; it was the temperature of atoms that sat and vibrated all on their own—which was to say, no temperature at all. But he assured her this didn't mean he couldn't feel warmth or coldness. On the contrary, the neutrality of his heart allowed every drop of his body to hold as much heat as desired, or as little as needed.

It was when he attempted to describe the texture of his heart that his interpreting machine started to falter. "My heart feels like—in the middle of—that is—are floating—but never—like—"

After a few breaths of this, Txyzna fell silent. "I'm sorry. When I composed the song, I wasn't doing it alongside my machine."

"That's all right."

"I examined all the songs that were passed down to me. There were many words in them that I did not recognize, that I never heard my parent use. Perhaps in trying to describe something indescribable, my ancestors had to invent many new words. Since now there is no way for me to learn their meanings, I decided to take whichever words tasted right to me, even though I did not understand them. But I suppose for you, they are even more impossible to understand."

A part of her had known this wouldn't be easy; she was no longer a stranger to the betrayals of the interpreting machine. But still, dread scratched at her cavities. "But you need me to understand you," she said. *How could I do so, if I don't understand your words?*

It took Txyzna several human heartbeats to answer. "My father used to say that in our ancestral homelands, we did not speak with sound, and we certainly did not speak with words. Our homelands were ocean planets much like Nusa, and we spent most of our days in the water; and when you are in the water the only vibrations you feel are those of the sea waves, and those were enough for us. We spoke in the language of sea waves. We did not listen; we vibrated, we attuned, we felt.

"My father used to say that in our ancestral homelands, when one of us was living through the forming of our hole, we would all swim together in our ocean, so together that our bodies blurred into one ocean within an ocean. We'd hold our new adult and their newly formed hole at our center, and as they sang their song in our ocean wave language, we'd vibrate along with them, ebb and flow with them. That was how we used to know each other, when we were still as vast as oceans."

Semau's eyes drifted to the center of the apartment, where the pool of blue water sat in quiet waiting. There wasn't even enough of Txyzna to fill this artificial body of water that would never be mistaken as the ocean.

"I'm sorry you only have me and this little pool," Semau said. "But could I still hold you the way your ancestors held your siblings? Would it help me know you?"

The waves of Txyzna's face eddied in a tranquil rhythm, almost hypnotizing in its repetition. "Yes," he said. "This we can try."

He ambled to the pool, lowering himself at the edge of the water, like how a child would sit and dip their feet before plunging in. But Txyzna didn't plunge in; he seemed to melt in. One moment he was his bulbous self; the next, a cascade of mercury slipping into blue water.

His interpreting machine remained in the air, and it said, "Come in, Semau. And when you're here, you can breathe as usual. I will give you the air you need."

Semau peered into the pool and found she could tell where Txyzna was, because even though he was now as liquid as the water, he also glowed faintly silver. His mass spread over the blue of the pool, like a loosely humanoid puddle of mercury suspended in liquid sky. Semau took off her shoes, trying not to think she was about to step on the body of a friend.

She dove in and wasn't sure what to do, but the silver puddle that was Txyzna parted to welcome her, circling around her. A part of her wanted to recoil as his mass inched closer to engulf her, but when the contact happened, it really didn't feel alien at all. It felt just like soaking in warm water that faintly pulsed like the blood in her veins.

A bubble of air formed where her nose was, and she took a tentative breath. She found she didn't choke, nor was she drowning. Txyzna held her tenderly, and as he'd promised, he gave her the air she needed to breathe. He was all around her now; she was floating in a cocoon of silver. She spun gently in it, and wondered if this was how a newborn plyzmorynox was buoyed to sleep, in the embrace of a physical lullaby.

Then, the singing started. She could feel it in her bones, like sea waves indeed, only that her marrow was as much the sea as the body of water engulfing her. She felt the vibrations on her skin and within her, gentle at times but a roaring crescendo at other times, a tickle and a punch, a whisper and a scream, a dance that swirled like streamers in the wind and twirled like the moon in its revolution chasing its own shadow. She inscribed in her mind and body every touch of the waves around her and within her, every vibration both atom-soft and earthquake-loud.

And in the middle of all that, as she spun in the buoy of her silver cocoon, she felt an emptiness, a negative space brushing against her arm. She recoiled in surprise. The cocoon that was Txyzna pulsed in reassurance, spinning her gently until she faced where she thought the hole was.

She reached out, a probe into deep space. The tips of her fingers touched the surface of her friend's heart. She knew it was her friend's heart because she couldn't sense it.

But it needed no sensing. It needed no knowing.

She twisted until she curled around the hole that was a heart, holding it with her whole body. She closed her eyes and let Txyzna's song wash over her, all as her fingers traced the boundary of his negative space. It seared her, the contrast between the nothingness of the hole and the vivacity of the song's vibration. She was the fine line between absence and presence, between oblivion and omniscience.

When the song ended, when every vibration had been recorded in the marrow of her bones, Semau floated in a quiet so thick she could touch it. Txyzna pulsed around her, warm like the embrace of a womb, and she felt like she was born anew.

"Thank you," she said, even though she wasn't sure Txyzna could hear her. *Thank you, and I hope this was enough.*

When she was back on solid ground dripping water on the apartment floor, she stared at Txyzna's bulbous body and felt the urgent need to hold him. This was the person who had a heart like storm clouds and salt, who spoke in a symphony of ocean waves. This was the person she got to know only because he was so unknown by the universe. This was the person she got to know despite not being able to know him entirely.

Txyzna opened his arms wide, his face rippling into tiny curves that looked like a thousand smiles. Semau fell into his embrace, and there she spent many minutes sobbing, her breath trembling to the echoes of his heart-song.

Later on, she asked him, "Do plyzmorynox cry, Txyzna?"

Txyzna answered, "Each of our bodies is one giant teardrop, Semau, my friend. But I appreciate the little ones you shed."

It surprised her how little effort it took to understand Txyzna, once she accepted she didn't need to understand him, only to hold space for him. With his heart-song still echoing in her bones, she thought back to her health model and the expansion pack, and how impossible it was to encode within them what she'd experienced with her own body.

And so, when the message came on her ferry ride back from Txyzna's apartment, Semau faced it with the calmness she'd learned just a few moments before, from a state of being that wasn't hers to perceive.

The message read: *MEDICAL BOARD OF ETHICS DISCIPLINARY CASE #891283: OVERSEER ASSIGNMENT. Overseer name: Prenter Gozzhanky. Charge: Pr. Dr. Semau Keo. Case update: Overseer arrived at charge's home planet. Charge is advised to remain at known address for detainment.*

On the heels of that notice came another message, this time from Mrs. Achterberg: *Legal counsels secured. Also, I've launched a fundraising campaign, quadrant-wide. My great-aunt's in on it too. One last ride, she said. We'll be along with you. Stay steadfast, dear.*

Semau nodded, even though she knew Mrs. Achterberg couldn't see her. She'd give her a call soon, but first, she had one last thing to sort out. A letter to her bank, then another one:

Dear Txyzna,

I can't give you back the money you spent on the expansion pack—they don't give refunds. But my mentor, who also raised me, left a bit of money for me when he died. It's the least I can give you.

I hope you can use it to maybe go and find other remaining plyzmorynox. They'll need a doctor too. Maybe you can be that. You'll be a better one than me.

It was an honor to know you. I'll remember your song forever.

Your friend,

Semau

She sent the letter, took a deep breath, and turned her gaze to the sky. Seagulls circled above, calling one after another in a language she couldn't understand. Under her feet, the sea was an undulation carrying her home—only that with the overseer waiting for her, home also meant somewhere she'd never been before, a fate undecided.

She didn't know—not yet—if there were any remnants of the Negative Scholars after the execution of their leaders. But even if there were none of them left, she was willing to shoulder the burden of being the first in a new generation of them, to find out how to know—or not know—outside the paths and boundaries set by powers beyond her reach. She wasn't sure if she was smart enough to do all that, but she would nonetheless try. If she could live the rest of her life stopping people from paying one million and eight hundred solars for nothing more than the trace of silence, then it would be a fine life indeed.

Guru Godang, this is your legacy, she thought.

This, and a song about how to hold, so very tenderly, that which you could not understand.

Anselma Widha Prihandita (she/her) is an Indonesian speculative fiction writer, college writing instructor, and PhD candidate in rhetoric and composition, with scholarly (and personal) interests in decolonial and transnational writing. She splits her time between the US West Coast, where she currently teachers and studies, and Indonesia, where she grew up and where her home remains. She attended the Odyssey workshop in 2023 on their Fresh Voices Scholarship, and the Clarion workshop in 2024 on their Octabia Butler Scholarship. Her stories are published or forthcoming in *Clarkesworld, Cast of Wonders*, and *khōréō*, among others.

KATYA VASILIEVNA AND THE SECOND DROWNING OF BABA RECHKA

Christine Hanolsy

Once, in a certain kingdom, at a certain time, a river flowed under a bridge. It flowed under a bridge and past a willow tree, and in that willow tree dwelled the spirit of a girl who had drowned. I dweeled in that willow tree, and I was content.

Oh, you river, my little river,
Oh, you swift little river of mine.

You flow, little river, without rippling,
Without overflowing your steep banks.

Without overflowing your steep banks,
Without disturbing the yellow sand.

Oh, you river, my little river,
Oh, you swift little river of mine.

I watched her from the river's edge. She was sturdily built, Katya Vasilievna, her skin ruddy and sun-kissed, her hips broad. She walked with a purpose that drew the eye. She lived at the big house, up on the hill. The house I could only glimpse in winter--a flash of color against the stark silhouettes of grasping branches. I only knew her name because I stole it from the wind one evening.

Girls often came to this spot along the riverbank—they had been doing so for as long as I could remember. They never saw me, else they would not come, I was sure. They came to cry under the oak tree, or to throw birch crowns into the water, or sometimes just to lie on their bellies on the wooden footbridge and tickle the minnows that darted among the cattails. They played their fortune-telling games and whispered their hearts' desires. Mostly, they wished for rich husbands and fat babies.

I had been a young girl once, but I had never had any interest in bearing children. They all looked the same to me, all soft cheeks and dimpled knees. I had no interest in men, either, despite the tales they told in the villages at night about the wickedness of my sisters. I had the river, and the little fishes that came to my beckoning hand, and the patter of rain on the forest canopy. The hidden folk trusted me with their ills and woes, and I helped them as best I could. I needed no more company than theirs.

At twilight I liked to sit in the crook of a willow tree, combing my hair with my fingers, untangling knots and picking out bits of plant matter. Here by the bridge the river was narrower, but it ran deep and cold, especially in the springtime. I would watch the people come and go, lovers meet and quarrel and reconcile, and I would think and I would *remember*. This evening I watched Katya cross the bridge and leave the path. She wore a blue sarafan embroidered in red at the hem, to protect her from evil spirits, and she hid herself under my tree behind a veil of willow branches.

"Katya!" A woman's voice echoed from the house on the hill, muffled only slightly by the new spring leaves and soft mosses that were only just starting to remember sunlight. "Katya Vasilievna!"

The girl—Katya—shrank in on herself, as though by making herself smaller, she would be less conspicuous. As though that were possible. Draped in shadows, she was sunlight. She smelled golden, like honey, like fine white bread. Even the trees noticed; they reached in her direction, turned their nascent leaves towards her.

There was no point in speaking to her, I knew. But I was as incapable of turning away as were the trees. I snapped off a slender branch, heavy with catkins, and brushed it against her shoulder.

"What have we here?" I asked. "A little fish out of water."

She stifled a startled noise with her fist and looked up at me. Her eyes were the same shade of blue as the flowers that grew along the riverbank.

I wrapped a bit of vine around my wrist and swung lightly to the ground. River water lapped at my ankles.

I knew what I looked like: my hair, long and water-dark, hanging to my knees; my arms, pale and slender. My eyes, too, were dark, like the deep pools by the riverbank where the sun did not reach. Young men had written poems about my eyes, once; women too. My clothing had long since rotted away, but what use had I for shifts and sarafans? I clothed myself in my own hair, in river weeds and trailing flowers.

Katya averted her eyes. "My mother... she is looking for me," she stammered.

"Let me guess." I drew closer, obliquely, the way I would approach a skittish fishling. "Your mother warned you away from the river. Your father forbade you to stand at the water's edge."

"I go where I want," she said, lifting her chin slightly.

"Do you?" Her defiance intrigued me, and I felt compelled to provoke her, just a little. "One should never lie to the forest spirits. They say Baba Yaga can smell a lie on one's breath."

"You aren't Baba Yaga." Her jaw was set, and she met my gaze squarely. Her dark eyes reminded me of something. Fog over the barley fields, perhaps. Storm clouds. The stone hearth at my mother's house. It had been a long time since I had thought of home.

"I am not." I studied her carefully. Warmth practically radiated from her. Her pulse fluttered at the base of her throat, and I imagined I could hear the blood rushing in her veins, like a river. I took a careful step back. "But there are other spirits in this wood. Other haunts. This river is mine. Your mother was right. You ought to take care."

"Rusalka," she breathed. On her lips, it was neither an epithet nor a curse. "Marya, who loved a prince. They say that she—that you threw yourself in. They say your heart was broken."

I trailed the willow branch through the water. My reflection, already distorted by the current, fragmented, coalesced. "Is that what they say? I remember it differently. A man wanted me, and when he couldn't have me, he threw me into the river. I drowned." My clothing had dragged me down. My belt had snagged on a submerged log. I remembered sadness, anger—but not fear. "Some time later, he found me here. I don't think he recognized me, not until just before..." I inspected my nails.

Katya's gaze darted, caught mine, darted away again.

"Sit," I offered. "Stay a while under my tree."

"You won't drown me?"

I considered this. "Have you caused me harm, or any other woman?"

She shook her head.

"Then there's no need. Besides—" I laughed— "this river is too small for two rusalki, don't you think?"

The woman's voice rang out again, this time closer. "I have to go," Katya said. She sidled around the tree, clearly unwilling to step closer to either me or the river's edge.

"You go where you want, of course."

She flushed, as though my jibe had struck a nerve. "Will you be here tomorrow?"

"Where else would I go?" I encompassed my world in one broad sweep of an arm: river, bridge, tree. The gesture dislodged my cloak of river weeds, baring my skin further. I laughed again, and I knew there was something sharp in my smile.

Katya fled, back to the warmth of hearth and home, back to the safe arms of her mother and father.

She came back the next day, just after sunrise. She brought her breakfast with her: rich black bread she had baked herself, slathered with sweet butter and sprinkled with salt. I could not remember the last time I had seen bread or tasted salt; she offered some to me, shyly, but I refused. I was a spirit. Hunger and thirst, heat and cold—these were things I remembered more than felt. She stayed an hour, then slipped away again, claiming to have heard her mother's call. I watched her go, tangled in my own memories like a bird among the reeds.

She returned the next morning, and the next. She visited only at dawn or dusk at first—the twilight times, when possibilities lingered among the shadows. She would stand on the footbridge until certain she wouldn't be seen, then slip away along the riverbank, around the bend to my willow tree. I soon came to expect her and even found myself watching impatiently for her arrival, starting at every snapped twig and rustle of leaves until, laughing, she parted the curtain of dangling branches and slipped through to sit beside me.

Sometimes, she would make up stories. She had a knack for it. The forest folk would creep up through the rushes and the underbrush: the leshii's children and the stodgy old bolotnik, who brought me herbs as a pretext before settling back on his fat haunches to listen. Katya was startled at first, but soon she grew to recognize them. I'd sit in my tree, or on a flat rock in the river, or—on particularly warm days—half-submerged in the water, and I'd listen too. She told stories of princes in their far-off kingdoms, of clever women and wicked stepmothers, of the notorious witch, Baba Yaga, with her black iron teeth and her double-edged favors. Even the birds stilled their songs to listen.

She told, also, stories of Muscovy and Kiev, of the bogatyrs and their adventures. These last made me laugh.

"Alyosha has always been a fool," I said dismissively, ignoring Katya's incredulous stare. "No matter what the stories say. And Dobrynya Nikitich is a liar." The bolotnik nodded sagely. He was the one who had told me so, after all.

Eventually, Katya told me about her family: her father, Vasilij, who doted on her with the sort of intensity only a widower left with a child could maintain; her father's wife, whom she called *Mother* and who was kind and beautiful but had hard eyes; her stepsister, who longed for marriage and babies the way small children longed for sweets. I listened greedily, hungry for the bread-and-salt taste of *home*. I couldn't bring myself to speak to her of my former life, of the lonely girl I had been before I had drowned or the home I had lost. Instead, I told her about the minnows and the frogs, the other spirits in the woods, the other haunts. When she finally asked about my family, I told her I did not remember them. It was too long ago, I claimed, my memory too waterlogged.

"How could you not remember?" Katya asked one morning, all curiosity and concern. "They must have loved you. Did you ever go to see them, after—?" She gestured at the river.

"Such a precious little fish you are. Do you think they would have wanted to know me like this? Better to be a quiet corpse than an unquiet spirit. I would have drowned any of them who came looking." It was a spiteful thing to say, meant to unsettle her. I was a rusalka, after all—everyone knew I was dangerous, vengeful. Unpredictable. Who knew what I might have done – what I might still do?

That evening she stayed away, and I told myself I was glad.

When she returned, two days later, I didn't offer an apology, and she didn't seem to be looking for one.

The sun was hardly above the treetops, but the buzzing of the bees and the lazy whispering of the aspens told me that it was already hot. Sweat beaded at Katya's brow. From time to time, she dabbed at her face with her apron hem.

"Come swim with me," I said. "It's not too cold, even for you, not this late in the season."

But Katya shook her head, drew back from the bank.

"I don't swim," she confessed. "And the river is so fast."

"There's a pool, small and shallow and fairly still. Safe enough even for a little fish like you."

She looked at me a long time, measuring, and I wondered if she still feared drowning by my hand.

"Where?" she asked.

It was less of a pool than a shallow spot at the next bend. A handful of boulders and a single half-submerged log protected it from the current; tall reeds swayed at the water's edge, and the soft murmur of ducks drifted out from between them. Across the water, an oak tree rustled its leaves.

Katya took off her shoes and stockings, rucked her skirt up above her knees and tucked it into her belt. "I don't swim," she said again, but she waded out into the water. She picked her way carefully across the pool to a flat boulder. When she had settled herself there, dangling her legs in the water, I hopped neatly from stone to stone after her.

"I could teach you, you know." I slipped into the waist-deep water beyond Katya's perch. The current was an old friend; I was used to it, and I had already drowned once. It swirled around me, supported me, but did not carry me away. I ducked under, came up again to float on my back, my hair swirling around breasts and belly. My nudity no longer made Katya look away. She looked, mostly, at my face, and if her gaze sometimes wandered, well, that was not unwelcome.

"I'm sure you could," she murmured, and something inside me leapt and fluttered with exhilaration—something half-remembered and strange.

I pulled myself up onto the rock next to her and began untangling my wet hair with my fingers.

"Here, let me." Katya drew a wooden comb from her pocket. "If you don't mind?"

I didn't answer, just let the snarled mess drape over my shoulder and flattened both hands against the sun-warmed stone. She started from the ends, gently picking at the knots until it all came smooth and fell over my bare chest like a silk robe. She leaned in, then, and kissed me there on a flat stone in the river under the early morning sun.

This I remembered, better than the taste of bread or salt or the thudding of my own pulse, better than the struggle for breath or the shape of apologies. I remembered the currents that had pulled me under the water, so many years ago. This drowning was different; this time I went willingly.

Later, we lay together on a bed of fescue and chamomile blossoms in the safe shelter of my willow. The wind had picked up, and I could hear the trees gossiping.

"Aren't you cold?" Katya asked, laughing, pressing her hand against my breastbone. The sun was high and it was past time for her to have returned to her father's house with an apron full of berries to excuse her tardiness. Her palm was hot against my cool skin.

"Not anymore," I said, and it was almost true.

I discovered over time that I liked to watch her eat. I found myself braving thorny blackberry canes and prickly gooseberry bushes just so I could watch her eyes close at the burst of sweetness on her tongue. When I kissed her, I could almost taste the fruit. We swam every day in the river—or rather, I swam while Katya watched and practiced the small magics she was learning from the leshii: how to coax mushrooms from a decaying log, how to listen to the trees. She still feared the deeper water of the river, despite my assurances that I would keep her safe.

Katya came to know my neighbors as well, or even better, than I did myself. She recognized the ducks that hid among the rushes and knew how many ducklings belonged to each. She tossed bread crumbs to them after breakfast, and soon they knew to come looking for her by my willow every morning. She tended the wildflowers along the riverbank; she fished bees out of puddles when they were caught in the rain. She left loaf-ends for the bolotnik and sometimes porridge in a cracked clay bowl. She left me her wooden comb and made me promise to use it.

"Would you have done any of this for them, if you did not know me?" I asked her. She had just spent a half-hour ferrying froglets from one tiny pool to a larger one. The adult frogs croaked their gratitude.

"I wouldn't have known to do it," she replied. "But I'm glad for it now. It gives me a purpose. If it were up to me..." Her face grew wistful. "I'd spend my days doing this. Tending the forest folk and all the river creatures."

"*All* the river creatures?" I said playfully, flicking water at her.

She drew herself up, haughty as the summer sun. "Some more diligently than others, maybe." And then she proceeded to show me how very diligent she could be.

As the leaves began to change color, it grew too cold, Katya claimed, for wading or splashing around in what I had come to think of as *our pool*. The oak tree began to drop its leaves well before the usual time. The chilly air didn't bother me, of course, but Katya traded out her linen shift for a wool one and wanted to stay out of the damp. I didn't mind spending our evenings gathering chanterelles for Katya's stepmother and listening to the nightingales sing their children to sleep, and the leshii didn't object. I still spent my days in or beside the river; I was bound to it, after all.

Katya began to pepper me with questions. "How long can you stay away from the river? Is it so difficult, being in the wood? The river runs all the way to the sea—could you swim there, if you wanted to?"

I answered as honestly as I could—*I don't know; it pulls, like a heavy fishing line; I've never tried*—but eventually I grew impatient.

"What would happen," she asked me one evening as I braided her hair, "if you left the river altogether? Is it even possible?" We sat together under the willow, Katya's wool coat spread out beneath us, the tree trunk pressing into my back. It was raining, a gentle drizzle that didn't penetrate through the branches.

"Do you think I would have stayed here, in this muddy river bend, had I any choice?" I pushed her away and clambered up into the crook of the tree where I could peer down at her. "I am bound here; I have no agency in this. Any choices I had were taken from me when I drowned." I bared my teeth. "You should learn to swim, little fish, else the same might happen to you someday."

She blanched. I waited for her to leave, to gather up her warm coat and her wooden comb and rush off to her warm hearth where there were no spirits to threaten her.

"I think it already has," she said instead, and lay the comb down at the foot of the tree. "At least, it feels like drowning. I can't feel the ground under my feet, around you. I can't breathe. When I'm not here, with you, the world is muddy and muffled, and something *pulls*."

I felt a pang in my chest, a ghostly flutter at the base of my throat: the memory of my own mortal pulse, perhaps, or the echo of Katya's.

"There are rules." The words tangled in my mouth. This was a thing I had never spoken about, had never needed to speak. "I'm safe as long as I can hear the river. If I go too far, I'll dry up and blow away, I think. Like a dandelion, or a cattail. A river isn't meant to leave its banks, and river spirits aren't meant to wander. The leshii stays in the forest, the bolotnik in his marsh. They call me Baba Rechka, Mother River, have you heard them? I am *bound*."

"Ah," she said, and drew her coat over her shoulders. "Then it's a good thing I love this river so much, isn't it?" She looked up at me, and if I was Baba Rechka, her smile was the sunlight that danced across our little pool.

Oh little green oak tree, why do you rustle so early?
It is not of my own accord that I rustle.
The fierce wind is rustling me,
And the terrible frost is crackling.

Oh beautiful Katya, why do you marry so young?
It is not of my own accord that I marry.
My father is giving me away,
And my mother-in-law is taking me.

I had been resting under the bridge, where shadows hid me from mortal eyes during the day, and daydreaming of Katya--of the scent of rye bread and woodsmoke and the kiss of heat against my skin on a cold night. *Remembering.* I imagined I heard the creaking of floorboards and the scrape of my father's chair; but no, it was the creaking of the bridge above me and the harsh murmur of an argument.

"You can't!" A girl's voice, raw with emotion.

"It's already done, child." An older woman, her diction crisp, her tone not unkind: Katya's stepmother. The footsteps ceased. The wood creaked again as someone leaned on the rail.

"But Katya doesn't even care for Yurij Grigorevich!" *And I do*, was the unspoken corollary behind the girl's words.

"And what has that to do with it? Your sister will do right by her family, just like I did, and so will you. She is older than you, too old, almost. Her father has indulged her long enough. Let Katya have the boyar; you are prettier, Svetochka, and the prince's second son is looking to wed."

"You married for love, not duty." Sveta pronounced that last word as though speaking around a mouthful of unripe plum.

Katya's stepmother did not respond right away, and when she did, her words were clipped. "Well. Be that as it may. What's done is done. The dowry has been agreed upon, and the priest has been informed. I suggest you make your peace." With that, she left the footbridge, and her weeping daughter, behind.

When Katya came to the river that evening, she found me up in my willow tree, combing out my hair with the comb she had given me. It was late, already near dark, the full harvest moon just rising. She pushed aside an armful of leafless branches and sat on the ground, leaning her back against the trunk.

"And what have we here?" I repeated my very first words to her, back when she was a stranger. I did not swing down from my perch. "A little fish, carrying news, I think."

She stared up at me. Even here in the shadows, in twilight, she shone, and her eyes reflected the moon. She did not ask how I knew, nor did she equivocate. "My father is sending me away to be married, my mother says. I'm to leave in the morning. He is a fine gentleman, and has a grand house and forty desyatinas of land. My mother says."

"Ah, I see." I inspected a twig, holding it between my fingers. "I loved a prince once, a fine gentleman. Or he loved me, I don't remember. His crown is buried in silt."

"Why do you always do this? Every time I say something you don't want to hear, you go all—" She looked over her shoulder at the river. "All wicked, and cold. It's a good match, the best my father could have made. What more could I ask for?"

"Nothing," I spat. "You could ask for nothing, and take nothing. Let your sister have the man, and let me have—"

"Have what? Shall I throw myself in your river, then? I can't give you a hearth or home, and neither can you give them to me. You can't even remember what a home is. You won't remember me, either, after I've gone."

I *remember the taste of bread,* I wanted to say. *I remember coming inside from the rain. I remember shelter, and I thought I had found it in you.* But the words would not form in my mouth.

"Little oak tree," I murmured instead. "Little Katya. You will put down roots, you will grow old and docile in that place, until someone comes to build a house of your bones."

Her face paled. "Keep your curses, and keep your river. I'm leaving in the morning, my mother says; I thought you should know."

She stalked off back to the path and over the footbridge. I took up her comb and threw it after her. It clattered against the bridge and fell into the water.

That night, the river iced over at the edges: just a thin sheen that cracked easily when poked with a stick, but that was only the beginning. A hard frost set in, turning soft mud to stone and shallow pools to mirrors. The reeds along the riverbank grew brittle. They rattled instead of rustling, bowing stiffly before the north wind. It sounded like the gnashing of teeth.

Katya didn't come again. She was gone, just as she'd said.

The days grew shorter, the nights interminably long. I did not feel the cold, but I watched it creep over the swampy pools and naked trees. Ice slicked the boards of the wooden footbridge and snow weighed down the limbs of the firs. On clear nights I marked the waxing and waning of the moon and wondered if Katya did the same, if she thought of me at all.

One morning just after the solstice, the leshii came knocking at my door – so to speak. There was an out-of-place rustling noise and a stomping of feet. I uncurled from my willow perch, where I had been moping all night long, to find him standing in the snow with a handful of willow branches in one fist. He shook them one more time, then pointed.

On the other side of the river, nestled in under the tall oak tree and just barely visible around the bend, stood a little hut where there had never been one. As I watched, it stood up on a pair of scrawny bird legs, turned around, and resettled with the front of the house now facing the river. Wind chimes made of small bones hung from the eaves.

"What is *she* doing here?" I recognized the hut at once and knew who was inside. I had sought to unnerve Katya with talk of Baba Yaga, but I never expected to encounter her here in my little grove. The leshii just shrugged and melted into the underbrush.

I considered, briefly, ignoring the hut and the witch within, but I didn't want to risk offending her. And besides, the glimmer of an idea began to take shape. *You ought to take care*, I had warned Katya when we first met. It was sound advice – I was a river spirit, after all, a rusalka. We were known to be vengeful. But also: *there are other spirits in this wood*. And so I climbed down from my tree, pushed aside the curtain of bare willow branches, and slipped into the icy river.

The door of the hut opened when I had crossed halfway. The ancient witch peered out. Her face was craggy and wrinkled, like a walnut. Her eyes were black, and her teeth as well. She leaned on a stick as she sniffed the air.

"What is that I smell?" She licked her thin lips and smacked her teeth. Her accent was archaic, as if she'd learned to speak long ago in some far-off kingdom.

I answered her politely, as I would a kinswoman. "Only frost and fir, Grandmother. There aren't any living souls here." I pulled myself up onto an ice-encircled rock and began to pick at the tangles in my hair, nerves jangling.

"No? Well, I know what I smell, and I smell the taint of a mortal soul. If it is not yours, then whose?"

"There is no one here besides me, Grandmother." But even as I spoke, I felt that familiar flutter, that tugging in my chest.

She sniffed again, wrinkling her nose in distaste. "Come closer, child." She pointed one bony finger to the riverbank.

I hesitated, but even if I had wanted to disobey, I don't think I could have. There *were* other spirits in the wood, older spirits, and Baba Yaga was stronger than me by far.

She looked me up and down, crown to ankle and back again. Took a lock of my hair between her fingers and brought it to her nose. I stood as still as I could; her scrutiny made me uneasy.

"I can smell her on you. She has infected you, that mortal girl."

Katya.

"She's gone," I said, and the words tasted like river stone, like a pebble beneath my tongue.

"Where?" asked the witch. I didn't answer, just turned my face to the east.

"Ah," she said. "And so you have come to me."

I could have pointed out that she had come here, to my river bend. I could have claimed that I had been content in my little pool under my willow tree. But Baba Yaga would smell the lie.

"I'd go to her if I could. But I'm bound to the river. Will you help me?"

The witch hobbled over to the water's edge, dipped a finger in and brought it to her lips. She broke off a dried-out bit of river grass, tasted that as well. She squatted down on the river bank, stared into the water for a good long time, then levered herself up with the help of her stick.

"I can give you what you need, rusalka. I can loosen your tether, somewhat, but it comes at a price. Will you hear it?"

The river seemed to grow quieter. The trees stopped their rustling. "Yes, Grandmother."

"First: are you here of your own will?"

"Yes, Grandmother," I said again, falling into a cadence both familiar and unfamiliar.

"Second: will you serve me true?"

"Yes, Grandmother." I felt as though I had come to a branching of a river in the dark, and before I could change my mind, I threw myself headlong into the current. "I will serve."

"And third: if she will not have you, your girl, you will give to me that sliver of mortal soul rattling about your ribcage, and you will content yourself with your fishes and your willow tree. Do you understand?"

"Yes, Grandmother."

She cackled, and an unexpected breeze lifted my hair. I was well and truly caught.

"Good, good. Well, then. My little hut is old and tired. Build me a new one, with snug walls and a warm stove and a new thatch roof, and I will give you what you need."

"But I don't know anything about building a hut!"

The witch shrugged. "You will learn, or you will not. But until it is done, and done properly, you are mine."

"But that will take—I don't even know how long that will take." And meanwhile, my Katya would be lost to me.

"She will be lost to you regardless," she said, as if reading my thoughts. "If you do not keep your promise."

The truth of this settled on me, and I could see the shape of the witch's gamble. If I failed to build this hut, if I failed to win Katya's heart, Baba Yaga would take that sliver of soul, and with it, my love for Katya. The taste of bread and salt. My memory of home.

"Well, then, Grandmother," I said. "Let's see your old hut, so I know what to do."

The enormity of the task I'd taken on filled me with despair. I knew nothing of woodworking or masonry and had only a rudimentary understanding of how to thatch a roof from watching the villagers make bundles of reeds and river grass to roof their own homes. What I lacked in skill and knowledge, though, I made up for in stubbornness.

The witch loaned me an axe in exchange for chopped firewood. She gave nothing freely, only bargained for something else first. When I needed a bucket to hold the river clay that plugged the chinks in the walls, she demanded a bucket of fish in advance—but only the ones with the blue stripe, mind, not the yellow. She crunched them between her iron teeth and gave the bucket back to me. When I needed a spade, she first gave me a chest full of bones and bade me sort them by length and resonance. The extra work slowed down my progress, but I had little choice.

Some nights, the witch locked the door of her chicken-leg hut, climbed into her oversized mortar, and flew off on some secret errand, and that's when the forest folk crept in to help. The leshii showed me which trees to fell and helped me notch the logs so they fit neatly together. The bolotnik brought me dry rushes and soft river mud. When the witch returned, she would cluck her tongue and peer at me disapprovingly, but by then the forest folk had made themselves scarce, and besides, she had not made me promise not to accept help.

One evening, the leshii's wife appeared with a domovoi in tow. It lived, I discovered, in Katya's father's house. Katya had always been generous, the domovoi told me, and had made a habit of leaving it a hunk of bread in the yard every night. It shook its head at my poor attempt at masonry and sent me to bed. When I woke in the morning, a gleaming white stove stood against the back wall of the hut where I had left a pile of stones. The stove was plastered neatly with clay, and there on top, tucked behind the chimney, was a narrow sleeping nook where an old witch might warm her bones in the winter.

I had no such respite. Snow fell, crusted over with ice, fell again. I wore a path in it between the witch's hut and the river. I gathered dried reeds by the armful and tied them into bundles. I worked until the river pulled me back, rested, and worked again. All the while I thought of Katya.

Katya, wading in the river, skirt tucked up over her knees.

Katya, her head resting on my lap, crowned in daisies.

Katya, combing my hair.

The trees began to put out new leaves, and new river rushes began to sprout. The hut's walls were complete, and the floor, and the great stone stove. All that was left to do was thatch the roof.

Course after course I laid, and pegged each one down with rods of withy cut from my own tree. I lost count of how many times I crossed the river to the willow tree and back again. The leshii's wife kept me company, handing up the supple willow branches one by one.

One morning I came out to survey what needed to be done that day and discovered that there was nothing left. The witch's new house was finished, from wooden floor to snug thatched roof.

I carried the witch's belongings from the old hut to the new, piling blankets in the sleeping nook atop the stove, hanging curtains, fixing her grotesque wind chimes to the eaves. Finally, the old hut was empty of everything but dust and scraps of old tales. The witch shut the door, locked it, and tossed the key into the river. The old hut seemed to sigh.

"That's that, then," the witch said, dusting off her hands as if she had done the work herself. "A winter well spent."

I hovered nearby, tongue suddenly tied.

"Ah, yes. Your payment. Your prize," she said, and bared her black teeth. "Your heart is bound in two places, child. You have two tethers. It is up to you to decide which is the stronger."

She fell silent; I waited, impatiently, for her to continue. For a solution, some bit of aid. Her eyes glittered, and she sniffed again, testing the air.

"That's it?" Incredulity and rage left a bitter taste on my tongue. "All this, and you give me a false choice?"

"False how?" the witch asked. "You stay here," and she pointed at the willow tree, "or you go there." Her arm swung east, upriver. "Fear is what keeps you here. This place is familiar; your place in it, comfortable. Consider this: you risk nothing, staying here. And if you ask me politely, I will relieve you of that bit of soul now, and you will forget your mortal girl right away. Or you can leave your comfortable place, for a chance at something else." She poked me in the chest with one bony finger. "Go, do not go; the choice is yours. Three days will be enough, I think, to bring your lover home—if she will come."

The witch clucked her tongue, and the house—the new house—rose up on chicken legs. It scratched at the dirt, impatient. With surprising nimbleness the witch leapt up onto the narrow stoop, pushed the door open, and shut it behind her. The house turned around twice, as if getting its bearings, and walked off into the forest, leaving me behind in the muddy clearing under the eaves of her sorry little abandoned hut.

I will go, I will go to the swift river
I will sit on the bank
I will sit through the whole night
If my beloved does not come

A white birch tree grows there
Bending over the river
Never will my heart
Be at peace again

All that night I sat by the river and thought. The moon slipped up into the sky, casting her wan light on the snowmelt-swollen river. The leshii did not visit me, nor his wife, nor the bolotnik with his tales and gossip. There was nobody to give me advice or counsel; there was nobody I could ask for help. I sat on the riverbank, waiting for something to change, to be decided.

Better a quiet corpse than an unquiet spirit, I had sneered at Katya. If I stayed, I would be no worse off than I was before I had met her. I had my willow tree – half shorn though it was – and I had my river pools, and the forest folk for company. I would have something resembling peace, if I stayed.

If I followed Katya, if she turned me away, the result would be much the same. Only, I would know that I had reached for something and lost it. What sort of peace could I know, after that? Even if Baba Yaga tore that bit of Katya's soul away from me, I would never unlearn the shape of it.

I missed, suddenly, fiercely, my mother, whom I barely remembered. I blamed Katya for the yearning in my heart, and I blamed the witch. I blamed myself for letting myself forget.

If I wanted something to change, I would have to do it myself, and I had only three days to do it.

I set out just before dawn, in the twilight time, hoping that it would bring me luck. I didn't want to admit to myself that I had been afraid to go at night, that I was afraid that in the darkness I wouldn't be able to make myself leave my little pool, my willow, my own history. The forest folk watched me leave. They whispered: *Stay, you belong here, spirits do not wander.*

But I was more than my history, and I was more than the choices that had been made for me. In the burgeoning light of day, I slipped the knot of my own fear and followed the river upstream.

I swam east, and then north, and then east again when the river branched. The trees grew sparser and sparser, and the river left my wood, becoming narrower and shallower at each fork. At first I swam, and then I waded: waist deep, knee deep, ankle deep, until the last damp tendrils of my hair dried out and began to tangle in river grass, until finally the river itself disappeared into a tumble of rocks at the edge of a wide, sprawling meadow. I could feel the place of my first drowning calling me back, back, back to my river and safety.

On the far side of the meadow at the top of a low rise was the boyar's manor. A cluster of smaller houses stood at the base of the hill, and in the distance, tiny figures worked the fields. Sunlight glinted off of a golden cupola that stood higher than any other building in the village. It was not so far, perhaps, but it was farther from the river than I could possibly walk.

I sank down to my knees in a little pool fed by the burbling spring. Wildflowers bloomed among the grasses and reeds. Lilacs and kalina blossoms nodded in the wind, occasionally dipping into the water, and the flowers were crowded with bees.

If Katya were here, I would weave a crown for her. I tried to guess the distance to the boyar's manor. I had come so far, but she was farther still. My mouth was dry, and my skin, and the tugging of the river, of my willow tree, was enough to make me gasp. I turned my face to the water and drank, wet my hair thoroughly, and felt a little better.

A ripple in the water materialized into a fat green frog.

"Baba Rechka," it croaked. "I thought I had come a long way, but I never thought to see *you* so far from home."

It was one of the froglets Katya had rescued from the puddle all those months ago, now full grown and no longer sporting a tail. I reached out, and it obligingly hopped into my palm. "I didn't come for myself. I came for Katya."

"Katya?" The frog blinked slowly and flicked its tongue. "She is at the boyar's manor."

"I know. Have you seen her? Is she well? Is she happy?"

"I saw her arrive," the frog said. "There is a fountain there, and a pond—not as nice as your pool, but the water beetles there are fat and slow. The boyar took her hand and led her inside the house. That was a long time ago." Though the winter had passed by quickly enough for me while I built the witch's hut, it must have felt like lifetimes to a frog. "I can go there and see, if you like. The stream goes underground here and you are too big to swim, but I know the way. If I leave now, I could be back by nightfall."

"You would do that for me?"

"For you," croaked the frog, "and for Katya." It leapt from my hand and disappeared into the underground spring.

I took refuge in the shadow of a lonely willow, comforted by the soft caress of its branches and the scent of green growing things. I wove a basket out of reeds and filled it with beetles and water skates and even a pair of crickets who wandered into reach. The sun dipped lower and lower, and I found myself anxiously watching the place where the stream emerged from the ground.

It was already full dark when the frog returned. I tipped the basket onto its side so the frog could make a good meal of the insects I had caught.

"Did you see her?" I asked, once the frog had eaten its fill.

"I saw her," the frog croaked. "The boyar sat with her beside the pool. He brought her fruit and cheese and fine white bread on golden dishes, and poured wine into a silver cup. When he wasn't watching, she tossed the bread into the pond for the fish instead of eating it for herself. I told her you were here, looking for her, but I don't know if she heard me."

The frog finished its meal and hopped back into the water. "Good luck, Baba Rechka," it said, and swam off downstream, away from the spring and towards the river that pulled at me. I curled up under the willow that was not my willow and waited for morning.

That was the first day.

I dozed, which of itself was unusual enough. A loud buzzing woke me well after the sun had risen. I felt frayed, wrung out; a scrap of linen forgotten on the line. All around me, butterflies and bees sipped at the morning dew.

One of the bees settled onto a flat rock in the sunshine and began preening its antennae.

"Baba Rechka," it hummed. "You are far from home, and unwell, I think. Why have you abandoned your pool? Why have you left your wood?"

With a start, I recognized one of the bees from the hive in the poplar by the bridge.

"Katya," I said, and her name coated my tongue like honey. "I'm looking for Katya."

"Ah." The bee's humming increased in pitch. "I understand. If you like, I will find her for you. She was kind to me and mine."

"She is a long way east, across the meadow and up the hill and in the boyar's manor."

"I can fly so far and back again," hummed the bee, and its antennae waved proudly. "I will bring you news before the sun sets. Only promise that you will return to your pool before you wither away."

I promised, touching my fingers to my lips to seal the bargain. "Once I know she is safe and happy, I will go home."

The bee rose then, pausing to fortify itself at a honeysuckle vine, and flew off east toward the manor.

The sun continued to climb, then began its slow slide down into the west. I spent the day tending the honeysuckle and other spring flowers, coaxing more vibrant blooms, until the entire copse seemed to shiver with the buzzing of the bees. The shadows grew longer and longer. One by one the bees flew off, their tiny bodies weighed down with pollen. Just before the sun dipped below the forest canopy, my little golden bee returned.

"I saw your Katya," the bee said. "She was walking in the boyar's garden, wearing a silk gown and silk slippers. There was gold about her neck and around her wrists and golden ornaments in her hair. The boyar walked alongside her."

I swallowed. "And did she look happy?"

"She looked very beautiful," said the bee, "but she didn't smile, and she didn't laugh, and she barely even *looked* at the flowers." The bee sounded affronted. "It is a glorious garden."

I thanked the bee, and it flew off, humming, to rejoin its fellows. I sank down into the water to think. Was Katya unhappy, I wondered, or might she be content? Katya was a serious girl, not one of those simpering, smiling chits from the village. I needed to know more. I needed to be sure.

That was the second day.

That night, the pull of the river nearly had me wading homeward again. My hair crackled, full of static in spite of the damp air, and it snarled with every turn of my head. I longed for the solace of my deep pool and the comfort of my own willow tree. But I kept my face turned to the east, towards the sunrise and Katya, and I stayed.

Fog lay heavy over the meadow in the morning of the third day. No breeze rustled the reeds at the water's edge, and even the singing of the birds was muted. As much as I loved sunshine, today I appreciated the cool dampness more. I sat myself on a mossy log and began to comb out my hair with a twig. A flock of ducks landed beside the stream in a flurry of wings and squawks and began to preen themselves in the shallow water.

One duck waddled closer, its webbed feet slapping against the mud. It dropped something into the stream.

"Baba Rechka," the little brown duck said. "The leshii's wife sent me. She said you would need this. She said to remind you that you have drowned twice, and you are tethered to the second no less than to the first." It was a long speech, for a duck, and sounded rehearsed.

I felt around in the water for the object the duck had dropped. It was a wooden comb, caked in mud and tangled in river weeds but otherwise utterly familiar: Katya's comb, that I had thrown into the river. One of the tines was broken. I cleaned the comb as best I could, pulling bits of greenery out and breaking another tine in the process.

Katya had given me this comb, made me promise to use it. She would know me by it and come for me. I hoped.

"Bring this comb to Katya," I begged the duck. "There, in the boyar's garden. Tell her I am here, and that I love her. Will you do this?"

The duck turned its head to look at me, first with one eye and then the other. "Very well," it said finally. "I will bring it to her. I will tell her. But you should really go home, Baba Rechka. The leshii needs you. Your willow tree misses you."

I knew this was true; I could feel it. Sliver of a mortal soul or no, I was still a river spirit. "In the morning," I promised the duck. "I will go in the morning, if Katya does not come." By then, of course, it wouldn't matter.

The duck returned a short while later.

"I gave her the comb, but then the boyar saw me and chased me off." The duck shook itself, ruffling its feathers. "I'm sorry, Baba Rechka."

In the distance, thunder rumbled, and the first fat raindrops splashed into the water. "You should go," I told the duck. "Before the storm comes."

The little brown duck flew off. The sky bore down on me, heavy with the promise of rain. Grief pressed against my eyelids, and loneliness, and I began to weep, tears with neither salt nor heat.

Let the witch find me here, I thought. I would wait the third day out, and if the witch wanted Katya's soul, she could come retrieve it. I wept long and hard. The willow grazed my shoulder with its branches in sympathy, but I brushed them aside. The rain sobbed and the wind keened, as though the storm itself were speaking for me. The spring burbled, oblivious, and no one came to see what sort of misfortune might have befallen a poor bedraggled river spirit.

A small hut appeared at the northern edge of the meadow, bobbing and weaving on its gangly bird legs. At the same time, I felt that fragile tugging in my chest: Katya's soul, reaching for its other half.

I looked east, and there was my Katya herself riding down the hill on a fine black horse, her skirts tucked above her knees and her hair loose and streaming behind her. She looked like a wild thing, almost feral, if not for the water-stained silk she wore. Water dripped from her hair and splashed up from beneath the horse's hooves as it slowed to a stop beside the little spring.

She slid down from the horse's back.

"I heard your weeping on the rain," Katya said. "The bolotnik taught me how to listen."

Now that she was here, my tongue felt thick, my limbs awkward and ungainly. "I hoped you would come." I gathered my hair over my shoulder, began to work at a knot with my fingers. Rain streamed into my eyes. I felt pulled in two directions at once. "I came to see if you were safe. And happy. Your boyar, he treats you well?"

"He is a good man, a kind man." She stared at something clenched in her hand: the wooden comb. "But Marya—he doesn't love me."

The way she spoke my name, the sound of it, filled me with hope for the first time. "And do you love him?"

"No." She said it without hesitation, simply, without guile, and I understood, suddenly, thoroughly, what it meant to drown a second time – not in the river, not in anger or despair, but in love. I saw that she understood this too.

"Come home with me, then." Thunder rumbled again. "Please, Katya."

She smiled at me, then. "Why else am I here?"

I forgot all the anguish, all the confusion and worry. I remembered what it meant to be cold and hungry, and I remembered sweetness and warmth. I remembered the taste of salt on my tongue for the first time in a long, long while.

"We should be quick," Katya told me. She gathered the tears from my cheek with a brush of her fingers and flicked them behind her. As if in response, the rain intensified, and lightning flashed. "I told them to tell Yurij Grigorevich that I wanted to go home, that I missed my mother. I hope the storm will slow him down, but he won't be far behind me."

Several figures on horseback appeared on the road leading down from the manor. The one in front wore a red coat.

Katya helped me onto her horse and leapt up behind me, wrapping one arm around my waist to steady me and holding the reins with her other.

Over my shoulder, I could see the rain start to come down in sheets between us and the boyar's men. "Where did you learn that trick with the rain?" I asked.

"The leshii's wife. Keep your head down." Katya kicked the horse into a gallop. Thunder rolled over us, and it began to rain in earnest.

We rode and rode, and I thought, how could I possibly have come so far on my own? Katya followed the stream through the meadow and between the rolling hills, leaping over gullies and low bushes.

I could hear hooves pounding not far behind us, and when I dared to look, I saw that there were at least a half dozen riders in pursuit. They rode in formation with the red-coated man, Yurij Grigorevich himself, well ahead of the rest. As swift as Katya's horse was, Yurij Grigorevich's was swifter.

Katya squirmed. "Hold on!" She tossed something behind her: the wooden comb. It bounced several times, but Yurij Grigorevich's horse dodged it nimbly. An immense forest sprang up behind him, cutting him off from his men. Katya muttered something under her breath about broken tines and urged her horse to run faster.

The stream widened gradually, joined up with another, and again, until it became a proper river once more. Finally Katya's horse slowed, planted its feet, and refused to go any further. Its head drooped, and its coat was soaked with rain and sweat. Katya dismounted, reluctantly, and helped me down. She stroked the horse's mane, whispering apologies.

"We can't stay here," I told her. My legs were wobbly, and the river's call was so strong that I nearly dove into it.

"I know." Katya turned to face the dark wood that had sprung up behind us, and the man whose horse had slowed but not stopped.

He was handsome, Yurij Grigorevich. His eyes were black, and his beard, and the shape of his face led me to believe he was quick to smile. He was not smiling now, however; he looked more sorrowful than anything else.

"Katyusha," he said, and I bared my teeth at him. "You should have waited for me. I would have gone with you, to protect you on the road." He eyed me, his hand drifting towards his belt knife.

I pushed Katya behind me. Her boots splashed into the river, and water lapped at my ankles. The strength of the river flowed into me. I knew what I was. *Rusalka.*

"Little princeling," I sang, and beckoned. He took a step towards me, enthralled. "Come take her, if you think you can. It has been a long, long time since I fed the river with the bones of a mortal man." The wind tossed my hair and lightning crackled along my skin. I knew what I looked like.

To his credit, he didn't so much as blanch.

Katya put her hand on my arm. "He is a good man," she reminded me. She clasped her hands at her waist and bowed deeply. "Yurij Grigorevich," she started. "Yura. You've shown me nothing but kindness, but kindness isn't enough for either of us, I think."

Yurij Grigorevich blinked once, twice, and I let him go. He stumbled back, swallowed several times.

Finally he asked, "Are you certain?"

"A river isn't meant to leave its banks," she said, "and I don't belong up there on your hill. Let me go where I am bound."

"What am I to tell your father? My parents? If you disappear, what could I possibly say?"

"Tell them I went to visit my mother," Katya said. "Tell them I missed my home too much. That you followed me here, and found my poor horse at the edge of the wood. Tell them," and her face softened, "that I bid you marry my sister instead. She will make you a much better wife."

His shoulders slumped then, as though a weight had been lifted off them and he wasn't sure how to hold himself. He nodded sharply. "Go, then," he said. "And peace be on you both." It was a kind thing to say, especially to an unquiet spirit, and I saw that Katya had been right about him.

Katya's hand tightened on my wrist, and she drew me, step by step, into the river. Yurij Grigorevich just watched us go. We were waist-deep in the water before I recovered from the shock of it.

"You can't swim," I protested. The current dragged against us.

"You'll keep me from drowning," she said.

"Ah, love." I laughed. "I think it's too late for that."

The water closed over our heads, mine and Katya's, and together we swam back to my river bend and my willow, to the witch's abandoned hut under the green oak tree and the hearth and home we would make there for ourselves.

Out of the dark forest, the green wood,
A thunderstorm came roiling—
A storm with rain, with lightning,
Full of terrible misfortune.
At the same time, at that very moment,
A girl came riding to visit her mother.
She rode and she rode, but she never arrived—
Her horse stopped at the edge of the wood, exhausted.

I was there at the wedding of Sveta and the boyar. I drank beer and mead; I tasted bread and salt, and it was more delicious than memory. And when the wedding was over and the bride and groom sent away, I went home with my Katya, to our little hut in the wood by the river bend, past the bridge and the willow tree, where the leshii's wife left chestnuts and chanterelles in a cracked bowl by the threshold.

Christine Hanolsy is a science fiction and fantasy writer who cannot resist stories about love in all its forms and flavors. Her speculative flash fiction and short stories have been published by EDGE Science Fiction & Fantasy Publishing, Atthis Arts, *Small Wonders*, *Worlds of Possibilities*, *Solarpunk Magazine*, *Beneath Ceaseless Skie*s, and more. She has worn many hats over the years, including editor-in-chief of an online writing community, Russian language scholar, composer, interpreter, and general cat herder. She lives in the Pacific Northwest with her wife, their two children, and a pair of very vocal cats, all of whom have been extremely patient with her. You can find her full publication list at christinehanolsy.com.

JOANNA'S BODIES

Eugenia Triantafyllou

The woman whose body Joanna is renting has a nosebleed. Joanna is about to get evicted again and she's cranky about it. She screams at Eleni in another woman's voice.

"Hey, this shit's burning!"

Eleni doesn't reply. She has been sitting on the toilet long after she's been done, counting supplies. Waiting for Joanna to get bored and go watch TV. There were ten rolls of toilet paper when they first set up here. Or was it twelve? Eleni swears the woman keeps everything in fucking dozens, she must have an obsession or something. Twelve tubes of mint-flavored toothpaste. Twelve red toothbrushes—two used by them. But does a toothbrush count as used by a guest if the mouth it's been brushing is the same as the host's? Does a new soul bring in new mouth germs?

One toothbrush used by them. By Eleni.

"I can't cook like this."

A whiff of burned butter and flour and whatever else Joanna is incinerating out there. Hopefully not the entire place.

"I'm coming!"

When Eleni comes out, Joanna is already slumped on the low leather couch by the window watching Eleni's ex-favorite movie for the billionth time. *Jennifer's Body.* Two girls who are best friends: Jennifer and Needy, one of them possessed by a demon, the other one possessed by the friendship itself. *Jennifer's Body* used to be their number one, but somewhere between Joanna's first death and her first resurrection, Eleni stopped caring for it. When fantasy becomes reality it's not as fun anymore. She prefers *Jurassic Park* these days—when Joanna lets her pick the movie—because there's no way in Hell dinosaurs are making a comeback.

Joanna is inside a short, fifty-year-old woman with unusually large hands. Joanna's hair used to be brown and sleek down her shoulders once upon a time, but this woman's blonde perm has a will of its own. Eleni tried to brush it into submission but the only thing she got out of it was a couple of bruises on her left arm from when Joanna got tired of the pain and pinched her.

The place smells like a gluten crematorium. Eleni runs to the kitchen and opens the window but it does little to help. Joanna has burned the pancakes and with them the pan that's currently swimming in soapy water. The pan that Eleni will need to find and replace with a similar one. She hates when Joanna does this. She knows the rules. She knows they are meant to protect Eleni and Joanna and the person whose body Joanna rents and she still does stuff like this. Whatever. They'll be out of here soon.

"I am sorry." Joanna's voice is barely a whisper under the sound of the jock's screams when Megan Fox, as Jennifer, dislocates her jaw and snatches him with her shark-edged teeth. "When it starts, I can't concentrate."

Joanna's telling the truth. It's hard for her to do anything when the body she inhabits starts breaking down. Looking at her, Eleni figures it's not too long now. They've got maybe another week before she needs to evacuate. And that's being generous. When too much time has passed—and that time is different for each person she inhabits—the body looks like a bodysuit a couple sizes too big. The flesh feels detached from the skeleton when Eleni rests a hand on Joanna, like it's sliding off in slow motion. It's at those times that Eleni can see the ghost of a face swimming under the flesh. Sometimes that face is slightly to the side of where the actual face is, but sometimes it's in other places, the neck, the small of the back, the stomach. It freaks her the hell out. Eleni usually gets Joanna to leave earlier than that, leave the person in as close-to-mint condition as possible. This is what they have agreed on.

Eleni plops on the couch and puts her arms around Joanna's narrow shoulders. There it is: the skin doesn't sit quite right on the bone, it's thin and slippery, like deli meat left too long on the counter. *It's okay. It's okay.* It always feels a little weird to comfort strangers but she's gotten better at it. This is body number ten. Joanna is wearing the woman's work clothes, meaning a pair of jeans and a white t-shirt that has the SuperEasy green and blue logo of the supermarket she worked at.

In the movie, Jennifer is looking at herself in the mirror. She's just fed and she is glowing. She has a *new* body for a while, until the power wears off and she needs to feed again.

If only it were that easy.

Joanna puts her head on Eleni's shoulder and sighs. Her sigh comes out heavy and a little wet. The woman was a smoker.

"I am so tired all the time," she says with that high-pitched voice that reminds Eleni of one of her aunts. One of her least favorite ones. "I don't want to do this anymore."

Eleni rests her chin on the bleached blonde hair to keep her jaw, and by extension her mouth, shut. She's tired too. So, so tired. Her breathing slows because she doesn't want to distract Joanna from what she is about to say. *I want to rest forever*, Eleni imagines Joanna confessing, *I want to go back to that place where I rest in between bodies and never leave again. It's nice there. Peaceful. I am ready.*

"I need someone younger, Leni." Joanna gently takes Eleni's hand into hers as if to show her how old and spotty her skin looks next to Eleni's twenty-year-old hand. One that fits their real age. On the TV, Jennifer looks like death and she is about to eat the emo boy. She won't stop until someone stops her. "I want to have fun for once."

Eleni's heart drops to her knees. She shakes her chin that still rests on Joanna's head and makes a mess of her hair all over again. "That's a stupid thing to ask and you know it."

"Why?" Joanna squeezes her hand with all the strength she's got. The way Joanna's skin moves against Eleni's flesh makes her queasy.

Joanna knows why. Eleni has explained this over and over. Middle-aged and above single women are more often independent. And that makes them safer. They live alone and can isolate themselves for a few months with little fuss. And if someone—a relative or a friend—checks in with them, they can tell them to go away and that's that. They are good targets.

"Let's try. Just this once. Promise me you'll try." Joanna squeezes Eleni's hand harder. Muscle and sinew and bone wobble under the surface. Her voice sounds like her real voice now that she's angry. It has the same tremor her real voice had before they got into a big fight. Joanna shouldn't get angry now. Not when the body is breaking down like this.

"Stop it." Eleni pulls her hand free and gets up. "I've got the next one lined up."

Joanna falls back on the couch which makes her moan but then she laughs in that mean way of hers. "Is it because you miss your mommy?"

"Shut up."

That's how Eleni messes it up. Again. She starts screaming in Joanna's face. "Shut up. Shut up. Shut up."

Joanna smiles with the woman's mouth but underneath the smile there's anger, Eleni knows. Joanna's teeth glisten, her spit is extra frothy, as if there's too much of it. Suddenly, she starts coughing so hard she stops smiling. She leans forward and coughs some more. She spits on the floor. Her nose starts bleeding again and now she coughs an inky-dark liquid that Eleni wishes were blood.

"It's happen—"

Eleni kneels in front of her. Grabs her by the shoulders to steady her and instead she feels untethered herself.

"Jo, you have to leave. Leave now, Jo, please."

She shakes her head and keeps coughing. Blackmailing Eleni like she always does.

"Fuck, Jo, you'll kill her. Leave now!"

Stubbornly, Joanna keeps coughing. There's so much inky mucus in her mouth now, it oozes between her teeth like she had been chugging mouthfuls of mud. And next to her ear Eleni thinks she sees a familiar nose materializing under the skin. Like a drowning person coming up for breath before they disappear under the ripples again. Eleni shakes her.

"Leave now! I'll try, okay? Leave!"

Only then Joanna smiles. Her teeth are stained black. Her brown eyes—it's her old eyes, the only thing she brings with her from body to body—turn pale gray as she leaves, so translucent you'd think there's no iris. A black pinprick-sized pupil is left staring at Eleni like a mite swimming in milk. Soon she stops coughing and fighting altogether and her body goes warm. Burning with fever. The woman—her name is Maria, Eleni can finally think of her name again—slumps forward and Eleni throws her own back out trying to pull her onto the couch. She immediately checks for the woman's pulse, and now she can breathe again because it's there. Faint but there.

It will take some time for her to come to herself, but she will be okay. Probably. Eleni will have to call someone, a friend or neighbor, to check on the woman eventually.

Eleni has at best a couple of days to return the house to how she and Joanna found it, or a close approximation, and then stuff her backpack with the essentials and get the hell out of there before the woman comes to her senses and starts asking questions.

The host—Maria—has lost her job at the supermarket and maybe burned a few bridges, but this isn't too bad as far as possessions go, Eleni tells herself.

"Thank you for being her host, Maria," Eleni says and kisses the woman's forehead like she's read in the spellbook. "You're now free."

On the TV Jennifer has found her next target. Her best friend Needy's boyfriend.

It isn't hard to summon a soul. All you need is an object that's easy to carry around—for Eleni that's a coin—a little blood, and the right kind of words. What's hard is having a strong enough connection with the person you are summoning. Visualizing them inside and outside as best and as accurately as possible. There must be billions or trillions of souls out there. And by *out there* Eleni means Hell or Heaven or wherever Joanna is vacationing when she is not here. Eleni never asked. Joanna tried to tell Eleni once but she stopped her. They both have gathered enough trauma for fifty lifetimes as it is. No need to open that can of worms. Visualizing Joanna as she was when she was alive is important, because it's like calling her special soul-fingerprint from the other side. Eleni doesn't even want to think what would happen if she summoned the wrong soul. Can you imagine? How embarrassing.

Eleni blames that movie and all the witchy, edgy stuff they were into during their teen years for at least some of it. Or maybe she doesn't really blame them. They were fun for a while. Like she and Joanna used to be fun together. They didn't know what they were getting into by buying all those spellbooks from the flea market in Monastiraki. They didn't know what they were getting into when they met each other in preschool either.

The books were fun for a while. They would call each other and read out loud the passages they found the most outrageous to spook themselves before bedtime. Then the witchy thing got old and Eleni stored the books at the back of her bookshelf so her Mom wouldn't find them, and almost completely forgot about them.

A couple of years passed and they found new ways to dare each other. This time it was all about who was going to leave the other one behind. Eleni's thing was drawing with permanent marker on every available surface and adopting a new wear-all-black-don't-give-a-fuck persona. Joanna went the other way by dressing up every morning for school while carrying around her duffel bag just to be able to casually drop that *oh, by the way I'm on the volleyball team, I've got hobbies and stuff.*

It all became a game of who was more interesting, or cute, or popular, or ultimately cruel enough to move on to new people first. And Eleni found she was losing on most of these tests, but at the end of the day they ended up together on the phone, judging the rest of the world for not being more like them while reveling in their own uniqueness.

Then one day Eleni's mom decided to sign her up to a cram school. Since she apparently lacked the motivation that would help her pass her college entrance exams with a good score, she needed the extra help. Cram school was a revelation. It was the first space where she had met people who didn't know Joanna, or didn't particularly care to listen to Eleni talk about her. A Joanna-free zone. No long phone-call conversations, no big personal secrets, no inside jokes between two people who have known each other forever, but no fights either, no jealousy, no fear.

Everyone there seemed brand new and sparkly to Eleni and she found they could all make up new inside jokes and the world would not fucking end. To them she was *artistic* and *chill* and sometimes *a dork* but in a cute way, and she toned down the emo-ness to something more average without feeling like a loser. It was the first place she could finally relax, even though it wasn't supposed to be a relaxing place. She started meeting up with her new friends after school; a part of her brain urged her to keep this a secret from Joanna. But it was all short-lived.

Eleni's next target is the woman who works at the coffee shop at the intersection of two of the busiest shopping streets. Her name is Elisavet—a name Eleni will try to forget once Joanna possesses the woman—and she lives alone in a house in the suburbs with a tiny garden and two cats. Divorced; her daughter studies abroad, like Eleni might have done if she had graduated from high school instead of messing up her own mother and then running away to create more mess elsewhere. Eleni petted the cats and chatted with the woman a couple of weeks ago. She passed by with her little backpack asking for directions that she didn't need. The woman was nice and even told her where she worked. Perhaps she sensed Eleni was lacking a mother and a direction in life—not only when it came to streets—and wanted to fix her. Then one of the cats, the oldest and fattest one, came and sat in Eleni's lap and that sealed the deal. Elisavet would be getting possessed.

When they were ten and Eleni's Mom was working night shift, little Eleni called Joanna in the middle of the night scared out of her mind. When she was alone at home everything seemed alive. The clothes, the lamp, that shadow in the corner. Her father had left them a long time ago so there was nobody to comfort her. Only Jo. That's how it started, their nightly ritual; sometimes until the early hours. Much later, when they were drifting apart, it phased out to mostly on weekends. High school was becoming too demanding to keep this up or, perhaps, they were using it as an excuse to take some space from each other. Eleni still isn't sure which one was true.

Their ritual led to Joanna calling Eleni that night and finding out from Eleni's mom that she wasn't home. Which made Joanna grab her bike and go looking for Eleni. Eleni hadn't thought to give her mom clear instructions on what to say in case Joanna called the landline looking for her.

Eleni isn't sure what Joanna was thinking that night. What Joanna thought she was going to do once she found all of them sitting around in the square drinking beers and talking about music and then sitting awkwardly in silence for a bit because they didn't know each other well enough. Neither of them got to find out. Eleni thought she heard sirens somewhere not far from where they were sitting but didn't think anything of it.

Later, after Eleni had summoned her from un-life, Joanna said, "Dude, you should have seen my face. Pure horror show. That truck messed me up big time. My nose got knocked all the way to the back of my skull and with my mouth and eyeholes it became one huge cavern full of blood, and teeth, and bits of brain. I could barely believe that was me."

"Weren't you already dead?" Eleni asked, which sounded cruel but deep down she really, really didn't want to know.

Joanna smiled as if she was still reading that spellbook. "I was hovering over myself for a moment. I was looking for you in the crowd. Too bad you weren't there to see the show. Guess you were busy with your new friends."

It's still very early but the store is already busy with people grabbing a coffee and a pie to go as they head off to their offices. There are four people working as far as Eleni can see. A man and three women, one of them Elisavet. The tall dude is cleaning the tables; one younger woman, the barista, her black hair up in a slick ponytail, is working the coffee machine. The third woman is cute, also very young, maybe the one closest to Eleni's age, with short-cropped pink hair. She is on customer service alongside Elisavet, taking orders behind the counter and working the cash register.

Eleni stands outside the store. Backpack resting against her back. She squeezes the coins in her hand as she finishes the dregs of her latte. There is a right time for these things. She always picks people who work some sort of cashier job because it is easier to give them the coins, especially the one she has marked with her blood. The ritual can work without the host-to-be touching the coin and by extension the blood, but there has to be some sort of bleeding by the summoner and in any case it's always safer if they touch it. Blood channels magic better.

Eleni's solution to the whole blood-touching thing was coins. Spill a drop of blood and give it to someone. Coins are dirty as hell anyway; who would notice a slight color tinge? And who turns down money? It turns out a lot of people did. Eleni had to find out the hard way that people weren't gullible like in the movies and if you yell *Sorry, ma'am, you dropped your fifty cents*, while running straight at them, arm outstretched, it's more likely that they will back away than gratefully accept the coins. So, cashiers it is.

When the last customer leaves and before anyone new comes in, Eleni sees her chance. The moment she sets foot in the café Elisavet seems to recognize her, and then becomes nervous for some reason. Or at least that's what Eleni thinks when the woman's face tightens and her eyes dart a little bit to the left to the other employee. The really young one. *Shit*, Eleni thinks. Was she too creepy that day? Too pushy? It doesn't matter much though because all she needs is for the woman to touch the blood and then Eleni will get her freddo cappuccino and occupy one of the tables in the back to have full view of the woman as she summons Jo's spirit.

"Hey," she says with the easiest voice she can muster.

Elisavet, the woman, gives her a nod of recognition and a cautious smile and takes her order. There is this awkward back and forth during which Eleni tries to sound not-creepy. It seems to her that the more she tries the creepier she looks, to the point where she has an out-of-body experience of herself as movie-Jennifer when she tries to lure the boys into quiet places for a snack. Eleni counts the moments with her heartbeat until the coffee is finally ready. Before the woman delegates to someone else, Eleni opens her now super-sweaty palm and drops the coins into Elisavet's hand.

Then they both smile at each other and the moment is over and Eleni isn't sure at all that the woman had been nervous or if it was a projection of her own nervousness. Eleni takes the coffee and leaves hastily for the table she has marked as hers. Now it's time for the really hard part.

Eleni was seventeen the first time she summoned Joanna back from the dead. It was a week after Joanna's funeral and she was sitting cross-legged on her bed, leafing through the books they had bought together in Monastiraki. It was one of Eleni's favorite memories of them, a day they'd both been in a good mood and holding hands and laughing, going around the stalls.

The friends Eleni had sneaked out to meet on the day of Joanna's accident did not talk to her after that night. They didn't know what to say to her, Eleni figured. They didn't want her pain. Her guilt. In an instant she stopped being the fake-emo girl and became the real thing. Nobody wanted the real thing. She had nobody and she needed Joanna again. Joanna was the person she knew the most intimately. Running to her when things got hard was like a natural instinct.

When Eleni turned the page of one particular book, she saw the spell. There had been other spells like that in the other books but this one felt truer. Probably all that visualization stuff it went on and on about for pages. And as Eleni sat there with her red eyes and that emptiness in her heart, she could see Joanna with her mind's eye. She could see Joanna inside and out as if she were standing right next to her, and her heart ached even more.

Perfect skin and long brown hair that caught the light right. Generous at times, clingy—but only when it suited her—and moody. Shrieking like a banshee when she was angry or to get her way with things. Lately she was getting distant with Eleni, chatting more with others at school, calling less often at night but expecting Eleni to pick up when she did.

Eleni pricked her finger with an enamel pin she had on her tote bag—probably not the most hygienic choice—and smeared blood on her bedroom mirror's glass. When she was done the room looked like it belonged in a horror movie. She had no clue what she was doing and she imagined that, if this ever worked, Joanna would appear in her bedroom mirror and talk to her like a Bloody Mary. Instead, she heard a knock on the door and before she could hide the bloody mess and tell her mother to go away, her mother's body barged into the room and fell into Eleni's arms.

That was Eleni's first thought when she saw her mom. Her mother's body. Not her mother, no. The body carried itself wrong. Like there was someone else inside her mom's skin. Someone with a different shade of brown eyes. Someone who clenched their jaw instead of half-opening their mouth. Someone who slumped their shoulders and shrieked and shrieked like a banshee on a full moon. *Mom, what's wrong? Mom? Mom.* It was more than a question. It was a hope that her Mom would confirm it was really her in there.

But when the body stopped wailing in her arms, someone who was definitely not her Mom whispered, *Why did you leave me?*

Nothing is happening. Eleni doesn't know why nothing is happening and her mind is racing as she takes the smallest of sips from her coffee, afraid that the woman—Elisavet?—will know when she has drunk it all and will expect her to leave immediately.

Eleni has gone through her list of things she knows about Joanna five times. She even dares to close her eyes and actually visualize Jo sitting right next to her at the coffee shop, the way they had done so many times when she was alive. When she opens them again the woman looks unaffected, meaning she looks like herself and not like a costume someone else is wearing. As far as Eleni can tell. No clenched jaw, no coppery-brown eyes, no scouring of the room to find Eleni and then a subtle nod to show her she is in there, inside the woman. Eleni decides to think of her as *the woman* just in case.

When Eleni left the previous *the woman*, now effectively renamed Maria, she took enough money from her to crash at a cheap hotel room for a few days. Pretty much in the same way Joanna was crashing the afterlife until it was time for her to be called back. That's what they always do between Joanna's bodies. Eleni pretends she talks to Joanna inside her head even when she is not here possessing anyone. In a way Eleni is permanently possessed.

There is a very specific window in which Eleni can call Joanna back and that window is two weeks. It says so in the book. If the two weeks go by, Eleni won't be able to call Joanna back from the dead. And although she has tried to wait the window out, she found out that she can't. She can't stop calling her back. The first time might have been love and loneliness and guilt, but now it's also that promise Joanna makes her give each time, before the body she is in starts breaking down. *You'll call me back, right?* is what she asks each time. The subtext is always the same: *I died because of you. Because you left me. So, you have to call me back.*

These thoughts give her already rising panic a nice tinge of desperation and since she can't hide it anymore, she gets up and paces back and forth in front of the woman, glancing at her, begging her to give her a sign that it isn't her anymore but Joanna. The woman looks increasingly uncomfortable and then she turns around and goes somewhere in the back, the place where customers are not supposed to go, and Eleni loses sight of her. Only the barista lingers behind the counter now.

"Is there something I can help you with?"

Eleni jumps at the voice on her right. It's the tall guy who has stopped mopping and looks at her with a mixture of concern and annoyance. Eleni eyes the cash register and thinks of the coin resting somewhere in there, her blood smeared all over it. There is a moment of hesitation, where she weighs her options. The man doesn't take his gaze away from her and now the barista is getting suspicious too. Perhaps they guess her intentions—although not all of them, her mind is a dark pit of unfathomable depth. Eleni is trapped and panic is clouding her mind. She looks at the cash register, at the customers coming in again, at her coffee cup, still warm and almost full on the table.

And then she escapes outside. She hides around the corner and inhales as if the concept of air is something she just discovered. Inhales like Joanna when she opens her old eyes in new sockets and realizes she has come back again, and again, and again. Until now, that is. Eleni counts the days. Three more days until she can't call Joanna back anymore. Three. And then what?

As her mind is brimming with questions, she feels the outline of someone familiar watching her. It's Joanna in the flesh. Eleni's mind freezes for a moment. Joanna finally did it. She made a deal with whatever entity exists on the other side. Or maybe it's the Devil himself coming for her own soul.

Eleni realizes she can't breathe. She is choking back sobs as Joanna approaches, languid. Her limbs don't seem to touch the ground for long, she is almost floating, soaring like a ghost, and now Eleni wonders how nobody else around notices. Is she already dead then? Only when Joanna comes close enough does Eleni see the things that aren't Joanna-like. Her hair is cropped short and pink while Joanna's was waist-long and dark brown. The woman still wears her uniform, only it's not *the woman* in there, is it? It is most definitely Joanna. Coppery eyes look down at Eleni and she can't stop staring at the person who is two persons and trying to merge the version in her mind.

"Hey, wake up, you goof. It's me," Joanna says. Lips peeled back in a smile, she opens Eleni's palm and slips in the bloody coin.

Joanna's new voice is deep and smooth and comforting, a voice Joanna would wish she had when she was still alive. Eleni can't deny that this is the most alive Joanna has looked in a while. Ever since this shit-journey started, actually. She can't find traces of that ghostly face underneath this woman's skin, but that's always how it is in the start. The woman's whole frame and Joanna's align so perfectly Eleni feels almost guilty she didn't find her a younger body earlier. Almost.

"Shit, Jo. How did you do it?"

Joanna shrugs coyly. "Do what?"

Eleni's eye catches the tall man from the coffee shop. His eyes dart around the busy street, looking for someone. She grabs Joanna's hand and pulls her in the opposite direction.

"Did you grab her stuff at least?"

"You bet."

Joanna pulls up the messenger bag, and shows her a laptop, a phone, and a couple of textbooks on statistics and machine learning. A student. After the first shock, Eleni feels the panic rising. Fucking great.

"She probably still lives with her parents, Jo. Did you think of that? Where the hell are we gonna go?" Eleni wants to make a break for it and never come back. But is there any place she can go?

"No, she doesn't. It's all in her phone." Nothing can break Joanna's calm exterior at this moment. If it's the body or just that she doesn't give a shit anymore, Eleni doesn't know. Joanna dangles a key fob shaped like the head of a crying baby. "I even know where she lives."

What Eleni didn't know or didn't understand back when she first called Joanna was that spirits don't go into inanimate objects. The same way water slides off glass but a sponge soaks it up. Living flesh absorbs a wandering spirit the same way a dish sponge absorbs water. When Eleni called Joanna's spirit, it bounced right off the mirror smeared with her own blood and went for her mother. The only other available body in the vicinity.

But if the water stays for too long the sponge gets moldy, slimy. It gets sick and eventually dies. Well, dish sponges don't die, but humans do. It's a bad metaphor but it's the only way Eleni thinks of spirits now. A few months into the first possession, Eleni's mother had a hemorrhagic stroke. The body lay on the bed, black tears running down her cheeks black snot from her nose, her irises glued to the ceiling, unresponsive. She was muttering something but it was too low and too unintelligible for Eleni to make out what it was. Through everything Eleni knew Joanna was still in there. It was the way she was wearing her mother. Like one of those paper masks they used for art projects in school, the skin deadly pale and fragile, ready to slip off at any minute. And somewhere under there, another face, made only of her mother's flesh, without discernible eyes, nostrils, or teeth.

Eleni begged Joanna to leave her mother's body before she finished her off. She promised to call her again before the time window passed while she waited for the paramedics. That turned out to be the only way Joanna would obey her from then on. Only after she had extracted Eleni's promise.

After making sure Mom would probably be okay, Eleni called her aunts, packed a suitcase and some money, and disappeared, going dark to everyone she had ever known in her short life. Everyone except for Joanna. She couldn't bear her mother's empty stare anymore and she dreaded to find out what she remembered from the time Joanna was subletting her. Maybe all the memories come back to the women eventually. Perhaps someone will recognize her on the street one day and call the police. She would deserve it. It might even make her break her promise to Joanna and stop summoning her. Or not. Calling Joanna back is all she can do now. All the company she has.

Knowing where the woman lives and knowing how to find the right apartment are two different things. They get the address from one of the delivery service messages. The apartment the woman rents is a condominium in one of the smaller neighborhoods in downtown Athens. Which means she might have friends and family at a walking distance, which makes Eleni very uneasy but when Joanna finds out, she replies with a *Sweet!*, as nonchalant about it as with everything else. Eleni guesses the apartment wouldn't be too big; the woman is still a student after all. One bedroom, probably. They gauge the ones they think fit the description through the windows during the day and when darkness settles, they try the locks as quietly as they can, half-waiting for the moment when someone catches them trying to break into their apartment and they have to scuttle down the hall, waking up the neighbors.

Only when the lock clicks open and they make sure there's nobody else in any of the rooms does the air leave Eleni's lungs full force.

"Thank God for no roommates," Eleni says, collapsing on the small blue couch, in the middle of the very sparsely furnished living room.

"Thank God for *Dr. Pepper.*"

Eleni hears Joanna opening a soda can in the kitchen and putting on some music she probably found in the woman's laptop.

"Keep it low," Eleni says as quietly as possible. "We're not ready to meet the neighbors now. Or ever."

She still prods at the events of that morning with her mind, trying to figure out what went wrong. Or which way it went wrong. Could be a number of things. A soul is like a water stream, and like a stream it needs direction. Eleni is the one doing that with her visualizing, but what if she was too tired that day? What if she was admiring the pink-haired woman more than she was focusing on Elisavet? What if, before she managed to channel the spirit into Elisavet, the other woman grabbed the coin to pay a customer, and boom, the deed was done. Was there even a single customer there while Eleni was visualizing? She doesn't remember, but there must have been.

What if none of the above is true and Joanna is hiding how powerful she is? What if, while Eleni was visualizing and calling her from the other side, Joanna's soul changed direction at the last moment into someone she fancied more, pretty much the way she had done with Eleni's own mother? If she had done it once she could do it again. How stupid of Eleni to think she had any control at all. Stupid, stupid.

In the background Eleni hears the gentle clicking of a keyboard and then giggling. It's coming from the kitchen.

"Jo?"

Eleni stalks into the dim-lit kitchen, fully covered in lime-green tiles. Joanna's face is the most illuminated thing in the room as she types furiously on the woman's laptop, feet resting on the kitchen table. She has already logged into a group chat. The usernames read Foxfire, Spider, HauntedTrails. Eleni doesn't recognize any of them.

"What the fuck, Jo? Are you talking to her friends?"

Joanna doesn't even turn or try to lie. "Relax, dude. I have to learn as much as I can about her. Plus, her friends are kinda cool."

"Why?"

"Because," Jo turns around this time and looks at Eleni. "I don't plan on leaving this body any time soon."

Eleni's jaw almost drops to the tiles. She knows that's what Joanna had wanted for a long time, but she wasn't expecting her to be so upfront and territorial about it. So calculating. It will be hell getting her out of this body in time. Her Mom's image flashes in front of Eleni's eyes and she thinks she can hear her own heartbeat.

"Ah, Leni, I am sorry," Joanna's tone changes immediately and the woman's deep voice becomes even deeper and silkier. She's already using this body like a virtuoso playing a melody on the piano. "It's just that we earned this. Both you and me. We've barely had a chance to enjoy life all this time."

Enjoying life isn't an option when you're already dead, Eleni wants to say. But she feels bone-tired. She isn't sure she can fix whatever is happening here. Perhaps there are parents close by that can pop in here at any time, or someone else with a spare key. Perhaps the friends Jo is merrily talking to will see right through her—very realistic—disguise. Perhaps they'll call from work and ask why the hell she ran away in the middle of her shift—never mind, that will definitely happen. Some of these people are bound to ask a lot of questions and they will know something is wrong. Eleni doesn't have the power to stop any of this and she's tired. She realizes too late she has slowly collapsed on the floor.

"You've been doing so much for us. Worrying a lot. Let me take care of things this time. I promise I'll be careful."

Crap, Joanna almost has her. The more Eleni looks at her, the more the woman transforms into Joanna. How Joanna used to look. How Eleni remembers her from the photos on her phone and her own subjective memory. She starts to speak but the question almost freezes in her brain.

"What if—?"

"If the body rejects me? I'll leave. We can go back to little old ladies after that. Just let me have a good time." Joanna leaves the chair and sits on the floor next to Eleni. She takes Eleni's hand in her own, gently, like when they were younger and she was asking for a favor only Eleni could do. The woman's face is iridescent, almost otherworldly under the lighting of the screen. Eleni can't stop admiring her long nose and the chrome stud ring that pokes out from the right side. Joanna gives Eleni a gentle nudge on the shoulder. Everything is gentle about her. "Listen—I am sorry about the Mom thing. Dying sucks and makes me all bitchy."

To that Eleni doesn't object. She's run out of comebacks and dead-end questions. Whether she wants to admit it to herself or not this is the most peaceful moment they've had for a while. The moment that feels the most right. They are both at the right age and in a student's apartment. Because they were both supposed to be young and in college. She doesn't speak because it will break the illusion. And Eleni loves the illusion. Whatever might come next.

Sometimes Eleni is movie-Jennifer, especially in the scene where she leaves Needy and gets into the van with the evil band. Their lives change forever after this. Although it's not really what Jennifer *wants* to do. It's not her fault. She is in shock after the bar catches fire and she follows along. Eleni, on the other hand, *wanted* to be with these people, her new and shiny friends—it also helped that they weren't demon-summoning murderers like the band in the movie—and she left that night to find them at the square, guilt drilling into her like Jennifer's teeth into boy-guts.

Sometimes Eleni is Needy, sitting in her room at night, finding Jennifer burrowed in her bed. Jennifer, freshly fed and freshly kissed, smiles at Needy like the teenage girl she used to be and says, *Best friends don't keep secrets.* This is what Joanna texted Eleni before Eleni left to meet the others. Before Joanna's accident happened. Needy loves Jennifer and Eleni loves Joanna and feels both guilty and scared out of her mind. She wants to stay with Joanna until the end—until some kind of end—and wants to drop everything and run away every second that passes.

Eleni is the worst parts of both of them: she is the one who gets seduced by the new people and leaves her best friend, setting off a series of events, *and* she is the loser who runs after the demon-girl. She doesn't want to think how she is the one who keeps summoning Joanna from beyond the veil. No, because that would make her someone with the power to end everything at any given moment and yet she is not. That would make her one of the evil guys from the band and that's the one thing she never wanted to become.

Adriana's friends are all right, nothing special. They remind Eleni of the kids at the cram school. They are all sitting around three tables made into a makeshift large one at a cheap ouzeri that attracts half the city's student population. There's this mixture of flirting, arguing, and drinking spread around the group that Eleni had only tasted for a very brief time but she dearly misses now. She is experiencing this scene as a stranger, an intruder. No wonder everyone has asked her if she has graduated already. She looks past her age.

Joanna manages to flirt, argue, and drink at random intervals with most of the people surrounding her, and they all love it.

"Seriously, computer science? Why I'd pick such a boring subject? I mean look at my hair. I should have been in art school or something." She playfully tucks away a pink lock. The guy Joanna is talking to (Eleni guesses he is the Foxfire dude from the chat), chuckles, incredulous, but plays along.

"...um, is everything all right up there, Adri?" He points an index finger at his own temple. "You're the one who wouldn't shut up about the awesome job you'd be set up with and that sweet, sweet paycheck. Remember all that?"

Joanna nods and smiles because of course she doesn't remember any of it. Eleni is about to tear the wax paper that covers their table to shreds.

"I'll look into art lessons anyway." She leans over the table like a cat trying to stretch its torso into an inverse question mark. "I am a different person now."

The guy still plays it cool but in a less look-at-me way. "I bet it's because of that new, fascinating friend of yours. I give you one month."

Suddenly everyone looks over to Eleni who feels like the least fascinating person around. She has already torn a piece of wax paper and is rolling it between her palms like a stress ball. How is she supposed to forget the woman is named Adriana if everyone around keeps reminding her? Joanna puts an arm around Eleni, like she would do when she wanted to claim her as her own.

"My friend is a great artist," Joanna announces to everyone. For a fleeting moment Eleni dimly remembers being seventeen and wanting to get into the School of Architecture. She was really good at drawing landscapes and was about to ask her Mom for extra lessons in line drawing if she could afford it. Then everything went to Hell. "But she's not new. I've known her since we were kids. She'll outlast all of you."

At that a short girl with long black bangs peeks out from the left.

"What? Since when?"

Shit, that's it, Eleni thinks.She remembers a few of them being high school friends with the woman. This is what she was trying to avoid all along by isolating both of them but she let down her defenses for a hot moment and now they are caught. Or whatever being caught body-hopping means. Probably something like calling the woman's parents and staging an intervention because she is acting weird. Eleni can't stop doom-dreaming about what comes next. Joanna seems to pick up on that because she touches her arm in a way that feels something like a code. It's not the same as when she hugged her; this is not for the others. This is a message shared between the two of them. *Relax, I got this,* it says.

Within twenty minutes Joanna has convinced everyone that Eleni is her childhood friend, which is true, and that they all knew and had interacted with her at some point in the past, which is a total lie and a kind of scary achievement. Eleni gets progressively more drunk and a horrible thought rises from her gut: what if Joanna is mesmerizing them? What if she is convincing them that what she says is true, but in a supernatural way? Nothing about her is natural—except for the body she is occupying—so why not this one too? Eleni regrets not asking more questions about where Joanna goes when she is not here. It's possible she has picked up a few tricks *down there*. It's also possible that she used them on Eleni the other day.

Eleni shivers and pulls her arm away. Joanna, thankfully, doesn't seem to notice.

The book has been sitting at the bottom of Eleni's backpack for years now. She doesn't need it—or at least she didn't think she needed it—the ritual is etched in her mind. She goes looking for it the moment they return home. Joanna might be renting the body, but the body still gets tired and drunk and needs to sleep. Eleni watches as Joanna stumbles forward, her destination the small double bed at the end of the narrow corridor. Even though she has invited Eleni to sleep on the bed multiple times, she prefers the small blue couch. It is better for them to keep some distance, healthier. If there is anything healthy between them at this point.

She waits until she hears the light snoring sound the woman always makes—it turns out possession cannot save you from snoring. Then she cracks the book open and tries to turn its pages. A tough job because they are both slightly sticky and hardened, like an old shoe you haven't worn for some time. The passages are even more horrifying than she remembers. She was seventeen when she first summoned Joanna and she is almost certain that at twenty-one, if she were to start all over again, she would have not summoned her. Almost certain. Her new-adult brain feels very disturbed by the passages in the book. There are several animals and even babies involved in some rituals. Their own ritual is actually one of the more PG-13 ones. She shivers thinking that all of them might actually be real rituals like the one that brought Joanna back. But what else could they be? She wonders how her teenage-self delighted in these horrifying descriptions. And then she quickly understands: teenage Eleni—and teenage Joanna for that matter—read this book as a horror story, a dark and strange fairytale some people used to believe. They shivered imagining the darkness breathing close to them, clinging to their skin, licking their palms with its long, bloody tongue, but once morning came, they were free from the monsters. Not anymore.

There's nothing in the actual ritual and its preparation that will tell Eleni what she needs to know. No warning about the demons being tricksters. Perhaps those were in the beginner's manual. Eleni tries really hard to avoid considering the implications of this. She puts the book back and slips into the kitchen to make coffee. The steady rhythm of the snoring almost lulls her to sleep but she feels too guilty and alert to let sleep take her. Over the murmur of the coffee machine Eleni tries to break down what happened earlier. Did Joanna magically convince Adriana's friends what she said was true or did they not care enough to challenge her? And was Joanna hypnotizing Eleni to do her bidding, or was she pulling all the right strings and was Eleni—being the weak-willed creature she had always been—more than happy to release some of her burdens? It all felt too slippery and vague.

"Did you know I can sleep and still be awake?"

Eleni almost poured the scalding coffee on herself. Instead, it was the green tiles that got the brunt of the spill.

"What the hell, Joanna? Don't you ever knock?"

"Uh, this is the kitchen?" Joanna gave her the weirdest look that Eleni had no word for. "Besides, you never demanded your mom knock before."

"What?"

Joanna grabs one of the ice cream sandwiches she has filled the freezer with and sits on the same chair she did the first time they were here.

"All I'm saying is that you are a mommy's girl. And it's not like she thought very highly of you. Like sometimes she was so tired of your clinginess, she was daydreaming about running away." Joanna takes a very toothy bite of the ice cream, which makes Eleni flinch at the idea of all the chill against her teeth.

"How would you know that?" A shiver travels down Eleni's backbone. She feels a kinship with the ice cream sandwich. They are both unable to resist Joanna's biting.

"It's a neat trick, right? Just like the one I discovered in this body. Come here, touch my pulse." She leans forward on the chair and bends her neck to the side, as if inviting Eleni to bite her back. Vampire style.

"Uh..."

Joanna reaches out and grabs Eleni's arm, pulling her down and close. Her pull is gentle but it implies far greater strength than she lets on.

"Come on, don't be shy. Touch here." She puts her finger on the bluish-green vein that runs down the side of the woman's neck, brushing against her clavicle.

Eleni obliges her. She presses two fingers where Joanna shows her and lo and behold, the pulse is very slow, almost untraceable. The breathing too is slow and shallow and as Eleni leans a bit closer to listen better, there comes the snoring out of Joanna's half-open lips.

Eleni jerks back. "What the—Are you kidding me?"

Joanna rests her finger against her lips now. "You'll wake her"

"Shit, is she still in there?"

"Yes and no. Sorta. She knows I am here and she's sad about it. So, she drifts in and out. We are all coping somehow, I guess." Joanna smiles a conspiratorial smile that Eleni instantly hates.

"Is this how you know about my mom?"

Joanna's smile turns mean now. But not openly mean. The quiet kind of mean that nobody else notices but Eleni, because they know each other so well.

"All these women have so many thoughts, El. They get tangled in my head. I can't help it when I rip them from their minds when I leave." She reaches out and touches Eleni's shoulders. "You don't hold it against me. Do you?"

Eleni feels the sudden urge to call her mom after four years. If her mom yells at her for leaving, if she cries and screams and renounces her, then maybe that means she is still herself. That would be the good outcome.

"It's like I have lived so many lives. I feel wiser now. All that wisdom can take us anywhere with this body. You saw what happened tonight."

"Jo." Eleni swallows and tries really hard not to show how terrified she is of her friend. "I think you should get out of there. In fact, I think it's time to stay on that other side."

Laughter bubbles and spills out of Joanna's throat. She laughs and then keeps laughing some more. Her arms fall from Eleni's shoulders as her whole body starts convulsing with the most hysterical laughter Eleni has seen. For a mere second—too soon in the whole process—the outline of someone's face surfaces on Joanna's chest. Then it disappears again.

"Other side? There's no other side. Don't you get it? The other side is here. Just shittier and dim and disembodied. After the crash and the pain and the sleep,

I woke up in this grey dense mass of a sea worming up my nose, ears and eyes and I kept swimming around with no end in sight, going through bodies and buildings and clouds like they were sketches a five-year-old drew. Only when you called me did I start seeing color, and followed your voice until I got to you and your mom. You were both full of the most beautiful color I've seen in my entire undead life. And, well, your mom was the only other person I could go into, since you were the one doing the calling." Joanna takes a lock of Eleni's hair in her fingers and looks at it like she is considering her body very seriously. "And I wouldn't want to go inside the caller now, would I? I'm dead, not stupid."

Eleni can't shake the faces. They always seem like they are swimming. And drowning. "How long can we keep doing this?"

"And what? You want me to drift too? You want me to swim forever? It's all your fault anyway, loser. After all I've done for you, you weren't even there to pick up the phone."

As if a switch has been flicked, Joanna lets tears stream down her face. The hysterical laughter turns into hysterical crying. Eleni can't tell the difference any more. She keeps very still, hoping that Joanna will forget about her.

"You owe me. You've got to give back what you took from me."

Eleni already sees their future ahead. A life with no rest for her, only a few-months-long breather before the next jump, without ever seeing her mother or anyone she's ever known before Joanna died. A life full of bodies, Joanna's bodies, strewn behind them like empty beer cans. Some of them live, some of them don't, depending on their stamina and Joanna's mood. Joanna takes from them whatever she needs and they move on to the next one and then the next. But most of all a life full of faces floating inside too-thin skin, reminding both of them what comes next no matter how much they try to outrun it. Now they both know and that's not something they can leave behind.

"Okay," Eleni says, resigned. She feels a million years old. She sits on the coffee-soiled tiles and opens her arms. "Come here."

After a moment's hesitation Joanna dries her eyes with the heels of her palms and rests her head against Eleni's chest. Trustingly, lovingly, they fall asleep.

It takes a little longer this time but Joanna is getting kicked out of the woman's body one party at a time. That's how Eleni counts their time here: in parties she and Joanna—but mostly Joanna—attend or crash, fumbling for their keys to their apartment later and avoiding phone calls from parents who, thankfully, live in another city two hours' drive from there. Joanna makes a half-hearted attempt at art, after buying supplies and falling behind on her college classes, but it's Eleni who ends up using them, when Joanna parties, when she sleeps in after a hangover, and the days that she is too sick to do anything else but complain and burn breakfast all over again.

Eleni avoids painting anything even remotely human-looking. Instead, she does landscape painting, forests, mountains, lakes, anything that's open and brimming with color because fuck it, she knows color is not in the cards for the future. The brighter and more misplaced the color in the painting the better. She spends all her money on tubes of acrylic named crimson red, cobalt blue, and primary magenta. She is busy painting the frothy waves of the Ionian Sea in Permanent Violet Dark when Joanna wobbles into the house, propped against a friend's shoulder, the name of whom Eleni forgets. A blonde girl, an engineering student if she remembers correctly. There's dark red coming down Joanna's nose; it has seeped into the blonde woman's pristine white shirt but she doesn't seem to notice.

"What happened?" Eleni doesn't need to ask but she does anyway. She is a pro at keeping up appearances.

"I don't know." The blonde woman sounds frantic and lost. "She was dancing. Maybe she hit her head or something? She didn't wanna go to the ER."

"It's okay. I've got her now. You can go." Eleni pats the woman on the shoulder although it doesn't seem to comfort her in any way, then picks up Joanna's crumbling body.

Reluctantly, the woman releases Joanna, and after standing there for a minute she quietly closes the door and leaves. As Eleni lays Joanna on the little blue couch, the strap of her blouse falls down revealing a violet-dark sea of bruises, skin rippling like waves, and underneath not only a face but fingers, a palm, nonstop movement.

"She's been trying to kick me out for some time now." Joanna's smile is laced with weakness and nausea. "But I am headstrong too. Oops."

"Jo, listen to me." Eleni cups Joanna's head in her hands and guides it to face her. Joanna's eyes are glassy and unfocused; they stare through instead of at her. "The party is over." You have to let her go."

Joanna shakes her head and presses her lips together. Her voice becomes high-pitched, close to what her real voice used to be when she was about to cry. "I don't want to go inside a little old lady again. I was having fun, dammit." When she manages to focus for a moment on Eleni she says, "Promise you'll get me another one."

"I promise."

"No, that's too easy. You're lying."

"I am not."

"It's all your fault.

"Stop. Look at me. Joanna."

Joanna makes another effort through all the pain, which Eleni guesses is a lot.

"I've been looking around. If you leave her okay, I promise I'll get you another one."

"...really?"

"A promise is a promise. I am never breaking this one. And you're right. It is my fault," Eleni says and she means it. She means every single word because Joanna will know if she's faking it.

Even now, she can't stop wanting to call Joanna. Breaking this promise feels wrong. Misshapen. She's the one who started everything, Joanna is right. But not because she didn't pick up the phone. Because she answered it every single time up until that day. That was another promise she had made without realizing it and she should have kept it. Eleni isn't sure if she is compelled in a magical way to keep this promise to Joanna. There's nothing in the book that says so. But she felt compelled to keep things as they were long before that, so in the end it doesn't matter. If she is not the person who calls Joanna back, then who is she? She has always been with Joanna. That's her one constant.

Joanna holds her gaze like a statue. Eleni feels her heart beating under her skin the way Joanna feels the other woman's soul. Then Joanna takes Eleni's hand in hers, kisses it and relaxes. And Eleni can breathe again.

"I already miss you."

Joanna lets go with the sweetest smile plastered on the woman's face. The bruised body takes the shape of the couch, like an empty shirt, like a ragdoll. Her fists unclench, her fingers curl, her face takes on the sort of calm expression someone might get before sleep, and her eyes turn a green-ish grey. Eleni checks for pulse and breath. The clock resets all over again.

"Thank you for being her host, Adriana. Be free."

Free. What a word.

Eleni takes one city bus, then another, to get to the third long-distance one toward the Parnitha mountain range, north of Athens. It's still early in the morning when the bus drops her on the side of a road snaking its way up. Backpack dangling from her shoulder, she sets off through the woods and walks until the road gives way to rocks, fir, pine, and the occasional abandoned building. She tries to fit all the beauty of the landscape in an imaginary picture she might one day paint. There are so many birds here. Eleni was never very good at telling birds apart.

When she reaches what looks like an abandoned playground or some weird art project gone wrong, she stops and drops the backpack to the ground. She never carries much with her. Some clothes, money taken from the previous host, and the book. This time she couldn't help but keep some of the brushes and the tubes, although she is not sure she'll even use them again. And a packet of sunflower seeds. The place seems sufficiently abandoned and sparse. Sparse enough for her to watch for any random person approaching. For any bird. She presses the coin with the blood in her pocket. The seeds feel heavy in her other hand. Soon a bird comes by as if swimming through the air, drifting. A swallow or a swift. Eleni can't tell. She tosses a few seeds on the ground. The bird hops closer.

It feels easy enough.

This is the last day to do the summoning. She wishes she had held off because she had second thoughts. That somewhere inside her she had found the thread that ties her to Joanna and torn it to shreds. But the reason was, she was building up the nerve to call her mom. Dreading what her mom knew about Joanna and her stay in her mom's body, dreading even more what she didn't know anymore.

"Mom?" Eleni asked when she picked up the phone, even though she could already tell by the breathing.

"Joanna?"

Eleni dropped the phone as if it had transformed into a giant cockroach and immediately threw up. Because her nightmare had come true. Where her mother's memories had been before, now there was a huge scar calling Joanna's name. That's when she became convinced everything was fucked beyond salvaging. She didn't stay on the line to find out how bad.

The bird cocks its head to the side and Eleni wonders if it can feel Joanna drifting. Waiting to take its body. Birds can't speak. They can't ask you to make any promises. They don't have houses with cats or money she can steal either, but that's birds for you.

Eleni rubs the blood-smeared coin. Then she lifts her arm, aims somewhere to the right and tosses. The coin ricochets off a jutting stone with a clang and she loses sight of it. The bird flies away. Even a bird's soul has value. And she has wasted enough of them.

There's a moment toward the end of *Jennifer's Body* that Eleni hates but once loved, where Jennifer is dead and gone but Needy still carries a part of her in the form of a bite. Gifted to her by Jennifer. She wonders what kind of shape this bite would take and then she visualizes:

Your name is Ioanna Balaska but you want people to call you Joanna because it sounds cooler.

You eat rotisserie chicken like a fiend.

You had a gazillion goth stickers on your desk and on your bedframe back home, even though there was a non-stop war with your mom over them.

You don't like vodka because it burns your throat.

You had a crush on half the class at one point or another but you always blew them off to see me.

You pretended you read manga but really you only liked superhero comics.

When we were eleven you took in the kitten I rescued from under a car because I asked you to and my mom wouldn't let me keep it. He ended up liking you more than me. More than anyone.

Before you died you didn't want to be friends with me anymore but you wanted to be the one to walk away. You hated that I found new friends first.

You were afraid that you'd be left behind. So I am taking you with me.

Eleni's feet crunch into gravel and dirt, bracing against the impact, as the world unspools around and inside of her. She leaves her mind unlocked and Joanna rushes inside like a drowning person latching onto driftwood.

Safe now. You're safe. I won't fight you, Eleni thinks. But she can't say it anymore. She will never use her lips again, or her mouth. She already can't see what's out there, only a roughly-sketched outline. Her own eyes are so far away from her.

Joanna feels sad once she realizes where she is. Abandoned, even. She picks up her backpack and heads for the road.

Eugenia Triantafyllou is a Greek author and artist with a flair for dark things. Her work has won the Shirley Jackson Award and has been nominated for the Ignyte, Locus, Nebula, and World Fantasy Awards. She is a graduate of Clarion West Writers Workshop. You can find her stories in *Reactor.com, Uncanny, Strange Horizons, Apex,* and other venues. She currently lives in Athens with a boy and a dog. Find her on Twitter @foxesandroses, or Bluesky @foxesandroses.bsky.social, her IG @eugeniatriantafyllou, or her website http://www.eugeniatriantafyllou.com.

ANOTHER GIRL UNDER THE IRON BELL

Angela Liu

There is no limit to the number of curses in theworld. For each one the monks try to exorcise, ten more take its place.

We are not here because we enjoy it though. Please don't misunderstand. As you dip into steaming bath waters, entwine your bodies under warm sheets, and dream of delicious sake under spring flowers, know that we are always burning.

The crows cawed from atop the shingled roof of the outer hall. Wind chilled through the branches of the plum trees, their early spring buds like tiny eyes.

Akechi stood in the garden in front of the temple's wilting tulips and gardenias, a pair of shearing scissors in hand. He frowned when he saw me. I wasn't allowed in the garden, but I'd already memorized the schedule of the others. This was the only time I knew we could be alone.

"It's done," I said, tossing him the left hand.

Akechi studied the blackening fingers, the flesh half-rotted from the journey back.

"Did he say anything before you slayed him?" he asked, casting the hand into the pond for the koi fish. I watched the swarm of fat orange and white scaled heads bob in and out of the water, their massive mouths puckering over the hand, dragging it down into the dark water.

I looked the monk in the eye. The humans always think you can't look them in the eye when you're lying.

"Not a word. I kept it painless, just as you requested," I answered, listening to the splashing feast.

Akechi and I first met on a spring morning just like this one at a crumbling seaside town, the kind where the bedsheets feel salty and unwashed. Where the hot springs are hidden behind broken wooden gates, and the streets are fogged with enduring misery.

He had been hired to exorcise a cursed spirit from a woman who worked at one of the inns. A staff member had seen her speaking to a painting in one of the guest rooms. The woman's husband had been trampled by horses two weeks earlier after falling asleep drunk on the road, and the staff believed his unhappy spirit had clung to her reflection, playing tricks on the other guests.

Akechi was done within the first two days. *The famed curse tamer of Eikando Temple*, I heard the staff whispering, half in awe, half in fear, as they washed the bloody sheets in the alley behind the inn. I found the monk cleaning the blood off his hands and tools in the river just outside of the town. Any hungrier beast would have devoured him then and there, but I had no interest in consuming someone whose skin was still stained with another's cursed blood. It added a disgusting aftertaste.

"You're not human," he spoke, looking into the blood-smeared water, the scarlet trails dissipating like ink against the burbling current. He raised his dagger more like a doctor than a hunter. "Are you looking for a new master?"

I laughed. It had been so long since I'd met a human who didn't shrink away at the true sight of me. Not since Ryunosuke.

"What could you do for me?" I asked, still smiling. I felt a rare tenderness toward this soft bag of overconfident meat and bones. "I am not in the habit of devouring those who cull my competition," I said, motioning at the cursed blood in the river, "but I'll gladly tear off your insolent mouth and feed it to one of the bears."

"I am offering you an opportunity because of your skill," he said, flicking the water off his blade and sheathing it back into its wooden scabbard. "Give me your name, and I will keep you alive."

My hair billowed up, blood pooling into my fingers, nails sharpening into claws. There is a fine line between an amusing rodent and a pest. "You dare ask for my name, human?" I growled.

"I am not asking anything."

A trick of light, a rustle of bare branches in the spring breeze, a chipmunk scurrying in and out of a beam of afternoon sun. I reached down, the blade embedded in the ugly pouch between my stomach and throat. There was no blood, but I could not move, my body petrified. It shouldn't have been possible. Was this Ryunosuke's final curse on me?

"My blade does not kill. It simply binds you to me. A cursed contract," the monk said, holding the handle of the blade with both hands as if ready to twist my insides. "But I have other weapons that could release you from this world. Do you wish to die or come with me?"

My hair fell back over my shoulders. A curse's strength lies in its pride, but also its bottomless desire for vengeance. And I was not ready to die before I killed the monk myself.

I don't know when I was born. If I'd replaced another girl, or if I'd simply devoured her waterlogged corpse by the river's end along with fragments of her memories. I only remember the sound of water. The whisper of voices coming and going like rustling leaves. The gash of light under a closed door. The smell of lilies. The longing for warmth. The overwhelming hunger.

Are curses born or simply distilled from collective misery?

The humans have many names for us. Demon, devil, cursed creatures, the damned, but every curse has its own True Name. That name is a key, an invisible chain around our necks. To share that name is to hand those chains to a stranger.

Akechi stole mine with his binding blade and contract, but I had a different name once too. One that was my own, not belonging to *her*, that miserable girl who forfeited herself to the river. Ryunosuke gave it to me.

Kiyo.

He said it was the name of a woman who had turned into a cursed serpent and burned to death under an iron bell after she'd fallen hopelessly in love with a monk who did not return her feelings.

I told him I'd make him eat his own liver if he continued calling me by that nonsense.

But in truth, I wondered about the woman.

It was only long after Ryunosuke was gone, long after I told myself I'd forgotten the strange warmth of our time together, that I wandered into that broken seaside town, starved, looking for a dim-witted traveler to consume, and instead, found a painting of a woman with a serpent's body hanging in one of the inns. The creature was enveloped in orange flames, but my gaze settled on her face, how serene it looked. She was beautiful, in that way all things are when they burn out.

Akechi had me do the jobs he was not interested in. False prophets, village leaders, novice assassins—tedious, messy jobs. Even miles from the temple, he knew the sharp pull of the contract would prevent me from trying to escape. So he sent me to Niigata, Kyoto, Yoshiwara, anywhere his clients paid him to go, sometimes as a warning, more often than not though, to kill and bring back evidence of the pathetic life I'd cut short. He preferred hands, claiming they were less conspicuous than heads. A dead body is all the same to me. Despite his warnings, I'd take small trinkets I liked too, beautiful things that seemed wasted on a corpse: a jade ring, golden bells, a silver pen from a foreign land, a silken scarf stored inside a straw bag that had avoided the splash of blood.

When I was not working, I was to stay in an old room stacked to the ceiling with handscroll sutras, away from the sun and the prying eyes of the monk's sycophantic disciples and overly generous believers. I suspected it was soundproofed.

The room was only accessible through a door in his study. I sometimes peered in when he was at work: the amber glow of his oil lamp, his eyes already on me the moment I found his silhouette in the dim light.

"Come in," he would call.

His study smelled of incense, star anise, and wet soil. Akechi wore a dark brown robe with an orange shawl draped over one shoulder down the length of his body. He was tall with broad shoulders and strong hands, a high forehead that the idiot humans celebrated as a sign of intelligence. The kind of man that was popular among both the human women and men. A part of me understood—I too would have loved to devour that torso, hands-first, then sip on strong rice wine from that skull.

"You seem to be in a good mood," he said, offering me a seat.

I saw it then. The dagger tucked in its wooden scabbard, poorly concealed inside a lacquer box next to a statue of Kannon, the bodhisattva of mercy. All I needed to do was slash his throat open or tear my claws through his gut, toss his flopping body to the side, and take the binding blade. No more enduring the humiliation of servitude to a human.

His hand was suddenly at the base of my throat. He didn't squeeze, but I could feel my own pulse under his fingers.

"Our contract doesn't just make you obey me in terms of taking others' lives," he said, his eyes tracing the curve of my neck down to the valley of my chest. "I know you cannot easily die, demon. But there are other ways a body loses meaning."

His fingers released me, but I would not give him the satisfaction of gasping for air.

"Come now, you're being more paranoid than usual," I said with a smile, imagining how pretty he would look rearranged into smaller, bloody pieces. "Bad day?"

"Don't waste your time with useless thoughts. The moment you touch the blade, our contract ends and your cursed life will end with it," he said, returning to his desk and his writing.

There were stories, of course. Of demons who had successfully severed their cursed contracts by destroying the binding relic that held their true name prisoner. How they'd rapturously devoured their former masters soon after. But stories are just stories. I'd seen one dissolve into blue flames in the back alley of the Pleasure Quarters, the cracked binding relic by its burning feet. How the body burned in such beautiful colors that anyone peering into the alley might have imagined it a woman dancing in iridescent robes. How the scavenging doctors happily shoveled up the cursed ash afterwards to sell as cure-alls to gullible patients. Nothing in this world is fixed, luck and unluck two parts of the same coin, and I wouldn't exactly call myself lucky. Akechi was a lying fool, but I was also not one to gamble with my own life.

"Am I supposed to stay here until someone else kills you then?" I asked, walking over to the shelf of books and sutras. Akechi didn't mind if I touched his things, but there wasn't a single item that could whet my appetite. There hadn't been in so long. Was that the result of being a demon or simply being a creature that had lived for far too long? I would've been more sated by the look on his face as I burned this place to ground with him inside it.

"Even if I die, the contract terms are unbreakable," Akechi answered, dipping his brush into the ink spool.

"Am I to follow you into the depths of hell then? Should I slaughter the king of the underworld for you as well? Or just the husbands of the women you wish you take to bed?" I said, smirking with satisfaction when he looked up from his documents with a dangerous gleam in his eye.

"Leave. Now," he said, the tip of his brush dripping ink onto the table. "Before I forget why I keep you here."

I kept a jar by me at all times, sang it songs tenderly at night like a sleeping infant. It was filled with precious things: centipedes, maggots, frenzied lice, and a beautiful baby viper I once found hidden in the brush by Arashiyama River at night.

There is only one way to cleanly sever a cursed contract. I learned this from a frog-faced exorcist in a Yoshiwara brothel. I saw him do it, the way he had the older staff hold the arms and legs down of a troublesome customer, how he then poured the contents of the kodoku jar into the person's mouth, everyone's heads turning away at the ghastly sight. A cursed contract can only be passed to another cursed spirit, and the fastest way to find a cursed spirit is to make one. A heart for a heart. A soul for a soul. A body remade bone by cursed bone.

I caressed the jar, running a long fingernail along the rim. It quivered, the creatures consuming each other, beautiful chaos unfolding inside.

"I know you're up to something," Akechi said, walking into my prison chamber as I pretended to read.

"If I am, it is your fault. I'm bored out of my mind," I said, putting down the stone sutra and uncrossing my legs. My muscles felt impatient, rusting, like a water wheel abandoned in a dried-out stream.

"I have a new job for you. From the imperial guard," he answered. "I want you to bring Arata along with you this time."

"Who?" I asked. I'd already seen the latest batch of new disciples, smooth-faced and wide-eyed like startled infants. Which one was he referring to?

"Arata Watanabe," he answered, his eyes trailing the shelves and tables as he always did, as if expecting to find evidence of some transgression. "He comes from a family of executioners, but he seeks penance."

"If he holds me back, I might just devour him. And you will have another woman to apologize to."

I smiled innocently at Akechi, but he was unfazed by my words this time.

"Arata is talented. He will not die so easily."

Akechi pulled a small scabbard from his sleeve. Rust-red engravings of centipedes and spiders curved up the lacquered wood, a black cicada made of stone clinging to the handle.

"I want you to kill him with this after you're done with the job," he said, handing me the blade.

"And what would be achieved by killing one of your own? Or have you truly lost your mind?" I asked, trying to hold back my grin, lips twitching. It was always a delight to watch the humans kill each other.

"Arata's father requested this. He claims the boy acted treacherously, lusting after his new young wife. The boy's mother is not a member of the Watanabe clan. Some claim she is a demon herself, another stain of shame for the clan. There is little to be lost in his execution."

When does a woman go from being a prize to a stain? How many stains could a man collect before the filth finally tainted the soft skin below?

Akechi gripped my chin in his hand and tilted my head up so I had to look at him. "The boy is talented with a sword, but his mind is weak. Try your best to kill him painlessly. He is still my disciple."

I jerked out of his grip, pulling the scabbard off the blade. The candle flames reflected in the smooth steel underneath like fire burning across a lake.

Painless is a subjective term, isn't it?

"Can I keep the blade after it is done?" I asked.

The first time I met Ryunosuke, I thought he had come to take my head.

He had hair like silver rivers down his back and a face the humans would call handsome. But what struck me most was the overwhelming smell of other people's blood, like a library of death on him. He was hired by the Emperor's imperial guard as an assassin, their unofficial executioner. The rebellion soldiers whispered stories about him to new recruits like warnings of evil spirits. *The one with snow-like hair who drenched the ground in crimson and then vanished. The one who slaughtered without hesitation.* He was swift with a blade, his attacks clean and majestic, the twisting arch of his arms under his navy haori as he swung his katana, the spray of blood, the way the energy inside him pulsed like dark suns after the bodies fell. He was a work of art to witness.

Ryunosuke found me devouring one of the soldiers behind the Yoshiwara brothel where I'd taken up the girl's identity. I'd been sloppy, too hungry. As he approached, I raised my claws, lips stained with blood. His blade was still sheathed, his hand on the hilt. He was overconfident, a delicious trait in a meal.

"I am not interested in your head," he said, studying the body on the ground before looking back up at me, undeterred by the bloodthirst in my eyes "I am just curious...about the taste."

"The taste?" I asked, licking the blood from my lips. I raised the dead man's left leg by the ankle. "Of this human?"

Ryunosuke nodded, his eyes tracing the fallen body again. "I've lived my whole life with death. Dedicated myself to it. Experienced it with all my senses. The loudness and quietness of it, the wet warmth of it, the stink of it, the pure color-lessness of it. Everything...except the taste." His coin-like eyes shone under lantern light, meeting mine again. "What does death taste like?"

I laughed, wiping my mouth on the back of my hand. How delightfully strange, this human who longed to be a demon.

"Why don't you try some then?" I asked, tearing off some of the flesh from the soldier's throat. "You may not survive your first time." I held the bloody offering up to him with a grin. If he was going to kill me afterwards, I at least wanted a good show.

To my surprise, Ryunosuke got on his knees the way I'd seen some of the humans pray. He took me by the wrist, his hands warm, and brought my fingers to his lips.

"My name is Arata Watanabe," he said, standing at the entrance to the garden, the morning sun searing against his back, his face inked in shadows. "I will be your escort to Jigokudani."

My first thoughts went to the similarities: the luxurious kimono that only government officials or those who killed for them wore, the large scarred hands, his long hair tied up neatly behind him, a sheathed sword corded to his side, the eyes that lacked light. They were both beautiful in the way fires that burn down entire villages are.

He had the scent of an executioner on him—I'd been around Ryunosuke long enough to know that scent of blood that never completely washes off. It was different than the smell of oil and ink that the other pig-faced disciples stank of.

"Pleased to meet you," I bowed gently, eyes on the cracked tiles under his feet, still wet from the earlier rain, unsure if I was allowed to speak. Men could get so easily riled up by small offenses.

"What is your name?" he asked.

I opened my mouth, the words spilling out before I could think.

"Kiyo."

The journey to Jigokudani was long and choked with dust. We wrapped our faces in too-thin scarves, our tongues still tasting the smog in the air.

It was nearly sundown by the time we arrived through the smoking gates of the town. The streets were alive with vendors peddling snacks, shiny trinkets, and embroidered silk robes. Tiny turtles swam in tiny glass tanks, ready to be drowned in medicinal jars.

The only inn in the town was connected to a windowless spa that offered everything a human body could want and more. In the wooden foyer, a young woman in a beautiful black-red kimono kneeled on a cushion, golden pins and carnations in her hair. Water spilled from a bamboo pipe into the small man-made pond. Another floating world. I wondered if Ryunosuke would have found her beautiful too. If he would've wanted her like so many of the men in this town. I squeezed the blade in my sleeve, tight enough that the stone cicada's wings dug sharply into my skin.

"Shall we?" Arata asked, offering his hand. I could hear the clinking of glasses and laughter from inside, a foreign world. I crushed all other thoughts from my mind as we slipped out of our sandals and greeted the innkeeper as a married couple.

After our first meeting, Ryunosuke came to visit me at the brothel every night despite my threats to devour him. The other girls asked if he was as rough as he looked, *was I scared of him,* they'd giggle idiotically. He'd bring fruits and breads, tasteless offerings to a demon. I told him to bring me good wine next time or I'd have to drink the blood from his bones instead.

He came the next night with the wine.

It was better than I expected, so I let him live. And the day after. And so we continued this until I began to wait by the barred windows each dusk, searching for the familiar crest on his navy haori among the crowds flanking the nightly procession of oiran on the streets. Until seeing him felt like breathing.

Ryunosuke longed for a greater understanding of death. Unlike the other humans who clamored for more time, more riches, more pleasure, he was obsessed with how a body ends. And what creature had a better understanding of death than a cursed body that had been forsaken by it?

A cursed spirit can live for centuries unchanged. We feed on the misery and regret of the land, on the creatures that inhabit and pillage it. In this way, we are a part of the cycle of life—nature's executioner.

"Is it true that all demons were once human?" he asked one day, his blade next to him on the tatami mat. He'd been gone for several days, and I could smell the accents of new blood on him.

I snickered, sipping on the Sudo Honke sake he'd brought, watching the fluttering shadows of moths against the shoji screen windows. I'd heard the same story countless times from other humans, always those begging for their lives.

"You humans always clamor for meaning," I said. "We demons seek human flesh because it tastes good. We have no grudge to settle, no nobler cause. Humans and demons are simply incompatible, so we kill each other. The moon assassinates the sun each evening when it demands the night, and the sun in turn incinerates the moon each dawn when it rises. And so it goes on and on."

I gulped the last bit of the sake, feeling it burn deliciously down my throat. I didn't tell him of the girl. Of locked rooms and the burn of probing strangers' hands, the coldness of a memory without an identity left to anchor it.

"Then I have a different question," he said. "Is it possible for a demon to love a human?"

"What a stupid question."

My grip tightened around the narrow neck of the gourd. There was a childishness to his persistence that irritated me. Still, a part of me was curious too. What would it be like? To live an entire lifetime among the humans in peace? To have a name that no one could take away? To be free of this curse, this hunger, this unrelenting rage? What would it be like to die quietly and have someone tenderly bury my bones into the earth?

I hated myself most during these moments of weakness.

I tossed the empty sake gourd back to him, and he caught it one-handed. The other hand, less confident, reached for my wrist.

"But," he said, a powdering of blush on his cheeks. "If a human can love a demon, don't you think the opposite should be true?"

In the room, Arata undressed in front of me as if it was nothing. He climbed into the white futon, turning his back to me, but I could feel the heat from his body through the thin sheet. He knew nothing of who I was. There was a thrill in this one-sided knowledge. I imagined the shape of my hand around his throat, prying open his lips, my jar of precious things tumbling down into his gut. He would be beautiful in a skin of curses. We would be the same, except I would finally be free.

When I woke, Ryunosuke was sitting by the window, one hand on his knee, the other cupping his long face, elbow on the low tabletop, the slight smile on his face I'd seen countless times before. I opened my mouth to call to him, but when I blinked, Arata had already taken his place. Magic. A cruel trick of the brain. A family of sparrows fluttered by the glass, shaking snow free from their wings. Arata glanced over as if sensing my stare, but I closed my eyes, still as a statue.

"If you're awake, we should leave for the Tower," he said low enough that I knew he thought I was still sleeping. After a few minutes, I opened my eyes again, watching him watch the birds, waiting for another trick of the eye.

The dusty streets were nearly empty during the day, the sun grilling down. Rusted shop signs swung on their chains in the rough winds. A lone old man drank sake from a sun-bleached gourd, his spine curved down like a bent tree, oblivious to the sand in his hairy ears.

The Tower of Jigokudani lay on the west end of the small town, a vulgar black aberration in the flat sandy landscape. A self-proclaimed Oracle lived at the top, worshipped by the residents. With his third eye, he was responsible for everything from reading the weather and harvest cycles to designating the job of each person in the town when they turned sixteen.

The job from Akechi was straightforward. I was to climb to the top of the Tower and take the false Oracle's life—chop off his long hair, pierce his heart with the monk's divine blade, spill open his slippery guts, and toss him from the tower window as a warning to the people. A direct request from the Emperor who proclaimed the people should not worship a mere man, or at least not one who dared to question his authority.

"The third eye is a fake," Arata confirmed, holding up the Oracle's bloody torso, pressing his thumb to the old man's forehead. Charcoal smeared on his finger. He tore open the old man's white robe, revealing the black kimono underneath. Embroidered into the dead man's sleeve was a three-claw crest inside a lotus flower, the imperial emblem.

The old man's blood was still warm on my blade.

"Why would one of the Emperor's men be here?" I asked, but the answer was already clear.

The Emperor could not forgive a man with too much power, one who might question his authority. Including a treacherous monk with too many generous followers.

And Akechi always sent me to do the jobs he never wanted to do.

I could be as far as Shimane by sundown, but the cursed contract would pull me back. The monk could command me to prostrate myself in front of the Emperor's marionette men. To do whatever they wanted until they were satisfied enough to look the other way. There were so many uses for a body that could not easily die, more than I cared to imagine.

I watched Arata as he stalked across the room to the window. He slid the shoji screen shut, the hall darkening. Most humans feel safer in the light, but some, not unlike demons, prefer the shadows.

"There is only one way to settle this," he said, unsheathing his blade. He looked up at me with the narrowed eyes of an executioner.

I took a step back, hand on the scabbard of the blade Akechi gave me. My grip tightened around the handle, ready to parry any attack—the perfect angle could break his sword in two, sending the metal into his throat.

Arata raised his sword. With one clean motion, he sliced off the fake Oracle's right hand.

"Put this in the jar you've brought with you," he ordered, dropping the severed appendage on the table with the dead man's teacup and stacked fortune cards. Blood stained across a diagram of the body laid out like a map of a human-shaped country to conquer.

"What jar?" I asked carefully.

He grabbed a hold of my arm as if to slice it off as well. "The one you've been keeping. The one Akechi gave you."

He released my arm, the pressure of his fingers still pulsing against my skin.

"We'll return with proof of the execution," he said. "That was our only job, was it not? There is no reason for us not to feign ignorance about everything else."

Yes, he was right. Ignorance was a man's greatest weapon.

There are few places a demon can live among the humans, but they exist. These are the lush houses of pleasure and discretion where money is exchanged for time and relief. Where there is less concern for where a body comes from and more interest in how much it can take. These are the blood fields of war where the sharpness of a sword buys a man or demon another day. These are the places where the humans allow themselves to become demons. The places where a girl must become a curse to survive.

Here a man's hands can open a girl up like a blade shucking open an oyster. Like the soft creature inside, she never even knows she has already begun the process of dying.

The first time I was taken from the only home I'd ever known to the Pleasure Quarters, I was no more than seventeen, and my existence was already a stain on someone else's life. I had not even been afraid. There was so much beauty at first. The bejeweled hair pieces and thin-toothed combs, the racks of kimono, the porcelain teapots painted and glazed with ancient landscapes, the music each night, the generous curtain of sunshine each morning on my face. Sometimes you can surround yourself with enough beautiful things to forget how ugly the world is. Sometimes that is all you can do.

Arata played the kokyū in the Crane Sitting Room next to the inn's hot springs-fed bathhouse. A group of elderly women gathered to listen, fanning themselves with paper uchiwa, still steaming from their baths, their husbands smoking outside or drinking hot sake in the tatami room. Everything in the foyer was covered in a thin layer of dust and sand, even with the doors closed.

Outside, the full moon bathed everything in a twilight blue glow, even the smoke pillars rising in the distance as men set fire to grass fields in hopes of alchemizing new soil from the ash.

In the Tower, just a few miles away at the edge of the town, the false Oracle was rotting in a pool of his own blood without a hand. We'd closed all the windows to prevent the crows from feasting, but the rats had likely started first pickings. The man's imperial comrades and their weapons would make their way up those dark stairs soon after, if they hadn't already.

I don't tell Arata how the jar had begun to transform. How the serpent had wrapped itself into a scarlet-threaded cocoon made of the clotted blood from the hand, a divine-level curse imbued into its tar-black scales. I felt its rage surging in the pit of my gut. It spoke to me through its ceramic prison, singing back my old lullabies as if pleading for freedom.

To the other side, to the other side...

Soon, soon. I promised the creature fresh meat for its first meal in exchange for its silence now.

I remember my own first meal well. A man from the girl's memories who had cruel hands. It was in the back alley of the Pleasure Quarters. The taste of well-aged wine mixed with tones of mint and the man's cigars. I remember the nausea. The way a body resists its first time in more meanings than one. For moment, I'd felt like I was dying again as I brought the man's bones to my teeth, revenge never quite tasting the way you expect it to.

The strings petered out like rain dimming to a drizzle. The room grew quiet. Arata put down the kokyū's horse-haired bow to hushed compliments and applause. He had the air of someone who knew how to fit in with common people, even if he would never be one of them. Even if he could cut down each one without hesitation. Like a god disguised as a human.

I followed him down the hall back to the room, the maple trees swaying in the relentless heat. I dabbed at my forehead with my sleeve, catching sight of Akechi's blade inside. Some of the other guests stopped to watch us, to watch him. He took my hand, looking at me as if we were the only two people left in the inn, in Jigokudani, two fugitives at the end of the world. "You are beautiful," he said as if putting on a show for our audience. "Let me free you from Akechi."

The moon shone into the room, a shuddering pool of light on the bed.

Arata was dressed in his coal-black hakama and crested haori, an armored mask over his nose and mouth as if ready for an assassination.

The jar sat in the middle of the bed, its glazed colors reflecting the light of the moon.

"Are you alright?" Arata asked.

I nodded, not wanting to hear my own voice. The inn had tired me out, the nonstop human interactions. The stink of the old inn's tatami floor swarmed over all my senses, drowning me. For a moment I could see the old Pleasure Quarters, the stained sheets, the bruised women in beautiful clothes, the lamps burning in dark rooms like ghosts.

Arata picked up the jar, cradling it against his chest. "Let's go."

The town was dead quiet. Even the sparse lanterns on the streets had been snuffed out for the night, the whining crickets in the shadows our only company. In the dark, I could still taste the dust in the air.

The last time Ryunosuke left the brothel, it had been so quiet that I'd wondered if the whole town had died and finally left us in peace. I remember watching him from the window as he made his way through the streets to the entry gates, the morning mist blanketed across the shingled roofs, how I caught myself wearing the haori he had left behind. How it still smelled of him when I fell asleep with it on. How I'd wanted to tear it to shreds when I woke up alone hours later.

Hand in my sleeve, I gripped the handle of Akechi's blade. The cicada-stone nestled between my index and middle finger, cold and hard against my pulse. Arata's pace increased, his strides long, elegant as a deer, as we made our way past empty glass tanks and smoldering fire pits toward the beech forest spilling out from the west gate of the town.

In the distance, the sound of the river's current echoed along the trees. My lungs burned with phantom water. A body never forgets how it leaves the world the first time, I suppose. A soul etched into the flesh. Some curses are not the ones you expect.

I stopped, listening to the throaty croaks of the toads in the misty path, the unearthly cries of raccoons.

Arata slowed, moonlight on the back of his haori, glossy against his black hair until it looked almost white. For a moment, I could see Ryunosuke in the profile of his face like a beautiful ghost.

I took one step forward, dead leaves splitting under my feet. I'd learned long ago that waiting for someone else to save you meant losing the opportunity to save yourself.

Right timing only comes once.

I lunged forward, throwing the scabbard past him. Arata eyes darted toward the flash of lacquer. My vision was swimming, tiny sprites at the edges of my eyes. I gripped the handle of the blade like a dagger, taking aim. All it would take was one sharp drive between the ribs to the beating wet muscle housed inside. The jar's contents would slide down his throat before he died, before his body became an unusable vessel and useless to me. We would be back at the temple by dawn. I would barter my freedom with my new cursed vessel, a sharpened blade pressed to Akechi throat.

I coughed, spitting up blood. Pain seared through me like fire blooming across my flesh.

Arata pulled his sword out of my chest, flicking my blood from his steel blade.

"Did Akechi order you to do this?" he asked, lowering his mask. He looked nothing like the man I had spent the past few days with, the veil of kindness gone from his eyes.

I refused to fall to my knees. I'd already spent so much time on the ground, far more than I would ever admit to a human. If I could buy enough time, I could heal this wound. I could devour him bones and all, I could—

"He doesn't deserve you." Arata suddenly gripped my chin. My body froze. I couldn't feel my legs or arms, my limbs encased in invisible concrete.

"What are you—"

He leaned forward and kissed my petrified lips, soft at first, and then deeply. My mouth opened, coaxed by whatever curse he had put on me. Something slid between my lips, warm and slippery. I fought the urge to gag as it slithered across my tongue, down my throat. Arata's lips pressed harder against mine as the *thing* crawled down to my gut. It thrashed against my insides. I forced my eyes open and saw Arata's gray ones staring right at me, grave-cold. On the ground by his feet, the jar was on its side, the lid open. Panic swelled in me. I willed my arms to move, but I could barely twitch a finger.

His hand and lips finally released me. I tried to raise the blade still in my hand, but it was no use. I felt depleted, boneless. As if I were drowning, again. Blood spilled from the wound in my chest. The thing inside me was growing, squirming, feeding on my strength.

"I was silent, just as you asked," Arata said. "Now it is time for you to keep your promise. To the other side, to the other side..." he hummed cheerfully.

I looked down at the empty jar, finally understanding.

I told him I wanted to meet in the forest to avoid trouble with the brothel owner. But in truth, I wanted no witnesses.

"I want you to leave," I said, handing him back his haori.

"Have I been a bother?" Ryunosuke asked.

Most cursed spirits are skilled at lying, but I could not move the right words from my chest to my tongue. "I don't know," I answered instead, an unfinished thought. What I wanted to say was: *I don't know what I'm becoming when you're around.* "Please leave. Otherwise, I will probably kill you."

"Could you do it?" he said, not looking at me as he put his haori back on. "Would you finally feel strong enough then?" His hand was on the hilt of his sword. His eyes narrowed, a familiar cruelty on his smirking lips. "You will need to be if you want to stop me from doing what they sent me to do."

At that moment, I remembered. He was still an assassin for the imperial guard. All this time we were just playing house. The world behind the walls of the Pleasure Quarters were no more real than the make-up we smeared onto our faces each morning, the carved masks the actors donned each night. It had been so long, I'd almost forgotten.

He pulled the blade out of his wooden scabbard. I laughed as he assumed the position of an executioner, sword raised.

Arata took the blade from my hand and held its sharp tip to my neck. The forest seemed to spin in dark blues, as if we were underwater.

"What did you put into me?" I asked.

"Just a piece of me. Nothing too serious. I'm still new and a little afraid of commitment," he grinned. "I'd planned to take that monk's body, but I wanted something to happen now. I was getting bored in there," he motioned to the open jar. "So, I made an agreement with the boy instead."

The boy? "Arata Watanabe?"

Something thrashed sharply in my gut. I dug a claw into my palm, drawing blood.

"No, no. The one inside *you*. The one sick with love for you."

Ryunosuke.

"He's dead. I killed him."

Arata waved dismissively.

"Whatever you say. Anyways, he did not like the *new* boy. He wanted to get rid of him."

Jealousy is a consequence of love. And love is a consequence of weakness. A blue-tailed lizard darted into view and then disappeared down a burrow. My vision blurred from the blood loss. I fought back the urge to vomit.

"He took over your body for just a moment. Just long enough to let me out. To let me crawl into my pretty new vessel while he slept," the creature in Arata's skin explained, leaning close enough to peer into my eyes as if I were the one inside a jar now. "The Watanabe family has a long history of demon hunting. Not my favorite clan. The taste of too much cursed blood on them makes them a rotten meal. I'm sure Arata or one of his spineless elders had already sensed you at the temple or during one of your jobs. He probably came to take your head under the guise of penance training. Under the guise of being friendly. Assassins really are the worst kind of executioners, don't you think?"

I opened my mouth to speak, but Arata held up a finger over my lips.

"Sorry, all that time spent keeping my mouth shut and now I've just got too much to say," he sighed. "Let's go do something fun. Your contract with the monk is still in place, is it not? Akechi is overconfident, which means he will not give up so easily. And I know you cannot stand that look in his eyes, that look like he thinks he has already won." He leaned in so close his lips grazed my ear. "How long have you been waiting to devour those eyes? Let me help you."

My claws lashed out, barely missing his throat as he leapt back. My arm had moved on its own, compelled by phantom strings.

The demon in Arata's skin grinned with his sharp teeth.

"So, the boy inside you breaks deals as easily as bones. Or perhaps you are his weakness. I can't say I'm surprised or even disappointed. We both know how delicious betrayal can taste. But a body is a crowded place for two souls, isn't it? Shall I pull him out of you and devour him piece by piece?" His grin widened. "Or will you do it yourself first?"

I was lying by the river. The sun was hot on my face, but my legs and arms were in the shade, cold and damp from the soil. Everything was sore from the fight. My mouth was wet, a sticky sweetness clinging to my tongue. I sat up and wiped my lips, the back of my hand staining dark red.

Several yards away, a bear was feeding behind a large stone. I walked over quietly, not wanting to start an unnecessary fight, but curious about what there was to eat.

Beneath the bear, obscured by its massive brown furred back, were two legs clothed in a bloody hakama, twitching in time to the bear's feeding. Wet smacking sounds filled the air. Chewing sounds. Bones cracking. Nearby, a sword was abandoned near the water, unsheathed.

Ryunosuke's blade.

There's a strangeness to a body without the glaring light of life in it, like an oversized sack of rice. I looked down at the thing on the ground, really looked at it. It was almost silly. Taking up so much space, all those limbs.

Crack. Crack. Crack.

The bear looked up at me, its eyes consumed in purple flames. A cursed creature. Possibly the unfortunate test subject of a twisted curse wielder. Or perhaps it had simply consumed the bones of a cursed body left to rot in the forest.

Begone.

I slashed the creature back with my claws. It howled, its bloody breath miasmic. I leapt back, noxious clouds ballooning around us. The creature's paw lashed out behind me, three new bloody welts streaking across my back. Pain seared over my vision. My sandals sank into the dirt. I blinked once, twice, my eyes re-focusing, then sprang forward. Instinct sharpened my teeth and hair into messy slaughter tools. *A cursed body is forged from misery. It is made to kill, to burn, to hate.* My claws sank into flesh, tearing fur and skin off the creature's throat. Blood splattered onto my cheeks and kimono. The bear fell back, stumbling over Ryunosuke's body. It ground its jaws, chewing on something still in its maw. Some*one*. A human that had once belonged to me. I grabbed the creature's jaw. Rage splintered my vision now. *Ryunosuke had been mine.* My eyes flitted over toward the lifeless bloodied body on the ground, the one I'd torn to shreds with my own hands. This is what I had wanted wasn't it? To be free of him? To be alone? *A cursed body can only kill, burn, and hate.* Isn't that what I had told him? The creature roared against my grip. With a clenched fist, I sent my cursed flames into its open mouth. They exploded in purples and then charcoaled to black. The creature stilled, crumbling to the ground.

Behind the crackling flames, Ryunosuke's body was still dressed in the haori he always wore. What remained of it anyway after the bear had torn through the smooth fabric. My hands still felt sticky as I pulled the body up. I tried to remember his face, but all I could picture was the slaughter, the calmness of his face as it happened. I wanted to ask him why he'd raised his sword to me with no intention to kill. Why hadn't he stopped me? Where was his pride?

Why wasn't I happy?

But a corpse has no answers for the living. At least he would finally know the true meaning of death. Wasn't that what he'd always desired most?

Sparrows rustled in the trees.

I laughed.

Good riddance. I would miss the expensive wine.

I wiped the creature's blood that had splattered onto my face. It mixed with the blood that was still on my hands, smearing across my lips.

An unfamiliar ache pulled on my chest. A feeling like sinking into a black sea. I swallowed back the copperish taste in my throat, but the feeling did not wash down with it.

Inside the bloody mess, something gleamed wet and red under the morning sun like a petaled flower after the rain. Another beautiful thing left behind.

Ryunosuke's heart was miraculously intact. I reached in and tore it free from its useless cage. All these bones and tendons. A body was nothing but a cage. I brought the heart to my lips. It was still warm. Was this how it felt to kiss a human?

"Is he really still in here?" I asked the cursed spirit in Arata's body.

I'd heard tales of consuming a soul, of obliterating a soul, but nothing of saving one to another body through consumption of the flesh.

A heart for a heart. A soul etched into skin.

"Will you rip yourself open to find out?" he asked, amused.

My hair flared out like hooks, wrapping around his arms and legs.

"Will this violence please you enough to forget about him?" He laughed as I lifted him off the ground. The strands of hair tightened around his chest, his ribs on the verge of snapping, but he didn't even flinch. He looked me in the eye as if he were delighted. Like a madman staring at a house he'd set alight. "Or are you that desperate to die?"

Pain ripped through me. Arata's sword swung back through the air as if wielded by the wind and sank into my arm again. Warm blood trickled down my elbows to my hands. My grip weakened, my hair dropping him back to the ground.

Arata brushed the black strands off his kimono coat, watching me sink to the dirt. "What could a cursed spirit want more than power and revenge?" he asked, standing over me. "Or have you truly relinquished your pride to that human inside you?"

Pride?

I raised my left hand, pain still throbbing through me like lava in my veins. For a moment, I felt the phantom welts on my face. The roaming hands of strangers on my body. The beautiful things that remained among the ruins. Pride was an armor I'd earned through blood. But when had it actually protected me?

Arata frowned, almost with pity. "Come now. It's time for us to feast on a treacherous monk."

He was right. I'd wanted vengeance so badly for so long. Hadn't I pictured it each night, dragging Akechi into that soundproofed room he kept me in, of all the ways I'd make him hurt?

But there are so many hours in a night, and a demon doesn't need much sleep. When the fog of anger settled, I was no longer in that temple. I was in the dark alleys again, with the crying women, on the dirty beds, in the locked rooms, a gash of light always just out of reach, a misery so deep it had no name.

Is it possible for a demon to love a human?

I thought again of myself devouring that stranger in the alley behind the brothel, the blood covering my tattered kimono and face, the face of a monster.

Was it possible for a human to love such an indisputable demon?

I thought of Ryunosuke's back, how he'd never taken off his haori until the night I asked to see the scars on his body. How he was the only man who never asked me to open my body to him as if it were an honor.

"I never understood why Kiyohime had been turned into a curse just because she'd loved the wrong person," he'd said like a fool.

"She should have just devoured the monk and gone to live a peaceful life in the mountains," I replied, lingering on the smile on his face.

Hadn't I just wanted to be rid of him? Hadn't his existence been like a curse on me?

The open jar glinted against the moonlight.

"Can you get rid of it?" I asked.

"It?"

"The boy inside me."

The demon that had possessed Arata's body pursed his lips.

"Is that what you really want?" he asked.

"Can you get rid of him or not?" I repeated, unable to meet his eyes.

"It will be a bit messy. But isn't impossible," he answered, the smile playing on his lips again. "If you are willing to make a sacrifice."

Akechi sat in the garden in front of the wilting tulips, sketching a sparrow perched on a browned petal. Beside him, gold-speckled koi fish flicked their monstrously long tails over the surface of the pond.

"It's done," I said, tossing him Arata's right hand.

He studied the blackened fingers, the flesh half-rotted from the journey back.

"Did he say anything before you slayed him?" he asked, imbuing an energy border around the rotting specimen.

"He begged for his life," I answered.

The sparrow took off. Akechi eyed the blade in my sleeve.

"I have a new job for you," he said, standing.

"What poor unsuspecting idiot is it this time?" I asked, peering over the pond. The cluster of white-orange koi scattered into deeper water at the sight of me.

When I looked back up, Akechi's face was close enough I could see the long scar on his neck, the flint color of his irises.

"You've lied to me," he said, lowering his head just enough so our eyes were on the same level. "Arata is alive." He stepped back and picked up the hand from the stone, glancing back at me as if I were a guilty human child, stolen sweets hidden behind my back. "How did you convince him to give you his sword-wielding hand?"

"I didn't. I just took it before he could stop me."

I pulled the blade from my sleeve.

"Oho, so you plan to use my own weapon against me?" he said, unsheathing the binding blade from under his orange shawl. "Very well, I will enjoy you for a bit, and then end your long suffering."

Our blades clashed, divine steel against divine steel. The monk had not earned his position and power through appearance and words alone. Steel grazed my scalp and sliced across the thick shoulder of my kimono, drawing blood. Koi fish gathered by the edge of the pond as if expecting treats. My muscles strained, still drained from my earlier battle with the demon in Arata's body. Akechi fought with his eyes closed, one hand behind him as if relaxing to music. Insolent creature. I took a step back, aiming my blade at his throat.

His mouth suddenly dropped open, unfamiliar words spilling from his lips in rapid succession. A cursed incantation.

The cicada on the handle of my blade fluttered to life, translucent wings batting against my fingers. It flew up, landing on my left eye. I jerked away, but it wouldn't move, blocking my vision. The centipede slithered to life next, down the hilt, sliding up my wrist and arm, up my neck and curled around my ear.

"*Tomare*," Akechi ordered, and the creatures halted their assault.

He walked over, leisurely. A lion in top form.

"The soldiers always say that a demon smells worse than the rotted flesh of their dead comrades, but I disagree," he said, lowering his head and taking a deep breath against my neck. "I've always thought you smelled like a river, like the sea. That wonderful aroma of something that takes everything that pours into it."

My body moved on its own, grabbing a hold of the monk's head. Two hands pulled by phantom strings. I leaned in, pressing my lips into his. The monk struggled, his dried lips squirming against mine. I opened my mouth, my tongue like a blade forcing his open, the creature sliding up my gut and my throat. It crawled into my mouth and then squirmed into his. A copperish, slimy taste. A curse looking for a new home. His body thrashed, but my hands, our hands, held tightly onto his head, claws grazing his scalp and ears. Akechi choked, the wet sounds of drowning as the creature pressed down into his throat, seeking warmth.

I wanted to ask him if he really understood how many ways a body could lose meaning.

The afternoon light was a heaven-like gash in the forest canopy. The river rushed from the previous night's rain, the smell of blood washed away by lush greenery. For a moment, I imagined myself as neither human nor demon, but as a songbird perched on a high branch, ready to alchemize the air in my lungs into music instead of fire.

Dead leaves crunched behind me. Arata walked into the clearing, his right hand wrapped in blood-stained fabric and bandages.

No, the cursed spirit had kept its promise, just as I had kept mine. It had no use for its former, damaged vessel.

Ryunosuke had walked into the clearing in the body of a stranger. He looked dazed, like the face of a newborn calf peering out from the darkness of its shed for the first time. His eyes moved from the burbling river to a fallen tree wrapped in wet moss to a weedish patch of wildflowers until they settled on me. His remaining hand reached for the sword corded to his side. Did he want revenge for what I'd done to him? I sharpened my fingers into claws, released my hair into a violent curtain of black. My eyes pooled into reds and purples. So be it. This is what I was, a demon, a curse, and I would devour him again if I had to.

"Kiyo," he called, taking a step forward. The name sounded familiar, warm on his lips.

"Aren't you afraid of me?" I asked even though I already knew the answer. It had always been the same.

"I have no reason to be," he said. "I'll stay as long as you'll have me."

"They'll hunt us until the end. Burn us. As cursed spirits, demons, monsters," I said. "Until there's nothing left of us but ash."

"Let them come," he said, the afternoon light like a torch against his face. "Death was always a price I was willing to pay to stay with you."

Angela Liu is a Chinese-American writer/poet who writes about intergenerational trauma and weird things. She is a two-time Nebula Award Finalist and Astounding Award nominee. Her work has also been nominated for the Hugo, Ignyte, and Rhysling Awards. She used to research mixed reality at Keio University in Japan with a focus on new narrative platforms and tangible interfaces for remote communication. Her stories and poems are published/forthcoming in *Clarkesworld*, *Strange Horizons*, *Uncanny Magazine*, *Lightspeed*, and *Logic(s)*, among others. Check out more of her work at liu-angela.com or find her on Twitter/Instagram @liu_angela and on Bluesky @angelaliu.bsky.social.

THE BROTHERHOOD OF MONTAGUE ST. VIDEO

Thomas Ha

At first I thought something had broken in my book.

I didn't notice until the afternoon light from the windows began to recede. I tried to increase the brightness settings of the page, but no matter how I thumbed the margins, they would not change. For the first time, I looked carefully at the gold printing along its spine. The book was dead.

What kind of library carried a dead book? I wondered.

No one responded to my calls for assistance. There were no working service-buttons near the shelves that I could see. I walked downstairs to the circulation desk. No one was present at the self-checkout stalls, and I assumed, like all other recent changes, that this was the result of cuts to the city budget.

The more I looked at the gold-laden book, the more I considered it may not have belonged to the library at all. It had no identification tag on the inside cover, no chip at its base. Perhaps someone had left it, hidden among the other inventory, for some unknown reason. There was no way to scan a book that didn't belong there, so I put it in my coat without checking to see if cameras were hovering over me and walked out the door.

The entire ride on the 2, I wondered if something would happen. I waited for an officer to pull me aside at the station exit. Or for a street drone to make me step away from the pedestrians on the icy sidewalk. But nothing came of it, my taking away the dead book. I was surprised, and even disappointed, in the nothing that seemed to follow.

"*The Winter Hills* by Carrigan Salt."

The owner of the video store studied the binding, the page edges, much as I did before. Alaric had an eye for dead things that I did not, and he understood instinctively the rarity of what I had brought him.

In the weeks after my mother's funeral, I had come to the video store more often, bringing boxes from her Court Street apartment. Recorded-over VHS tapes, floppy disks, and undeveloped photo rolls. The Brotherhood on Montague was always eager to collect physical effects and would accept donations of any kind, I had been told. Even if they could not use or preserve them, they often had a sense of who could.

I was curious if he would buy the dead book from me, given his obvious interest.

"I'll consider it." Alaric paused, then he redirected the conversation to my mother's things. Some of her belongings I had chosen not to donate outright. One in particular, I had requested the Brotherhood try to restore and copy.

"The digital video disc, the DVD, you asked about—we'll need a 650 nm red laser to create a copy from the scratched original."

"Just as it was? No optimization?"

It was important to emphasize this. Every other data center had been unable to pull the file without automatic edits to the image settings and content.

"That's right." Alaric nodded. "No optimization. Just as it was. The Brotherhood's burner is on loan. It'll be a week or two."

He was about to give back the dead book, but he kept touching the textured cover. "I never read this, the original, in ink on pulp," he said. "It's part of Salt's Long Wanderer series."

"Oh," I said, as if I had heard of it before. Salt's name had been vaguely familiar to me when I plucked the book from the library shelf, but if there were more volumes like this one, I didn't recall seeing them.

The old man turned several pages. He was reading, but it was apparent that he was thinking of other things. I could feel his mind split between the words and wherever else he was. His breathing slowed, and then he closed the book and put it in my hands. There was some sound in a distant part of the shop, behind the shelves and stacks of preserved things—spinning racks of cassette tapes, mounted pinhole cameras, an old standing arcade cabinet. A rhythmic rustling, there, that continued until I left.

Elii met me at the promenade after dark, not far from Montague.

We sat on a bench and watched the East River behind the slow-moving bodies on the walkway. I tried to show her the dead book, and she thumbed the margins before giving up when it wouldn't brighten. It was clear she had no interest in the thing.

I'd been hoping after several months of dating we'd be able to take off our amp-glasses, but she insisted we keep them on. I'd already snuck little peeks of her around the edges of my frames. I knew she did not look all that different without her themes. Her cheeks were less contoured, her lips less plump. The alterations in the glasses were only slight. Nonetheless, she had only ever let me take them off when we were in total darkness together. For people who kept glasses on, it was never really about looks alone.

She asked if I was almost finished with my mother's apartment. There were just a few more boxes, some paperwork, and the deposit to get back. My bereavement leave was done, and I had borrowed from next quarter's vacation time. But I'd be back in my apartment soon.

We began talking about the scratched disc I'd sent to Montague St. Video, how it contained, among other things, old footage my mother had shot and saved. Clips of us up at Lake George in the years after my father had left. I offered to show Elii some of it once it was restored and copied.

"It sounds like your mom held onto a lot," she said. "That's a lot to go through and settle up. A lot of things."

"Right. That's true. It is a lot. A lot of things. Too many, even."

"Yes, maybe too many," Elii agreed. "I was thinking, because there's so much, we should probably hold off on visits and videoconnects—until you're done settling everything, at least."

"Oh? I mean, sure. That does make sense."

"It just seems like something you should finish first. Don't you think?"

"You're right. No. You're right. I should focus and finish. That does make sense."

"Sorry again. For your loss."

"Of course." I went back to watching the dark glass and cement shapes of the city across the river instead of her, already half-forgetting whatever it was that we were saying. "I appreciate that," I said. "Yes, I appreciate that. I do."

Later, in the stillness of my mother's apartment, I began reading through more of *The Winter Hills*. I sat in her old chair, her scarf still draped over the arm and barely brushing against the rug. Lost in the pages, much as I'd been in the library.

Carrigan Salt's protagonist, the unnamed rider, rode his gray horse across flat and rocky lands and through sparse little towns. The character had a peculiar way of going from one place to another without a sense of purpose. In any other book, I would have known the shape of the narrative at this point. But not here.

He did not understand the urgency with which others lived. They all seemed so eager to reach a conclusion, no matter how partial or incomplete, but in his mind there were always more questions forming like eddies in a stream. Every town the rider visited, he liked to ask himself these three things: What is it these people want? What is it these people need? Are they striving toward one, or the other, with what they do each day? And in examining these things he usually came to a clearer understanding of the people in that particular place.

I fell asleep reading about thundering horses and cattle and sizzling heat. Outside, the heavy trucks on the BQE rattled the icy apartment windows, but I imagined them as hooves over hollowed rock. I dreamt of a man on a gray horse standing at a lake, watching a mother and her young boy at the water's edge throwing rocks. I woke up crying for reasons I did not understand.

My days had already lost normal proportion before the dead book. They were little eras contained within odd chambers that did not begin or end with a sunrise or sunset. There was the unlocking of my mother's online accounts. The post-funeral cremation and retrieval of remains. Notifying various agencies and sending copies of death certificates. Finding an attorney to settle any outstanding issues with her estate. The time spent reading *The Winter Hills* in meditative stretches felt no different. Just another era to add to the ones before.

Alaric had not yet finished with the disc I had given him on my next visit to Montague. I found him stooped over an album of postage stamps, carefully arranged on each page in airtight little sleeves. Behind him, a black-and-white movie played on a CRT, and a modified VHS player appeared to be recording the contents for the Brotherhood's archives. I asked Alaric, while he inspected the postage stamps, if the store sold any paper.

"As in, sheets? Uncoated? No pixelated surface? The Brotherhood has a relationship with the mill in Tarrytown, so we do have some supply, yes."

He did not ask why I needed it, so I assumed this was not too extraordinary of a request. I bought one ream with some store credit I'd accumulated.

My mother kept an old Trapwood typewriter she had gotten as a gift from her grandmother. She had shown me, when I was very young, how to replace the ribbon, but I still had to spend some time watching videos online before I could do it. Once I'd had everything, I put the copy of *The Winter Hills* next to me and began typing its words on the fresh paper.

The town was nothing like he knew. There was a solemnity to the way the miners at Copper Hawk lived. Their existence was like a duty they bore begrudgingly but also would not relinquish. The rasp of dust in their nostrils and mouths, the lines of their skin. They did not enjoy the brilliant bang of the white sun. It was only the swollen blackness of the shafts before them, and they could not remember what had been there before the mines had been birthed beneath them.

I didn't know why I'd begun this project of copying the dead book's text over onto fresh sheets. My day job as a freelance re-writer meant I often studied material like this. But typically I would be cleaning up inarticulate copy, trying to make output from some desk producer into something people could understand. My agency mandated simplified phrases and strict grammar rules we had to know by heart.

The Winter Hills did not have any of those phrases or rules. There were long turns that were not necessarily about efficiency or meaning, but about rhythm. It was a voice I wanted to transpose for myself to feel the words. I was getting lost in the book, but at a pace and flow that felt more like a dissolving comfort than the listlessness of despair.

It was also during those quiet days when I began to suspect something else was happening, especially when I left my mother's apartment.

Walking along the slushy sidewalk, past naked black branches waving like claws at the curtilage in front of the brownstones, I heard that distant sound, that rustling, I remembered from the shop. Not like soft wings, but something like plastic or the scrape of faux-leather.

There was a presence I could not explain.

I'd take breaks from typing and go down to one of the corner stores. No one would be working there in person, of course. The camera would dangle from tracks in the ceiling, following over my shoulder and monitoring every item I picked from the shelves. I'd scan my items at the self-check registers, and I'd think, for a second, that someone was in one of the aisles. But I also knew if I looked, I would be wrong.

The iron-handed sheriff of Copper Hawk did not take kindly to the rider or the differences between them. In his mind, every stranger was a new element to be carefully accounted for, and the sheriff was not one with the patience for it. He did not ask questions about what people wanted or needed, only what they could do. No, he and the rider were not the same at all.

The ending of the dead book was as mystifying as the rest.

The rider spent weeks in the mining town of Copper Hawk, slowly coming to the realization that the sheriff there, working under the auspices of a metals corporation, was bleeding the people of their wages and exploiting their labor. The last chapter involved a shootout, as these kinds of books tended to have. But instead of a decisive victory, the rider ended up winged and bleeding. The book finished with the rider, delirious, on his gray horse, barely escaping with his life out into the desert. Nothing resolved. No one in Copper Hawk saved. Perhaps the rider would return to the town and set things right in another book, but somehow I didn't get that sense. So the ending felt haunting, strange, and unfamiliar to me.

I found a living reprint of *The Winter Hills* for comparison. It was encased in shiny plastic, the spine with the usual rechargeable port. I scanned and skipped along the various digital chapters to see what had been altered by the publishers posthumously. It wasn't uncommon for the estate and rights holders to periodically update these kinds of stories. The benefit of a living book was that they didn't have to contact readers to update the content. Alterations would sync in the pixelated pages whenever the book went online next.

The biggest difference I noticed in the new electronic copy was the ending.

There was a shootout in Copper Hawk like before, yes. But instead of the loss and the blood and the shame of the rider, the iron-handed sheriff was the one to take a bullet. The miners of the town staged a revolt against the metals company in the third act. They set fire to some of the shafts with an explosion at the end of the action, to punctuate the triumph. I could almost sense the hand of audience-score maximizer programs in the plot. It could even have been a re-writer at my agency that oversaw the edition, for all I knew.

I felt better in some ways, having read the new, happier ending, but I forgot it promptly, like some garbled conversation I'd overheard on the subway, something that made me chuckle and then escaped my mind.

In my dreams, I kept going back to the image of the original ending—that rider bleeding, leaning over on his horse, clutching at its neck, and whispering softly to the beast. And then I remembered my mother wearing sunglasses, on a towel at Lake George, reading a magazine, while I ran back and forth on the white-hot sand.

"Why would they change it that way, *The Winter Hills*?"

Alaric was inventorying one of the last boxes of my mother's belongings. He held up a record and inspected its sleeve. There were also a series of digital postcards, rewritable electronic messages in thin plastic film, some from Cabo, others from Denmark, sent by my mother's younger sister who had never stayed in one place too long.

"People have a tendency to confuse change with improvement. So alteration seems like creation to some." The old man peered down the glasses dipping at the end of his nose. "We like the feeling of progress, and folks figured out a while ago that you can always tweak things in your surroundings to heighten a perceived movement through time. Even if, in truth, you haven't advanced anywhere meaningful at all."

"I don't know what that means."

Alaric laughed, to me or to himself, I could not tell. "I've never been accused of clarity." He typed something on his dust-covered computer and studied the digital postcards from my aunt. "It seems counter-intuitive, but it's really the preserved things—fixed markers that never move—that are the more meaningful measure of change. A traveler on the road can look at mountains, forests, other landmarks, and he understands the difference in his positions the farther along he goes. Just like when I listen to a song, look at a work of art, read a book. And then later, return to that same piece. Something will be different, will have moved, in me. That's the benefit of the work we do in preserving things in particular forms, I like to think. We remember who we were then, so that we know who we are now. Does that make a little more sense?"

His words did feel right. Like something I'd been thinking but didn't know how to articulate in the weeks of going through my mother's things. Again, I removed the dead book from my coat pocket and offered it tentatively to Alaric.

"Have you considered, by the way..." I felt almost embarrassed asking. "Whether you'll buy? The dead book, I mean."

He did not answer quickly. The question appeared to weigh on him. "I'm making inquiries, but I have to be frank. We may not be able to offer a fair price. Not what you could get elsewhere. We will do our best to get back to you soon."

"I understand."

"In the meantime, you should be careful."

"With the book?"

"With who sees it. Not everyone appreciates these things the way the Brotherhood does. Materials that can't be modified, adjusted, or updated. Some enjoy true things like that. Some can't stand them."

"I see," I replied, but again, he had lost me.

"Where did you find this copy, again?"

"Just an old place in the city. My mother used to go."

"Your mother...she was from this neighborhood, you said?" The old man studied my face and the postcards, like he was trying to figure something out. But if he put anything together, he didn't say a word about it or give any other indication. After we'd finished with the box, and as I was about to reach the stairwell, he called out to me.

"West Nyack."

"Hm?"

"There's a Brotherhood in West Nyack," he said. "Not that far out of the city. They know dead books and sometimes teach others about them. If that sort of thing interests you, maybe those are the ones you should go and see. They might have something to offer or to teach you too."

I thanked the old man for the information. There were other things I probably should have asked, but that I just let go. I suppose I thought there would be time with other visits. I did not think too much then about leaving Montague St. Video behind.

Caliper John approached not long after that conversation. Or rather, he decided to make himself known, I suppose. Even then, I should have known he'd been listening for some time.

In the days that followed, typing and re-typing passages from *The Winter Hills*, I found myself awake in the quietest parts of the night. Sometimes, as my mother and I used to do when I was a kid, I made my way to a small Greek diner a couple of blocks from the apartment that was open at all hours. The owners had changed a couple of times over the years, but the kitchen stayed the same through each transition. No automated preparation. Just staffed by a few older men who rotated shifts. My mother had always gotten the fries and the coffee, oil and acid, she'd call it, and read at the blue booths closest to the radiators. So I took to doing the same on these chilly nights too.

He came to my table while I was reading, alone.

"Excuse me, but that book you have there. Have you ever considered selling? It's been some time since I've seen an original Carrigan Salt."

His voice was weak, almost a whistle, and did not fit, because he was so unnaturally large, bigger than any man I had seen. Something animalistic in my brain went off. I felt threatened by his shape and the way it towered above me. He wore tiny glasses and a tailored jacket, little signs of seeming gentility. But they could not obscure the physicality and power of his frame.

He introduced himself as Caliper John and said he had seen me reading *The Winter Hills* and felt compelled to come by. Later, I realized he did not specify when he had seen me reading the dead book.

I asked if he was with one of the Brotherhoods, and he shook his head.

"Not quite."

His eyes would never rest for too long on the cover of the dead book, like he could not take in too much of its details. I noticed, then, a special watch on his wrist, running applications I could not read from where I sat. The watch was similar to mine and other personal computing devices, but it was clearly more expensive and technically advanced. This one seemed like a tiny bracelet on that beefy wrist, and yet he managed to tap and swipe at the watch's face and pull up several programs with ease.

"Physical depreciation might impact its value, but you could get quite a high price from specific collectors. For example..." A few taps into a search bar on the watch and he pulled up a store profile, which he projected just above the watch screen. An antiques and rare editions shop called Satoshi Print. It looked like it was somewhere on the Upper West Side, based on the address. "Just an example, you understand," he said.

"You work for them? Satoshi Print?"

The large man did not meet my eyes. He was listening to the sounds from the kitchen, the sizzle of a frying pan, or maybe the clang of utensils.

"I could make inquiries for you. This is, you understand, not the sort of establishment where individuals can approach. Mine is a tricky business with very little trust. But I am something of a known entity. So if I should broker something, they will make serious offers. It could be quite a lot. Potentially five or even six figures. And you and I could work out a percentage for my commission."

"I...I appreciate that. I'll have to think about it. Mister..."

"John. Caliper John."

"Right."

"Right." He repeated, not mockingly, but more like an uncontrolled echo. The large man, Caliper John, seemed to sense a need to adapt his approach with me, so he smiled. It felt practiced, and he appeared to think it would be reassuring. "People do not often hesitate when I tell them there is that kind of money involved. You understand what I am telling you, about the money involved."

"Sure. I don't know. I've grown attached, I guess."

"Ah. Grown attached. Yes." He touched his small glasses. "I understand what you are saying about growing attached. But items can be replaced. Similar ones bought. That is, after all, what all of the money is usually for. There is a substitute for everything. A meaningful replacement. Everything. You understand what I am saying too?"

He touched the strange watch, and something beeped on my own. I realized he had sent me his contact information, which now appeared on my watch display. I had not accepted any link or pairing, which was usually required for such transfers.

He was smiling, but there was something violative in that otherwise innocuous gesture. I realized he was showing me, in his own way, how insubstantial the separation was between us, and how easily he could pass through it, if, or when, he wanted.

The large man stood and buttoned his jacket around that swelling frame. "I will circulate this, on your behalf, and let you know if there is any interest. If I come back with a number, I ask that you please consider it seriously."

I looked away from his stare until he disappeared, and then I very slowly finished my coffee and fries. I wanted time to pass, to put more space between me and that man. I left my tip and thanked the kitchen and headed out into the cold. As I crunched on the sidewalk slush I felt it again, that hovering presence somewhere about, though I could not track it at first.

The rider felt an unsettling and restless quality to the iron-handed sheriff. There was a hollow in the man that went deeper than eyes could see. He did not operate outward from a source but took things from around himself to sustain an internal void.

Beside the trash cans of a nearby restaurant, I saw something move close to the ground, making that rustling sound. It went quickly, but from what little I could see, it looked like a lizard with hundreds of legs, and yet it was the size of a small dog. There were strange translucent wings up and down its back, rubbing against itself like plastic sheeting while its body undulated further into the darkness.

Between the shadows, I thought I saw its nearly human face staring out at me from behind one of the wet dumpsters, but I did not stay long enough to be sure.

What surprised me most was not the offer from Caliper John, but how it came.

Elii contacted me wanting to meet, not on videoconnect, but in person, despite our previous conversation. In fact, she chose a nice restaurant, next to the bridge and overlooking the East River—*Oubliée*. I told her that place seemed a little out of our reach, but she said that it was taken care of. I didn't have the presence of mind to ask her what that meant.

I only knew *Oubliée* was the type of restaurant that required a jacket and reservation and a certain demeanor. Everyone there was intentionally and strategically thin. The patrons who seemed uncomfortable and sharp-eyed and on their watches were likely of the working layer of the city. The ones who were slower and well-rested carried electronic notebooks like they were serious or artistic people, but leisure was clearly their business and everyone knew it. I kept thinking about the rider in *The Winter Hills*, his three questions, while we were seated and studying the menus, which seemed to have no prices.

What is it these people want? What is it these people need? Are they striving toward one, or the other, with what they do each day?

The waitstaff was clearly informed to take good care of us.

A young man came by with a tray of pills—relaxers and enhancers and different kinds of stimulants. The right elevating component could brighten flavor and become the perfect complement to a meal, I had always heard. Non-addictive. Neurotropic. Personally designed. If you could afford it, why wouldn't you? That was the implicit tenor when these things were presented.

Elii picked two bright blue pills the waiter explained had been manufactured in Fukuoka and would go well with the fresher ingredients on the menu tonight. I struggled with the decision but ultimately went with the yellows, which were supposed to be mildest.

Elii kept her amp-glasses on, and talked very animatedly about the food, which was some fusion of several cultures that I did not understand. At a certain point in the meal, though, it became clear that she was supposed to talk to me about the dead book. The dinner reservation, all of this, came about because she'd received messages from Caliper John.

"I'm actually not sure how he found me," she admitted. "I would've, you know, told him to pound sand, but he said he wanted someone you trusted to give you the number."

"Right." I drank some wine.

"It's a big number."

"Right."

She told me what it was, the offer for my copy of *The Winter Hills*, and it was, in fact, a big number. More than I could earn as a re-writer in a decade.

"I don't feel comfortable, to be honest."

"Selling?"

"Selling to him."

Elii closed her eyes, like she was feeling some pleasant effect of the meal. "Do you have another buyer?" She hummed. "One of those video stores, maybe they have some kind of offer?"

"No. That's not it." I shut my eyes too, feeling dizzier than I expected to feel. "I just don't get the sense that good will come of giving anything to that man. I don't know why."

"Well, he's just a broker. The buyer's someone he knows at Satoshi P—"

"Satoshi Print. Right."

The problem, of course, was that there was no Satoshi Print.

The large man had shown me its information at the diner. There were numerous corroborating sites, reviews, mentions for Satoshi Print I'd found since. But when I went on an early Sunday up to the neighborhood out of a percolating curiosity, just to get a sense of what kind of business this really might be, I found only a half-empty parking lot.

No, there was no Satoshi Print in the physical world to speak of. And if Elii were being honest, I think a part of her already could have guessed it too. This

Caliper John and people like him using digital husks, they were not the type of people who usually meant well.

"I get it." She cleared her throat and tucked her hair behind her ear. "You don't like it. That kind of thing. The smoke and mirrors. Shiny and empty. Even if they paid you upfront—did I say he said he'd pay upfront? Anyway. You still wouldn't take it. Not you. Because you like things solid. Things to hold onto. Like the book. And so, you hold on."

"I guess that's right," I agreed. "Yes. Things like the book. I do prefer to hold on, at least, for a little while. Sure."

"Of course. For a little while." She nodded. "But not in the long run. You don't want to be that kind of person in the long run."

"That kind of person?"

"You know. With too many things. Didn't you say that, about your mother, how she held onto too many things? And you don't, you know, want to be too much like that."

I stopped eating, and Elii seemed surprised. I wasn't angry. I just couldn't remember if I had said that about my mother the other day. It sounded like something I would say, but I just didn't know anymore.

"Listen, I understand," Elii began again delicately. "Right now you've got something of value. Something that feels important. But nothing's all that important, when you get down to it, in the end. Books fall apart. Memories of books fall apart. Nothing is solid or lasts, right? Nothing. Not that and not us."

"No. Not us. That is true."

"So at least with the money—and it's a lot of money—you get to have some fun and enjoy. That's all I see when it comes to this. So long as he pays you first, I say you might as well go for it while there's an offer out there. Why hold onto something you know is going to end up as more nothing eventually anyway?"

Across from us, a couple laughed. The woman bent over and vomited quietly into a little silver pitcher with a lid and daintily wiped her mouth. One of the waiters came by discreetly and picked it up off the floor and took it away. Other customers seemed to have an easier time averting their eyes than I did, familiar with erasing unpleasant things like these.

The enhancers I had taken began to hit their full stride. My head felt like a gigantic bowl, expanding and curving and stretching. The music and dim lighting of the restaurant seemed untranslatable in my brain. But I kept thinking about what Elii said: why hold onto something you know is going to end up as nothing anyway?

Yes, I thought, there was some truth there: why?

At some point, Elii took me from the table and led me somewhere out into the cold with our coats. She said that there was more for the evening, that Caliper John had not just taken care of the dinner, but had set out more for us to see.

We rode together in an automated cab uptown, light flickering and streaming through the pristine plastic windows; then we were in a white marble lobby; then in a gold-colored elevator that was almost as large as my apartment, rising up to the top of a hotel.

Elii had a watch on her wrist that I did not recognize. It was sleek and well-fitting. She used it to swipe us through every scanner and walk-gate we passed in the area. I briefly saw IDs on one of the hotel screens for a "Mr. and Mrs. Uqbar." More digital husks like Satoshi Print, or were they real people, somewhere? I wondered but did not think about it for too long.

There were no employees at the front desk to verify anything. No one kept us from going up to the penthouse suite, so long as Elii's watch kept opening the doors. Each door after the other we just...went on through.

There was too much space between everyone now, and it was too easy to advance like this. That was how Caliper John did the work that he did, I knew. He and others like him, they were people who worked their way through all of this space.

From the suite's living room, I could look out and see much of the lower part of the city, everything unpleasant at a distance, small. This, too, like much of this evening, felt unreal. And I suppose that was part of the point of this, his point, and maybe Elii's point too.

What did any of it matter, if it came and went with so little effort?

"Wait," I said, before Elii's slender arm could reach to turn off the lights. "I just—I just feel a little woozy, and I want to take these off." I touched my amp-glasses and hers. The yellow pills were still spreading through my body like a kind of sickly heat, and I felt like I could almost see through the walls.

Elii did not say anything for a moment.

"Why don't we just—"

"No."

Her face went still.

"No?" I laughed. "But I thought—I didn't really think you would care. Nothing lasts anyway, right? I just want to—"

"No."

In the silence that followed I knew that something had shifted in Elii. She had spoken so glibly before, about the transience of everything. But maybe that was something she'd heard before or been told to say. This, on the other hand, was very much her. This thing she couldn't do, with the glasses, was real, and I could feel it. There was something in this that mattered. Something she could not share.

I was a little surprised, but I think I understood.

I couldn't explain, but I understood.

I told her so, too, before I left the hotel room.

Yes, that was something, for the first time the entire evening, I could understand. A reminder of something similar, in me, that I could not get rid of easily either. There were still real beliefs, in her and in me, that couldn't be reasoned out of existence, no matter what others told us. There were parts of us, still real, and remembering that was good. I needed to remember that. So that was good.

Outside of the lobby and back in the cold, I found that a rising unease had returned. It could have been the yellow pills taking a turn. But no, I could sense it elsewhere, and I was sure. The large man who called himself Caliper John was unhappy with the way things were going, the way I was withdrawing from what he had prepared. I felt again that presence that had been with me over the days and weeks. There, in the delivery drone that buzzed at 6th Avenue. In the red camera ball floating in the department store window. In every mechanized eye between here and the East River and beyond.

I touched the dead book in my coat pocket, its textured surface, and I felt even more certain than before. I had to make my way downtown and across the river, back to Montague Street. Whether the Brotherhood could pay or could not pay for the copy of *The Winter Hills*, I wanted to go to Montague Street with the dead book. They would know better what to do, I thought, because of the care they took with things like this. Better than me, and certainly better than Caliper John.

I swiped my watch at the handle of an automated cab at the curb, but it did not open. *APOLOGIES. A PROCESSING ERROR, MR. UQBAR*, the taxi's window flashed. Over at a store, I tried an ATM, but scrambled data or a bad connection kept me from completing the transaction. *UNABLE TO READ YOUR INFORMATION, MR. UQBAR. SORRY FOR THE INCONVENIENCE.* This was the opposite of what happened earlier in the evening. Someone wanted to show me how quickly these impediments could appear. Just a few changes, and I could not get where I needed to go.

The iron-handed sheriff made sure there was no welcome. No respite. Everything Copper Hawk did was done at the sheriff's instruction, and the rider could feel the town shifting away from him in every direction, no matter where he went.

When I was a boy, my mother and I used to play a game.

This was before the city had fully transitioned into an extended network. She had taught me how to look for the dead spots underneath stationary cams. How, if you could not avoid a stretch with monitors, to cheat your face at an angle so that programs had issues scanning you to completion. She knew that certain brownstones with a specific pre-war style were historic, and therefore adding machinery to their exteriors was not permitted. The alleys between them were best for cutting routes. Certain subways would probably never be fully up to date, because the infrastructure had been done a particular way decades ago and could not be changed without significant cost.

I thought of her, and all of this, when a four-legged police-walker trotted by, stopped, then turned in my direction. Something flickered across its head panel—the pixelated outline of a facial expression. I moved back and away, between two buildings across from the hotel, and down an unmonitored street that led to a service entrance to one of the older underground stations. My mother had shown me this one, years ago, when we had been caught uptown in the rain.

The tunnel below was empty, and I studied the mosaic tiles of one of the walls.

In the dark, a familiar rustle trailed behind me—a sound I realized had followed me long before Caliper John introduced himself at the diner. He'd been watching me since the video store, maybe the library, I realized, though I couldn't say exactly when it began. My mind was only now piecing it together, those hundreds of legs rubbing against translucent wings, the sound of a synthetic, plastic multi-limbed surveillance device, getting swallowed by a rhythmic scraping of metal and rumbling of *klak-klak-klak*ing of an incoming train.

I couldn't see it, that thing, whether it was below the platform or somewhere behind the stairs. But I knew Caliper John was in the remote device, within that little body, controlling and looking out. An empty shell where there was enough space for him to operate.

Flickering light spilled from the moving train windows as it pulled up to the platform, and I could see the lizard-body beginning to lean out from the dark. That face and neck hunching forward, extending itself out from that long shape with its little legs. The face had too many lines. Little seams where plating and pieces were fitted together to look like a person but could not quite pull it off.

The lifeless lens-eyes, like dark little bubbles, fixed on my coat, as though he could see through to the dead book in my pocket. And I could feel Caliper John fixating, so palpable and alien. Alaric had said there were people who despised materials like the dead book because they could not be conveniently compromised or manipulated or remade. I could see it. Caliper John did not want to acquire and preserve *The Winter Hills*. He only wanted to contain or destroy it, if given the chance, and I knew now I could not give him that chance.

I got onto the subway car before that shape could slither out further into the light.

In the rattling, turning, and bumping as the car pulled away from the shadowy station, that long thing withdrawing back to somewhere I could not see, I looked down at my watch, thinking again about how Caliper John had accessed everything within it. I placed it under one of the seats and left the train at the next stop, then got on the local train behind that one instead. It would take longer, but it would not be anywhere near where he'd be watching, I thought.

By the time I got back across the river and up onto the surface, I couldn't feel it anymore—the presence behind me. I clutched the dead book in my coat, and I kept thinking about dropping it through the mail slot of the video store, thinking it was just narrow enough, maybe, to fit its way through that slot.

The rider wanted no fight. But he also knew the sheriff of Copper Hawk knew nothing but. And for people accustomed to using violence, there was never going to be any other way. For them, it was a natural repercussion of moving in the world.

The two men shared a drink together from a bottle, as a courtesy. But the rider took very little. He was afraid of what sharing too much might mean. And he was no longer thinking about the people of Copper Hawk and their troubles, or about the people he'd met out in the flat country. He wasn't even thinking, really, about the blood and gunfire to come. The rider thought only a cold thought.

This might be it.

He had found nothing in the sands or the plains, nothing in the towns or settlements and farms that he'd seen that he could take to heart, and this might be it.

There were fire trucks gathered on Montague Street, splayed at crooked angles and with ladders raised. Men yelled at a deep blackness that barely hid a roaring sound, a rapid whirl of orange light that moved in and out of holes in the crumbling surface of a familiar building, pressing against the cold air like an animal beating against the bars of a cage, something wailed from behind the billows. I stood there on the street with others, knowing it was too late, and it was all gone.

Montague St. Video and everything that had been saved there, burning.

Decoupled and scattered into the smoke and air.

Everything I'd given of my mother to the Brotherhood.

Just smoke and air now.

Nearly all that was left of her, now just smoke and air.

I never saw Alaric after that. Never learned, with certainty, what had happened to the store. The news articles were vague, specifying neither casualties nor cause, though I had my beliefs. Still, somehow, despite the fire, the old man found a way to deliver what he had promised.

There was one last piece of mail from Montague St. Video in the lobby when I got back to my mother's apartment. I didn't know why he hadn't called me to pick it up, or when he had sent it. But it was there. The restored copy of the DVD, just like we'd discussed.

I used my mother's old laptop, one of the only things left in her otherwise empty place, and I watched the file. Not optimized like all the other copies I'd tried to make after she died. Not cleaned up so that I wasn't crying in it. Not edited so that she didn't have those dark circles under her eyes.

My mother looked tired. She had insisted on the getaway to the lake, recording it all, the way she liked to collect things. But she didn't know, in those early days, how to handle me without my father around. I could see the veins in her hands when she applied sunscreen in the video. A cigarette dipped in her lips. She was stretched out on a beach chair, trying to look calm, even though we'd been screaming at each other moments before the camera started going.

Right before she hit record, I had been asking her where dad had gone, why she'd been so mean about him, why he didn't want to come back to us, and she had slapped me.

It was sudden. And without the video, I almost wasn't sure it had happened. But it was there, minutes later, when the camera shifted in her hands and I came into view. I could see it in the aftermath on that little boy's face in the video, in the red almost-welt on my jaw and part of my neck. I recalled the bright sting, the hot tears spilling, no matter how hard I tried to keep them in. All those little things you wouldn't have seen if they'd improved upon the file. I watched her, how she was, exactly as she was back then, on the terrible lonely edge of something. And now, with less resentment, and a tiredness of my own, I felt it all.

The dark circles under her eyes, her hands, my burning face. Nothing lasts, Elii had told me. Nothing lasts, that was true. But I also didn't have to give everything up so effortlessly, the way everyone else did, either. Erasing the bad felt only a step away from erasing the good, and I just didn't have it in me to do that. Especially with the people I loved most of all.

My mother did what she could, and I did what I could, in the years we had together. So I wanted to remember as much as possible, even hurtful things—the oil and acid, the scarves, the games, Lake George. Because I knew I would never remember nearly enough. No number of discs or books or notes or typewriters or boxes sorted through and preserved would capture it all.

I would try, but I would never be able to remember enough.

Before I locked up, I wrote Elii a digital postcard like the ones my aunt used to send, telling her I was leaving the city for a short while. I hoped to see her when I got back. I didn't think we were done talking about what mattered and what was real. I don't think either of us really knew enough yet to know what mattered or was real. But maybe the next time we found one another, we would. Or maybe not. I supposed we would see.

The trip uptown, working my way around the cameras, I kept thinking I saw a large shape, much too big, following me from behind. Something like Caliper John would be there at a park bench, or at a bus stop, but then would be gone. Only able to do so much in the cold brightness of day.

I got to the bus station, cheating my face away from the self-checkout when I bought the ticket. I watched the gray highways rise and the glass disappear behind me. There were fewer cameras in the small neighborhoods and roads out in West Nyack; at a certain point, when I got to walking the main streets, there were none.

From the outside, the Brotherhood video store looked almost identical to its Montague Street counterpart. The color of the frame, the style of window, everything, like it had been plucked out of time. Alaric had said they taught others here. The idea of that, of maybe joining in remembering what was dead drew me to this place, and I kept thinking of a passage toward the end of *The Winter Hills*. The one I'd typed more than any other, from that ending that stayed in my dreams and mixed with memories of Lake George and the heat, the image of the rider slumped on the gray horse, bleeding and delirious as he wandered away from Copper Hawk.

He knew that the world was unspeakably broken and turbulent and ill-formed in its foundations, a violent and material realm, ever coming apart. But he had to believe that the pain and impermanence was a kind of lie. Because there was something buried within him, somewhere, and with it a feeling that even if he were to disappear some fragment would echo beyond this time and place. Yes, he told himself. They could take everything substantive from him, but not that. They would get many things from him, but they would never get that.

I stepped into the store and put down my bags. I could hear the slight clunk of my mother's Trapwood inside hitting the floor. I clutched that gold-laden dead book in my hands and walked to the counter, where an old man looked up at me.

He did not seem at all surprised.

"Come on in," he said. "Let's see what you've got."

Thomas Ha is a Nebula, Ignyte, Locus, and Shirley Jackson Award-nominated writer of speculative short fiction. You can find his work in *Clarkesworld, Lightspeed Magazine*, *Beneath Ceaseless Skies*, and *Weird Horror Magazine*, among other publications. His work has also appeared in *The Best American Science Fiction & Fantasy* and *The Year's Best Dark Fantasy & Horror*. Thomas grew up in Honolulu and, after a decade plus of living in the northeast, now resides in Los Angeles with his wife and three children.

WHAT ANY DEAD THING WANTS

Aimee Ogden

The third week of a planetary exorcism is the hardest—at least if the planet in question has megafauna to deal with. Enthusiasm wanes even faster on worlds that never evolved past microbes. Hob's crew always comes in like a team of intrepid explorers, swapping stories with the outgoing terraforming crew as they run down the handover checklist. But after ten, fifteen days, the work slows down, as the crew moves farther from the terraforming origin nexus. That's where the ghosts are densest, the hauntings the most intense. Along the meridian lines that the crew follows around the planet to the secondary terraforming nexus, only the most stubborn haunts linger—the ones that won't clear out at just the first reminder of their own recent mortality. The ones that don't seem to give a shit that Hob and his crew are working to a strict deadline. Exo megafauna have, unsurprisingly, absolutely no sense of human decency.

And of course Hob, as team captain, gets stuck with the stubbornest beasties of all. "Got one," shouts Maseley over the comm, and Hob winces. They're obliged to wear suits out here along the meridian, where the vestiges of the pre-transformed world remain, albeit with open visors to let them breathe the brand-new, thaumaturgically generated, human-friendly atmosphere. Still, Maseley yells through the grove of old-growth trees to Hob instead of talking to the suit comm that's right next to his twice-damned mouth. "It's another of these cabbage-faced motherfuckers."

Shit, thinks Hob, but he keeps that unhelpful thought to himself. They're running behind on this job as it is, and the last thing anyone needs is to suspect the boss is cracking under the pressure. "Got it, Maze. Flag it and keep moving. I'll take a look."

He moves off in the direction of Maseley's map marker as soon as it drops into his visual overlay. Soon he's forced to leave behind the yellow-white light of the G3-type star that wanders bloatedly across the sky, in favor of the shade of a grove of trees. The grove is unusually quiet, only a few brave birds gossiping back and forth, the vanguard of earthly fauna seeded here by the skilled thaumaturgists on the terraforming team. Usually there are more of them, little mammals too (whose species Hob can't remember), flitting from tree to tree and chattering irritably and shaking the branches. Most of them make themselves scarce when a haunt passes through, though.

The grove has a certain sameness that bothers him. The regularity of the placement, the symmetry of the branches—it looks like the terraforming team took a basic flora incantation and rubber-stamped it all over the area without the least effort to differentiate one tree from the next.

He lifts a hand and half-heartedly taps into the source—it's all the *same* source, whether you're creating life or banishing it, and it's not like the Process audits are going to catch a little unauthorized application of thaumaturgy. Tongue between his teeth, Hob concentrates on a minor incantation, *growth* threaded through with an urge toward *chaos*. After a moment, new branches unfurl, new leaves mutter in the wind. Probably no one but Hob would notice the way that the edge has been taken off the grove's unnatural conformity, but it's the principle of the thing.

Principles. Right. Such as, perhaps, doing the job you're getting paid to do and handling yet another CFM haunt. Stubborn-ass beasties. The survey crew that preceded the terraforming event would have documented this flavor of megafauna, collected and stored a few representative specimens at one affiliated research institution or another. You never know, after all, if the resident microbial mat of Planet Terraformed-Out-Of-Existence produces the miracle molecule that'll cure blister-lung, or metabolize bionatriline faster than it can accumulate in topsoil, or whatever. At some point, researchers will assign the species a proper scientific name. As far as the exorcist crew is concerned, though, they're just cabbage-faced motherfuckers. Or CFMs when they're feeling lazy.

Cabbage-faced motherfucker is somewhat euphemistic, though. Nothing about them even vaguely suggests what humans would think of as a face. The globular organs appended at irregular intervals along their fat, toroid bodies do, however, write *cabbage* in bold font. Hob doesn't spot the CFM in question, but he does find tracks in the soil and some deep scratches in the bark of a tree near Maseley's marker. Ghosts experiencing intense responses—anger, fear, confusion—can exert some influence on objects in their environment. Responses like that can be enough to trigger acceptance, or understanding, at whatever level exolife can comprehend: *Oh gosh, would you look at that, I'm a dead cabbage-faced motherfucker!*

It's a good sign, and a bad one. Acceptance is the only way to permanently clear a haunt. On the other hand, Hob himself very much counts as an "object in their environment." The terraforming team has already been through, wiping away poisonous atmosphere and clouds of unfriendly microbes, but there's still a reason he wears this protective suit.

The tracks peter out a few meters deeper into the trees. Hob doesn't see any movement beyond the wind riffling through the leaves overhead (his ocular overlay tells him these trees are chestnuts). Not a single glimmer of ghostlight.

He takes some time to explore outward from the marker, but he doesn't find any more tracks, nor any further damage to the grove. His educated guess is that there's only the one CFM left in this area. Pair-bonded fauna are more likely to wind up in a co-haunt situation, anyway, and according to the info in the survey team compendium, CFMs exhibited mostly solitary behavior outside of a prolonged parental-care stage for newly hatched spawn.

It's enough recon for now; he doesn't have time today to set up the incantations that a full megafauna exorcism will demand. He adds notes to the marker and trudges on in the direction the rest of the group has moved. A black and white bird scolds him noisily, and he walks faster, feeling appropriately chastened. This sector isn't going to clear itself, after all.

After a few dull but productive hours of exorcising alien microorganisms, Hob is ready to call it a day. (Microorganisms are *so* easy. Show a microbe a substrate it can sense but not digest, and it's immediate game over. Like, its only job is eating and reproducing, take that away and *bam*. It's not as if single-celled wannabe bacteria have a lot to live for.) He's the last member of the team to report back to the modular habitat that they currently call home; the others have been trudging in on foot or trundling up in their fleet of transports for the past hour. There's no airlock, not like on terraforming dome habitats, so before Hob can even step inside, he can hear Maseley and Yettal in the mess, arguing over whose turn it is to prep dinner. "It's Yettal's turn," Hob shouts, tossing his helmet ahead of him into the locker room. "It's on the goddamn duty roster, Yetz, does it have to go down like this *every single rotation?*"

Then of course they mob him by the suit lockers, because Yettal has to lay out her whole rationale. Something about swapping turns on transport maintenance last rotation, although it's hard to follow her logic when Maseley interrupts every other word. Hob absolutely cannot muster up a single shit to give, but Maseley and Yettal are so occupied with each other they don't seem to notice.

They both jump when Jaara's voice booms out behind them. So does Hob, for that matter, but he doesn't think they notice. "Flip a fucking coin or something, you two," Jaara barks. "Your petty squabbles are not Hob's problem." She produces a tablet with an eye-crossing spreadsheet arrayed across the screen, as Yettal and Maseley retreat to the margins of the locker room. "Can I borrow you for a moment, boss?"

"Yeah, of course." He glances at Maseley and Yettal, and turns his shoulder toward them to hang up his suit. It's not that he's trying to be dismissive, it's just that they're being annoying as all hell. "See you both at dinner in a few."

Once they've slunk away, he takes the tablet from Jaara and flicks two fingers over the screen, zooming out to a less migraine-inducing resolution. It's not like he needs to read the actual numbers to know where they stand; Jaara *lives* for color-coding and the spreadsheet is a screaming eyesore of yellow, orange, and pink. "None of our metrics are in the red yet. That's something."

"It might be something if this was a routine colonization." Jaara shoves her hair out of her face for a better view of the tablet, as if she doesn't have every row and column committed to memory. She had gray hairs before this particular job, but they've gotten more noticeable, silver spangles in the undergrowth of her severe side-shave. "Zetharin's days are numbered. If this place isn't cleared in time—"

"It'll be cleared." Almost unconsciously, Hob pulls up the most recent news pull in his visual sidebar and scrolls to coverage of the poor, doomed planet in question. The exact nature of the thaumaturgical experiment that disturbed Zetharin's orbit escapes him—partly because orbital astrology isn't his field, and partly because the official reports have been purposely vague so that no one else can attempt the devastating effort to modify a planet's orbit. But any layman could interpret the effects. Temperatures are dropping, crops are failing, energy sources can't keep up with the increased demand for light and heat. Zetharin is a dead planet spinning; Hob has to clean up "Zetharin 2" well enough that a review team deems it safe for human habitation. "We can always jump ahead to the secondary nexus if we need to, and backtrack..."

"Sure." Jaara takes the tablet back and glares at it. If you could change metrics by sheer force of will, they'd be comfortably in the green by now. "The company loves it when we deviate from Process."

"Could be worse." He nods toward the door, and toward the smell of questionably prepared mealmix. "You worked the Kadecur job, didn't you?"

A notoriously messy terraformation. She winces, acknowledging the hit, and follows him to the mess. It's barely big enough for all of them, twelve chairs packed around a pair of flimsy tables in a square that's two meters on a side at most, a daily appetizer course of jostled elbows and accidental footsies. Hob and Jaara squeeze into the last two empty seats, a small bastion of quiet amid the chaos. They both abstain from the traditional mockery of Yettal and Maseley's culinary prowess: Hob because he's the boss, Jaara because she's Jaara.

"Looks good," he says diplomatically, when Maseley unloads a tray of mealmix portions in front of him. Maseley rolls his eyes, so Hob adds: "Better than it smells, anyway." What's the point of being the boss, really, if you can't get a good one in now and then?

It's the third night in a row eating the same variety of mealmix—someone did a shit job setting up the supply cabinets before takeoff, and Hob suspects it may have been him—and he tucks in without enthusiasm. Before he gets past the first bite, though, someone's standing over him. It's Rathana, his hair wet from the showers.

"Uh," says Rathana, looking over the full mess. "Who the fuck is in my seat?"

Whatever routine joviality had been on hand in the mess, it falls away now. Hob's gaze rivets to the seat wedged into the far corner—to the guy in a nondescript jumpsuit, whose braided-back black hair and beaky nose bear only superficial resemblance to Rathana's.

"Hi," says the stranger apologetically. "Sorry for showing up uninvited." Embarrassed under the sudden flood of attention, he goes to nudge the spoon sitting in the portion of mealmix in front of him, but his hand passes straight through. "But I think I'm dead."

Nothing in Process covers what to do if a dead human being waltzes into your exorcism site, because why the fuck would it? Still, while he waits for a reply from HQ on the subspace comm, Hob leaves Jaara to manage the rest of the crew and spends an hour searching and double-checking the handbook. No one terraforms a world already inhabited by humans—that's the whole *point* of terraforming.

The ghost, who has followed him to his quarters, watches with interest while Hob panic-scrolls. "What are you looking at?" he asks, inspecting the various jumpsuits and socks and underwear crammed into Hob's cubby. He speaks Standard Spanglorin with the fluidity of long practice, and Hob can't place his accent from its crisp plosives and not-quite-suppressed uvular trill. There are as many human languages as there are settled worlds—quite a lot more than that, actually—and trying to nail one down without a few more clues is a loser's game. "If you're reading to relax, I don't think it's working."

Hob pages into the part that covers the reasons that a Process Investigator might be required, then skips ahead to the next section marker. "I am not reading to relax."

"Okay." The ghost cranes his neck to look at the handbook over Hob's shoulder. "Maybe you should try that, then."

The tablet chimes, and Hob swipes away the handbook to read the message from HQ. No salutation, no advice, no assigned Process Investigator (not yet, at least). *Additional information requested before proceeding. Is the haunt a deceased terraformer?*

When Hob looks up from the tablet, the ghost is studying Hob's private stash where it protrudes from the bottom of his cubby. "Are those Arjali buttersweets?" he asks with interest. It's a small mercy that Hob's pornography collection is tucked away under a layer of emergency snacks. "Damn. I haven't had one in *years.*"

"Help yourself," says Hob. A pathetic effort at exorcism, really, and one that only earns him an unimpressed look from the ghost. "Sorry. Uh. I have to ask: Were you one of the terraformers assigned here?"

The ghost's face scrunches thoughtfully as he plants himself next to Hob on the bunk. "What answer are you hoping to hear?"

"No. I think."

"Oh." A shrug. "That's too bad. I was."

Hob squints. "Okay. Explain how to calculate the optimal number of meridians for full planetary coverage."

The ghost makes a deflating noise. "That's not fair," he complains. "I didn't know *you* were a terraformer. Isn't this an exorcist crew?"

"It is. And I'm not." Anymore. Hob keys into his tablet: *Haunt is not an exorcist.* Before sending this fragment of information, he glances sideways at the ghost's implacable face. "How did you get here, then? If you're not a terraformer?"

"I crashed." A ghostly finger gestures at the tablet. "Pretty sure that's also how I died, if that's helpful for your bosses to know."

"The company wouldn't have authorized any other spacecraft to be in this system until the terraformation was done."

"Oh, no. By all the Thousand Gods of our ancient home," says the ghost, without the least inflection, "I would hate to think I'd died doing something the company hadn't authorized." And he flickers out like a tablet screen gone dark.

Hob adds to his message: *Victim of crash (craft origin currently unknown). Please advise.*

Staring at the subspace comm does not, unfortunately, make the messages travel any faster. Nor does it make them any more helpful when they finally do arrive: *Unauthorized entry is a forfeiture of legal standing in-system. Continue with exorcism as planned.*

Hob would continue staring at the delivered instructions, hoping his tired eyes were playing tricks on him, but he's all stared out. He keys in a few simple requests to the system while he's here, basic boss-guy shit: running a projection for sector clearance time, sending out a couple of recon drones. Then, tablet in hand, he wanders back to the mess, where only Jaara remains, watching the doorway. If he hadn't expected her to be here waiting for him, with the whole Process handbook behind her eyes, he would already be melting down. In a boss-like fashion, of course.

But Jaara will know what to do. "Which Process Investigator are they sending?" she asks, as he hesitates in the doorway. The mealmix in front of her has been cut into precise quarters, exactly three of which have been eaten.

"None of them." Hob shrugs, somewhat more pathetically than behooves the lead exorcism specialist on this assignment. "The higher-ups are saying that this doesn't change anything. 'Continue with exorcism as planned.'"

He waits for her to remind him that that's crazy, that's ridiculous. Because they both know it is! No one here signed up to exorcise a *human being.* Certainly no one has trained for that kind of thing. There should be Process for this, there should be someone coming in to look into how a random guy not only ended up on a world mid-exorcism but ended up there as a corpse. If Jaara can just look him in the eye and say, in her own way, *what the fuck, Hob, we can't just exorcise a whole person,* he'll turn around and get back on the subspace comm and demand someone (he doesn't care who) do something (he doesn't care what) to figure out what happened here; and if she added *this flies in the face of Process page 103 paragraph 4 line E,* that would help a lot too.

But Jaara doesn't quote Process at him. "Okay," she says, which is not what she's supposed to say, because she's supposed to be better than Hob, and not just at Process. "So. Who's going to handle the dead guy?"

"Well," says the dead guy himself, from behind Hob. "I like to think I'm pretty self-sufficient."

Exhaustion does Hob the small favor of suppressing his startle reflex. "I've got to take care of that cabbage-faced motherfucker—"

"Wow." The dead guy makes an aggrieved noise in his throat. "My *name* is Ozzi. Not that any of you asked."

"—so I can handle our new friend here too, while I stay on site. No reason for the rest of you to hang behind; we're cutting the margins close enough as it is." If he didn't know Jaara as well as he did, he might have missed the minute relaxation of the lines in her face. "You're in charge of the others till I catch back up."

"Okay, boss." What Jaara means is *no shit, boss.* Imagine Maseley taking the lead. The rest of her mealmix disappears into her mouth in one, two, three bites. Before she clears out of the mess with her empty tray in hand, she adds: "Good luck."

"Nice to meet you," calls the dead guy—Ozzi, that is, assuming he's been more truthful about his name than about his work history—before throwing his translucent hands in the air. "Oh, damn, I didn't ask for her name either. Or yours. Because I'm definitely not calling you 'boss.'"

The next sector scheduled for clearance—the next seventy miles along the meridian—is still accessible from the modular habitat, so it stays behind for now when the crew leaves Hob behind. He waves the truck fleet off before setting out on foot toward the chestnut grove.

No sign of their new pal Ozzi yet today. Hob woke once in the middle of the night, certain he would find a ghostlight-bright body looming over him, but his compartment had been empty except for himself and the nearly corporeal scent of some unwashed socks. Exorcising exolife has never been a cushy gig, but at least he didn't use to worry about a haunt following him home.

Without the human ghost on hand, he has some time to deal with the CFM problem. He takes his compendium out of its padded pocket and flicks the stylus over the screen. A cataloged list scrolls past, flora and fauna of all kinds, filtered and sorted by their current location. The fruits of the survey team's labors, and the fodder for Hob's job now. Previous interactions with the CFMs have shown them to be a scavenger species, which simplifies his task now. He selects a thumbnail of a different species of megafauna from the compendium, studies it for a moment, and steps back.

The illusion that he generates looks just like the picture in the compendium; he hasn't bothered to modify it from the base model. It's sort of crescent-shaped, the hump of its back reaching higher than its shoulder. Its lacquered-looking scales catch and refract the meager light under the chestnut canopy, with hundreds of small, knobby, leafy protrusions poking up in between. The crew calls these things "battle slugs," probably because "gemmiferous sprout-faced mother-fuckers" is too much of a mouthful. Also no one but Hob knows that gemmiferous refers to sprouts, which are sort of like miniature cabbages; and Hob only knows because he specially sent a data request on the out-of-system relay. That's what dedication to one's craft looks like, baby.

No reason to take the time to animate shallow trembles in the leafy knobs or a ripple over the shiny scales—that kind of artistry is wasted on a CFM that would have eaten dead prey just as happily as live. It looks like a dead battle slug. It smells like one, or as close to one as he can make it based on the chemical signatures noted in the compendium. That's going to have to be good enough.

There'd been a time when Hob wouldn't have illusioned up a single blade of grass without that kind of eye to detail. That time ended roughly somewhere between earning his certificate in technical thaumaturgy and his first day on an exorcism campaign.

"Come and get it," he calls, on the breathtakingly small chance that a) the CFM's cabbage-y sense organs are tuned to the frequency range of human speech, and b) it understands a language resembling Standard Spanglorin. He feels like he has to say *something* when he attempts an exorcism, and he can't think of anything with the right amount of gravitas right now.

A few of the chestnut trees have low-slung branches that let him get a foot-hold and climb higher, even in the cumbersome suit—some terraformer's idea of a playground for kids from the settlement planned for nearby, maybe. Either way, he's clear by the time the CFM comes snuffling-whuffling along, a lumpy yellow donut wriggling in wide sweeping arcs around the grove as it centers in on Hob and his illusion. There *are* haunts with less efficient movement patterns, but there sure aren't many.

It's probably just as well he didn't spend much time on the details, because the cabbage-faced motherfucker's cabbages don't appear to be feeding it much in the way of visual data. It rotates ungracefully through the trunks of several trees as if they aren't even there. Stupid CFM doesn't know: *it's* the only thing that isn't even there.

Only when it approaches the make-believe battle slug corpse does it pause in its ineffectively circuitous route to investigate. A few cabbages unfurl, the leafy appendages on the outside slackening and pulsing unpleasantly as it...tastes?...the air. It must like what it finds, because the skirtlike flaps at the bottom of the toroid lift, and it tries to envelop the battle slug in its prehensile stomach.

It doesn't work, of course. That's the whole point of the exercise. The CFM vibrates in distress, a painfully high-pitched frequency that Hob's suit quickly blocks. It knocks around a few times, rebounding off tree trunks as it gropes for the delectable dinner that remains outside its reach. It's mad enough to become corporeal; that's promising. *Come on,* Hob urges silently, as he watches its hide flush green and orange in a patchy, bruised-looking pattern. *Figure it out and go to haunt hell already.*

"That's the first exo I've ever seen in person," says Ozzi.

Hob leans back, looking for the ghost. Sure enough, telltale ghostlight surrounds a human shape on the branch above him—but as he swings his head around, he overbalances himself. Gravity's hand seizes him by the collar and gives him a good yank. His grasping fingers strip slender chestnut branches of their leaves as they slide through his fingers and then he's in the air.

The fall is shockingly brief; his shoulders bounce off a solid branch and he hits the ground on all fours. Right on the spot where his own illusion is even now dissipating, as his concentration fragments.

The CFM shrieks in outrage, its toroid rippling in circular waves. Although it's not intelligent enough to recognize Hob as the architect of its untouchable meal, it's not so brainless that it can't at least spot a convenient target for its current rage. It whips around into Hob, sending him flying. Branches break—unless those snapping sounds are bones—as he crashes face-first into a stand of younger chestnuts.

Dazed, he thrashes around: for a weapon, a hiding place, a tree that's climbable in his current state. But the CFM is already on top of him, cabbages pulsing. Its stomach peeks out of its maw, then retracts back in. Hob must not smell like dinner. With one last squeal of ear-piercing disdain, it turns and slinks off into the trees.

"Oh my god. Oh my *god*." The shape that looms in his vision sheds more light than it blocks. When Hob's vision clears, the shape resolves into Ozzi's shocked face. His eyes glitter with more than ghostlight; Hob wonders if a haunt can cry real tears. "Are you okay? What can I do? I can go find the others—"

"Fuck," says Hob, more as punctuation than a response to the fall. Exorcism is rarely as easy as that, anyway. He gets up off the ground carefully, checking for injuries. Bruises, minor cuts, scraped knees; his left wrist is sore, but not, he thinks, broken or sprained. He dusts off his suit. "I guess there's a reason they make us wear these things."

"I'm so sorry." Ozzi hovers a short distance away, within arm's reach, if his arms could actually reach anything. "I'm not any happier about the situation than you are. Probably less. But I wasn't trying to get you *killed*."

"Well, you didn't. So no harm done." Reaching for his compendium pocket, Hob's wrist twists unpleasantly, and he winces. "Not much harm done."

At least the compendium landed in better shape than he did; the last thing Hob needs is to have replacement equipment fees levied against his paycheck. While he flicks up and down the entries related to CFMs, Ozzi peers over his shoulder. "I didn't know they could still...*do* things," he says, and gestures vaguely with both hands, flexing his fingers. "Touch things."

"Mostly they can't. Only when they're experiencing strong emotional activation." Hob chews on his tongue, lingering over the entry on CFM mating behaviors. His next attempt at exorcising this exo haunt will require a little more effort than a half-assed illusion of dinner.

A swath of ghostlight cuts between him and the compendium. "Hyah!" yells Ozzi, then steps back shamefacedly when his arm passes harmlessly through Hob's hand. "Okay. Sure. Stronger emotional activation than that. Got it."

"Eh, you're new at this exorcism thing." Hob jams his compendium back into his pocket, making sure to zip the padded pouch closed around it. "You'll get the hang of it."

"Can't wait." Though Ozzi says it with the cadence of a joke, a frown flits over his face before he yanks a lopsided grin back into place. "Got as much time as I need to improve, now."

Maybe knowing a little more about Process will help shuffle things along, or maybe it'll just get in the way. Hob creates a mental compendium entry for his human haunt and starts entering data: *Thirty to forty years old at time of death. Occupation unknown. Business in-system unknown. Doesn't like the idea of exorcism. Got upset when he thought he'd harmed a human being (me).*

With that limited data entered, he makes a decision. "The emotional activation is the key." It sounds almost like a confession. A conciliatory gesture, grudgingly offered. "That's what lets a haunt finally break through to acceptance." Before Ozzi can verbally process that, Hob adds: "I'm done out here today." He jerks one shoulder in the direction of the modular habitat. "You coming back to base with me?"

He doesn't have a plan yet on how to get Ozzi out of here. Not yet. But he has a plan on how to *make* a plan.

When Ozzi hesitates, Hob shrugs his understanding and sets off on his own. But as soon as he starts moving, Ozzi calls after him: "Fine. But only because you're a better conversationalist than that exo." When Hob looks over his shoulder, Ozzi drifts in his wake, slipping through shadows and tree trunks with equal ease. "The name 'cabbage-faced motherfucker' makes a lot more sense now, by the way."

Quiet is a rare commodity in the habitat. Hob takes a moment to bask in it after he's shucked his suit into the first empty locker. A friendly electronic hum— from the air circulation fans, the water recycling system, the pair of cleaning drones—takes the edge off the silence. As does the occasional scuffle from the ever-expanding family of field mice that's made a home under the northwest solar array. Hob really does need to take care of that too, at some point: another little undesired exorcism.

A few kinks linger in his back, all the muscles that clenched up in anticipation of his fall, which haven't figured out yet that they can let go. While he massages the sore spot over his hips as best as he can reach it, he pulls up the latest download packet from HQ and flicks through it. Blink, a pay stub deposited in his account. Blink, the smiling faces of the latest set of new hires, terraformers and exorcists alike. Blink, a sample serving of news headlines. A blurb about rapid changes in Zethari weather patterns careens past him, and he double-blinks to dismiss the rest of the packet before the news has another chance to leave a mark.

After a series of stretches and matching grunts (his toes are farther away than they used to be), he shoves his feet into his module shoes and stands back up. "I'm going to warm up a mealmix," he says, and hesitates. "Sorry I can't offer you anything. This situation sucks for both of us—but mostly for you." He scratches the back of his head as if he's speculating on the fly. "Are there...do you have people somewhere? Someone you'd want to send a posthumous message to?"

Ozzi trips over his own insubstantial feet, which is quite an accomplishment when you think about it. "A message?" he repeats, following Hob into the galley. "To let them know where I—how I—oh." His eyes narrow. "Oh, nice try, though. I thought maybe you'd start by offering me some holographic injera and doro wat."

"They're not holograms. They're illusions. We tap into the same source that any thaumaturgist does. Exorcists, terraformers, cosmological augurs." Someone (Maseley) has left the pantry door ajar; Hob replaces the mealmix boxes into neater rows as he rummages around for the shrimp-flavored packages that no one else likes. Jaara complains that they don't actually taste like shrimp, which is one hundred percent correct, but whatever they *do* taste like is delicious. "I'm not trying to sneak one past you. I already explained how it works." He's been told he has a reassuring voice. That's why he's mission boss, probably. You need someone who can say whatever shit you need him to say and make it sound true. "I mean, if you think you can keep yourself calm, you can dictate a message saying whatever you want, and I'll send it to whoever you want."

Add water, add extra salt and pepper and a packet of chili sauce, put it in the heater, wait. Ozzi phases in and out of his sight a few times while Hob waits, tapping a fork against the countertop. The heater dings; Hob opens the door and gingerly removes the hot mealmix, peeling back the lid to let eau de not-quite-shrimp waft out into the otherwise empty galley.

He's picked his way through about half of the mealmix when Ozzi drifts back into quasi-existence opposite him at the table. "No," he says slowly, as if he wasn't sure what he was going to say until he opened his mouth. "No, I don't have people. No one who wouldn't be more upset to hear from me again than not to."

Hob swallows a mouthful of room-temperature printed protein. "Sounds complicated."

"It is." Ozzi's head tilts, and he swipes a finger through the soggy vegetables dangling from Hob's fork. The finger passes through un-shrimped, and he makes a weird face that Hob can't interpret. With CFMs and battle slugs, he doesn't have to scrutinize the expression beneath the ghostlight glow to guess how the beasties are feeling. "How about you? Do *you* have people?"

"Nah." Hob anoints a wad of noodles with the last sauce puddled in the corner of the mealmix packet. "Not anymore."

"Sounds complicated."

"About as simple as it gets, actually." In Ozzi's patience silence, Hob's chewing sounds obnoxiously loud. He pushes the noodles into his cheek to say around them: "My parents were old. No siblings. Not married, not seeing anyone—they wouldn't see much of me anyway, if I was. I don't really keep in touch with the folks from my old job, and they don't keep in touch with me." He drops his spoon into his empty-enough mealmix and stands. "Except Jaara, I guess. We weren't on the same squad back then. And she's stuck here with me anyway."

When he heads to the galley to throw away the packet and toss his spoon into the wash bin, Ozzi follows him—albeit through the wall instead of the doorway. "Sounds pretty fucking depressing if you ask me," he says seriously, while the bottom half of his face is occupied by a shelf of beverage pods.

"That hits hard coming from a dead guy."

Ozzi makes a deflating sound, sort of like a belly laugh that got round-house-kicked halfway through. "Jatya!" he swears (or at least it sounds like a swear to Hob, who has a working vocabulary of swear words that borrows from five or six different localects and languages). "I thought we were having a moment here." A ginger attempt at a slap passes harmlessly through the side of Hob's head. "Then you had to go bring up the whole dead-guy thing again."

"Damn." Hob dumps the rest of his mealmix unceremoniously into the bio-composter and leans his arms on top of it. "I guess that means we're still a ways out from acceptance."

They swap half-hearted smiles, and Ozzi dissipates like morning fog. Hob hangs on to the smile for a moment, staring into the empty space. Then he dusts his hands off on his pants and pulls up a side-tab for the compendium in his visual overlay. With the images and notes as a guide, he starts putting together a new illusion, from the bones up. This one has to walk the walk more convincingly than his poor battle slug carcass.

Every now and then, he flicks over to Jaara's metric files. Orange, yellow, 250 kilometers per day, yellow, 87% first-attempt clearance rate, orange. The colors don't change, of course, nor do the numbers underneath. But he can't stop checking anyway.

The next morning, Hob stands alone in the shadow of his own personal module detachment, waving. No sign of the ghost yet today, which means he can claim this spare moment to see off the rest of the crew—and the rest of the habitat. Dozens of smaller modules school around the big central unit as it trundles over the open plain along the meridian. "Let us know if you need anything, boss," says Yettal's voice, in Hob's ear. "Or if you think you're starting to go crazy being out here with only haunts for company."

"Dumbass," hollers Maseley, "how's he gonna *know* if he's going crazy?"

A crackle of static precedes Jaara's appropriate-volume command to keep the comm clear. They're her problem now, and Hob only manages to work up a little guilt over that.

When he turns back to his module, a little yellow notification circle starts blinking in the bottom left corner of his overlay. One of his recon drones has identified a site as worth investigating.

"It's not going to investigate itself," he says, to no one, which is also who he has to convince that his illusion mock-up work-in-progress can wait. On foot, foregoing his protective suit in favor of a little extra mobility, he sets out into a pastel yellow morning.

The site is a few kilometers off the meridian, down a ravine that slouches through a section of the forest where the chestnut trees are gradually overtaken by some other species, slim white-trunked trees with dozens of eye-shaped black patches: silent watchers tracking Hob's progress. They're so spooky-looking that he has to wonder if they're actually an Earth tree and not a remarkably staunch haunt—which should be impossible anywhere other than along the meridian. But it wouldn't be the first impossible thing to happen to him this week, so he double-checks his compendium. "Birch?" he reads incredulously. In the localect he grew up speaking, the word is an egregious insult: a leech, a saboteur, someone who acts in selfish interest to the detriment of the habitat.

"Are you talking to me?" The haunt—Ozzi—falls into step alongside Hob without missing a beat. "Or yourself? Or another, secret, third person?"

Ozzi's...wispier than usual, a clot of mist that vaguely suggests a person. An ex-person. "You look like shit," observes Hob, "even for a dead guy."

"Well, we're pretty far off the, what do you call it, meridian." Ozzi pulses, the shape of a shrug. "But I didn't want you to get lonely."

It's not uncommon for a haunt to attach itself to an exorcist, follow it around until it can be safely dismissed, but usually exorcists hang pretty close to the meridian themselves. Such an activity might loosen Ozzi's tentative grip on the afterlife; Hob weighs whether or not he should bring that up and finds staying silent to be the heavier option.

"So?" Ozzi prompts, for want of a response from Hob. "What's the deal? Taking a day off? Mental health walk in the woods?"

"Afraid not." They emerge from the birches at the top of the ravine on Hob's map. Below, a scabby black line cuts diagonally across the creek at the bottom of the slope. Dark wings flare to either side, a pattern of leafless once-white trunks that have burnt to a dark, ashy gray. At the terminus point of the line lies a hunk of wreckage, blackened at one end and stained metal at the other. A ship. Or the haunt of one, maybe. "Look familiar?"

"Oh—no." A breeze sends ripples through Ozzi, and Hob loses sight of him altogether for a moment. "I remember it better *before* it was on fire."

They make their way down the side of the ravine: Hob picking his way carefully over dew-slick rocks and steep leaf-littered slopes, Ozzi glittering vaguely in his wake. At the bottom, Hob walks a wide circle around the wreck itself. He can make out the last few digits of the ship's registration number, which he subvocalizes to record in his notes. Whatever the ship's name was, the paint there has peeled unreadably away in the heat from the fire.

"Small," he says. "Couldn't have been more than four or five of you on board. So that rules out one of my theories."

Ozzi, no longer beholden to the same laws of gravity as Hob, floats upward without responding. The sunlight that breaks through the canopy refracts at the suggestion of his misty shape, and Hob has to squint to see him. For want of a better idea, he keeps expanding on those defunct theories. "My first thought was a squatter ship. Dump in a load of your own colonists before anyone's paying attention, claim a chunk of freshly terraformed land, hope no one notices until you can get some sympathetic news coverage."

He speaks louder as Ozzi drifts around the curve of the ship's hull. "Then again, I thought, maybe a thrill-seeker. We get a heads-up from HQ about those, once in a while. How close can we fly to the terraforming origin without getting wiped out of existence, ooh isn't that fun; let's race the meridians to the secondary nexus, this is a very good idea that has definitely never gotten anyone killed."

Ozzi hasn't made it back around the hull yet, so Hob follows in the direction he went. The haunt is, well, haunting the part of the ship where—Hob thinks—the cockpit would have been. "But you don't fit the profile for that," he goes on. Ozzi twitches, shrinking by a few centimeters. "Usually they're either dumb kids or dumb old people who have outlived all the fucks they had to give. Which really only leaves one possibility."

"Oh yeah?" says Ozzi. "And what's that?"

"You and your crew were symps."

A laugh ripples Ozzi's outline. "Symps."

"Exo-sympathizers," Hob amends, and racks his brain. There are half a dozen groups, each with its own self-aggrandizing title for itself. "You're with Sparrowfall, or the Hundred Thousand Suns, or—"

"You should just stick with symps." Ozzi's voice has lost its usual coat of cheerfulness. What's underneath slices ice-cold into Hob. There are tender points even a protective suit wouldn't cover. "It's more honest. Excuse me a second."

The ship's hull shimmers once as Ozzi slides through it. Through the pitted wounds in the hull, Hob can hear him muttering to himself. He can't make much out—the distance aside, Ozzi doesn't seem to be speaking Spanglorin—but curse words have a certain texture that transcends language barriers.

While he waits for Ozzi to peter out, he picks his way around the wreck for a second, closer look. The front is in pretty bad shape, but the top looks more or less intact. Well. In a better state than he'd honestly expected. If he had the right safety equipment, he could probably get in through the wounds in the front of the ship and check out the rest.

A ferocious clang echoes inside the ship, scaring away the rest of his coherent thoughts. It's followed up by Ozzi's shout: a distinct Spanglorin "Fuck!"

Hob waits. It's another couple minutes before Ozzi coalesces beside him; might be he lost his ability to hold on to his haunt-self after he failed at whatever it was he was doing in the ship. "Anything I can help with?" Hob asks mildly. "Being in possession of actual physical hands as I am."

"No."

They stand (and float) in contemplative silence. When Hob risks sidelong scrutiny of Ozzi's expression, there's not much there to see. Drifting, detached. Grief wakes an anger in some people, gets their fists up, starts them swinging. With others, grief books them a one-way ticket to a destination far from the immediacy of pain. With what he's seen of Ozzi so far, Hob would have marked him as the first type, but both *fight* and *flight* tend to dig down to a deeper level than what most people display on the home screen of their personality.

Well, what the hell; he decides to take a chance. "I could've respected squatters," he says, and heaves a sigh. "The survivors of Caloteru IV, or the folks left behind in the Trei Belt after the iridium interests dug everything dry? There's no one looking out for those people."

Ozzi's expression solidifies into incredulity. "No one's looking out for exos, either. Not the ones that got mowed under to make room for New Bania, or Syfonica—certainly not the ones you casually deleted to make room for Zetharin—oh." His voice, which had been gaining in volume and intensity, returns to conversational tones as he takes in Hob's poorly hidden smirk. "Was that the laziest ever attempt to exorcise me the fuck out of your life?"

"Pfft. No. I could have kept egging you on *way* longer if I was trying to get rid of you." Hob nods his head toward the wrecked ship. "Seriously. Is there anything you want me to look for in there?" He hesitates. "Or anyone?"

"Still no." Ozzi's eyes lift to the hole in the cockpit, then slide past, to the sky-spangled green canopy beyond. A bird calls quizzically in the distance, and another answers with the same curious chirp. "I don't suppose they'll just let it stay here."

Even though he already knows the answer, Hob calls up his visual overlay. "We're standing right in the middle of the lumber preserve for a planned settlement," he says apologetically. He calls up a minor illusion, replicating the map in the air between them for Ozzi's benefit. "See? They'll probably haul it off to a dump. Maybe back up to space, if the settlers, the uh, refugees, make a big enough deal about having it here."

"Well." Ozzi puts a hand up as if to pat the blackened metal. He keeps his hand as close to the hull as he can without letting it pass through, so that it almost looks like he's really touching it. Just for a moment, his arm is solid enough that Hob can barely see the trees through it. "All orbits decay in time. Shall we go?"

The walk back is either boring, exhausting, or both: Ozzi bleeds out of existence about a kilometer in. He doesn't reappear until after Hob has gotten back to the module, scraped lunch out of a mealmix packet, put the last few finishing touches on his new illusion, and shoved his feet back into his still-sweaty boots.

"No rest for the wicked," Ozzi says cheerfully, as if this morning never happened, as if the crashed spaceship is still just a curious blip flagged by the recon drone. "Where are we off to this time?"

"'No rest for the wicked' is a funny thing for a ghost to say." Although the lemon-yellow afternoon suggests heat, the air is cool on Hob's face and arms when he steps outside. He sets out toward the CFM's grove, noticing that he's starting to wear a track through the grass in this direction. He knows the spells that would call new grass up from nothing and cover the scuffed dirt, of course. Ground cover is a basic incantation, one that every two-bit thaumaturgist knows. But he smooths over that corner of his thoughts and leaves the spell uncast. "Don't you have anywhere better to be? Like, I don't know, the afterlife?"

"I wouldn't leave you to go alone. It can get dicey out there. Last time, you fell out of a tree!"

Hob snorts. "I think that was because I *wasn't* alone." The conversation is easy enough for him to run out of the background of his thoughts, banter operating on autopilot; most of his brain is occupied with watching out for CFM tracks, listening for the telltale crack of branches. "What did you call them?" he says, cultivating an air of absence. "The CFMs, I mean. Did you have a name for those?"

"Naming species was a little outside our scope. Temrethalin was our only biologist, and she was busy enough with other—" Ozzi cuts himself off, and Hob politely lets the name slide past as if he hasn't heard it. "We all had better things to do," Ozzi concludes instead. When he lifts a hand to flick a drooping chestnut branch, his fingers pass straight through.

"What *do* symps get up to? Was there an Adopt-a-Battle-Slug campaign in the works? That ship didn't seem big enough to whisk away a whole herd to greener pastures." The terrain is starting to look familiar; they're not far from the tree where he had his first close encounter with the CFM. He slows down, listening, looking. The spell that usually helps him locate a haunt is useless right now—when he opens the source and thinks the right words in the right cadence, his thoughts light up with neon red arrows pointing right at Ozzi. "If you wanted to get up close with real exos, get your graduate degree in CFM-ology or whatever, you could apply to one of the affiliated research institutions."

"We didn't care about the individual species—no, let me rephrase. Our *focus* wasn't on the biology of any given flora or fauna or bacterium or—or cabbage-faced motherfucker." Ozzi barks a laugh at his own joke, hard enough to send ripples through his vaporous body. "For us, it was more than the loss of biodiversity. It's the *inhumanity* of the process."

"Yeah, obviously; exos aren't humans." The words slip out of Hob's thoughts and into his mouth, only too late does he realize it's obviously the wrong thing to say. Ozzi sheds a cascade of glittering sparks, and Hob doesn't know either human haunts in general or Ozzi specifically well enough to know what that means—surprise, shock, outrage? He steps on the heels of his own ill-thought-out comment in his haste to leave it behind: "I think we're getting close. I'm going to set everything up, and then we can make ourselves scarce."

He puts his back to Ozzi as he closes his eyes and calls up the idea he's created. More than a mere image, this is a not-living-but-breathing rendition of a CFM. It casts a shadow; it gives off a sweet, swampy reek. As it solidifies and separates from the source that Hob used to make it, it rolls in a looping, wandering arc around the small clearing. Its cabbage-y appendages ruffle, and if Hob hadn't been the architect of those delicate movements, he would think it looked as if the CFM was feeling out the shape of its own surprising new existence.

"Interesting tactic. I didn't think they were social creatures." Ozzi makes himself the opposite of scarce, reaching out to touch one fluttering appendage. Hob almost expects his hand to make contact, as if two things that weren't quite real and physical must meet on some other plane than the one Hob's life operates on. But of course his fingers slide right through, and the CFM continues past him. It wasn't designed to react to the kind of stimulus presented by Ozzi.

Even though it ended poorly last time, Hob finds a foothold to haul himself up onto a low tree branch again. It'll be harder for Ozzi to surprise him this time around. "You stay down there if you want, but I'm getting out of the CFM smash zone."

When he pulls himself another branch higher, Ozzi is waiting for him. "How many planets did you flip?" he asks conversationally. Like this is a job interview and he has some concerns about Hob's work history. "As a terraformer."

The easy lie catches in Hob's throat. His instinct is to spit it out, but he knows, in the long run, it would only do more damage.

Being honest with Ozzi means being honest with himself.

"One. Just one."

A rumbling vibration spares him from Ozzi's reaction. The CFM has arrived, and it's headed straight for Hob's illusion—as straight as its bizarre method of locomotion will allow. The frequency of the vibrations increases to a trill, and the cabbages bloom a darker color, purplish black, as it approaches the puppet-CFM. A query, or a request, perhaps, asked in color and sound.

And answered in kind. The illusion does exactly what Hob designed it to do, burning source as it flushes pinkish-purple, buzzing its encouragement. It everts the net of membranes tucked under a flap beneath the bulk of its body. The membrane shines wetly, the bluish veins within it pulsing, as it protrudes toward the haunt. The haunt everts a membrane sack of its own, from which spongy, branching tubes emerge, and—

"Oh, what the *fuck*," says Ozzi in dismay. His indistinct form twists, head one way and torso the other, as if he's not sure whether he's supposed to avert his eyes. "Are you kidding me?"

The CFM—the dead one—continues to slide up the musical scale until its trilling becomes a full-on shriek. This isn't a question, it's an exclamation, and it's roughly the same one Ozzi just made, translated into CFM-language. Its colors change again, dappling and then muting, as it gropes around its would-be mate. But there's nothing there to grope, nothing real. Look, but don't touch. The proboscis—penis-sponge-thing—flexes, spasms, recedes. The CFM wails once more, in confusion or anger or both or neither; Hob doesn't care what emotion it's feeling as long as it's feeling a lot of it.

Then it shrivels in on itself, and dissolves. The illusory CFM remains, still presenting its ripe membrane sac. Hob resents that he knows the phrase "ripe membrane sac," let alone that his eye for detail spent so much time familiarizing itself with the concept. He lets the illusion go, unspent energy sliding back into the source's fathomless reserves.

"Was that it?" Ozzi's voice comes out strained—not tense to the point of snapping, but certainly with whatever else he wants to say pulling the words tight. "Did it...work?"

"It's work*ing*." Not as much progress as Hob hoped for, but Ozzi's going to try to guilt him for every hard-earned inch. "You're lucky you didn't have to see this on Victory. They had these, uh, what did we call them—oh, bug-eyed hairbrushes, and do you want to guess what the *dick* on one of those things looks like?"

Ozzi follows Hob when he descends, carefully, from the tree. "This isn't empty prudery. It's not like I grew up in a sex-neg culture, I just—fuck."

He's not behind Hob's shoulder when Hob looks up from examining the site of the CFM haunt's disappearance. Could he have—? No, there wasn't enough emphasis behind that "fuck" to trigger a transition. Hob makes his tight chest relax enough to draw in a full breath. Make some notes. Write down his ideas, make a vague sketch, in case he forgets before he gets back to his mobile unit.

He's finishing up, tucking his compendium back into its pocket, when Ozzi speaks up, from far overhead in the trees where he can't see. "I've never really understood why they can't just terraform the dying planet itself. Like Zetharin. Divert a couple blocs of the Transit Fleet, load everyone and everything that matters onto a ship—all at once instead of in waves, like they'll move people here. Send in the terraformers, reset everything back to factory defaults. One happy healthy brand-new sparkling-clean planet, zero dead planets, everyone wins."

"They don't take guys like me aside to explain company policy." He looks around but can't find a spark of ghostlight anywhere in the shadows. His line is a weak one, and he knows it. He doesn't need a primer on the economics of it all. It's only a matter of how you draw your lines of cost. C-suite execs see a bottom line that has to accommodate valuable and often perishable freight—freight that would only lose value while Transit Fleet ships serve as apartment buildings instead of cargo transports. It's much pricier to house a planet's population for the months and months it takes to execute a successful terraformation and clearance than it is to just leave them in place for the time being. And if you waste a planet that didn't offer any economic value in the first place, then it's hardly a waste at all. Folks like Ozzi do their accounting differently, and that's fine for him, if he wants to go start his own pro bono terraforming organization, and in the meantime other people like Hob have to live in the real world where food doesn't fall from the sky and engine fodder doesn't grow on trees.

"It's expensive," he says, to a knotty chestnut tree, since he still can't tell where Ozzi is. "That's all. It would be too expensive."

A rustle shakes the branches somewhere overhead. A pair of leaves, still green, flutter idly down. They settle silently to the forest floor. Hob calls Ozzi's name without really expecting an answer.

Not because he's crossed. Hob doesn't think so. He *really* doesn't think so. It would take more than that. There are lines that haven't been crossed. All of this today was about exorcising a CFM, not a human being. But Hob walks back alone anyway, following his own tracks homeward.

The next morning, Hob wakes himself before his alarm. There's a lot to do today, and their schedule is only getting tighter. He reads through updates from Jaara first—the next sector has been quieter, thank goodness, and they've made up a little of their lost time. He signs off on a few decisions, crew schedules, and supply drop requests.

The last thing in the packet is a list of potential rendezvous points, depending on how soon he thinks he can clear the ground here. With time, they get farther apart and closer to the secondary nexus...except for the final point, which is right where he's sitting now.

It's not as if they couldn't get by without him. It's not as if they aren't getting by without him right now. Jaara feels better if she can point to his signature on the things she's already figured out; he's just her magic ballet shoes or magic feather or magic magnetic boots, depending on which version of that story the grown-ups in your habitat told. It's not the end of the world if he stays here, circling the drain, a while longer. The world already ended, a long time ago now.

He fusses for a while over a new illusion, recycling some parts from the previous version where he can, altering scale and paint colors and textures as needed, but his heart isn't in it. In the late morning, he loads a too-heavy bag and heads out, under a sky scabby with clouds, in the direction of the wrecked ship.

Before he comes within sight of it, he changes tack. Back and forth, wide swings, keeping himself between the meridian and the ship. He kicks up underbrush as he goes, silencing the creak of crickets; he rifles through piles of leaf litter and sends flocks of startled birds skyward. There's no guarantee he'll find what he's looking for. All creatures come into the world with a hunger, whether they arrive as squirming squalling nestlings or fully formed adults. Surely one of them, surely a whole swarm, has been through here before him.

In the end, it's because of that hunger that he finds the body. He thinks it's a mushroom at first, a swell of white tucked between the roots of a tree. But when he gives a testing poke, his fingers find something smooth and hard. He tugs, and the roots grudgingly surrender the gape-eyed skull. It's streaked with dirt, but there's not a molecule of flesh clinging to it. No way to know if it's actually Ozzi's, but a quick analysis from Hob's overlay tells him the markers of age and size are a match.

So.

He takes his time spiraling outward from that spot, and turns up a few more odds and ends. Most of an arm, a few desiccated shreds of ligament holding humerus to radius, or ulna, Hob can't remember which is which. Three rib bones and a vertebra, scattered at distant points, all of which show signs of tooth marks. He doesn't even try to distinguish carpals and tarsals from pebbles, overlay or not. Everything he finds, he adds to a growing pile alongside the skull, and stands back, wiping his dirty hands on his shirt.

The modular habitat doesn't have a shovel. It'll have to be a flattish rock and bare hands. The hole doesn't get very deep, not even after a great deal of effort on Hob's part, but then, with remains this thoroughly picked over, he probably doesn't have to aim for a full two meters. Once he's thrown dirt back over, to fill in the big empty spaces around the bones, he stands for a moment. Maybe he should throw a couple flowers on it. Maybe he should say something.

Maybe he should get on with his work.

In the shadow of the shipwreck, he unfolds the ladder from his pack and counts the sections of Process he's about to violate. Jaara would have known specific page numbers, probably, but he contents himself with ticking off on his fingers. One: Don't enter potentially unsafe terrain alone. Two: Always have a plan for safe evacuation. Three: Don't scale a ladder without a crew partner at the bottom to hold it steady. Well, he's kilometers outside Process by now, and it's HQ that sent him there, so to all seven hells with Process at this point.

It takes some maneuvering to get him inside the cockpit in a way that he's (fairly) certain will let the charred metal take his weight. Once he's there, he finds himself in the company of two of Ozzi's late friends: a pair of half-melted spacesuits with blackened bones peeping through at separated shoulder seams. The industrious creatures that tidied up Ozzi's remains haven't been at work in here: the unpleasantly organic smell of decaying flesh asserts itself over the ozone stink of the fire.

Hob eases them, one at a time, out of their seats and totes them toward the hole in the hull. "Sorry," he says helplessly, but there's no way he can navigate the ladder safely with a corpse on his back. He tips them out onto the dirt below and doesn't look to see them land.

There's not much else to see in the cockpit, except smoke stains and cracked computer screens and the flame-retardant emergency kit under the main console. Hob opens that and peruses the contents: a first-aid kit (bleakly hilarious), next-of-kin contacts (not that funny at all, actually), and the datasafe that probably backed up their reconnaissance or research or whatever they did, which might also tell Hob something about what happened to the ship. He slides everything into various internal pockets on his suit for safekeeping, except for the respirator mask in the first-aid kit, which he slides over his face, enjoying his next breath of trimethylamine-free air.

There's one more body in the cabin behind the cockpit, and Hob hauls that to the front of the ship too. Once he climbs down, he apologizes again to the three corpses, and arranges their limbs a little less pathetically: straightening legs, folding arms across chests.

"Oh, sure, I see," says Ozzi. It takes Hob a moment to locate him, a crystalline spangle of ghostlight in a shaft of pure sunlight. "I'm supposed to try to fuck them, yeah? That's your M.O.?"

"Don't be a dick." Hob takes a deep breath. Even in the respirator, the flavor of rot clings to his skin. It's enough to make a guy a little edgy. "I'm trying to be human. Do you want me to bury them? Do you want to just say a few words, or—?"

"I've already said everything I need to say to them." Ozzi coalesces a little: the suggestion of a shoulder, a face. "Are they going to let a grave just stay here in their nice neat new forest?"

"They might. If I request specially."

A red glitter shivers through Ozzi. Hob says, reluctantly: "No. Probably not."

"Okay." Ozzi fades again, then pulls back together, even clearer than before. "Sure. Yeah. Bury them."

Hob isn't going to get any less tired standing here. He starts, again, to make a hole. This time, there's a fragment of the hull that makes for a halfway-acceptable shovel, and the ground is softer here too, deep lodes of a friendly and eminently diggable silt. Maybe this is where the terraformers planned to put a green cemetery. He probably needs to dig deeper this time. And his back is already tired from his earlier efforts. It's going to be a long day, an extra long one in a series of long, long days.

He stops more often for breaks, to wipe the sweat from his face, to see if Ozzi is still there. After a few of these, he stops to sit on the side of the growing grave and takes a crewcake out of his pack. These things are supposed to provide on-the-go energy for a day of heavy work, but mostly they just seem to work his jaw muscles to the point of drooling exhaustion.

"So," he says, gnawing a corner off. "What was it like? Up there?"

Ozzi pauses in his lonely, drifting vigil over the silent bodies. He's almost a full haunt now, even this far from the meridian. Hob can see the lines in his forehead as his eyebrows rise. "You've been there," he says. "At least we only saw it through the drones. But you've been *right there*. You know better than I do."

Hob thinks about waves of light washing over a world. He thinks about scarlet snake-whales the height of a man, screaming and writhing as they fight the inevitable. He thinks about iridescent flowers a cartwheel in circumference, whose petals immediately droop and wither and relinquish their hold on life, not enough substance to their soul to demand their own right to existence. He takes a bigger bite of the crewcake. It takes him longer to chew, so his tight throat has a chance to relax.

"Real nightmare shit," he says, once he's worked his way through the mouthful.

The sound Ozzi makes is a little too desperate to be called a laugh. The conversation feels over, but Hob isn't ready to pick up the shovel again yet. He nods toward the three crumpled spacesuits. "Who were they, Ozzi?"

"My friends." Ozzi thinks a moment, then adds: "My coworkers. My family. The lines get blurry in our line of work."

"That can happen with people who care a lot."

"Not that you would know."

"Not that I would know."

They grin wearily at each other across the clearing, across the line of bodies. Hob pushes himself to his feet and picks up his makeshift shovel.

Ozzi parts ways with Hob when the first thing he does upon returning to the habitat is to start stripping off all his clothes. Alone, he opts for an irresponsibly long, hot shower. He can eat cold mealmixes for a day, if the mini-solars can't make up the energy deficit. Then he sits down with his compendium. First he plugs in the datasafe—but no, not today, he can't look at any of that footage right now. Instead, he pulls a connection to the satellite. He sends a series of data requests to be forwarded to the quantum relay, eats fully half of his buttersweet stash, and folds himself into bed.

When he wakes up, Ozzi is at the foot of his cot, swiping fruitlessly at Hob's blinking compendium. "I have so many emotions, I should be able to interact with this fucking thing," Ozzi says, as Hob blinks at him in confusion. "Unfortunately I think they're all just annoyance."

"Move." Hob reaches around Ozzi instead of through him to grab the compendium. His data requests have been fulfilled, and he has a series of messages from Jaara too:

Please see attached requisition list for approval. You missed yesterday's check-in. Is everything okay?

Per page 41 paragraph D of the Process Manual, the crew commander is expected to handle all approval requests within 12 hours. Can you let me know when you get this?

Boss, if I don't hear from you in the next hour, I'm sending Maseley and Rathana to come collect your deceased ass.

This last is timestamped forty-five minutes ago; Hob hastily sends an apologetic reply and a promise to look at her requests soon, before he turns to the packets he received from the relay. The files are titled: Ozzi Sagar, Amindal Sagar, Temrethalin Ta, and Einda Malliso. Even without the biodata, it's clear from the attached photos that Amindal is Ozzi's older sister. The other two, both middle-aged women, are a partnered pair. Hob flicks aimlessly through the rest of the information, not sure what he's looking for, scanning their histories of activist work, family and relationships, university studies, previous habitats of residence.

"Find anything juicy in my life story?" Ozzi peers at the compendium over Hob's shoulder.

"Pretty boring stuff, to be honest." Hob turns off the compendium and tosses it onto his wadded-up blankets. "I have no idea what to do now."

"Sorry?"

Hob pushes up out of bed and crosses to his drawers, rifling through for a clean shirt. "A thoughtless exo is one thing. But you're a person. Or you were. Are. Don't make me get into the grammar of the situation." He throws aside holey socks and an equally holey pair of boxers. "And we're just stuck with this mess, and my bosses want me to make you go away, and I want—I want—there should be something I could do to at least help, you know? But the terraforming is over, nothing to be done about that; the exorcism is pretty much done too." A slight exaggeration for dramatic effect, maybe, but hey. "There's nothing either of us could do about your friends, except see them laid properly to rest, and if you've got something to say to whoever out there is still living and gives a shit about you, you're being kind of weird about withholding it at this point since I already know way more about you than you wanted." There's nothing in his drawer that qualifies under any definition of clean. He balls up the dirty odds and ends briefly in his fists, then wads them back into the drawer and slams it shut. "I don't know how to help you. I don't know what you *want*. I don't know anything."

"I guess I want what any dead thing wants." Ozzi's shoulders bounce helplessly up and down. "The impossible."

Hob sits down harder then he meant to against the drawers, banging his back against the raised edges. Something Ozzi said before pops back into his head, and he repeats it: "All orbits decay in time."

"You're helping more than you think," says Ozzi, and he pops like a soap bubble.

Hob sits where he's landed for a while, sifting the silence through his thoughts. By any objective measure, he's alone either way, but the texture is different when Ozzi's not there.

When his leg starts to fall asleep, he makes himself stand up, and puts on the least grubby shirt.

Though Hob woke early after his early bedtime, he's not moving fast in the morning; every part of his body expresses its regrets in the form of delayed-onset muscle soreness. There's something in the module medi-kit that helps speed muscle repairs, but its effects are far from instantaneous, and it's a good two hours before Hob drags himself back outside. This CFM isn't going to exorcise itself any more than Ozzi is.

It's only when he catches the first glint of ghostlight through the brush that he remembers: he hasn't spent any more time on developing this new illusion. Well. There's something to be said for the rawness and on-the-fly reaction of improvisation. He ducks into the cover of a massive, yellow-flowered bush and throws the bones of the illusion up behind him as he goes.

At first, it's only a smaller version of the CFM. Smooth nubbins in place of leafy cabbages, a paler, more delicate color than the full-grown specimen. It crawls around in wandering circles, bumping curiously into trees and plants. Hob's careful to make sure it avoids his hiding place. As he watches, he feels his tongue between his teeth. It needs something. A little more *touch*.

He shifts the connection to the source, drawing a little harder, and the baby CFM's vague path takes on new urgency, frantic geometric patterns in place of curious circles. Its gray-white skin flushes even lighter, and Hob adds a noise. There's nothing in his compendium about the vocalizations of juvenile CFMs, but he takes the sounds he's heard the adult versions make and modulates them: altering the frequency, smoothing the texture. A mewling, bleating tremolo echoes in the clearing, and Hob's heart clenches in spite of himself. He wrote and directed this little movie, so it's pretty fucking silly to let it upset him.

It's supposed to upset someone else, after all.

The haunt crashes into the clearing, bellowing a challenge, shrieking terror of its own. A cacophony of voices from various CFM orifices, but the meaning is pretty clear: some CFM version of *you come after my kid, I'll wreck your shit.*

The shrilling dies away as the CFM recognizes—piecemeal?—that the juvenile is here in front of it, alive (well, "alive") and apparently unharmed. It broadcasts another earsplitting challenge to the woods around it, as it approaches the juvenile for a gentle nudge.

But of course, when it reaches Hob's illusion, it slides straight through. There's nothing there to be touched; there's nothing there to do the touching with. It retreats backward, shrilling, and its cabbage appendages dilate fully, flexing and flaring. Trying to comprehend the incomprehensible.

Hob sends the illusion after it. What does a hopeful baby-squeak sound like coming from a CFM? He makes his best attempt as the baby CFM trundles forward, its smaller body struggling over the rough ground. All over the universe, small creatures want a parent when they're lost and confused and frightened, and this make-believe exo is no different. When the haunt runs out of room to retreat, Hob lets the illusion roll right through it—then triggers the fear-trill sound over again. *Why won't you help me?* it seems to beg. *What did I do wrong?*

The CFM rolls in panicked circles, as if to flee—but then it stops. With the oscillation of its own body, it begins to dig. Dirt flies around it in wide, round waves. Some of it pelts Hob in his hiding place, some of it rustles like rain in the foliage.

The CFM stops. It opens the cabbages on the side nearest the juvenile, and it closes them again. It calls once more—a vocalization Hob hasn't heard before, a croak that slides up and down the musical scale.

Its child is unreachable, beyond its ability to touch or comfort. A biological imperative, to make more of yourself, to protect the fruits of your reproductive labor—there's a reason this thread is woven so thoroughly into life forms across a thousand planets. The fundamental disconnect is enough to penetrate into whatever limited version of a brain the CFM has.

It understands. And it accepts. What else can it do, at this point?

The whole world seems to squeeze, the swell of source beneath a successful exorcism. Hob winds his fingers into the branches of the brush, as if the haunt could take him with it when it goes. He blinks, and everything around him releases the breath it was holding. When he opens his eyes, the CFM is gone. *Gone* gone. He can feel the difference, as reality loosens up around him. He's witnessed a successful crossing a time or two in his career; he knows what they're like.

He lets go of the baby-CFM illusion as he stands and shakes off the debris of leaves and dirt. His knees pop to let him know they're not happy about how long he spent on them. "If you're going to haunt me," he announces to the clearing, "do it to my face, please."

Ozzi walks out of the shadows, a full human shape outlined in ghostlight, and steps to the hole left by the CFM. "Man, you're really running short of options. I've never been particularly food-motivated, I'm ace, and I never had kids or younger sibs. What else you got up your sleeve?"

Hob sits beside him, letting his feet hang down into this donut-shaped hollow. He wonders what drove the CFM to dig it—trying to hide from its inevitable fate? Making a hiding place for the little one it couldn't otherwise protect? It reminds him of all the graves he dug yesterday, but nothing in the compendium suggests that CFMs or any other exos here had anything like funereal practices. A waste of energy on the CFM's part in any case, but then he's neither a xenobiologist nor a psychologist. Nor a xenopsychologist. If there's another explanation, it's past his understanding.

"Maybe I'm stuck with you," he says. Ozzi glances sidelong at him with a sad, quizzical smile.

That makes this a little easier for Hob. You see your opening, and you step through it. He who hesitates, etc., etc. Something's lost already and it's not going to be Hob.

He takes the datasafe out of his pocket and sets it on the ground next to himself, on the lip of the hollow. "Or maybe I'm not."

Ozzi lurches. "Is that—?"

"Of course you weren't food-motivated. Not to an exorcism-worthy extent. But *work*-motivated?" Hob takes a hammer out his other pocket and holds it contemplatively in one hand. "That, I could believe."

"No. No!" Ozzi drops down into the hole, putting him eye-to-eye with Hob. Hob meets his translucent gaze indifferently. "Don't do it. The footage is—you've *seen* what the footage is like!"

"Nightmare shit," Hob agrees. The hammer slips a little in his grasp; he tightens his fingers around its handle. "You think that matters? People care about human lives. Not exos. Not fucking CFMs." Not dragonflowers, not Matisiran serpents. Not skymoss or jellybags or scissor-toads or twelve fucktillion weird little microbes. He looks away from Ozzi, toward the datasafe. "It's all acceptable losses to them. Whose mind did you think you were going to change?"

"Yours would have been a good start."

The datasafe rings resoundingly when Hob lands the first blow on it. It's designed to absorb shock, after all, designed to take a hit. He strikes it again.

"Stop!" Ozzi paws uselessly at—through—Hob's arms, the hammer, the datasafe. A faint crack opens in its case as Hob lands another blow. "Fuck! *Stop.*"

"Make me." Hob brings his hand high and puts his whole shoulder into one more blow.

The datasafe shatters. Tiny crystalline pieces go flying: into the brush, onto Hob's clothes, into the hole.

"No!" Ozzi howls, and grabs for the shards where they've fallen.

He scoops up a handful of dirt and wasted computer parts, lifting them toward his chest. For a moment, Ozzi is a black hole, one that pulls everything in the clearing toward him. His fists close, and Hob leans away, bracing for a blow.

The only thing that hits him is Ozzi's resigned, weary look. Then the dirt tumbles through the space where Ozzi used to be, and Hob is alone.

He waits, hearing his own loud breathing in his ears. Ozzi hasn't crossed, not yet. It hasn't worked but it's work*ing*, he tells himself. He stands up, when he's sure his legs will take his weight, and flings the hammer as far into the woods as he can. It crashes, metal against wood, and some kind of typical Earth-origin woodland hellbeast chatters its outrage at him.

He wonders whether he'll see Ozzi again before he goes. Neither possibility is comforting.

He takes out his compendium and calls up the files he pulled from the datasafe. He watches wave after wave of purifying light wash over CFMs and banana turtles and cloud-weed, peeling them out of existence layer by layer until it's like they were never here at all. It's been a long time since he saw terraforming from this end. He doesn't like it any more than he did the last time.

Remaking a world in your own image is only a good idea if you aren't ugly as shit to begin with.

If Jaara is surprised that Hob makes a vidcall request to go over the day's progress reports and requests, she doesn't show it. Together they catch up on all the minutiae that Hob has let slide. He asks how the team is, and she says they're fine; she asks how the ghost is and he hesitates.

"I'm working on him," he tells her finally, and she nods, as if that's all she needs or wants to hear.

Before she can cut out of the call, he catches her with one more thing, and this time even Jaara can't mask a startled expression. "You used to be a terraformer too, way back when."

It's not a question, but Jaara answers it. "I was." She's already back in control of an alert-but-unconcerned expression. "For a while."

"What made you switch over to cleanup?"

She hesitates, and he knows she's trying to figure out what he expects of her, what he wants to hear. Finally she says, reluctantly: "I was having trouble sleeping during jobs."

"Bad dreams?"

"No." She looks down at her hands, or whatever's in them, just off-screen, then back at Hob. "It was the noise. You know what I mean?"

He does. He can handle hearing that noise one-on-one, but a worldwide chorus, an entire planet's death-scream in unison—it's too much. Even too much, apparently, for Jaara. "Okay," he says. "Thanks. Good work over there. Keep it up."

"Okay," she says. No *thanks, boss*; no *you too*. She ends the call first and he sits with the dark compendium in his hand for a while before he gets up in search of a mealmix and a clean fork.

He should get out of bed. He should figure out what it'll take to finish Ozzi off. He should eat something. He should plot out a rendezvous point for Jaara and the rest of the crew.

He gets up and pees. He goes back to bed.

He watches the footage from Ozzi's drones. Over and over again. He scans through the dead ship's maintenance logs, gives up, and directs a script to scan through them and ping his overlay with the results. He watches the footage again while he waits, closes his eyes, sees dragonflowers and CFMs disintegrating side by side in the darkness of his imagination.

When he opens his eyes again, a notification is blinking to let him know that his search has run. He wanted it to be company sabotage, wanted an obvious flashing "here there be monsters" neon red flag, but analysis suggests otherwise. The ship was cobbled together with what a bunch of starry-eyed symp believers could scrounge up with spare change. They'd fixed a faulty connection between gas exchange and ventilation systems a few times before, but this time the failure was catastrophic. A spark, an explosion, an impact crater that would soon be smoothed over and tidied up by an in-progress terraformation event.

He would have known what to do, if there were *obvious* bad guys.

If there were *obvious* bad guys, it would be easier not to be one of them.

Ozzi reappears while Hob is in the head, his dick in one hand and his compendium in the other. "Shit!" Hob bobbles the compendium and narrowly avoids soaking it in piss.

"You shouldn't use your comp in the toilet," scolds Ozzi mildly. His voice is different, coming from farther away. "It's getting harder to stay. I wanted to say…" His ghostlight throbs like a pulsar. "Well, fuck you, first of all. And also goodbye."

"You can't!" Hob zips his fly and turns the compendium's screen to face Ozzi. One of his rewatches is frozen there, a battle slug curling in on itself, its tissues unraveling even as it hunkers protectively down. "You can't go yet. You have to tell me where to send it."

"Oh," says Ozzi softly. He reaches as if to take the compendium, then remembers. His hand falls back to his side. "Really? You think it's going to matter?"

"I think it matters to *you*," Hob says.

Ozzi studies him for a moment. Hob can see his own face in the mirror, through the back of Ozzi's head. He looks, even more than usual, like shit. "Okay," says Ozzi finally. "Sure. Give me access to the relay. I have a destination code."

Hob enters his company password, and looks up, waiting for Ozzi to give him the next string of information. Instead, Ozzi frowns intensely. Mustering the emotions that still tie him to this world, his last reserves of want and need and hope. He reaches out and takes the compendium from Hob's hands. "This might take a second," he says, as if from the other side of a tunnel. "Sorry."

After keying in a few strokes one-handed, he thinks better of it, and sets the compendium on the corner of the tiny countertop. Tongue between his teeth with furious concentration, he enters the destination code one digit at a time. The air is heavy, so heavy Hob can barely breathe. He holds on to the clean-water pipe for balance.

Ozzi finishes with the code and straightens up. "For what it's worth? I don't think I'm the only one it's going to matter to."

He gives Hob one more lopsided grin, and he stops.

Stops existing, stops haunting. Just plain stops. The air goes back to normal, but Hob still can't breathe. He listens, but all he can hear is his own all-but-fibrillating heart. This is the first time in his life it's ever been weird to be *alone* in the john.

When he's sure he can pick up the compendium again without another risk of dropping it in the urinal, he scoops it carefully off the counter. The destination code has been input and the compendium recognizes it as valid, but Ozzi fucked off to the afterlife before pressing send. He's left that for Hob to do.

"Asshole," says Hob, and laughs—maybe a little hysterically, but he's the only one who has to hear it—and covers the button with his thumb.

He skulks around the habitat, waiting for Something to Happen, but of course nothing does. Data takes time to travel, vid takes time to be seen. Difficult conversations take time to hold. He picks at a cold mealmix and goes to bed early, leaving his compendium in the head so that he can get maybe his last good night's sleep for a long time.

When he wakes up and sidles tentatively into the toilet, he's got a dozen message notifications waiting for him. All blinking urgent—several from HQ, a few more from reporters or government officials or whatever. He glances through them. Interview request, a demand for official testimony, also he's *super* fired. One of the notices from HQ lets him know that the appropriate section of Process has been triggered and that he has been logged out from all access to company files, machinery, even the habitat itself—if he leaves, the missive warns, he's *not* getting back in.

He makes himself a cup of tea and goes to sprawl in the grass and drink it. It's a nice day out. Maybe rain later, one of those brief midafternoon spritzes that seem to keep this planet watered. But for now it's peaceful, and the sky is a striking lavender-blue.

By the time the transport rolls up, he's long finished his tea and started to wish he'd stayed inside so that he could have brewed a second cup. "About time," he calls to Jaara, as she steps down from the driver's seat.

"I'm supposed to take you into company custody, boss." She doesn't sound mad at him, or even annoyed. Embarrassed, maybe, at the situation. Or maybe just because of that reflexive "boss" that slipped out.

"Makes sense." He tosses the dregs from the empty plastic cup over his shoulder. "Are you going to?"

"Why did you do it?" Not like her to answer a question with a question, but he's already set the precedent on going rogue. "The people who want to know what it's like, they already know. The rest don't give a shit. Why bother?"

"I don't know," he tells her honestly. He contemplates the bottom of his teacup. People read their fortunes in the bottoms of teacups, don't they? He read that somewhere, but he's not sure what a single red-brown droplet means to him. "I guess...*I* wanted to give a shit. A little bit of one."

Her perfect posture sags a little. Probably only Hob would've noticed. She sits down next to him on the grass and digs her fingers into the topsoil. "What now?" she asks. "Any other pointless nonsense you need to get out of your system?"

They chase all the critters they can find away from the crash site and a couple square kilometers around it: rabbits and chipmunks, birds and even one snake that scares the absolute shit out of Hob on its way out of there. His compendium tells him it probably wasn't poisonous (he didn't exactly linger for a good hard look at the thing), but that would have been quite a way to go, wouldn't it? Only after they're sure things are fairly clear do they pull on their full protective suits— the things are useful, but too bulky when you want to move fast.

"What about the trees?" Jaara asks wistfully, laying her gloved hand on a birch tree that's grown around the scar left by the wrecked ship's passage. "We can't move any of them."

Nor can they move all of the worms, the microbes, the crawly little nasty things that burrow through the soil. On a subconscious level, trees want to go on living just as much as anything else does. Hob shrugs helplessly, and Jaara rests her head against the white bark for a moment before moving on.

"Are you ready?" Hob asks, when they've spent about as much energy as they can afford clearing things out. The sun is high in the sky and the wrecked ship doesn't offer much shelter.

"Sure," she lies gamely. She puts out her hand, and he squeezes it convulsively. You might think you're ready for a terraformation, fresh out of training and ready to un-save the world. But no one really is.

The light is too bright, rolling outward from the nexus of their joined hands. Hob's suit tries to protect his eyes by darkening his visor, but he double-blinks to dismiss the change. He wants to see.

In the flare, the trees bleach to clawing skeletal hands; untold trillions of unseen lives panic as they dissolve back into the source they came from, not so very long ago. Hob tries to ignore the noise, tries to tell himself *it's different this time*. But the familiarity comes at him from an unexpectedly tender angle; reaching into the source to create *life* rather than its illusion doesn't feel so different. This is an illusion-plus, really—take your idea of a CFM and then surrender control. Let your wants and demands recede, let its own break through. Give it enough source not just to *seem* but also to *touch*, not just to *sing* but also to *listen*.

New foliage shoulders up through the crumbling remnants of chestnut and mulberry: yellow leaves, serrated and sharp enough to cut yourself on. Out of sight, strange and different single-celled life pulses into existence between grains of soil, within the veins of plants. There's a faint greenish tinge to the air; Hob knows it's poisonous, but he still wonders what it would smell like, how heavy it would sit in his lungs.

Without intervention, it'll just blend with the human-friendly air outside this place. He cocks his head, feels around for the source whose touch he knows so well, and calls up a spinning, stirring wind. It spirals up from around his feet and spins wider, pelting him and Jaara with clots of dirt and broken bits of vegetation until its radius expands past them. Under his concentration, the wind swells wider—wide enough to wrap around this entire wacky little project of theirs. When he lets go, it stays in place: a spinning globe of gray, dirt-flecked currents. Lazy spirals, storms in miniature, curl through and collide. He's never seen anything like it before. He's certainly never *made* anything like it before.

It's pretty, in a fucked-up kind of way. He hopes it gets to last a little while.

With the perimeter set, he lets Jaara put the finishing touches on what they've created. As she works, he begins to record on his compendium.

"This is a preserve," he declares, the compendium pointed back toward himself and held at arm's length. "Put up walls, put up barriers, but do not fucking touch a cabbage on these cabbage-faced motherfuckers' heads or we will put up a *fight*." He keys in the destination code to match the one Ozzi used and releases the footage into the ether.

"Yettal's calling. I was supposed to be back with you by now, probably." Jaara glances at her compendium, then shoves it deeper into a pouch on her suit. The work has left her face gray and clammy with sweat. Hob can only guess what *he* looks like right now. It's easier than speculating about what Yetz wants to say: *fuck you, boss; you're under arrest, boss; where do I sign up for your doomed-ass little rebellion, boss?* "Won't they just plow it under again?"

"Don't know." The shipwreck is gone, the buried bodies, presumably, too. There's a swell of purplish soil, he thinks (he t*hinks*) where the wreck lay, but it's hard to be sure now that he's overwritten the landscape so thoroughly. "I don't know, Jaara." There are a lot of things that he doesn't know, and a few things he does. One is that this isn't enough. The other is that it's better than nothing. Has to be.

A yellowish flash illuminates the freaky alien jungle—but it's no ghostlight, only a battle slug, warning off other challengers in its territory.

"It matters," he says aloud.

He's not sure who he's trying to reassure, because Jaara doesn't look like she believes him and he doesn't sound like he believes himself. Maybe the battle slug feels better for hearing it. He wonders if they should stay here and try to guard this weird little zoo, try answering some of those interview requests before they're both locked out.

"Maybe just for now. Maybe just to you and me."

"But it matters," she echoes, and it sounds truer coming from her mouth instead of his.

They sit side by side on a stumpy, rubbery chunk of vegetation that doesn't seem to be secreting anything that'll eat through their suits. Idly, Jaara pats the plant matter under her legs. The stump doesn't seem to mind.

"You want to talk about metrics while we're waiting?" Hob asks, after a while, and Jaara chokes on an incredulous laugh.

He pictures shiploads of Zetharin refugee-settlers, corralled behind safety perimeters until the secondary nexus can be cleared. Maybe someone will catch a glimpse of a CFM from behind the barriers, and maybe that person will come up with a better name than *cabbage-faced motherfucker*. Oh, damn—he should have brought something to carve the crash victims' names into one of the quasi-trees in the jungle.

"I don't think we're going to make deadline. They're going to dock our pay, probably."

Neither Jaara nor Hob has enough energy left to laugh at that. All they can do is cave vaguely in toward each other, shoulder to shoulder, partly out of exhaustion and partly because the shape of the stump-thing makes this kind of lean inevitable. From out of sight among the wool-trees and pipe-orange plants, a trumpeting call rises, and another harmonizes with it. Two more calls, smaller and shriller, echo the first set. A mated pair of CFMs and a couple of young to round out the set.

"Just like I always say." Hob cranes his neck for a glimpse of the CFMs, which stay stubbornly out of view. "The third week of an exorcism campaign is the absolute fucking worst."

"Yeah." He can just see the crescent-moon glint of Jaara's smile through her sweat-fogged visor. "But you're leaving off the next part."

"I am?" Hob racks his empty brain and comes up, unsurprisingly, empty-handed. "What else do I always say?"

She clinks her helmet against his. "That if we can survive the third week? The rest is cake."

"That might have been an exaggeration on my part," Hob cautions, and clinks her in return.

They both subside into silence. Waiting. Listening. Watching the yellow sun wrap itself up in green clouds and settle to sleep beyond the horizon. The CFMs have moved away, it seems; and if there are any ghosts lingering out there, well, they're quiet tonight.

Aimee Ogden is an American werewolf in the Netherlands. Her debut novella "Sun-Daughters, Sea-Daughters" was a 2021 Nebula Award finalist, and her short fiction has appeared in publications such as *Lightspeed, Strange Horizons*, and *Best American Science Fiction and Fantasy 2022*. Her newest novella, *Starstruck*, arrives in June 2025. She would make for a very annoying ghost.

LONELINESS UNIVERSE

Eugenia Triantafyllou

From: Nefnef_baby@lyons-edu.org
To: Cara Hasani CaraMia1990@mailbuddy.gr
September 18, 2015, 5:36 am
Subject: I am drifting, but thank you for the photos

My dear Cara,

Thank you for sending me the photos, I never thought I'd feel this way again. But the pictures help. They really do. I can't stop looking at them. Thank you for scanning and emailing them to me. These photos and our old videos are all I've got in this place.

Before your messages stop coming through, I want to tell you this: It's all my fault, Cara. It's my fault because I ignored you and let us grow apart. But it's also my fault for trying to reconnect with you. That was a stupid idea. I don't know if we would have hit it off again like when we were kids. Perhaps it would have been super awkward and by the time I got on the bus home I'd have this weird taste in my mouth like eating a lemon raw, skin and seeds and all. Or perhaps we'd be best friends again and you'd invite me to your house for Easter and I'd see your family and we'd keep in touch until we grew disgustingly old and died. (Perhaps part of this will happen anyway. I am afraid that if I stop getting your messages I will be lost forever.)

But we'll never know. Because despite what the scientists may say, I believe I broke the universe by coming to find you. I broke it and I don't know how to put it back the way it was. Or even close. I defied some sort of unspoken law of the universe, Cara, and the universe pushed back and then kept pushing. I know that now, in this place that isn't a place.

Your oldest friend,
Nefeli

Nefeli paced back and forth the whole five steps from one side of the bus stop to the other, sneaking glances at the passersby while typing furiously on her phone. She was trying to guess which passing woman in her mid-twenties Cara had become. Rehearsing what she would say once they met face to face. In the one and only blurry picture of her grown-up-self Cara had posted on social media she was a blonde (Cara, a blonde! How times change), three-quarters profile, leaning casually against a wall. But that photo had been over two years old, based on the timestamp. She could have looked like anyone now. They had agreed to meet at the bus stop more than one hour ago but they were still working on it.

Nefeli: Lol, nice one, Cara. Now come on. I am hungry.
Cara: U sure you can't see me? I am sitting right here? Are u even at the right bus stop?

Nefeli looked around at the people arriving in Korinthos, her hometown. She had gotten on a similar intercity bus as a child with her parents many years ago and moved to Athens. She left everyone and everything behind, including her best friend. She might have forgotten a lot of places and people but never this bus stop and never Cara.

Nefeli: Yeah, I am sure. This place is pretty much the same.

Nefeli started typing another answer, then stopped. This was the only place Cara could have been waiting for her. The only intercity bus stop. When Nefeli found the courage to message her, Cara had agreed to meet up but said she couldn't come to Athens to see Nefeli, because she had to keep her parents' store now that they were old. *We can't all be feathers in the wind*, she had said to Nefeli and that stung a little, but Nefeli might have deserved it.

Another bus came and people rushed in. There was no one at the bus stop now. No way Cara was hiding here unless she was transparent. Or she was lying.

Nefeli looked to her right, to the rest of the bench. Empty. There wasn't even the occasional passing woman in her mid-twenties that Nefeli could have mistaken for Cara. She was alone on the bench and it was starting to feel like a bad joke.

She called Cara but it went straight to voicemail.

Then a message appeared on the screen and Nefeli's face turned red and pink. Once for anger and once for shame.

Cara: Are u ghosting me again in ur own weird way or something? Just like with the letters?
Nefeli: No, I am really here. Where are you?

Nefeli didn't technically ghost her when they were kids; ghosting was not a term that existed in their vocabulary at the time. But before her family moved to

Athens she had promised to write and rarely did. Cara had actually written her several letters (the pre-internet days were rough) but she had gotten maybe one response from Nefeli who was in her own rat-race of trying to fit in with the big city kids. Perhaps if the internet had been a thing back then, they would have still kept in touch.

When she tracked down Cara again, a few months back, it was through social media. One day she just found herself googling her and she felt a little bit like a stalker. Cara's profile picture was a tiny auburn-haired Cara sitting on the beach, facing the camera with the sun on her back, pouring water from her plastic bucket straight onto a hole in the golden sand. There was also a tiny Nefeli in the same photo, standing right behind her, pouring water over Cara with her own plastic bucket. This was a sign, Nefeli thought then. Next thing she knew, she was sending Cara a friend request.

Then, an impossible selfie came through. One where adult Cara was sitting on the same bench on the exact same spot Nefeli was occupying at that very moment. A poster loomed over Cara's head in soft blues and eggy yellows.

Cara: Right. The fuck. Here.

"Can you fucking believe it? The audacity of it all!" Nefeli kept talking too loudly and gesticulating too much, making Antonis, her brother, readjust his position on the couch next to her every minute or so. The bright blues and purples of *TinyCastle*™, the video game they were playing, cast a light that made the room look like some kind of nightclub. In the midst of it all loomed Antonis's avatar, a very sinister-looking ghost.

Antonis could not believe it. In fact, he had probably stopped listening to her rant right about when his werewolf neighbor had sent him a new wallpaper pattern. A thank you gift for watering the roses outside the werewolf's castle. Antonis said that he'd prefer to be paid in teeth, the currency of *TinyCastle*™, but as he had explained to Nefeli, *you have to roll with the game, that's half the fun.*

Nefeli didn't know why he played that viciously cutesy game instead of going out and meeting people in the flesh. Like she just had, even though it blew up in her face.

"Told you that friendship had gone stale. Just let it go."

"And do what? Play games on my days off? Do you even see any people?"

Nefeli felt the skin-warmed plastic of the controller in her hands. She didn't know what to do in the game. How to build her own castle and how to befriend her stupid monster-neighbors. (She didn't know how to befriend anyone apparently. Human or monster.) It was why she never liked playing video games with Antonis or with anyone.

"Hey, these are my friends I'm playing with. Technically, I see more people than you."

That was factually true. Between the delivery job for a local pizza place, his gaming community, and his occasional outings with his buddies from college, Antonis's social life was light years ahead of Nefeli's. Nefeli used to justify this by telling herself she had just returned to Greece from her Graphic Design MFA abroad and was trying to make her one-person company take off. After she had settled in her new life, she would have time to reconnect with old friends. It was time to do it. Cara was the first person she thought of, even though she was the one she hadn't seen the longest. If she was going to fix her life she would start from the beginning. Nostalgia plays weird games.

Fuck Cara.

Nefeli left the controller at the coffee table and watched as her vampire avatar got stuck in the rose bushes Antonis's ghost had made blossom.

"You know what I need right now? All the potato chips. Like, literally every flavor ever put on a shelf? I need them."

Antonis looked annoyed for a second but then his face lit up. "I was going to go on a quick supermarket run. I'll get you the chips if you go chill in your room and let me play in peace."

Nefeli grunted but got up nonetheless. When half, then a whole hour passed by, and there was no other sound in the house but Nefeli's own breathing, she reluctantly left her bed and shuffled back to the living room like a potato chip-hankering zombie. She would have rocked that character in the game. The living room didn't look fun anymore. Instead, it was half in shadows and half drenched in a light the color of crème pâtissière as her mom called it, curtesy of the old beige chandelier. The TV was off, both the controllers were left on the coffee table, and Antonis was nowhere to be found. There were however three bags of potato chips waiting for her: regular, BBQ, and sour cream. She grabbed them all greedily and hurried to her room in case Antonis changed his mind and came back for them, but she thought she should text him just in case.

Nefeli: Hey, little ghost, thanks for the chips. Too bad you aren't here to share. I guess you took my advice.

Antonis: …? When did u steal the chips? I should take ghost lessons from u.

Nefeli: What do you mean steal? You left them on the couch before you went out?

Antonis: I'm right here? Building stables. Got so many teeth from a swamp creature. Just bring back the BBQs. K?

Nefeli stalked to the living room so fast she didn't stop to think about chips. Chips were suddenly the last thing on her mind. The whole house was exactly as it had been five minutes ago. Cemetery-quiet. No Antonis anywhere. She reached a shaky hand in the pocket of her sweatpants and pulled out her phone.

Nefeli: Tell me you're fucking joking right now.

Antonis: What's going on?
Nefeli: This is messed up, Antonis. After everything I told you.
Antonis: Look, I don't know what's up but I'm coming for the chips. U should get some sleep.

Nefeli, as if in a dream, dropped on the couch and stared at the dark screen until at some point she fell asleep. It must have been sleep, right? Because when she opened her eyes again, the first thing she focused her gaze on was an empty, crumpled bag of BBQ-flavored chips left on the coffee table.

She looked around as if she'd been introduced to the apartment for the first time. In fact, this was the place where her parents had raised her and her brother after they arrived in Athens. Nobody had passed through here. Nefeli was sure of it. Even if she had fallen asleep, she would have at least heard her brother and startled awake again. She wasn't sitting in the most comfortable sleeping position and Antonis was never mouse-quiet.

Nefeli picked up the misshapen bag like it was an imaginary object and crushed it in her hands just to feel its existence. To know it's there. Then she found her phone and messaged her brother again. She didn't have the courage to call him because deep down she knew it would go to voicemail or to nowhere at all. Just like with Cara.

Nefeli: Where are you now?

It took half an hour for him to respond.

Antonis: Just woke up. Making coffee.
Nefeli: On the stove?
Antonis: Nope. On my PS5.
Nefeli: Don't move.

Nefeli waded down the corridor as if in a dream and even though deep inside she knew what she was going to see when she turned the corner to the kitchen, it still broke something inside her when she faced nothing. The stove was cold and unused and the briki was still inside the bottom drawer. There was nobody there.

Nefeli wasn't proud of what she did in the weeks that followed but those were desperate times.

The first people she visited were her parents. They now lived in a smaller apartment in Peristeri, one of the western suburbs. They had claimed that was all the space they needed and they even had a small yard, since their apartment was almost semi-ground floor. Their windows overlooked a small park. It didn't take

Nefeli too long to get there. It was a half-hour subway ride and she had texted them before she left her house, but she was still afraid she would be too late. Or that's how it felt to her. Like a race against time and space. Her mom had texted back that she would bake ravani for her. The building had a side entrance, where her parents' apartment was. As she crossed the yard, walking down the small, stone path to the main door, she saw the kitchen lights were on and then rang the bell. They buzzed her in but the buzzing was cut very short. Like someone had slapped her mom's hand away from the button.

Nefeli ran up the few steps and knocked on the apartment door as if she was being chased and in need of a hiding place. The longer the silence stretched the louder she felt her heart beat in her ears and the harder she knocked on the door. She resorted to the spare key she had brought with her for this reason, although she'd hoped she wouldn't have to use it. Everything inside the apartment was pitch dark. Even the kitchen, although it did smell like someone had been baking. Nefeli stood on the doorstep for an undetermined amount of time, unable to lift her hands and turn on the lights. Then her phone buzzed.

Mom: Where are you? I buzzed you inside, didn't I?

Nefeli looked at the text miserably and responded with something about forgetting to turn off the stove back home. There was no point going through another round of this. Something was wrong. Irreversibly, inevitably wrong. And worst of all: the wrong thing began with her.

What added insult to injury was how she had left things with Cara—the beginning of everything. For a second time she let Cara down. Even if not on purpose. What's worse, she let her anger get the best of her even though Cara wasn't the person she was really angry at. That was mostly herself.

Over the course of the next few weeks, she stalked friends from college, relatives, and neighbors she had known ever since she was a kid. Or, more accurately, she stalked their houses and jobs and social media or messaged them to figure where they would be at a given time. It didn't matter, really. They were nowhere to be found. Not in the flesh at least, or face-to-face through the screen of her phone. She would only see their avatars and pictures on social media like the ghosts of relationships past, and occasionally exchange a message or two.

The world was still filled with people, of course. Just people she knew nothing or very little about. And just because of that she felt the world shrinking, become a tiny thing, even if, physics-wise, as far as she could tell, it remained the same.

From: Nefnef_baby@lyons-edu.org
To: Antonis Galliatsos, Mariza Galliatsou, Cara Hasani, Apost ..
July 5 2015, 7:36 pm

Subject: What the hell is happening to me? (An explanation)

Hi everyone!

I know this is a very weird mass email, but please hear me out first. For some of you (all of you?) it might seem like I've fallen off the face of the Earth. But guess what? I literally fell off the face of the Earth (ha ha). I don't think you and I are in the same place anymore. And by you, I mean all the people I care about. (Yes, that's every single one of you. Really.)

What I think is happening is...I am in some parallel universe situation? I've been doing some research about it. I watched over a hundred science videos. Okay, some of them were reels (I've only got this much time on my hands) and I can almost tell the point in time that the rift started. Suddenly it's like I am in one room and all of you are in another. Our rooms are identical and have clones of the same people who I know casually or not at all (for example the blonde barista in the coffee shop around the corner is still there), but none that I am connected to intimately. I call it Loneliness Universe. (Dad, look I am finally, *finally* into science!)

I can sort of feel all of you being somewhere close by, mostly from the stuff Antonis moves around. It's like our rooms overlap sometimes and sometimes they drift apart. Antonis, I'm eating from the food you've been leaving around in the fridge (sorry!). Also our rooms can communicate through social media (electromagnetic fields?) but not when I try to phone or video call you. The Loneliness Universe is doing its own thing, I guess. I am not 100% sure if all of you are together in that other room. I don't even know if you are okay. I really hope you are okay, guys. Please let me know? I love you and I miss you. Even the ones I haven't seen in years. At least I know you exist somewhere. I still remember all of you. I wish I could get everyone back.

Anyway, I don't know how to come back to you, but I am hanging in there. Maybe if I wait long enough the rooms will sort of settle into each other again? One can only hope. Please don't freak out too much when you read this email. I am not having some sort of meltdown (yet). Mom, I am okay and I eat well (as well as Antonis's eating habits allow). I even go shopping myself sometimes. For some reason I still have my clients who pay me for stuff. Yay for capitalism in any universe!

P.S. I KNOW you won't believe me, although I desperately hope you do. It doesn't matter if you don't. Just humor me, okay?

I love you in any universe.

Nefeli

If this was not an email but instead an instant message service, she would have seen the *several people are typing* notification stuck at the bottom of the screen. Because pretty soon her email was overflooding with panic-stricken sheets of text (mostly from her mom, to be honest) of people most definitely not humoring her. The responses ranged from Mom-responses, to a polite *That's horrible! Whatever is happening we are spiritually with you!* from a couple of Nefeli's old high school classmates, to a few college friends privately sending their therapists' contact information, to Cara doing the most Cara-like thing and trying to call her. And then when that didn't work as expected, she tried again and again and only then did she send an email saying: *I don't know what the hell is happening but please call me whenever. I mean it.*

Cara, had always been a boomer at heart and Nefeli loved her all the more for it. She loved all things old and never wanted to change. Like when she made Nefeli watch all the black and white Greek comedies or dressed all retro in her much older sister's hand-me-downs. Nefeli realized that she still did love her, no matter how far behind Nefeli thought she had left Cara and their small town. Suddenly she found herself wishing they had never left when she was a kid and wondering if that was the moment the real rift happened. If that was when two Nefeles were born. One that wrote back to Cara and one that didn't. And when she tried to be there again and fill that gap between her universe and Cara's, that void reacted and backfired. She had been gone for too long anyway. She ought to have not cared, and because she did, the world tried to fix her empathy or perhaps her neediness by locking her outside its borders. Suddenly Nefeli thought she was on to something but didn't have time to complete the puzzle in her head because her phone buzzed.

Antonis: Can u like, log into the game for a moment? I need to show you sth.

Before Nefeli had time to roll her eyes the phone buzzed again with a message from Dad.

Dad: Listen kiddo, I know that you left home. It's okay. Take some time off. I get that you're bummed that you have no close friends. Don't let it get you down.
Dad: Go out and meet new people. Don't get stuck on the past. Just take care of yourself for me. Okay?
Nefeli: Thanks, Dad.

It was like she was texting with herself. Suddenly Nefeli remembered where she got her buckle-up-and-get-over-it attitude from. Dad had told her something similar when she had been feeling nostalgic about their old life in Korinthos. About Cara. *Don't let it get you down. New friends are always better!* It was a little cruel both to Cara and to herself, but Nefeli knew he was only trying to cheer her up. Make her do something with her new life. And by taking his advice and forgetting about Cara she had set off a cascade of events that, years later, would blow up in her face.

But there was something helpful in what her father had said, both back then and now. She *should* go out and meet people. As much as she hated feeling exposed like that, she hated being utterly alone more. There were only new friends to be made now. Everyone else had disappeared.

The blonde barista's name was Katya. She only worked weekend afternoons. On weekdays she studied production design. Working on weekends sucked because she couldn't catch a film with her friends but she made up for it by making their coffee just the way they liked it and sending them silly capybara memes every morning. She was worried they would bond without her and leave her behind. Nefeli was actually surprised by how many things she learned about Katya in such a short span of time.

It helped that their areas of interest had some overlap. Katya loved art and they spent the first couple of hours at the coffee shop arguing on and off about color theory and how much leeway one could have with their color scheme. On the second day they discussed the best graphic design software and ended up commiserating on the current job market for creatives.

On the third day, Nefeli decided to come earlier and bring her sketchbook along, hoping to catch Katya's attention once more. She set her phone on silent mode, annoyed by people asking *isn't it time to show her face again?* And *whatever it is there must be something they could do.* Her brother—having his priorities straight—kept texting her to log into the game. This was Katya's work and she shouldn't be seen ignoring the other customers, so Nefeli made an effort to look occupied until the barista came to her first. Lately, Nefeli's sketchbook had been filling up with theories about her situation. She had drawn pages upon pages of people stuck in rectangles Nefeli thought of as rooms. The rooms were arranged in various ways on the paper Nefeli had renamed *the Elsewhere*. Parallel to each other, opposite each other, in some cases the rooms neighboring each other but the people in them looking only to the front, like some sort of people-stable stalls. Nefeli was looking for a way back to her friends and family by drawing various lines connecting the boxes.

"Is that a Pepper's Ghost?"

Nefeli jumped at Katya's question, accidentally pushing the biscuit that came with her coffee off the edge of the countertop. Katya smiled and brought her a complimentary brownie instead.

"I'm sorry, I was distracted," Nefeli said apologetically. She hoped this wouldn't stop Katya from chatting with her again. She hoped they were still friendly. She sounded too needy in her head so she stopped thinking about it.

Katya seemed eager to explain, which made Nefeli sigh with relief. "Pepper's Ghost is an illusion used in theater. It's basically two actors being in two different but identical rooms but appearing like they are in the same room together. One room is hidden and the image of the hidden actor is projected onto the visible room. But the audience can only see one room and one actor in the flesh. The other one was never really there."

"An illusion," Nefeli repeated. As Katya explained how the lighting in the rooms worked to get the trick right, Nefeli was certain her eyes had grown to the size of coffee saucers. What if everyone was really an illusion? What if the universe did break but not when she thought it did, but earlier? She was just the only one who noticed because she has been lonely and had needed a friend. So she accidentally made the lights in the visible room brighter while looking for Cara. That made the mirage of the people she loved disappear. Because every illusion needs the right angle or lighting to work. Could she find that switch and turn the light down to low again? She didn't know.

"It's a really old trick." Katya wiped the countertop to a shine and pointed to her own reflection. "See? I look like I am in two places but only one of me is here."

Nefeli decided she already knew enough about Pepper's Ghost so she made up an excuse of looming deadlines to head back home. The illusion theory was gaining more ground the more she thought about it. Perhaps that was the reason everyone else was still here. She didn't need them as much as the people close to her and so there was no light cast upon them to show that they weren't really there. Was anyone there? Was she? Nefeli was standing in the middle of the road and felt like screaming but then everyone who was or wasn't there would think there was something wrong with her—a different something than what was actually wrong with her so she put her head down and picked up her pace.

On the fourth day Katya was not there. Or more accurately she was and she wasn't. Nefeli had walked into the coffee shop with an imaginary script in her mind. She'd pretend her situation was a movie she had seen and then pick Katya's brain on the Pepper's Ghost theory and how theoretically someone could get out of it. Two brains were better than one and Nefeli's brain was already reaching its limits. The minute she stepped foot inside though, she felt it. The room was slightly wrong. Nefeli wasn't sure what was happening. Her senses had grown sharper perhaps. Recognized a familiar pattern. She walked straight to the counter and asked the short guy in the too-big shirt about Katya and he stopped in his tracks for a moment. He looked around, as lost as Nefeli.

"She was right next to me a minute ago," he said while peeking at the back where the kitchen was. "She's taking out the trash probably. Can I get you something?"

Nefeli nodded and placed her usual order. She sat by the counter and waited for Katya even though she knew Katya was Elsewhere. She sipped her coffee and got up couple of times to ask the guy if Katya had returned and every time he was just as surprised to not find Katya by his side. That was the confirmation Nefeli needed, that and that feeling of wrongness. Katya was and wasn't really here. Nefeli's presence was pushing her away from this reality but Katya was still here for everyone else. She realized she didn't have Katya's phone number—they hadn't known each other long enough—and she felt a weird relief because she would be tempted to text her and go through the same motions as with everyone else all over again and that wasn't healthy anymore.

No more, she thought. No more.

From: CaraMia1990@mailbuddy.gr
To: Nefeli Galliatsou Nefnef_baby@lyons-edu.org
July 20 2015, 12:03 am
Subject: I worry

When I said you could call me anytime, I meant it. I don't really know what's going on in your life right now, we've only exchanged a few DMs on socials, but whatever it is I know you can get through it.

I am sorry I snapped at you at the bus stop. You have to admit it was a pretty weird situation and I was a nervous mess that day. I was thinking mostly about myself when I should be remembering that other people go through their own stuff.

Remember that day, it was someone's birthday, yours or mine I am unsure, when we tried to eat the freaking candles off the cake? You told me they were made of the most delicious candy but all I tasted was wax. It was hilarious and embarrassing and we picked bits of candle from our teeth for a week. I pretended I believed you but I only half-did and went along anyway. Because that's what you needed at the moment. Someone to believe you. I can't promise you I will believe everything you say but I'll try if you let me.

Please let me. Or at least send me a message that you're still holding on.

Love,
Cara

Nefeli moved through the world like a shadow. Fast and immaterial, trying to leave everything as undisturbed as possible. When she had to go out for the occasional grocery shopping, she avoided chatting with the person buying the box of pasta next to her, with the fishmonger at the corner, with the cashier at the bakery. Sometimes she didn't feel like going out at all and subsisted on Antonis's pre-made meals and the occasional gyro he brought home from work. The fewer people she pushed to Elsewhere, the better. But sometimes she needed to go out, to listen to people's chatter, the sound of their feet on the pavement, the marble floors, the grass. The restaurants and the bars in the afternoon were packed with people, old and young. Big groups of friends sitting around a tiny table, trying not to bump each other's knees and dissolving into laughter moments later. She ate it all up because she needed to know someone was still there. But she never interacted with anyone for fear of breaking the illusion. She felt like a spy overhearing conversations in a strange world. A lonely spy in a lonely place.

From: Nefnef_baby@lyons-edu.org
To: Cara Hasani CaraMia1990@mailbuddy.gr
August 15 2015, 1:00 pm
Subject: The world is empty

Dear Cara,

Thank you for your honesty, my friend. Not everyone is like you and I mean it in the best of ways.

You know what day it is. It's the day of the Assumption of Virgin Mary's body. The day that Athens becomes a ghost town. If you turn on your TV right now, you'll see videos of empty streets baking in the sun. The absence of sound in a city that houses more than three million people is astonishing. Then you'll catch the same vanished people jostling against each other on a beach somewhere in Greece, the on-site reporters asking about the weather. Others you'll find in Tinos or other holy places, praying for this miracle or that (perhaps I should be following their example).

This is how it feels being me right now. I constantly live in a void and there is nowhere to turn. The blinds on the windows are always closed. Where has everyone gone? For you the answer is straightforward. For me it's more complicated.

When my body finds the strength to reunite with my spirit even for a little bit, I will message you again.

Your oldest friend,
Nefeli

Antonis: Dude, log into the fucking game. U can do it. I believe in u.

It was at one of her lowest points that Nefeli shambled one morning into the living room to find the bags of chips resting on the couch. When she was feeling down, she liked to huddle in the couch under the blanket and leave the window half-open just to get a glimpse of the people rushing outside.

The flavors were BBQ, oregano, and vinegar. Nefeli scrunched her nose at the idea of the last one, but she took out her phone and texted Antonis.

Nefeli: I know what you're doing. Thanks. Why vinegar though?
Antonis: Sorry, it was a late-night run. I thought you wanted all the chips!

Antonis: Will you please, please, log into the game?
Nefeli sighed.
Nefeli: Fine, but after I've had my coffee.

FangGirl: Hey, I'm here. What's going on?
Hauntcules: Finally! Stay right there! I am coming!

Nefeli couldn't go anywhere. Once she opened *TinyCastle*™ two things happened: first, the room filled with the indigo hues of the game's graphics, taking her back to the first day she realized there was something wrong with the world. With her world. And two, she remembered she had been stuck in a rosebush the last time she had been there. She ditched the controller and connected the keyboard to send a "telepathic" in-game message to Antonis to come and get her out.

The bushes seemed to be faring quite well since she last saw them, as opposed to Nefeli herself. The rose buds had grown little mouths and two rows of tiny needle-teeth and were now trying to eat her.

"Hey, cut it out!" she yelled at the screen and instantly felt weird talking to herself. But what was wrong with that? In a way it was liberating.

And then she saw Antonis in the game. Not the ghost avatar with the trailing sheet, the evil red eyes, and the mischievous smile Antonis had chosen as an avatar when they were playing. It was a tiny avatar of her brother, tall and lanky, with long hands and a slight hunch from years of trying to see her eye-to-eye. Nefeli had no idea up until that time that a silly game avatar could make you cry. But it did. The avatar made a barely noticeable movement that to Nefeli seemed like breathing and there was a gust of wind every few seconds that shuffled Antonis's curly hair like in real life.

Hauntcules: Sorry about that! The bushes are buggy but I found a walkthrough. Sending you a link.
FangGirl: I missed you, jerk. Nice avatar.
Hauntcules: My avatar is the same. This is a Halloween costume. I am still a ghost underneath.
FangGirl: You dressed up as yourself? That's so you.
Hauntcules: That is me! I figured you might want to see my face.

She did. Nefeli realized how much she had needed to see everyone's face and if this was the closest she could get, she'd take it for now. There had been texts, DMs, and emails from her family and friends the past few weeks and even though they were worried, and kind, and a little sad, there was always something in them that would remind Nefeli that she was not believed. They did try to pretend they believed her but it was obvious they didn't. Her experience was hers and hers only.

Hauntcules: Looks like you're free! Don't worry about the ear. It will grow back tomorrow. The perks of being a vampire!
FangGirl: Hey, do you believe me? About the universe thing.
Hauntcules: Yes.
FangGirl: Why do you believe me?
Hauntcules: Because you're either telling the truth or I am living with a ghost who's been stealing my stuff. A real one.
Hauntcules: Do you know how many days I've gone sleepless to see where my food disappeared to? I've been testing your theory for a while. That's why I've been begging you to log into the game.
Hauntcules: Also, I've missed you too.

This time playing the game wasn't such a slog. It was comforting in a way she couldn't appreciate before. She got to meet people she hadn't seen in ages, like Antonis's high school friends. She went skull-digging with them. She even befriended a couple of new neighboring critters. It turned out Antonis was a minor tycoon in the game, a proper teethillionaire, and although he couldn't transfer her his teeth, he bought stuff with them and helped turn her tiny castle into a mini version of their apartment. She even got her own Halloween costume that looked like her real self. She needed everything to look normal even if the game itself wasn't meant to be normal. If she could see it maybe she could feel it too.

Hauntcules: Nefeli what did you do to my garden?
FangGirl: I thought a few carnivorous roses would look nice. They can't eat you. You're a ghost, remember?
FangGirl: Where's Mihalis? Did he lose connection? We should go ghost hunting.
Hauntcules: Hello, ghost here! Show some respect!
BrainsForBreakfast: Sorry guys. I've got to go. Something is wrong. I can't find my mom. She was cooking and now the food is burning and I can't find her.

Ever since she had returned to the game, Nefeli kept catching herself daydreaming that everyone would just give up on the outside world and stay with her around the clock. She found herself feeling abandoned every time Antonis had to go to work, even though she had to work as well. Wouldn't it be nice if they could just all beam themselves inside the game and have fun and leave their corporeal forms behind? According to her Pepper's Ghost theory, they were not really there anyway. So, wouldn't it be nice if they just stayed in the game? Wouldn't it be fun?

That's why it hit extra hard when she got all the messages. Her dad sent her a short, scared text about having lost Nefeli's mom for a week and was he losing his mind too? Was there collectively something wrong with his family in a psychosomatic way?

Nefeli felt anger burning on her cheeks and texted: *There's something wrong with all of us. We aren't listening to each other. Please don't stop texting Mom. She needs you.*

Mom was sorry too but only because she didn't know how to fix things. She was even sorrier she hadn't realized what kind of fixing was needed or she would have done it. Nefeli didn't know what she could say to her, so she wrote: *Sadly, Mom, you're not an astrophysicist. You did nothing wrong. I love you.*

Her long-lost high school friends texted her asking for tips and tricks to beat this.

She texted: *There is no beating this. I am sorry but I am as lost as the first day. Get yourselves some chocolate because this will be brutal.*

Nefeli emailed Cara before her oldest-ex-newfound friend got the chance, saying: *I guess phone calls are out of the question now for both of us. But if you find the time in this chaos you can email me anytime. This time I will always reply. You are still my oldest friend.* To make a point she attached a photo of Cara's infamous eighth birthday party when she and Nefeli ate the little pink swirly candles.

Then she sat on the couch and turned on the news. The confused mess of the news anchor as he was trying to contact the on-site reporter was pitiful. Perhaps because they shared a bond with the news anchor they were now lost to each other. It was not one place where all of this was happening. Nefeli read post after post on public forums and she finally decided to add her story. She couldn't really claim she was the patient-zero in this but she did share what little she knew. She even mentioned the term Loneliness Universe that became instantly viral. Everyone felt like this now. Trapped in loneliness like bugs in resin.

Antonis managed to somehow get the whole family in the game and that helped a little. Her brother was surprisingly the most level-headed one in this situation. Dad became a swamp-monster, complete with moss growing out of his ears and nose. Mom on the other hand turned into a gigantic spider. At first, nobody knew what to do with themselves in the game, but Antonis gave them a project. They would build a castle for the family. Just like the time they tried to raise a giant sandcastle on a beach in Crete but there was too much water and it kept collapsing. This time they'd do it right. As grim as it sounded, it was the closest they had been in years and Nefeli could not shake the urge to visit a beach and stick her toes in the warm mud.

From: CaraMia1990@mailbuddy.gr
To: Nefeli Galliatsou Nefnef_baby@lyons-edu.org
September 5 2015, 1:35 am
Subject: I am lonely

This sucks, Nefeli. I didn't know someone could feel like this. Everything feels nonsensical and a little fluid. I'm sorry I didn't believe you at first. How could I? I don't believe myself right now. I don't know how to find anyone. I miss my family and my boyfriend. I haven't told you about him yet. I was waiting until the time we'd meet (lol). Now it's too late. He sleeps in the same bed where I am typing this email from right now and yet I can't see him, touch him, or smell him. I only see the ripples the sheets make sometimes. They hold the shape of him. The soft outline of his body and I could swear the ripples change every night. Can you believe it? Of course you can.

I feel immaterial, like the wind or the froth of the waves. Or I just might be delirious. I haven't slept in a couple of days.

I never asked about you though. Even through our instant messages I didn't seem curious about your life and I am sorry about that. It's because I would prefer to talk about important things face to face, so I could see you crack that sideways smile of yours as you told me your whole life story. But I am asking now. Do you have someone in your life that you miss in that way? Even if you don't I hope you know that you have me. Only one email away.

I loved that picture of us by the way. I didn't know you had it. The funny thing is I would gladly eat a birthday candle just to go back in time and space and join you again. But maybe it's not wise to wish for more scrambled-up physics.

Tell you what. I'll make a project for us. I'll make myself go out and take pictures of the places we used to visit as kids. Then I'll tell you everything that happened this past two decades. I need this or else I feel my brain will turn into goop. Please do the same for me even though I have never been to Athens. I want to know all your usual spots.

I have already forgiven you for the letters. There is nothing to be mad about.

Love you,

Cara

Loneliness Universe was now the standard term of each new iteration of the universe, when someone lost someone new. There wasn't really an official scientific term for this particular multiverse or series of bubble universes. Scientists published scores of perspective and opinion articles but a particular one caught on, one that described observable and unobservable universes, where observable is the subjective universe each person objectively exists in and observes the rest of humanity from and unobservable are the parallel universes where the individual projects themselves onto so that others observe them but they are not physically there.

All of this until the moment of rapture or dimming happens, where the individual stops projecting themselves onto an unobservable universe and that's when people assume a bubble universe has appeared, but in reality, they were never really there. Which to Nefeli's ears sounded like a super complicated way to describe Pepper's Ghost but whatever.

And then the world started drifting further apart.

It started small. First as a glitch in the game. The rose bushes were still trying to eat Nefeli but the avatars of Antonis, Mom, Dad, and the rest stopped moving for a few seconds. It was the closest thing Nefeli had seen to silence, nothingness, the end. Then the slowed down pace spread to the entire internet, phone texts, and emails. The theories started popping up immediately (as immediately as they could have appeared in this new pace). Everyone agreed on one thing. The universes were somehow moving away from each other. Like charges repelling.

After that, silence. This time because the world turned inward. People needed the precious time left before everything was lost to say their goodbyes. Some scientists offered a glimmer of hope: they said that this was a cycle of sorts. Like the revolution of the Earth around the Sun. Only this must happen every one million years instead of one. Soon it would all be over. All anyone needed to do was hang on a little longer. The hope was so small it was barely there, but it was the only thing people wanted to think about.

Nefeli and her family lit a bright bonfire in *TinyCastle*™, a virtual BBQ with friends which very much felt like the last family dinner they all had together before Nefeli left Greece to pursue her MFA and came back a couple of years later. Meaning, they all pretended they would meet again. They had to. Hopefully in less than a couple of years. Hopefully very soon. It's amazing what people can adapt to when need arises. How so little can suddenly become so much.

Nefeli took a picture of *Six Sins*, the now-closed goth club she drank her first cocktail in when she was nineteen. It would probably be the last picture she'd be able to send Cara for who knew how long. She used to daydream about bumping into Cara in that club by accident, in a scenario where Cara had come to Athens to study. But that would be just another reality that never came to be.

From: Nefnef_baby@lyons-edu.org
To: Cara Hasani CaraMia1990@mailbuddy.gr
September 22 2015, 11:00 am
Subject: A passing

Let's play a game.

Not like the one my whole family now lives in. Let's play one inside our minds. Like we used to do back in the day.

Pretend you remember this picture I am sending you. Remember it as in, you've been there with me when we were in college. You left one afternoon and took the bus to Athens just to have a drink with me in that goth club I could not stop talking about. I called you nuts because you'd have to catch the 6 a.m. bus back to Korinthos but you just stared at me and giggled, without a care in the world.

Now imagine it again with all the pictures I sent you and I'll do it too with all the ones you sent me. That's how we'll measure the passage of time. And hopefully by the time we run out of made-up stories the world will be one again, and I won't have to concern myself with the laws of physics for the rest of my life. I need to believe that this is a winter season and that spring is within reach.

Our memories together were a handful of overexposed Polaroids my mom took of us, all at various places. Now we have added ours to the canon. Perhaps if I look at those pictures really hard. If I plunge myself into the texture of those memories, the creature that runs the universe(s) will believe I mean it this time and will stop drawing us apart. These pictures are my last hope, Cara. And I won't stop looking at them—at you, at me, at our families, at our past—until I can dream of a future again. Until something good fucking happens. I will still be here.

Still waiting.

Love you always,

Your oldest friend

Eugenia Triantafyllou is a Greek author and artist with a flair for dark things. Her work has won the Shirley Jackson Award and has been nominated for the Ignyte, Locus, Nebula, and World Fantasy Awards. She is a graduate of Clarion West Writers Workshop. You can find her stories in *Reactor*, *Uncanny*, *Strange Horizons*, *Apex*, and other venues. She currently lives in Athens with a boy and a dog. Find her on Twitter @foxesandroses, or Bluesky @foxesandroses.bsky.social, her IG @eugeniatriantafyllou, or her website http://www.eugeniatriantafyllou.com.

NOVELLA

THE DRAGONFLY GAMBIT

A.D. Sui

If you're listening to this then we have arrived at our ends.

We kept our promises as women of our constitution should. I have ended the twenty-year-long uprising against the Rule in just six months, just as you've asked of me. And you, the Third Daughter of the Rule, Eternal Rightful, both beautiful and deadly, have ended me. Regrettably, this means I wasn't there to witness the instance when your façade came down, when all control seeped through your fingers.

Alas, we were never meant to live in the future we were carving from the decaying carcass of your empire.

Now you can rest. We can both rest. We did the best with what we had.

The Opening

Chapter 1

By all accounts, I should be scared.

Intelligence and Investigations boys are overzealous. They like to break things: doors, people, entire local governments if they get the chance. Five more flights of stairs until they're at my door. After three weeks of stealthily tracking me, taking shifts to shoot unflattering photographs from the flashing billboard across the street, my day of reckoning is finally here.

I can't complain. It's nice to feel wanted.

They pass from one glowing screen to the next, slithering along the chipped walls. Their silhouettes scurry up the stairwell, tasers drawn, back-to-back, like they're in some sort of an active shooter situation. The cameras I set up in the months prior are paying for themselves. Who's the paranoid one now?

Shay will do the knocking. He's here to ease the blow. Ten years ago we were friends, in the way where you know how the other sleeps, in the way where I know he's about to puke by the way he stops talking. He arrived not a full cycle ago to close the deal, I'm sure.

When he knocks, it's an official rattle, the sort that lets you know you're in trouble, the sort that's followed by a black bag over your face and a trip to an undisclosed site. Shay knocks like he carries the authority of the Rule with him, like it will back him up on any decision. Little does he know, the Rule will break him just as well, if necessary.

I limp over to answer.

"You're not a delivery bot." I give him a sour smile. Shay is stiff as a board, his own taser unholstered. He strategically avoids staring at my bare chest, or the rest of my naked body. The slumped shoulder and the hoisted arm, far too atrophied to look functional.

"Nez, I'm on orders to retrieve you."

"That's no way to greet an old friend, *Captain*."

"Don't make this harder than it needs to be. I have guys in every stairwell, armed, ready to take you out."

"On a date, I gather?"

"Don't be difficult. Be glad I knocked."

"Be glad I didn't blow you to bits while you were climbing the stairs."

Shay's face darkens for a moment. Okay, the camera*s an*d the traps are paying for themselves. He retraces the stairwell, his eyes darting from left to right as he replays his ascent in slow motion. Every turn, every step. "Third floor?"

"Third floor."

Shayrocks his weight anxiously between his feet, pretending not to notice the projected hologram and the floating code behind me. "Look—" he says, visibly uncomfortable. "We gotta get moving, so you need to put something on. The guys—they're—"

I disappear into my apartment and Shay follows like an oversized puppy. He steps cautiously over a box of moldy takeout. I bet he gets danger pay any time he docks on any non-central planet. "This wasn't my idea," he says, and I've never wanted to punch him more. Not his idea. When was the last time he *had* an idea?

Investigation and Intelligence has him dressed to the nines. In his grey uniform and gold cuffs, Shay is a walking, talking propaganda poster. The jawline helps. No wonder him and Kaya—no, there's no sense going there.

While I saunter around the room, Shay stands awkwardly in the center. His pin camera is recording from his chest, so this conversation will remain lukewarm. "If it were up to me, I'd leave you alone, but the Rule needs you."

"The Rule doesn't need *me*, it needs a way to turn a stalemate."

Shay flinches. "Nez."

"*I* said it, not you."

"I should correct you. The Rule is not in a stalemate. The Rule is winning."

I throw a shirt in Shay's general direction. "It's been *winning* for twenty years now."

Every empire falls. You can kick and scream, and whine, and plead, but every empire will have its fall. The Rule has been doing well for over a thousand years, expanding at an impossible rate, absorbing small and medium system-level governments into itself. Sometimes peacefully. Mostly not. But it got too big, and the edges began to fray. Shay knows this. Anyone with half a brain knows it. It took a few hundred years for systems to actively rebel and break away. It took less than a decade for full-out war to ignite after that. That was twenty years ago, and the Rule has yet to reclaim the systems. Two generals have already fallen, the First and the Second Daughters. The Third doesn't have much time left either.

"Safe to assume you're not going to tell me where we're headed?"

Shay affirms with a shake of his head. What a good little soldier.

I find a passably clean shirt and shove it over my head. My left arm goes in elbow first, and then inertia takes it the rest of the way. If I flail too much my shoulder will pop out. You gotta learn to get around these things if you want to get by on your own.

"Nez, something more substantial, *please*."

I'm willing to put just as much effort into my appearance as the Rule did into summoning me. I slide on my pants with my right hand, do them up. I take a sharpened pencil and plunge it through my hair, twist it around and stab through the bun.

Shay watches the entire routine silently. Then, when I'm done, he half-heartedly asks, "How's the—"

He means the arm. Everyone *always* means the arm. He fails to acknowledge the limp, the slight toe drag, the way my left eyelid never fully opens, the upward curve of my lip. The devil is in the details. Shay could never even begin to comprehend the extent of the damage. Just one ruptured vertebra and any dreams of piloting anything other than a desk are gone. *Poof!* I shrug at Shay with my right shoulder. "It's fine, won't get in the way of whatever it is you want me for, I'm sure."

Shay gestures out of my apartment and down the long, shadowy corridor I've crawled through many times, too drunk to stand. He's a real gentleman, and as of a man of such constitution, he lets me wrap up my projected code and schematics before we leave. By which I mean he lets me "accidentally" pour a litre of coffee on the CPU while he turns his back and politely stares out into the hallway. I watch it fizzle and die without making any small talk. Then, he leads me down the corridor and into the stairwell, where I'm greeted by the wrong end of a rifle.

"Down," Shay says, and the boy in dark grey coveralls lowers the muzzle.

"There's a transport waiting for us downstairs. You will be hooded and handcuffed, and taken to an undisclosed site." I'd really hoped we could do without the undisclosed sites. "Don't bother staying awake, it's a long trip. You can ask for a sedative once you're inside, I highly recommend it." Shay slips into the Intelligence persona as easily as a snake into a rabbit's burrow. Ten years and the Rule still has him running errands like a recruit—either Shay's gone and royally fucked up or this is important to the Third Daughter.

"For once I'll stay sober." We start down the stairwell, boy-with-rifle ahead of me, Shay behind me. I'd be stupid to make a run for it. I haven't run in nearly a decade, today would be hell of a day to start.

"Rule Eternal," Shay greets the driver once we're outside. A sleek, black transport has been bestowed upon me, the interior of which I will never see. Shay pulls a hood out of thin air. "You know the drill."

"Wait—"

In the early hours of the day, suns still safety tucked beyond the horizon, the rain lashes frigid droplets against the exposed parts of me. If I tilt my face skywards, it patters against my eyelids, my lips. I can taste the acidity as the water seeps into the corners of my mouth.

"What are you doing?" Shay looms over me, impatiently.

"I have a feeling this is the last time I'll see rain," I tell Shay and let him pull the black-out fabric of the hood over my face. Immediately, it's difficult to breathe. It's going to be a long ride.

Shay slips inside the car beside me. He presses cold steel to my wrists and at once they are bound and immobile. Based on the sounds of shuffling, there are four of us in the car. I manage to keep my mouth shut for what feels like an hour. "What does the Third Daughter want me with?"

"What makes you think it's the Third Daughter?"

Oh, I don't know. Maybe it's because if this was an Intelligence and Investigations solo assignment, I'd be missing half my fingernails by now? "Let me take a gander." Sometimes, I really need to keep my mouth shut. "The Rule is at a stalemate. You've pushed your tech as far as it will go and it gave you, what? A marginal advantage? One that you wasted because the breakaways have much better pilots? You're matched in tech and now you want someone like me to come in and fix this problem for you, you want an edge, you want—"

Shay stabs me with a sedative. *Rude.* The last I remember is the artificially melodic launch countdown , and then everything disappears into a chemically induced black-out.

Hands.

There are hands on me, and I have no energy to fight them off. Strong hands. *Cold.* They're moving me. Somewhere? Moving me up? Where is up anyway? Someone shines a blinding light into my eye.

"Stay still." A commanding voice comes from above and I obey by habit. I just can't rinse the soldier out, no matter how much I try. The sedative keeps the panic at bay. My heart rate never goes past seventy.

"Buy me a drink first," I slur, and the world disappears around me.

Shay hands me a plastic sippy cup filled with sweet juice of an unknown variety.

"I don't blame you, you know," I say, still slurring. Oh no, what am I replying to? "All of us had to find ways to survive. You found yours in uniform. I don't take it personally."

Shay watches with wary eyes and nods along. Whatever sedative knocked me out must have produced hints of unwanted amnesia. My brain started recording only now, but we could have been chatting for hours. Oh *no*. The room is anything but cozy. A two-way mirror shimmers in the dim lights and there are at least four cameras by the ceiling that I can count. Five, if you include the pin camera on Shay's chest.

I flex my legs and drive my heels into the floor. Wherever we are now, we're not planetside. Shay has given me magnetic soles and left my arms uncuffed. This just might be more of a conversation than a beating.

"Now that we've put some distance behind us, let's have a chat," Shay says. Detached. Professional.

I nod along as I tense various parts of my body to test their function. Looks like the sedative is the only thing that was used. They transported me in a rush, probably unconscious; my left shoulder aches as if I've been laying on it for too long. I have yet to piss myself, but honestly, I'm not even sure I'm wearing the same pants as when I left my apartment. Which, by these estimates, puts us between six and eight hours travel time. With an extra half an hour to throw my unconscious body like a sack of potatoes on and off shuttle, I'd say we're halfway to the frontlines.

Normally, I'd agree that everything they've done to me so far was a well-deserved consequence to my actions (the usual: sabotage, treason, I dabble in a few), but the lack of actual consequences is unnerving.

"I wouldn't go as far as to say it was treason," Shay says. "Broadcasting the details of Vice-Admiral Treped's divorce to every station that would listen hardly constitutes a crime against the Rule, although I did find it highly entertaining." He grins and I break into a sweat at how little control I have over keeping my thoughts inside my head where they belong.

Shay's aware of this. "You've been busy since we last saw each other."

Yes, I wasn't exactly sitting there twiddling my thumbs for a decade.

"You developed shield-penetrating drones, you obtained and revealed classified locations of the major fleet operations, you shut down payroll on three major Rule carriers, and of course—" Shay raises his eyebrows, "—you managed to leak fighter schematics to the breakaways."

"They had those already. First Daughter herself armed the annexed systems."

"I don't believe that to be true."

But the thing about the truth is that you don't have to believe in it for it to still be the truth. Truth shouldn't bend to favouritism. One such truth is that the Oran system, my home, faithfully adhered to the assimilation agreement, allowing their children to be conscripted for the Rule's fleet as long as the system itself was allowed to maintain some of its governing power. Shay, Kaya, and yes, me, ended up in the Rule's ranks thanks to that requirement. That is a truth. One, I begrudgingly accept.

Once there were suspicions that Oran might break away from the Rule, all assimilation agreements were thrown out. The entire system, all fifteen planets that comprised it, was vaporized sometime before I was discharged. It wasn't personal, just like Shay coming to collect me wasn't personal. This is also a truth I must accept. Kaya and Shay continue to serve despite what happened to our home. I still struggle with that one.

"We're not here for the First Daughter," I say.

"We're here to put an end to pointless fighting."

"Oh, has the Third Daughter decided to surrender?"

A faint smile flickers across Shay's lips. "Nez—" Shay warns.

The air grows thick between us, and I brace for a thunderstorm. "I'm not going to help you optimize your baby killing."

The sudden pain is blinding. It twists my insides with an iron claw as I double over and hurl all over my pants. Then, hurl again on to the floor. When my vision returns, my forehead presses against the metal table and there's rust in my mouth. I force a laugh. "When did you implant that?" There's a shaved patch at the nape of my neck which also happens to be the epicenter of the pain.

There's no answer. A second shock shatters my world. Something about where the implant sits in my neck causes it to impact the left side more than right. My arm convulses with bone-shattering strength. Luckily, my stomach is empty and I just dry heave until the shock passes. "Oof" is all I can manage.

Shay swivels in his chair, back and forth, like a bored toddler. "Years away from any real action have made you soft, Nez." He leans over and gives me a pat on the shoulder. "Don't forget, you were once a baby-killer in training too, eager to see some baby-killing action. Don't get all high and mighty. The Third Daughter doesn't need, nor want your loyalty or any sort of change of heart, she simply wants you to optimize our fighters."

"Shock me all you want," I pause to spit out a piece of protein I ingested two days ago (three? Time is weird right now), "but you've pushed your fighter tech to its limit. There's nothing more I can do. You won't squeeze much else out of it." Or me. I promise you there's nothing more left of me.

Shay shrugs. The creases around the corners of his eyes weren't there when we last saw one another. We share in the damp silence, inhaling the putrid smell wafting from the floor. "Well," he says at last, with a wistful smile "you do have a talent for making something out of scraps. Try and apply yourself. The Third

Daughter might have a gentle hand compared to her sisters, but Intelligence and Investigations tends to correct for that."

He leaves me alone then, with the puddle of bile and the contents of my stomach on the floor, and if I could, I'd cry, but there's nothing in my stomach, not to mention the rest of me. For the first time in what I think is two days, there is a moment of silence, of reprieve. And I wish for nothing more than it to end. I dig my nails into my forearm, but the pain barely registers. One fucking vertebra. One vertebra bursting was enough to end a career, enough to end a future.

But then what kind of future would it have been, flying for the Rule?

I shouldn't blame Kaya for what happened, but I do.

Kaya.

Kaya Laux. The Iron Fox, the ace of the Rule, the best fighter pilot in the galaxy—supposedly, according to the Third Daughter and to the millions of propaganda posters around any space port. But it wasn't always like that. She wasn't always spewing militant garbage from an impersonal hologram, the face of the Rule's fleet, a million miles away.

I rest my head against the table again. No matter how tightly I shut my eyes, the world spins. No, she used to be much closer. The door opens and even without raising my head I can tell that Shay is back for me.

"Time to go," he says, cold and rehearsed, just as they taught him in the academy and enforced through years of service. Money well spent.

I have a feeling he won't let me change. "Will Kaya be there?"

"Don't worry about that right now."

I take it as a *yes*.

Chapter 2

The problem with military hangars is that they are designed to withstand a direct hit from a nuclear warhead and yet, no one has the mind to reinforce and improve the very soft people that inhabit them. People that easily perish from the tiniest stab wound or a drink of contaminated water. The dichotomy has begun to bother me for a reason I've yet to place. Maybe I'm getting too introspective in my age. People are soft and fallible; people start wars they don't have the strength or endurance to win. Maybe it's the softness that bothers me after all, the sheer waste of it all.

This particular hangar belongs to the Rule's flagship, which is barely two gate-jumps away from the frontlines. The ship sits in a cluster with five other cruisers, and a handful of smaller vessels, waiting for a golden chance at a counter-offensive. People, rations, ammunition, even the shocker in my brainstem are all delivered here from their manufacturing sites on Rule colonies. The Rule itself makes nothing except for war. I'm not supposed to say any of this out loud, of course. The fact that I even know it is probably what got me in this mess to begin with.

Shay is still by my side, wearing fresh-pressed blues against all odds. He must have shaved and eaten while I was asleep on the cot the Rule so kindly provided (bless the Rule Eternal). I think I ate. Yesterday's assault on my brain has severely impacted my short-term memory.

I've been issued a pair of standard issue blues with no insignia on them. Here, I have no rank. Not anymore. I pull my collar away and take a sniff. I must have also showered at some point. With the two middle buttons undone, I drape my arm through the hole and into the makeshift sling. Good enough to relieve the tension.

The walls of the hangar curve all the way to the ceiling and I have to crane my neck at a painful angle to follow their silhouette all the way to where they end. Kaya's eyes follow me from the hundreds of posters plastered around the hangar. In the most egregious, she is seductively propped up against her fighter, helmet in hand. The text reads *Invest in Our Daughters, Invest in the Future!* Another is a close-up of her face that reads *Ready! Fire! Victory!*

I might just puke again.

Hundreds of fighters line the floor, indiscernible grey against grey. Ignoring both Shay and I, thousands scurry between charging stations, pilots in black flight suits and techs in their brown coveralls. There are faces from all of the Rule here, joined together by the very conscription requirements that brought Shay and myself into the fleet. I can pick out a few native to Oran, techs mostly. They chat amongst themselves in a language I can no longer understand, that neither Shay, nor I, nor Kaya can understand. Still, I dream of it, singing songs I make no meaning of.

The Rule makes nothing. It only takes. Shay blends in effortlessly, like he's molted everything Oran from himself. Out of the three of us, he had the least trouble shortening the vowels of his speech, adopting the right diction. Speaking the right way, eating the right way, the oval of his face, the lightness of his hair make it easy for him to blend in with the central residents. Although, anywhere in the Rule, from the blinding center to the perpetually frozen outposts everyone avoids an Intelligence uniform.

I give a long whistle to get Shay's attention.

"What?" He frowns.

I tilt my head upwards until I lose my balance and stagger backwards like a dumb bird. "They didn't make them this big in our day."

Shay *hmms* in agreement and extends his arm in the direction of the middle lane of fighters. "This way." Even with me, he never points. Pointing is *aggressive*. It's much better to use a knife-hand, a softer gesture when directing your captive ex-friend to a fighter that has probably claimed the lives of thousands of your system neighbours.

The hangar is large enough that towards the corners, where the air is space-stale and heavy, a miniature climate forms, and condensation drips down my neck, half-environment, half-exertion. One of the fighters is pried open by the wall, its entrails spilled across the metal floors. Around it, three boys in brown coveralls are struggling to replace the warheads and set up the changing station.

Shay knife-hands towards the fighter. "This one is yours. You can play with it as much as you'd like. Take it apart, put it back together, whatever, just make it shoot faster or something."

"Or *something*, he says."

"Or go faster, whatever. Make it into a better fighter so we can finish winning this thing."

Or whatever. I run my palm against the hull. It's smooth and shimmering and matches the temperature of the hangar impeccably. All fighters are finished with a UV- and Gamma-resistant coating for longer fights or transports. If I close my eyes, I can still reconstruct the schematics of a fighter in my sleep, in any nightmare. This one is far newer than what I'd had the pleasure to fly, but the shape of it, the feel, is like stepping into my childhood home. Beneath the initial coating there are layers and layers of armour matrices interwoven with a network of intricate electronics. I walk along the hull, fingers gliding along the snakeskin-like coating. From touch alone, it's a good fighter. She'd handle beautifully with the right pilot.

"She's something, eh?" A reddish patch of hair pops from the cockpit. The boy is no less than a decade my junior and far too enthusiastic to be a pilot. Pilots usually have an air about them, a mix of superiority and martyrdom, like they're better than everyone else and aren't afraid to die to prove it. They are—better that is—but they also don't need to telegraph it so much. "Private Carte, Mechanic, First Class." The boy hops from the fighter and stretches out his hand towards mine.

"She still overheating after ten seconds of hard-burn?" I ask as I shake his hand.

Private Carte beams at me. "Ah, you've been around the Model 2s. We fixed it with a constant coolant wash. As long as the coolant is fresh, she can hard-burn as long as you want. Although that raised our coolant demands. Some solutions can create more problems, you know how it is."

I glance over at Shay who has wandered off and crouched against the wall. *Rest when you can.* He's picked up a few good habits since I've last seen him.

"And what's the charge like on her? 500?"

Carte laughs. "You know your stuff, but you're obviously from the last generation. The charge is in the thousands. It technically re-charges whenever it fires. Saves us time on resupply."

A lot has changed, and yet. "Then how are you losing?"

Carte pales. "Ma'am?"

"How are you losing to the breakaways when they have nearly decade-old schematics?" I glance over his shoulder and into Kaya's face, on yet another poster. This one has her features superimposed over her fighter, the *Iron Fox*. I wonder what the penalty is for setting one of these on fire.

"Ma'am, the Rule Eternal is not losing. We are winning a little more each day and will continue to win until the galaxy is again united and at peace."

Behind me, Shay stirs. "Leave the boy alone, Nez," he calls out. "You're just gonna upset him."

Carte freezes, mouth half-open. He's done his diligence in reciting the correct answer, the one any sane person would give in the presence of an Intelligence uniform. But I'm not here to throw around comforting platitudes.

Still, it *is* a good question. The Rule is technologically superior. They have pushed their fighter tech to its limit. The schematics that the breakaways have are nearly a decade old, and even if they worked on them and made their own improvements, they still shouldn't be able to compete with the Rule's manufacturing power. The sheer discrepancy in numbers should be enough. Maybe the breakaways just want it more. Then, before I can have a singular coherent thought, the hangar drops dead silent.

"The *Iron Fox* is back," someone bellows.

Shay leaps from his spot by the wall and grabs my arm. In a tone that's both warning and a plea, he whispers, "Let it go." The *Iron Fox*. My stomach churns. Shay squeezes my arm tighter. "Move along before you give yourself a stroke," he says.

But how can I let Kaya have her welcome parade without knowing I'm here? "I'll behave, just let me see her."

Shay doesn't buy a word I'm saying, but his fingers loosen their iron grip a smidgen.

"It's been more than ten years. I know the two of you are fucking. I'm over it. I'm not carrying a torch for her or anything, just let me see her."

Still unconvinced, Shay searches my face for any sign that I'm lying, telling the truth, anything in between. Meanwhile, the hangar erupts with deafening cheers and clapping. Dozens of pilots and technicians rush to the far end of the hangar where a fighter just pulled through de-com—fighters are basically radioactive by the time they return. Measures need to be taken so that the techs don't get cancer every time they set one up for a re-charge.

Even from nearly fifty meters away, when the cockpit hatch slides open I recognize the flight suit-clad figure climbing out. Even with the opaque helmet and faceplate, it's unmistakably Kaya. There hasn't been a pilot, and arguably, never will be a pilot, who exits their fighter with such pizzazz. In a smooth motion, Kaya pulls the helmet from her face, and her long (very-much-not-up-to-code) hair spills down and past her shoulders in an obsidian waterfall. Even as a cadet, Kaya had the swagger of an ace. Even in simulation, Kaya performed as if it were her very last battle, leaving nothing on the field. Unless, of course, it was me.

Eyes blazing with a victorious high, Kaya surveys her adoring fans. "Twenty direct hits, fifteen kills, and two full-sized cruisers. Today we drink to the Rule Eternal!"

"Rule Eternal!" The crowd erupts louder still.

I manage to pry my arm away from Shay and stagger through the rear line of onlookers. I shove a few aside with my shoulder, ducking under pumping fists. Thanks to my dodging and weaving there's now only one line of enthused spectators between me and Kaya. By now she's climbed down from her fighter and is receiving good natured punches to the shoulder.

She's parked *Iron Fox* right above a copper spot on the floor, one that I imagine had been crimson not too many hours prior. Sacrifices have been long carried out by the fleet before major deployments. It's not uncommon for privates to volunteer their lives to assure safety of a Rule ace. If I ask anyone about it, they will all lie and insist that those are just rumours, but the floor begs to differ.

Then, Kaya sees me and her expression shatters.

The Dragonfly Gambit by A.D. Sui is available from Neon Hemlock Press

A.D. Sui is a Ukrainian-born, internationally raised speculative writer, and Nebula, Aurora, and Theodore Sturgeon Memorial Award finalist. She is the author of *The Dragonfly Gambit* (2024), *The Iron Garden Sutra* (2026), and more than two dozen short stories. A failed academic and retired fencer, she spends her days wrangling her two dogs and tending to her myriads of tropical plants. You can find her on most social media platforms as @thesuiway.

NOVELLA & NOVEL FINALISTS

THE 2024 NEBULA AWARD FOR BEST NOVELLA

The Dragonfly Gambit

A.D. Sui

The Butcher of the Forest

Premee Mohamed

A world-weary woman races against the clock to survive a deadly forest in this dark, otherworldly fairytale from Nebula and World Fantasy Award-winning author Premee Mohamed.

At the northern edge of a land ruled by a merciless foreign tyrant lies a wild, forbidden forest ruled by powerful magic.

Veris Thorn—the only one to ever enter the forest and survive—is forced to go back inside to retrieve the tyrant's missing children. Inside await traps and trickery, ancient monsters, and hauntings of the past.

One day is all Veris is afforded. One misstep will cost everything.

The Tusks of Extinction

Ray Nayler

When you bring back a long-extinct species, there's more to success than the DNA.

Moscow has resurrected the mammoth. But someone must teach them how to be mammoths, or they are doomed to die out again.

Dr. Damira Khismatullina, an expert in elephant behavior, was brutally murdered trying to defend the world's last elephants from the brutal ivory trade. Now, her digitized consciousness has been downloaded into the mind of a mammoth.

As the herd's new matriarch, can Damira help fend off poachers long enough for the species to take hold? Or will her own ghosts, and Moscow's real reason for bringing the mammoth back, doom them to a new extinction?

Meet Toadling. On the day of her birth, she was stolen from her family by the fairies, but she grew up safe and loved in the warm waters of faerieland. Once an adult though, the fae ask a favor of Toadling: return to the human world and offer a blessing of protection to a newborn child. Simple, right?

But nothing with fairies is ever simple.

Centuries later, a knight approaches a towering wall of brambles, where the thorns are as thick as your arm and as sharp as swords. He's heard there's a curse here that needs breaking, but it's a curse Toadling will do anything to uphold...

Lost Ark Dreaming

Suyi Davies Okungbowa

The brutally engineered class divisions of Snowpiercer meets Rivers Solomon's The Deep in this high-octane post-climate disaster novella written by Nommo Award-winning author Suyi Davies Okungbowa.

Off the coast of West Africa, decades after the dangerous rise of the Atlantic Ocean, the region's survivors live inside five partially submerged, kilometers-high towers originally created as a playground for the wealthy. Now the towers' most affluent rule from their lofty perch at the top while the rest are crammed into the dark, fetid floors below sea level.

There are also those who were left for dead in the Atlantic, only to be reawakened by an ancient power, and who seek vengeance on those who offered them up to the waves.

Three lives within the towers are pulled to the fore of this conflict: Yekini, an earnest, mid-level rookie analyst; Tuoyo, an undersea mechanic mourning a tremendous loss; and Ngozi, an egotistical bureaucrat from the highest levels of governance. They will need to work together if there is to be any hope of a future that is worth living—for everyone.

Countess
Suzan Palumbo

A queer, Caribbean, anti-colonial sci-fi novella in which a betrayed captain seeks revenge on the interplanetary empire that subjugated her people for generations

Virika Sameroo lives in colonized space under the Æcerbot Empire, much like her ancestors before her in the British West Indies. After years of working hard to rise through the ranks of the empire's merchant marine, she's finally become first lieutenant on an interstellar cargo vessel.

When her captain dies under suspicious circumstances, Virika is arrested for murder and charged with treason despite her lifelong loyalty to the empire. Her conviction and subsequent imprisonment set her on a path of revenge, determined to take down the evil empire that wronged her, all while the fate of her people hangs in the balance.

The Practice, the Horizon, and the Chain
Sofia Samatar

Celebrated author Sofia Samatar presents a mystical, revolutionary space adventure for the exhausted dreamer in this brilliant science fiction novella tackling the carceral state and violence embedded in the ivory tower while embodying the legacy of Ursula K. Le Guin.

The boy was raised as one of the Chained, condemned to toil in the bowels of a mining ship out among the stars. His whole world changes—literally—when he is yanked "upstairs" and informed he has been given an opportunity to be educated at the ship's university alongside the elite.

Overwhelmed and alone, the boy forms a bond with the woman he comes to know as "the professor," a weary idealist and descendent of the Chained who has spent her career striving for validation from her more senior colleagues, only to fall short at every turn.

Together, the boy and the woman will embark on a transformative journey to grasp the design of the chains that fetter them both—and are the key to breaking free.

The novellas of The Singing Hills Cycle are linked by the cleric Chih, but may be read in any order, with each story serving as an entry point.

THE 2024 NEBULA AWARD FOR BEST NOVEL

WINNER

Someone You Can Build a Nest In

John Wiswell

Shesheshen has made a mistake fatal to all monsters: she's fallen in love.

Shesheshen is a shapeshifter, who happily resides as an amorphous lump at the bottom of a ruined manor. When her rest is interrupted by impolite monster hunters, she constructs a body from the remains of past meals: a metal chain for a backbone, borrowed bones for limbs, and a bear trap as an extra mouth.

Badly hurt by the hunters, Shesheshen's nursed back to health by Homily, a warm-hearted human. Homily is kind and would make a great co-parent: an ideal place to lay Shesheshen's eggs so their young can devour Homily from the inside out. But as they grow close, Shesheshen realizes that eating her girlfriend isn't an option.

Just as Shesheshen's about to confess her identity, Homily reveals something else: she's hunting a shapeshifting monster that supposedly cursed her family. Has Shesheshen seen it anywhere?

Shesheshen didn't curse anyone, so now she has to figure out why Homily's twisted family thinks she did. As Shesheshen's hunt for the monster becomes increasingly deadly, the bigger challenge remains: learning how to build a life *with*, rather than *in*, the woman she loves.

Sleeping Worlds Have No Memory

Yaroslav Barsukov

A science fantasy noir tale from the Nebula-nominated author of "Tower of Mud and Straw."

Refusing the queen's order to gas a crowd of protesters, Minister Shea Ashcroft is banished to the border to oversee the construction of the biggest defensive tower in history. However, the use of technology taken from refugees from another reality makes the tower volatile and dangerous, becoming a threat to local political interests. Shea has no choice but to fight the ruling hierarchy to ensure the construction succeeds—and to reclaim his own life.

Surviving an assassination attempt, Shea confronts his inner demons, encounters an ancient legend, and discovers a portal to a dead world—all while struggling to stay true to his own principles and maintain his sanity. Fighting memories and hallucinations, he starts to question everything...

Sleeping Worlds Have No Memory is a thought-provoking meditation on the fragility of the human condition, our beliefs, the manipulation of propaganda for political gains, and our ability to distinguish the real from the unreal and our willingness to accept convenient "truths." Praised for its gritty realism and literary qualities, the novel is a compelling exploration of memory, its fragile nature, and its profound impact on our perception of identity, relationships, and facts themselves.

Rakesfall

Vajra Chandrasekera

Rakesfall is a groundbreaking, standalone science fiction epic about two souls bound together from here until the ends of time, from the author of *The Saint of Bright Doors*.

Some stories take more than one lifetime to tell. There are wrongs that echo through the ages, friendships that outpace the claws of death, loves that leave their mark on civilization, and promises that nothing can break. This is one such story.

Annelid and Leveret met as children in the middle of the Sri Lankan civil war. They found each other in a torn-up nation, peering through propaganda to grasp a deeper truth. And in a demon-haunted wood, another act of violence linked them and propelled their souls on a journey throughout the ages. No world can hold them, no life can bind them, and they'll never leave each other behind.

Tracing two souls through endless lifetimes, *Rakesfall* is a virtuosic exploration of what stories can be. As Annelid and Leveret reincarnate ever deeper into the future, they will chase the edge of human possibility in a dark science fiction epic unlike anything you've read before.

Asunder

Kerstin Hall

We choose our own gods here.

Karys Eska is a deathspeaker, locked into an irrevocable compact with Sabaster, a terrifying eldritch being—three-faced, hundred-winged, unforgiving—who has granted her the ability to communicate with the newly departed. She pays the rent by using her abilities to investigate suspicious deaths around the troubled city she calls home. When a job goes sideways and connects her to a dying stranger with some very dangerous secrets, her entire world is upended.

Ferain is willing to pay a ludicrous sum of money for her help. To save him, Karys inadvertently binds him to her shadow, an act that may doom them both. If they want to survive, they will need to learn to trust one another. Together, they must journey to the heart of a faded empire, all the while haunted by arcane horrors, and the unquiet ghosts of their pasts.

And all too soon, Karys knows her debts will come due.

The Book of Love

Kelly Link

In the acclaimed first novel from short story virtuoso and Pulitzer Prize finalist Kelly Link, three teenagers become pawns in a supernatural power struggle.

The Book of Love showcases Kelly Link at the height of her powers, channeling potent magic and attuned to all varieties of love—from friendship to romance to abiding family ties—with her trademark compassion, wit, and literary derring-do. Readers will find joy (and a little terror) and an affirmation that love goes on, even when we cannot.

Late one night, Laura, Daniel, and Mo find themselves beneath the fluorescent lights of a high school classroom, almost a year after disappearing from their hometown, the small seaside community of Lovesend, Massachusetts, having long been presumed dead. Which, in fact, they are.

With them in the room is their previously unremarkable high school music teacher, who seems to know something about their disappearance—and what has brought them back again. Desperate to reclaim their lives, the three agree to the terms of the bargain their music teacher proposes. They will be given a series of magical tasks; while they undertake them, they may return to their families and friends, but they can tell no one where they've been. In the end, there will be winners and there will be losers.

But their resurrection has attracted the notice of other supernatural figures, all with their own agendas. As Laura, Daniel, and Mo grapple with the pieces of the lives they left behind, and Laura's sister, Susannah, attempts to reconcile what she remembers with what she fears, these mysterious others begin to arrive, engulfing their community in danger and chaos, and it becomes imperative that the teens solve the mystery of their deaths to avert a looming disaster.

Welcome to Kelly Link's incomparable Lovesend, where you'll encounter love and loss, laughter and dread, magic and karaoke, and some really good pizza.

A Sorceress Comes to Call

T. Kingfisher

From *New York Times* bestselling and Hugo Award-winning author T. Kingfisher comes *A Sorceress Comes to Call*—a dark reimagining of the Brothers Grimm's "The Goose Girl," rife with secrets, murder, and forbidden magic.

Cordelia knows her mother is…unusual. Their house doesn't have any doors between rooms—*there are no secrets in this house*—and her mother doesn't allow Cordelia to have a single friend. Unless you count Falada, her mother's beautiful white horse. The only time Cordelia feels truly free is on her daily rides with him.

But more than simple eccentricity sets her mother apart. Other mothers don't force their daughters to be silent and motionless for hours, sometimes days, on end. Other mothers aren't evil sorcerers.

When her mother unexpectedly moves them into the manor home of a wealthy older Squire and his kind but keen-eyed sister, Hester, Cordelia knows this welcoming pair are to be her mother's next victims. But Cordelia feels at home for the very first time among these people, and as her mother's plans darken, she must decide how to face the woman who raised her to save the people who have become like family.

ANDRE NORTON NEBULA AWARD FOR MIDDLE GRADE AND YOUNG ADULT FICTION

The Young Necromancer's Guide to Ghosts

Vanessa Ricci-Thode

Lusi is a perfectly normal 12-year-old wizard except for the part where she can talk to ghosts. But everyone knows ghosts aren't real, so at best they think Lusi is lying and at worst that she's lost her mind. Her big sister Marsi is the only one who believes her, but Marsi is running away to escape Uncle's terrible plan to make her marry his creepy nephew. Lusi can't imagine being separated from her sister and leaves behind the rest of their family to flee with Marsi via merchant caravan to the Wizards Guild for help. All their plans are dashed to pieces when Uncle catches up to them in a matter of days.

Uncle's connections to powerful wizards make him far more dangerous than Lusi initially realized. But Lusi isn't crazy or a freak for talking to ghosts: she's a necromancer! Marsi is worried-they've always been told that necromancers are monsters. Lusi needs to learn more to set both their minds at ease. She must enlist the help of a ghost girl, a dragon, and a strange wizard from the other side of the world if she wants to control her unusual talents and keep her family safe.

Daydreamer

Rob Cameron

An eleven-year-old boy copes with the challenges of his city life by weaving his reality into a magical realm of dragons, foxes, and trolls—until he must use the power of his creativity to save both of his worlds from destructive forces. This stunning debut is a profound exploration of imagination, community, and how the stories we tell both comfort us and challenge us to grow.

Charles' life is split between two worlds: one real and one fantasy. In the real world, he is a lonely, bullied kid who can't keep up with school when the letters refuse to stay still on the page and is constantly in trouble for getting distracted. He lives with his mom in an apartment building, where Glory, the grumpy old superintendent, fills his head with stories about the Dream Folk.

In his fantasy world, the Sanctuary, Charles adventures with faeries and sprites and his two imaginary best friends. There, Charles's bullies become ogres, and Glory opens his arms wide to transform into a dragon. But when trolls move into Charles' apartment building and bring with them a terrible secret, the stories he has been told and the ones he brings to life grow more complicated. To protect everyone he cares about, Charles must harness his imagination in ways he never dreamed, in this unique story of the spaces and narratives we create for ourselves, and the ways in which fantasy and reality collide and blur.

Braided

Leah Cypess

The fifth book in the Sisters Ever After series of fairy tale retellings from the point of view of the siblings in the background, this is the thrilling and mysterious story of Cinna and her older sister, Rapunzel, who was stolen from their castle as a baby. Now she's back, leaving Cinna with more questions than answers.

Princess Cinna has grown up longing for her older sister, Rapunzel, who was kidnapped before Cinna was born. Now that Rapunzel has returned home, Cinna couldn't be happier. She can't wait to help Rapunzel take her rightful place as heir to the throne.

But Rapunzel is not what anyone—including Cinna—expected. And whoever took her might still be lurking in the castle. When magical creatures begin attacking both princesses, Cinna finds herself with no one to trust...except, maybe, Rapunzel herself.

Will she risk everything for a sister with whom she may have nothing in common except their long, magical hair?

Benny Ramírez and the Nearly Departed

José Pablo Iriarte

Benny Ramírez can see dead people...Well, one dead person, anyway. A hilarious and heartwarming story about a boy who can suddenly see the ghost of his famous musician grandfather!

After moving cross-country into his late grandfather's Miami mansion, Benny discovers that the ghost of his famous trumpet-playing abuelo the great Ignacio Ramírez, is still there...and isn't too thrilled about it. He's been barred from the afterlife, and no one can see him except his grandson. But Benny's got problems of his own. He's enrolled in a performing arts school with his siblings, despite having no obvious talent.

Luckily, Abuelo believes they can help each other. Abuelo has until New Year's Eve to do some good in the world and thinks that teaching Benny how to play the trumpet and become a school celebrity might be the key to earning his wings. Having no better ideas, Benny finds himself taking Abuelo's advice—to disastrous and hilarious results.

Benny and Abuelo will find that there's more than one way to be great in this un-forgettable, laugh-out-loud tale of family, music, and self-discovery.

Moonstorm

Yoon Ha Lee

Trust the Empress. Move at her will. Act as her hands.

Hwa Young was just ten years old when imperial forces destroyed her home, among the rebel clans of the Moonstorm. Now, years later, she is a citizen of the very empire that orphaned her, dreaming of getting back out among the stars and piloting a lancer—the fleet's deadliest, most advanced fighting craft.

When a rebel attack leaves Hwa Young stranded on an imperial starship, her dreams become a reality. A military ship has no space for civilians, and the fleet badly needs lancer pilots—and Hwa Young and her friends are quick to volunteer for the demanding programme.

But training is nothing like what they expected, and secrets—like the fate of the fleet's previous lancer squad, and deeper truths about the rebellion itself—are mounting up. When Hwa Young uncovers a conspiracy that puts their entire world at risk, she's forced to choose between a past she's put behind her and an empire she no longer trusts.

Puzzleheart

Jenn Reese

Get ready to solve the mystery at the heart of this captivating new middle grade adventure about family—and a house with a mind of its own—from the award-winning author of *Game of Fox & Squirrels* and *Every Bird a Prince*, Jenn Reese.

Twelve-year-old Perigee has never met a problem they couldn't solve. So when their Dad's spirits need raising, Perigee formulates the Plan: a road trip to Dad's childhood home to reunite him with his estranged mother. There's something in it for Perigee, too, as they will finally get to visit "Eklunds' Puzzle House," the mysterious bed & breakfast their grandparents built but never opened.

They arrive ahead of a massive storm and the House immediately puts Perigee's logical, science-loving mind to the test. Corridors shift. Strange paintings lurk in the shadows. Encoded messages abound. Despite Perigee's best efforts, neither the House nor Grandma will give up their secrets. And worse, prickly Grandma has outlawed games and riddles of any kind.

Even the greatest of plans can crumble, and as new arguments fill the air, the House becomes truly dangerous. Deadly puzzles pop up at every turn, knives spin in the hallways, and staircases disappear. The answer lies at the heart of the House, but in order to find it, Perigee and their new friend Lily will need to solve a long-lost, decades-old riddle... if the House itself doesn't stop them first.

MULTIMEDIA AWARD
FINALISTS

RAY BRADBURY NEBULA AWARD FOR OUTSTANDING DRAMATIC PRESENTATION

Dune: Part Two

Jon Spaihts and Denis Villeneuve

Paul Atreides unites with the Fremen while on a warpath of revenge against the conspirators who destroyed his family. Facing a choice between the love of his life and the fate of the universe, he endeavors to prevent a terrible future. (*from IMDb*)

KAOS

Charlie Covell and Georgia Christou

Zeus has a wrinkle. He's worried it might mean the end of the world...and it might.

Because on earth, six humans — unaware of their importance or their connection to each other — learn that they are component parts of an ancient prophecy. Will they discover the truth about the gods, and what they're doing to humans? And, if they do, will they be able to stop them?

A darkly funny, contemporary spin on the Greek myths, *KAOS* is an epic 8-part series about love, power and the Underworld. (*from IMDb*)

Doctor Who: "Dot and Bubble"
Russell T. Davies

The world of Finetime seems happy and harmonious. But an awful terror is preying on the citizens. Can the Doctor and Ruby make them see the truth before it's too late? (*from BBC*)

Wicked
Winnie Holzman and Dana Fox

Elphaba, a young woman ridiculed for her green skin, and Galinda, a popular girl, forms an unlikely friendship at Shiz University in the Land of Oz. Their bond deepens as they encounter the Wizard of Oz, leading to a series of events that ultimately shape their destinies, transforming them into the Wicked Witch of the West and Glinda the Good. (*from IMDb*)

Star Trek: Lower Decks, Season 5
Mike McMahan

The fifth and final season of the adult animated television series *Star Trek: Lower Decks* is set in the 24th century and follows the adventures of the low-ranking officers with menial jobs on the starship U.S.S. Cerritos, one of Starfleet's least important starships. The final season culminates with the Cerritos crew needing to work together as they face a universe-ending space anomaly. (*from Wikipedia & TrekNews.net*)

I Saw the TV Glow
Jane Schoenbrun

Teenager Owen is just trying to make it through life in the suburbs when his classmate introduces him to a mysterious late-night TV show—a vision of a supernatural world beneath their own. In the pale glow of the television, Owen's view of reality begins to crack. (*from A24 Films*)

GAME WRITING

WINNER

A Death in Hyperspace

Stewart C Baker, Phoebe Barton, James Beamon, Kate Heartfield, Isabel J. Kim, Sara S. Messenger, Jingjing Xiao, Natalia Theodoridou, M. Darusha Wehm, Merc Fenn Wolfmoor (Infomancy.net)

As an embodied ship Intelligence and fugitive former warship, you've faced many challenges.

But when your captain dies suspiciously halfway through a hyperspace transit, you know you're in trouble. Not because you need a captain — you can pilot yourself just fine — but because, as an aficionado of mysteries and detective stories, you know there's only one explanation: murder most foul.

Investigate your rooms.

Interrogate your crew and passengers.

Solve the mystery.

Will you find your way back to reality—or be stuck in hyperspace forever? (*from IFDb*)

Elden Ring: Shadow of the Erdtree

Hidetaka Miyazaki

Shadow of the Erdtree is an expansion to *Elden Ring*, the 2022 Game of the Year.

Dark and intense, *Shadow of the Erdtree* has players continue their quest with the freedom to explore and experience the adventure at their own pace. (*from Steam*)

Pacific Drive

Karrie Shao and Paul Dean

Pacific Drive is a first-person driving survival game with your car as your only companion. Navigate a surreal reimagining of the Pacific Northwest and face supernatural dangers as you venture into the Olympic Exclusion Zone, an abandoned, anomaly-filled research site. Each excursion into the wilderness brings unique and strange challenges as you restore and upgrade your car from an abandoned garage that acts as your home base.

Gather precious resources and investigate what's been left behind in the Zone; unravel a long-forgotten mystery while learning exactly what it takes to survive in this unpredictable, hostile environment. (*from Ironwood Studios*)

The Ghost and the Golem

Benjamin Rosenbaum

Can your magic amulet save your Jewish village from destruction? Uncover the truth and forge alliances with soldiers, peasants, bandits, anarchists, and demons!

The year is 1881. Life in your village on the border of Poland and Ukraine is sweet as raisin pastries and bitter as horseradish. But it is a tense time in the Russian empire, with antisemitic riots spreading across the land.

And inside your pocket is a magic amulet, revealing visions of the future, omens of your village in flames. When you hold it, you can see the blood and the bodies, smell the gunshots, and hear the marching songs.

How could this future come to pass, and how will you stop it?

The Ghost and the Golem is an interactive historical fantasy novel by Benjamin Rosenbaum. It's entirely text-based, 450,000 words and hundreds of choices, without graphics or sound effects, and fueled by the vast, unstoppable power of your imagination. (*from Steam*)

1000xRESIST

Remy Siu, Pinki Li, Conor Wylie

1000xRESIST is a thrilling sci-fi adventure. A thousand years in the future, humanity is all but extinguished and a disease spread by an alien occupation keeps the survivors underground. You are Watcher. You dutifully fulfil your purpose in service of the ALLMOTHER, until the day you learn a shocking secret that changes everything.

Born from an eclectic set of inspirations, including the games of Yoko Taro (*NieR:Automata*), the anime of Satoshi Kon (*Perfect Blue*) and Naoko Yamada (*A Silent Voice*), and even the theatre of Robert Wilson (*Einstein on the Beach*), *1000xRE-SIST* tells a story in ways only a game can while simultaneously bringing fresh ideas to interactive storytelling from theatre, dance, performance art, and cinema.

Enjoy more than 10 hours of playtime brought to life with over 15,000 lines of fully voiced dialogue from a brilliant cast of Asian-Canadian actors and an incredible soundtrack from two composers. (*from Fellow Traveller Games*)

Restore, Reflect, Retry

Natalia Theodoridou

This is a haunted game about a haunted game. You've played this game before. You may not remember, but the game does.

Open the door. Enter the maze. Ignore the ghosts.

None of you remembers who first found the game: the black rectangular box with the small screen on which instructions appear. Of course it piqued your interest: this is the 1990s, after all, and there isn't much for teenagers to do in your small town. Your friends were intrigued, and so were you. So you started to play. And play. And play.

What does it matter if no one remembers exactly how you discovered the game, or if the story changes ever so slightly each time you tell it? Or if you change ever so slightly too, every time you emerge into the real world once more?
All that matters is that you keep playing.

Restore, Reflect, Retry is an interactive horror novel by Natalia Theodoridou. It's entirely text-based, with 90,000 words and hundreds of choices, without graphics or sound effects, and fueled by the vast, unstoppable power of your imagination. (*from Choice of Games*)

Slay the Princess—The Pristine Cut

Tony Howard-Arias and Abby Howard

You're on a path in the woods, and at the end of that path is a cabin. And in the basement of that cabin is a Princess.

You're here to slay her. If you don't, it will be the end of the world.

She will do everything in her power to stop you. She'll charm, and she'll lie, and she'll promise you the world, and if you let her, she'll kill you a dozen times over. You can't let that happen. Don't forget, the fate of the world rests on your shoulders.

You're not going to listen to him, are you? We're supposed to save princesses, not slay them...

Slay the Princess is a choice-driven psychological horror visual novel/dating sim with dramatic branching, light RPG elements, and hand-penciled art. (*from Steam*)

Yazeba's Bed & Breakfast

Jay Dragon, M Veselak, Mercedes Acosta, and Lillie J. Harris

While it's hard to say whether there's any one particular day that's best for running away from home, if forced to choose, one would probably say the 15th of September would be as good a day as any. But on the other hand, to the mud-soaked and water-logged girl stumbling through the woods, the fifteenth didn't feel particularly good for anything whatsoever.

After all, it was her birthday, and nothing good had ever happened on it before.

In the rainy damp woods, full of rainy damp thoughts, the girl wove past a broken-down wooden gate in an old stone wall without even taking notice of either. She did notice the house beyond them, though, and might have hesitated a moment if not for a sudden peal of thunder. A little bell chimed as she stepped inside, boots stomping against the small welcome mat, ignoring all the signs on the front door except for the words **Yazeba's Bed & Breakfast**.

Welcome to *Yazeba's Bed & Breakfast*, a slice-of-life tabletop RPG about a heartless witch, a peaceful house, and all the folks who have made their home inside.

Yazeba's Bed & Breakfast uses pre-set characters, quick-play chapters, and an adaptable ruleset unlike anything else out there. It takes less than a half hour to learn how to play and get started, but with new chapters and secrets to unlock folks can stick with the game for years and years. (*from Possum Creek Games*)

WITH THANKS TO THE TOP SPONSORS FOR THIS YEAR'S NEBULA AWARDS CONFERENCE

PLATINUM TIER

TOR PUBLISHING GROUP

SILVER TIER

ABOUT THE SCIENCE FICTION AND FANTASY WRITERS ASSOCIATION

The Science Fiction and Fantasy Writers Association, Inc. (SFWA) was founded in 1965 by the American science fiction author Damon Knight under the name Science Fiction Writers of America with a charter membership of 78 writers. Today, SFWA is home to over 2,500 authors, artists, and allied professionals worldwide, and is widely recognized as one of the most effective non-profit writers' organizations in existence.

The mission of the Science Fiction and Fantasy Writers Association includes the promotion, writing, and appreciation of science fiction, fantasy and related genres and field; informing, supporting, promoting, defending, and advocating for writers of science fiction, fantasy and related genres; and to promote and defend the interests of writers in these genres within the publishing industry. Each year, SFWA assists members in various legal disputes, administers grants to SFF community organizations and members facing medical or legal expenses, and hosts the prestigious Nebula Awards at our annual SFWA Nebula Conference.

All authors can benefit from our Information Center and well-known Writer Beware® website. Between online discussion boards, private convention suites, and a host of less formal gatherings, SFWA is a source of information, education, support, and fellowship.

SFWA Membership is open to authors, artists, editors, and other industry professionals who meet our eligibility requirements. To learn more about SFWA or to apply for membership, please visit our website, www.sfwa.org.

ABOUT
THE NEBULA
AWARDS®

The Nebula Awards, presented annually at the SFWA Nebula Conference, recognize the best works of science fiction and fantasy published in the United States as selected by members of the Science Fiction and Fantasy Writers Association. The first Nebula Awards were presented in 1966.

The Nebula Awards are voted on and presented by full, senior, and associate members of the Science Fiction and Fantasy Writers Association. Categories include awards for outstanding novel, novella, novelette, and short stories, as well as for game writing, the Ray Bradbury Nebula Award for Outstanding Dramatic Presentation, and the Andre Norton Nebula Award for Middle Grade and Young Adult Fiction.

SFWA also administers the Kate Wilhelm Solstice Award, the Kevin O'Donnell, Jr. Service to SFWA Award, and the Damon Knight Memorial Grand Master Award, SFWA's highest honor for lifetime achievement in writing science fiction and/or fantasy.

Over the years, the Nebula Awards banquet grew to become the SFWA Nebula Conference, one of the premier professional development conferences for speculative fiction industry professionals and people aspiring to become one. It takes place each spring. For more information on the awards and the Nebula Conference, please visit the Nebula website at nebulas.sfwa.org/nebula-conference.

www.ingramcontent.com/pod-product-compliance
Lightning Source LLC
Chambersburg PA
CBHW031441200726
48289CB00007BB/2066